THE WAVE WALKERS

Pirate Wars

THE WAVE WALKERS

Pirate Wars

KAI MEYER

Translated by Elizabeth D. Crawford

Aladdin Paperbacks
New York   London   Toronto   Sydney

❧ ALADDIN PAPERBACKS
An imprint of Simon & Schuster Children's Publishing Division
1230 Avenue of the Americas, New York, NY 10020
English language translation copyright © 2008 Elizabeth D. Crawford
Die Wasserweber text copyright © 2003 by Kai Mayer
Original German edition text copyright
© 2004 by Loewe Verlag GmbH, Bindlach
Originally published in Germany in 2004 as *Die Wasserweber* by Loewe Verlag
Published by arrangement with Loewe Verlag
All rights reserved, including the right of
reproduction in whole or in part in any form.
ALADDIN PAPERBACKS and related logo are registered
trademarks of Simon & Schuster, Inc.
Also available in a Margaret K. McElderry hardcover edition.
Designed by Paula Russell Szafranski
The text of this book was set in Centaur MT.
Manufactured in the United States of America
First Aladdin Paperbacks edition December 2008
10 9 8 7 6 5 4 3 2 1
The Library of Congress has cataloged the hardcover edition as follows:
Meyer, Kai.
Pirate wars / Kai Meyer ; translated by Elizabeth D. Crawford.—1st U.S. ed.
p. cm.—(Wave walkers ; [3])
Summary: Jolly, Griffin, and other brave warriors return to battle in one last attempt to save their world from the evil Maelstrom as, despite major setbacks, they finally realize that only courage, love, and loyalty will see them through.
[1.Pirates—Fiction. 2.Magic—Fiction. 3. Fantasy.] I. Crawford, Elizbeth D. II. Title.
PZ7.M57171113Pkw 2008
[Fic]—22
2007025867
ISBN-13: 978-1-4169-2476-0 (hc.)
ISBN-10: 1-4169-2476-0 (hc.)
ISBN-13: 978-1-4169-2477-7 (pbk.)
ISBN-10: 1-4169-2477-9 (pbk.)

Contents

The Dreaming Worm

On the morning of her last day in Aelenium, Jolly visited the Hexhermetic Shipworm.

His house in the Poets' Quarter of the sea star city was narrow, just wide enough for a low door with a window beside it. As everywhere in Aelenium, there were no right angles here and hardly a straight wall. The city's buildings were formed from the ivorylike material of the coral, some having grown in a natural way, others created by stonecutters and artists.

"It's me," she called as she walked past the guard and opened the door. "Jolly."

She didn't expect an answer, and she received none. She knew how things stood with the worm. If his condition had changed, she'd have been told about it.

Jolly closed the door behind her. What she had to say to

the Hexhermetic Shipworm was none of the sentry's business. Furthermore, she was afraid Munk might have followed her and stolen into the house behind her, unseen. The last thing she wanted was for him to overhear what she said to the shipworm.

This was her farewell. Hers alone.

She mounted the uneven stairs to the upper floor. There, in the largest room in the house, the worm hung in his cocoon and dreamed.

The room under the peaked roof was largely filled with the fine web being secreted by the worm's motionless body—the only sign that he was still alive.

A few days before, when the first signs of his transformation became visible, Jolly had begged for him to be housed in the palace, even in her own room. But Forefather and the Ghost Trader had refused. They'd given no reason for their decision.

Jolly wasn't really surprised. She and Munk were the two most important people in Aelenium, they were told over and over again. No unauthorized person was allowed to come too close to them. Certainly not some unknown thing that might hatch from a cocoon when the worm had finished his pupation. *If* something should hatch.

"Hello, Worm."

Jolly stopped at the wall of silken threads. The windows of the roof chamber were covered with translucent material to impede the view from the houses opposite, but also because it was feared that hungry gulls might discover the helpless worm. Windows were glass only in the palaces of

Aelenium's rulers, not in the dwellings of the simple folk; here they used wooden shutters to protect themselves from wind and weather, but those also blocked out the light. Instead, the fabric that had been stretched across the attic's windows turned the light streaming in milky, dissolving the edges of the shadows. There was no longer any sharp delineation between light and dark in the entire space; everything blended together, mingled.

"Hello," said Jolly once again, because the sight of the eerie thicket of silk affected her more than she'd expected. Buenaventure, the pit bull man, came here twice a day to make sure everything was all right. He'd told her of his visits, but this was the first time she'd seen the extent of the cocoon with her own eyes.

The silken threads were woven into a mighty net stretching from the floor to the peaked ceiling—not unlike a spiderweb, only with much finer mesh and without an obvious pattern. The uncanny thicket of threads was several feet deep. In its center hung an oval thickening—the worm's cocoon. He seemed to float. The threads that held him over the floor at shoulder height were almost invisible.

The Hexhermetic Shipworm was no longer recognizable in the center of the cocoon, his form buried underneath a layer of silk a handsbreadth thick. Only a weak pulsing showed that he was still alive.

"This is quite . . . impressive," said Jolly tentatively. The sight seemed to glue her mouth shut, as if it were filled with the webs too. "I hope you're feeling all right inside there."

Pirate Wars

The worm didn't answer. Buenaventure had warned her that conversation with him at this time was a one-sided affair. Nevertheless, the pit bull man was convinced that the worm could hear them. Jolly wasn't so sure of that.

"You gave all of us quite a fright," she said. "You could at least have warned us that something like this was going to happen. I mean, none of us knows a whole lot about Hexhermetic Shipworms." She sighed and stretched out her hand cautiously to touch the foremost threads of the web. The surface billowed like a curtain. It was as if a slight breeze had stroked her fingertips.

"I've come to say good-bye." She pulled her hand back and hooked her thumbs awkwardly into her belt. "Munk and I, we're going to start out. To the Crustal Breach. Everyone here in Aelenium—the nobles, Captain d'Artois, the Ghost Trader, Forefather—is hoping that we manage to seal the source of the Maelstrom. We do too, of course. And I don't know . . . Munk is really good at mussel magic. Perhaps he actually will manage it." She stopped for a moment, then went on. "Myself, I'm not ready yet, even if no one wants to admit it. Anyway, no one says it to my face. I'm not half as good with the mussels as Munk. He . . . well, you know him. He's so ambitious. As if he's possessed. And he's still mad at me—because I turned the mussel magic against him on the *Carfax*. But did he give me any choice?"

She began to walk back and forth in front of the web. She'd rather have had this conversation with someone who could give her advice. But even if the companions here in Aelenium were on her side—the pirate princess Soledad, Captain Walker, and his best friend, Buenaventure, the giant with the head of a dog—none of them could really put themselves in her place.

Except perhaps Griffin. But Griffin had vanished. His sea horse had returned to Aelenium alone. At the thought of him, Jolly felt her knees grow weak. Before they could give way, she dropped down onto the floor, rather clumsily, and sat cross-legged. It was too late to hold back the tears that were running down her cheeks.

"No one can tell me what's become of Griffin. Everyone thinks he's dead. But that can't be. Griffin's not allowed to be dead. That's just how people talk, right? I mean, *not allowed to* . . . pretty silly, huh? As if there were some sort of rules and regulations." She shook her head. "I firmly believe he's still alive."

The cocoon in the heart of the web pulsed on undisturbed. With every faint expansion, every contraction, a wave ran through the silk like a deep breath.

"What will you have turned into when you come out of this stuff?" she asked. "Do you have any idea yourself? What about the wisdom of the worm *now*?"

She noticed that as she spoke her fingers were clutching her knees so hard that it hurt. Frightened, she let go.

"Forefather and the Ghost Trader whisper together from morning till night. They say the attack on Aelenium is about to happen. And this morning they decided."

She brushed a strand of hair out of her face. "We're leaving," she said wearily. "The practices are finished. I don't think Munk and I can do half of what we're *supposed* to be able to. But there's no more time. Tyrone's fleet will be here in two or three days, at the latest, and the deep tribes will probably attack at the same time, or even sooner. No one knows how long the soldiers of Aelenium can hold out. Maybe a few days. Maybe only a few hours."

Again some time passed in which she said nothing, staring thoughtfully at the attic floor in front of her. She imagined what would happen when the servants of the Maelstrom reached the city. The monstrous whirlpool thundering on the open sea out on the horizon had brought the kobalins under his rule. Thousands of them were advancing on Aelenium in mighty swarms. And the dreaded cannibal king, Tyrone, would fight on the side of the Maelstrom with his fleet.

Sooner or later Aelenium would have to acknowledge defeat. Sooner than ever if she and Munk weren't successful in conquering the Maelstrom. But the fight for the sea star city was supposed to create the necessary time for them to do just that. Dozens, perhaps hundreds, would lose their lives to gain precious hours and minutes for the two polliwogs to try to close the Maelstrom back into his mussel deep on the floor of the sea.

And besides everything else—Griffin's disappearance, Munk's ambition, and fear of the gigantic whirlpool that was bringing all the evil to Aelenium and across the Caribbean— that was what concerned Jolly the most: the fact that men would die in order to support her and Munk. Because they placed all their hopes in two polliwogs.

THE DREAMING WORM

"I don't deserve so much trust!" she whispered sadly. "They must know that, mustn't they? That I'm going to let them down for sure."

She was just not ready yet. Maybe she never would be. But it no longer mattered. Her departure was decided.

She'd resisted, rebelled against it—all in vain.

The Crustal Breach awaited her.

Her fate.

Jolly stood up, blew a kiss to the cocoon in the center of the web, and wiped the tears from her eyes.

"The rays are ready to leave," she said. "Captain d'Artois is going to lead us to the Maelstrom. The Ghost Trader is going with us." She smiled wearily. "And Soledad. You know her—she insisted on coming with us as far as possible. No one dares to contradict her."

She pulled herself together. "Farewell," she said sadly. "Whatever you are when you hatch out of that thing— farewell!"

Then she turned, left the cupola chamber, and walked slowly down the narrow stairs. The eyes of the sentry at the door widened when he saw that she had been crying. But he said nothing to her, and for that she was grateful.

"The whale is being attacked!"

Griffin started up. He lowered the hammer with which he'd just struck the first blow and turned his eyes from the coarse wooden chair that lay in front of him on the floor. The twenty-eighth. He'd counted as he went. Twenty-eight chairs for Ebenezer's Floating Tavern—the first tavern in the interior of a giant whale.

"Harpoons, Griffin! They're attacking Jasconius with harpoons!"

"Who is?"

"Who, who . . . kobalins, of course!" The former monk had appeared in the doorway, arms flailing.

Griffin had believed himself to be looking certain death in the eye when he was swallowed days before by the gigantic animal. But in some amazing way he'd landed in the stomach of the whale very much alive and had been rescued by Ebenezer.

The monk must have gone crazy in the long years of solitude down here, of that Griffin was convinced. His plan to open a restaurant in the stomach of the monster was the best evidence of it. This mad plan was the reason that Griffin was spending his time making chairs and tables. Until he was finished with the job, Ebenezer had threatened, Griffin would never walk on land.

"Harpoons, Griffin!" the monk repeated excitedly. "The kobalins have harpoons."

Indignant, he was running back and forth in the wood-paneled room. Outside, in front of the opened door, stretched the dark stomach cavity of the giant animal. But here inside, on the other side of the magic doorway, the atmosphere of a solid country house prevailed: very cozy, very comfortable, very well appointed.

"How many kobalins are there?" Griffin asked.

"How should I know? Have you ever heard of a whale that could count?"

Griffin opened his mouth to reply, but at that moment there was an earsplitting noise in the dark grotto of the whale's stomach. Something shot toward the open door like a wall of shadows, accompanied by a roaring and raging as if someone had torn a hole in the body of the whale.

"Flood!" Griffin bellowed, and then they both plunged forward, threw themselves against the door, and together pushed against it with all their strength.

The house-high wave crashed against the outside and brushed aside the man and boy along with the door. Water shot into the room, swirled over the parquet, flung tools and finished chairs together, and smashed some of them against the walls. Griffin and Ebenezer both howled with pain as their heads and backs were shoved against corners and wooden edges.

The water withdrew just as quickly as it had come. A second flood wave never came. In no time the water began to seep away through the cracks in the floor. When Griffin staggered to his feet with a groan, a damp film over everything was all that was left—but it was enough to make it slippery. With a wild pirate oath he sailed backward onto his behind, landing on his tailbone, and wanting in his pain and rage to throw around all the dumb chairs he'd just made so laboriously.

Ebenezer's breathing was wheezy. He was sitting on the floor, his back against the wall, listening to the voice of the whale. He claimed that he and the whale understood each other through the power of their minds alone, and Griffin had become convinced that there was something to that.

Suddenly Ebenezer gasped. "He's swallowed them," he said. "Griffin, he's swallowed the kobalins!" His eyes swept worriedly to the open door and searched the splashing, gurgling darkness out there.

"How many?" Griffin was on his feet in one leap.

Ebenezer groaned. "Not many. But they're hardly likely to have drowned. It might be that he's squashed a few of them."

Griffin hurried to a chest where Ebenezer stored some of the weapons that had collected in the whale's stomach over the years. Whole shiploads of sabers, daggers, flintlock pistols, and rifles had been swallowed by Jasconius. Unfortunately, the guns were of little use in the whale's stomach—the dampened powder made it impossible to fire them. And besides, the danger of missing the target and wounding the stomach wall was too great.

Griffin pulled a saber out of the chest, tried its weight in his hand, and also stuck a long knife into his belt. Ebenezer looked from the door back to Griffin. "Are you really going out there?"

"Got any better suggestions?"

The monk was torn. "Jasconius has never swallowed a kobalin. Until now they've always given him a wide berth."

Griffin picked up a lantern and pushed through the door past Ebenezer. "Stay here and bar the door. I'll see what I can do."

"We could both hide."

"And what would become of your tavern? Besides, we'll

have to go out anyway to look for food soon. The supplies in the kitchen won't last forever."

Ebenezer nodded, but he didn't seem convinced. Griffin was unexpectedly touched by the older man's concern. Until now he'd rather felt himself the prisoner of the whale and his occupant, just good enough to cobble together the chairs and tables for Ebenezer's cockeyed dream. But now he realized that the monk liked him. And he couldn't really deny that it was the same on his part. Ebenezer was certainly a little crazy, quite definitely odd, but he was a lovable fellow.

"I'll be back soon." Griffin said it more to himself than to Ebenezer. The words made him sound braver than he really felt. His voice wavered, which Ebenezer must have noticed.

Kobalins with harpoons. Even if they'd lost their weapons when they fell into the throat, that didn't make them any less dangerous. Their long claws and sharp teeth were as lethal as knife blades.

Griffin walked out of the light of the room and climbed slowly down the hill with his lantern. He looked watchfully about him, taking pains to appear determined as he did so. No victim is more preferable to kobalins than one in deadly fear; it makes it easier for them to strike at their prey from ambush.

Ebenezer closed the door behind him. Griffin heard the bolt snap. The rays of brightness around him were cut off and only meagerly replaced by the weak shimmer of the lantern. The edges of the circle of light were just three or four yards apart. Beyond it, all was darkness.

Everywhere there was bubbling and splashing as the water

dripped off parts of wrecks and seeped into the mire. The sounds were hardly distinguishable from the whispering speech of the kobalins.

Griffin nervously shoved some of his braids out of his face with the crook of his arm. His blond hair was plaited into dozens of them. That was really a hairstyle of the slaves brought over to the New World from Africa. It was only rarely seen on one of the white inhabitants of the Caribbean, so Griffin was especially proud of it.

He'd just reached the foot of the hill when he heard a snarl. From the right. Out of the darkness.

He raised the saber high, and then something shot at him as if it had been slung in his direction with a catapult—a spindly, thin body with scaly skin on which the lamplight broke in oily rainbow colors. The kobalin's hands, with their long claws, were wide open, and his mouth gaped like the jaws of a shark.

Griffin let himself drop, and as he did, he thrust the blade upward. Steel cut through skin and muscle, a scream sounded, then the body disappeared somewhere in the shadows and moved no more. A long-drawn-out smacking indicated that it had sunk into the mud of the stomach.

That was easy, Griffin thought as he struggled to his feet. An oily shine gleamed on his blade. The kobalin must have taken him for a confused, starving castaway. But now the others were warned.

If he only knew how many he had to deal with!

He held the lamp on an arm stretched over his head. A

rustling was audible somewhere in front of him, followed by the lightning-fast *splish-splash* of rushing feet.

At least one, thought Griffin. *Probably two or three.* He hoped not more.

Something hit him in the back and made him stumble forward. He cried out, stumbled into a depression between the wrecks, and plunged forward. A moment later it was clear to him that the fall had saved his life: A claw swished through the air over his head. The blow would probably have broken his neck.

But then he rolled onto his back and hit his spine on something hard. The lantern slid out of his hands and sank into the morass a yard beyond him.

In its last light Griffin made out his opponents. There were two of them. Their furrowed grimaces were like unfinished accessories arranged around their wide-open mouths—as if the creator of the kobalins had concentrated all his powers on the gigantic throats and sharp rows of teeth, like a child who loses interest in a piece of clay and apathetically squashes the rest of his work together.

Griffin struck blindly over him with his saber in the darkness and at the same time tried to prop up his body with his left hand. But his fingers sank into the dark muck with a sound like a smacking kiss. Again he slashed, but his blow went wild. Instead he felt something grab his right ankle in the dark and pull on it, just outside the range of his reach. A second hand gripped his other leg, and now the creatures began to pull in opposite directions.

Pirate Wars

They're going to tear me apart! The thought flashed through Griffin's mind in a fraction of a second. Without stopping to think, he sat up and slashed a desperate stroke across his spread legs toward his feet. The pain that seared through his back with the abrupt movement was murderous.

Then—resistance! A cutting sound, followed by a mad kobalin screech.

His left ankle came free. But the strength of the creature to his right forcefully pulled him farther, away from the wounded one.

Kobalins are sly, mean creatures, but they are stupid and a little childish. If they can kill an opponent slowly and painfully, they prefer to, rather than slaughtering him the quickest way—because killing is like a game for them and the longer it lasts, the greater their pleasure.

This characteristic came to Griffin's aid now. The kobalin could easily have killed him in the darkness. But the feared attack did not come.

Griffin tried to kick away the claws that held his leg. In vain. The creature's long fingers sat as firmly as C-clamps. Now the kobalin was pulling him along through the bog, through puddles and mud holes, over hard wooden edges, fish skeletons, and bones, which broke beneath him and tore his clothing and his skin. Once it seemed to him that his face was being brushed by grass—until he realized he was lying with his head on the matted fur of a lion cadaver.

The cries of the wounded kobalin behind him became softer, turned to gurgling and sobbing. Then they broke off.

Suddenly Griffin's leg was free.

Stuffy darkness surrounded him on all sides.

Smacking steps to his right.

Before he could spring up, claws seized his braids and pulled his head back into the mud. But still the kobalin did not kill Griffin. It snatched the saber from his victim with one grab. In a twinkling, Griffin was disarmed. Steel clattered in the distance. The kobalin had thrown the blade away.

Dumb, thought Griffin. *Kobalins are really terribly dumb.*

Not that this insight was of any help to him now.

He tensed his neck muscles, supported himself on his arms, and sat up swiftly. There was a fearful jerk, and with a yell he realized that he had sacrificed patches of his scalp and at least one or two braids—they remained behind in his opponent's claws. But he was free.

Somehow he got onto his feet, while behind him the muscular kobalin arms snapped into emptiness like scissors.

This time Griffin didn't stop to fight. He'd learned his lesson. He ran, almost blind in the darkness. Suddenly in the blackness he saw a narrow strip of light, floating behind the parts of a wreck, which looked like huge ribs: Ebenezer had opened the magic door, a torch of light by which Griffin could orient himself in the darkness. The monk must have noted that the lantern was out. He knew that Griffin needed a signal that would point the direction to him.

"One's still alive!" Griffin called, panting, toward the doorway. "At least."

If he received an answer, it was lost in the smacking and

splashing of his steps. The kobalin storming behind Griffin was also now entangled in pieces of wrecks and trails of algae. A shrill gabbling sounded at Griffin's back. Was the kobalin laughing? Or was he summoning other survivors of his brood?

Griffin ran. Stumbled. Fell. Jumped up again and rushed on.

He reached the foot of the hill. The door at the top stood wide open. Flickering light poured over the slope and the makeshift board steps. The door stood isolated at the highest point of the rise, merely a frame with an oak panel and, except for the brightness, betraying nothing of what could be found behind it. Quite certainly not a room, for the hill on the other side was empty. Nevertheless, the glow of the great fireplace fell through the frame.

Where was Ebenezer?

Griffin was now clambering up the steps on all fours. His boots were full of mud, and he was afraid of slipping off the boards if he didn't support himself with his hands, too. He looked over his shoulder and saw the kobalin not six feet behind him—also on front and back claws, except that this posture looked natural for him. The light from the doorway bathed him in a scaly shimmer, an iridescent play of color. Even while climbing he waved his claws, trying to grab Griffin's leg, feeling, snapping, and snarling.

"Griffin!" Ebenezer's voice. "Stay where you are!"

Stay where he was? He wasn't about to.

"Watch out!"

Something large flew over him, missing him by only a

hairsbreadth. Because that did make him halt, it didn't hit him. It hit the kobalin instead.

There was a hollow *klong*, then the creature cracked backward onto the steps, finally lost his grip, and disappeared into the depths. Griffin turned around and saw him land at the edge of the light, caught between two timbers and half buried under a mighty sphere, almost as big as he was.

Ebenezer's globe! The monk must have rolled it out of the back room and flung it out the door with both hands.

The kobalin stretched out a trembling claw, then the movement slackened. His clawed fingers fell onto the globe, sought a hold for the last time, and then slipped down with a shrill screeching. The malice in his glowing eyes was extinguished. A broken spar had bored through his body from behind.

Ebenezer's hands seized Griffin and helped him up.

"Was that all?"

"I think so . . . yes."

"Are you wounded?"

"Yes. No. Not really." He had the feeling of having to dig for each word through walls of pain in his head. Dizziness threatened to cloud his consciousness. "Only a few scratches. Otherwise nothing."

Ebenezer pulled him over the threshold into the light. Griffin fell onto his knees on the floorboards and supported himself with his arms.

"Kobalins have never attacked Jasconius before!" said the monk, while Griffin blinked up at him. "The deep tribes never dared to in the old days."

Griffin gasped for air. "I told you the kobalins are going to war. You wouldn't believe me then. This won't be the last attack. The Maelstrom has taken control of the kobalins. They won't stop for the whale, or for much larger things either. They're going to destroy everything."

Ebenezer took a few undecided paces through the room before he stopped. "I mustn't allow something like this to happen again," he said, as if to himself. His face hardened as he turned to Griffin. "And I will not allow it." There was a new decisiveness and seriousness in his voice. "Looks as if we have to change our plans."

"*Our* plans?"

Ebenezer nodded slowly, as if his head were heavier than usual, and at the same time his words seemed to have more weight. "The tavern must wait. Now we have to deal with cleaning up this filthy lot first."

Griffin swallowed, then the corners of his mouth twitched into the beginnings of a smile.

"Does that mean——," he began.

"We'll help your friends against this pestilence," interrupted Ebenezer as decidedly as a captain who was laying out a new course for his crew. "Jasconius will take us to Aelenium by the fastest route."

Ray Flight

The stalls of the flying rays were located in the hollow dome of the coral mountain cone towering over Aelenium. The steep peak, dozens of waterfalls plunging down its sides to lose themselves in canals and ponds below, looked as if someone had cut off its natural tip ages ago. Instead there was a broad plateau at the top. In the center of it gaped a circular opening, fifty feet in diameter. It served the rays for flights in and out of their refuge.

It was the not first time Jolly had been up here—Captain d'Artois had already taken her and Munk up with him—but the sight of the countless ray pits arranged in a ring around the cave walls still appeared to her as impressive as it was disquieting.

The hall was roofed all over. Light, and sometimes rain, came in only through the large opening in the center.

Although flying rays didn't live in water, they liked their environment damp—and so the rainwater was directed by channels to their pits, where it collected. There the remarkable animals lay flat on the ground in the dampness most of the time and appeared to sleep until someone woke them to ride out on them.

There hadn't been time to find out much more about the amazing creatures, and Jolly treated them with hesitant respect. Unlike the hippocampi, which in spite of all their differences were similar to horses—not only in appearance but even more in behavior—she didn't feel at ease with the rays. Spread on the ground in the corral pits, they seemed torpid and heavy, but when they lifted themselves into the air, they possessed a majesty that took one's breath away. They were slow—the sea horses glided through the water a great deal faster—and yet they commanded enormous strength. Every ray could carry three riders, even more in a pinch. A blow of their sharp tail would kill a man within seconds.

Two rays were all ready to leave when Jolly and Munk entered the shelter. The animals lay outstretched on the floor, side by side, not in their pits but in the middle of the circle of light that fell into the shelter through the roof opening. The captain waited beside one of them.

Jolly cast a backward glance over her shoulder. She looked straight into the face of the morose Captain Walker and had to smile for the first time that day. He, Buenaventure, and the princess were staying close behind her. They looked as if they intended to attack anyone who came even one step too close to their protégée. Jolly felt deep affection for the three people who'd been so much to her in the last weeks: friends, comrades, and not rarely her protectors.

The three were not the only ones who'd come to take leave of the polliwogs, however. A whole train of people followed them on their way to the rays, among them Count Aristotle and the members of the council in their splendid robes, cloaks, and silken shawls.

Jolly didn't particularly like any of these men and women. She found them arrogant, spoiled, and ungrateful. Certainly they all recognized what Jolly and Munk were prepared to do. And yet most of them clearly considered the plan to be the polliwogs' duty—as if it were the unavoidable fate of the two of them, no matter what Jolly and Munk thought about it themselves.

But Jolly had long ceased to fret about that. She worried about other things. The Maelstrom. And the masters of the Mare Tenebrosum, those powers over another, incomprehensible world who had first created this gigantic whirlpool. Originally the Maelstrom was intended to serve as a gate into this world. But he had closed himself to his creators and now practiced his reign of terror without them.

Jolly walked up to Captain d'Artois. Out of the corner of her eye she saw the one-eyed Ghost Trader in his dark robe pull Munk aside and speak to him. The blond boy nodded again and again.

The two were beginning this journey together. They'd known each other for many years. The whole time, the Trader had tried to prepare Munk for this mission without his knowledge.

"Everything all right?" asked Soledad.

Jolly half turned around to the princess. In spite of their age difference Soledad had become a true friend. "No," Jolly replied.

The princess smiled sadly. "Believe me, if I could, I'd go."

"Munk and I will do it."

"Of course."

Neither one of them sounded especially convinced, but there was nothing more to say.

Walker detached himself from the others and touched Jolly on the arm. He seemed to feel even more uncomfortable in the presence of the flying animals than she did.

"Good-bye," he said simply, but his face was grim with concern. "Good luck."

"We don't need it. We're polliwogs, after all."

He stared at her for a moment in surprise, before her sarcasm got through to him. Then he laughed, forgot the closeness of the rays, and bent forward far enough to hug Jolly one last time. "See to it that you get on my nerves again soon, all right?"

She couldn't answer, merely nodded and waved to Buenaventure, who stood there the entire time with eyebrows raised.

With him you never knew whether that was a sign of concern or skepticism or whether it merely belonged to his dog face. He scratched behind his left ear—which made him look even more animal-like, though he did it with a human hand—then he tilted his head and actually looked as though any moment he was going to let out an anguished howl.

Jolly lowered her eyes. She didn't want to burst into tears now, not here and not in front of the members of the council. The captain seemed to sense what was going on in her mind. Quickly he grasped the reins, swung himself into the saddle, and motioned Jolly and Soledad to mount behind him. While the Ghost Trader and Munk took their places on the other ray, their animal also came alive. The first movements traveled through the animal's outspread wings like waves.

A moment later the ray bore them gently upward. Jolly felt the heartbeat of the animal beneath her, very quiet and steady. And with each beat she regained a little bit of her composure.

She sighed and looked down just as the second ray left the ground and sailed through the ceiling hole to the outside.

Walker and Buenaventure stood close together looking after them, their faces betraying their anxiety and helplessness. The council members waved exuberantly, but Jolly took no notice of them at all. Munk, on the other hand, calmly waved back, like a king taking leave of his subjects. He'd taken on many such gestures in the past weeks. It pleased him to be revered by the nobility of Aelenium. Didn't he realize that they'd forget him just as quickly as they'd welcomed him into their ranks? If the mission of the polliwogs were unsuccessful, they'd just be two more victims of a hopeless war.

Pirate Wars

"Captain d'Artois?" Jolly bent closer to him as the ray floated over the edge of the plateau and the chasm of the coral cliffs appeared beneath them.

"Yes?"

"If Aelenium survives . . . I mean, if the Maelstrom is defeated, but I don't come back, can you do something for me?"

He nodded seriously without turning around to her. "If I survive—of course."

"Can you look for Griffin and tell him . . ." She was silent, thought for a moment, and then took heart. "Can you tell him that I liked him very much? Much more than he can imagine?"

"I will gladly do that."

"Tell him that I've often thought of him in these final days. I would really like to have seen him again before we left."

"I understand that."

Jolly was about to add something, but then she thought that d'Artois had certainly grasped what she meant. If he ever really did meet Griffin, he'd find the right words.

She cast a last look back. From the air the protective walls of the city were clearly recognizable. There were two—one at the foot of the coral mountain cone, at the beginnings of the points of the giant sea star from which the city of Aelenium rose. The second barricade wall lay a few hundred yards higher in the maze of narrow streets, only a short distance above the Poets' Quarter. If that broke, the city was lost. Then the inhabitants could only defend themselves with house-to-house fighting, and it would only be a question of time before the kobalins, cannibals, and pirates overran the last positions.

With a heavy heart Jolly turned her eyes away and looked ahead. The rays were bearing them toward the fog wall that surrounded Aelenium on all sides. A moment later the animals plunged into the clouds and were flying through the uppermost layer of the fog wall. Up here it was as if they were floating over the clouds, a woolly white and gray that stretched below them as if it could catch anyone who fell out of the saddle without any difficulty. Misty tentacles stretched out toward the rays, which now and then touched them with their undersides or cut them to pieces with their wings.

Jolly cleared her throat. "May I ask you something, Captain d'Artois?"

"Ask away."

"Is there someone . . . I mean, do you have someone down there waiting for you? For whom you're doing all this?"

Suddenly d'Artois's neck muscles grew clearly prominent, his back visibly tensed. "I'm fighting for . . ." He stopped. Perhaps he'd been going to say "for all the people of Aelenium," but at the last moment he probably realized how empty those words would have sounded. "My wife is dead," he said after a short pause. "She was killed when the kobalins attacked the north arm of the sea star. She was riding a hippocampus that was pulled under by the kobalins."

Jolly's throat became even drier. "I'm sorry."

D'Artois seemed to be concentrating on guiding the ray

again. But she saw that his knuckles were white as he gripped the reins. He was breathing deeply, as if he could free himself of the bad memories that way.

Soledad laid a hand on Jolly's shoulder, very briefly, only to clutch the saddle again immediately. The flight made her uneasy.

"Each one here has made a sacrifice," she whispered in Jolly's ear. "Munk lost his parents; you, Captain Bannon; I, my father. The soldiers are no exception."

Jolly knew that, but still it was good to have Soledad say it aloud. Absorbed with her own fear and uncertainty, she tended to forget that others had to live with loss and with sorrow. She was only one of many. She was nothing special, she'd always said that. Even if Forefather and the Ghost Trader had tried to talk her into something different.

Just a girl.

Somehow she found the thought more comforting than all the talk of polliwog powers and mussel magic. If they should ever succeed in defeating the Maelstrom, it would not be because they were different from others. If they conquered him, it would only be because they didn't forget what they were. Who they were.

And that it was worth it to fight just for that.

"Can you see anything?"

The whale was drifting on the waves with his mouth open. Ebenezer stood between two teeth, holding fast with one hand and bending so far forward that he could look up past the animal's gums. The sky was deep blue, like a concave gem. Swarms of gulls circled over the whale. They followed him along all his pathways through the seas of the world. When he came to the surface, they picked algae and small shelled animals from his back.

Griffin was high up on the whale's head. It had been a difficult and frightening journey through the tunnel-like gullet up into the mouth. From there he'd jumped out into the water, and the whale had dived and then come up again right underneath him, thus lifting Griffin onto his back.

"Griffin!" called Ebenezer from the mouth down below. "Come on, tell, can you see the fog?"

Griffin was shading his eyes with both hands, but the brightness still blinded him. He squinted in all directions, searching for the fog wall behind which Aelenium was concealed. Jasconius might have a substantial intelligence for a sea monster, but his sense of direction left more than a little to be desired.

How would a whale know the points of the compass? Or degrees of longitude and latitude?

"I don't see anything!" Griffin yelled back. "Everything is so bright."

"Wait for a minute," replied Ebenezer, making an effort to be heard over the crashing of the waves against the mighty columns of teeth in the open whale mouth. The monster's gums stretched over him like a black dome. "You'll get used to the brightness pretty quickly."

It wasn't easy to find enough hold on the skin of the

whale's upper surface. Griffin had taken off his boots so as not to injure the animal. Barefoot, he crouched on the highest point of the mighty body, which stretched away under him like the hull of an overturned boat, as black as tar, with patches of thousands of tiny crabs and mussels.

Only now could Griffin comprehend how mighty the whale actually was. He estimated that the body measured more than double the size of a four-master—even without including the gigantic tail.

Griffin peered at the horizon through the whirling flocks of gulls. The more his eyes got used to the daylight, the bluer and more brilliant the sky seemed to him, as if azure dye were being unendingly pumped into it.

But still he couldn't see the fog anywhere. Hadn't Ebenezer explained to him that Jasconius chose his routes randomly? The monk could steer the whale in a general direction, and during the past night Griffin had checked the course by the stars—this was the first time that Ebenezer led him through the throat into the mouth. After that they'd dived again and begun the journey. To be certain, however, Griffin had insisted that they look for their destination once more by daylight. They might be closer to Aelenium than they thought, and he didn't want to risk missing the sea star city.

But except for the gulls, the glittering brightness, and the black monstrosity beneath him, he couldn't make out anything. No fog, nothing. Maybe he was still too close to the surface. That was the reason for the lookout being on the highest mast of a ship. Yes, if he could have flown like the gulls, then maybe—

A hellish noise startled him. About ten paces away, a towering column of water shot up from an opening in Jasconius's back, with a rushing and rattling that hurt his ears. Seconds later Griffin's clothes, which had just dried in the sun, were soaked through again. The masses of water had nearly rinsed him off the whale's back.

He lay on his stomach, cursing, and tried to hold on while the last fountains from the monster's interior poured down on him. He closed his eyes to protect them from the salt water and pressed his cheek firmly against the whale's skin.

"Griffin?" said Ebenezer from below. "Everything all right?"

Griffin struggled to his feet with a groan. "Why didn't you tell me he does that?"

"I thought you knew about whales."

Sighing, Griffin shook his head, rubbed the water off his face, and looked over to the opening in Jasconius's back. The fountain of water had been at least ten fathoms high. The pressure to expel such masses must be enormous.

"Griffin?"

"Wait. Just a minute." A crazy idea was taking shape in his head. Really *quite* crazy.

"Ebenezer," he called finally, "how often does Jasconius do that?"

"Oh, I can ask him to wait a while to do it."

"No, no . . . the other way around!"

"Is it too hot for you?" Ebenezer sounded concerned. Perhaps he thought Griffin had gotten sunstroke on the shadeless back of the whale.

"I only want to try something out."

"Try what out?"

"Can you tell him to do that once more? Blow out all that water, I mean."

"Certainly."

"On demand?"

Down in the mouth, Ebenezer was silent for a moment. Griffin was very happy not to have to see his face at this moment.

"Yes, very likely," replied the monk after a while. He sounded skeptical.

Griffin shooed away a gull that was taking him for an overgrown hermit crab and made his way over to the opening. From up close he could see that the edges had closed.

He took a deep breath. If he wanted to get up higher to search for Aelenium, he had to try it.

And if the water pressure was too strong and broke all his bones?

He hesitated again, then he climbed onto the opening. It looked like a gigantic, pursed-up mouth that could open beneath him at any moment. Griffin took a moment trying to find the best position, and finally he knelt, legs and knees pressed together and hands crossed in his lap.

"Ebenezer? Now!"

"What the devil are you *doing* up there?"

"Just tell him."

The monk hesitated. "Be glad I can't come up there to knock the nonsense out of you, boy."

Griffin grinned. "Just try it, old man."

"The hand of the blessed is led by God's will, don't forget that. Even when it takes the hide off the backside of a braggart."

"Who says so?"

"One of the blessed."

"Go on, Ebenezer! We have to hurry."

Griffin expected new arguments, but instead he felt movement in the whale muscles under his knees and feet.

He braced himself, tensed his whole body, and feared at any moment to be hit by a hammer of water so fast that he might not even feel his crash landing on the sea at all.

"Easy does—" he was beginning when suddenly he was raised as if by a giant hand, as gently as if Jasconius were trying to balance a breakable piece of china.

In his surprise, Griffin let out a jubilant sound, which Ebenezer, down in the mouth, misinterpreted.

"Are you dying?" came through the rushing of water.

"After you, Ebenezer."

Now Griffin concentrated on controlling his balance on the growing column of water. He stretched his arms out to the sides and relaxed himself a bit to offer the pressure more surface. It went better than he'd feared. Wavering, swaying, and with an intense discomfort in his stomach, he was lifted up high by the stream of salt water with a gentleness that he wouldn't have dreamed possible in a monster like Jasconius.

"This is fantastic!" he shouted, laughing.

Five feet, then ten, he now floated over the whale's back—all told, certainly some dozen fathoms over the surface of the sea. Gulls flew away, screaming, upset over this intrusion into their domain. Water sprayed up around Griffin, and yet he succeeded in looking in all four directions.

He discovered the fog. A gray stripe like lead that someone had sprinkled over the horizon. Far away, but certainly reachable within a day, perhaps faster if Jasconius hurried.

Scarcely had he seen the fog when the pressure decreased, and the water stream gradually subsided beneath him. Griffin floated down as if on a magic carpet and was set back on top of the blowhole almost tenderly.

A little dizzy, but relieved, he let himself slide down the curve of the whale's body on the seat of his pants and splashed into the water. With a few strokes he glided alongside Jasconius's gigantic eye, which regarded him curiously. At first Griffin was going to swim on, but then he stopped and trod water and turned toward the mighty black eye, at least twice as large as he was himself.

It was the first time he'd been able to look directly at the whale's eye. Its curving surface was like a mirror—it looked as if Griffin's image was imprisoned in a dark glass ball. But there was more than curiosity in the animal's eye. A trace of melancholy?

Griffin lingered so long in front of Jasconius's eye that Ebenezer called to him in concern. Even then he wasn't able to detach himself from that gaze right away. He had never seen anything more beautiful, and yet it filled him with inexpressible sorrow. Perhaps the monster's centuries-long loneliness was rubbing off onto him. What was going on in the whale's head? What was he thinking about the tiny beings in his interior? Was he pleased to have a little company after so long a time?

A deep booming sounded, almost a trumpeting—the voice of the whale. It was a warm, friendly sound, and suddenly Griffin could do nothing else but smile at the whale eye and wave to him with one hand. It was a wonderful, confusing moment. Only then did he shed his heavyheartedness. He felt as if the whale wanted to share something with him, thousands of stories from thousands of years.

Ebenezer reached both hands out to Griffin and helped him climb into the whale's mouth.

Griffin pointed. "That direction," he said, and then he and the monk fell into each other's arms with relief.

Swiftly they made their way back into the whale's stomach and to the door on the rubble heap.

Jasconius shut his mouth and waited until they had reached the magic room. Then he dove and swam with mighty flipper strokes toward the sea star city.

Into the Maelstrom

Jolly didn't know how long they'd been under way when Captain d'Artois turned his head toward them and pointed wordlessly ahead. She sat up and squinted her eyes into tiny slits to discern anything in the glaring light of the sun. But the spectacle in the distance was impossible to take in at one look. She had to turn her head in order to see it from one end to the other.

"It's so big," she whispered.

Far, far away the line of the sea dissolved into a gray fog, not unlike the fog wall around Aelenium, and yet much higher and inconceivably wide. The water below them was churning, but it had nothing about it of the unrest of an approaching storm, and anyway the air was almost windless. The farther ahead Jolly looked, the more clearly she could see that they were already over the outermost currents of a titanic whirlpool: The sea moved in broad, sweeping orbits from west to east, like the annual rings on a severed tree trunk. And it inclined very gradually downward, which was really impossible according to all known rules.

Over and over, towers of foam sprayed into the air, for no apparent reason, for there were no reefs or sandbanks to break the waves. The surface boomed and raged, and here and there the waves seemed to possess wills of their own, for they also turned against each other, as if there were something beneath them resisting the terrible suction. Foam lay in streaks on the water like scraps of skin on boiled milk, and not even the blue of the heavens was mirrored here anymore, the sea was so stirred up, so scarred. Instead the endless expanse beneath them had turned a purplish black, as if the disturbance of the waters had washed up the darkness from the depths like the camouflage color of ten thousand octopuses.

"It would be much worse if we flew closer," said d'Artois. His voice sounded hoarse and thick.

"Do you intend to?" asked Soledad. "To fly over the Maelstrom?"

Jolly shuddered at the thought.

"Of course not. That would be much too dangerous. But I thought it would be good if we all finally saw what we're dealing with. *Maelstrom* is only a word. But that down there, that's . . ." He shook his head when no suitable expression occurred to him. "A chasm between the worlds, the one-eyed one says. But it looks to me more like the *end* of the world."

He was right. If Jolly hadn't known better, she'd have been

convinced they'd reached the end of the ocean, that place where, people had once believed, the water poured over the edge of the flat earth. Jolly's foster father, Bannon, had explained to her that the world was round and that there was nothing like an end of it. But the sight of the Maelstrom could convince a person that the opposite was true.

Jolly felt horribly small, much too tiny to cope with such a force of nature. Mile after mile of roaring sea stretched out down there, and that was certainly nothing compared to what awaited her in the center of all this chaos. In the Crustal Breach, in the heart of the Maelstrom.

D'Artois gave a wave to the soldier flying the second ray, and the two animals simultaneously turned in a wide curve.

"We're now flying back to a place where the sea isn't so churned up," he explained over his shoulder. "It's important for you two to be able to dive vertically so as not to get caught in the suction."

"But we have to get closer in any case," Jolly countered. "Sooner or later we're going to feel the suction anyway."

"Not necessarily. A maelstrom is shaped like a funnel. Up here it might be fifty miles wide, but it decreases on the ocean floor. You'll be able to walk on the ground unharmed, straight underneath its outer edges." He paused for a moment. "The one-eyed one says that in the center, where it rises from a gigantic mussel on the floor of the Crustal Breach, the Maelstrom isn't much wider than a tower."

Jolly looked over at the Ghost Trader, the one-eyed one, as d'Artois called him. The Trader was talking urgently to Munk, but at this distance she couldn't hear what he was saying. Perhaps he was giving instructions similar to the captain's.

"How many miles do we have to go?" Jolly asked.

"If we set you down at the edge of the Maelstrom . . . well, about twenty or thirty. It's not possible to say exactly, because it's getting bigger every day and we've given up measuring it."

Thirty miles, thought Jolly, shaken. The Crustal Breach itself supposedly lay at a depth of thirty thousand feet, Forefather said. And they were supposed to cover all that without any help? They couldn't even take a compass with them because the water pressure would immediately destroy the glass.

"Don't forget that you mustn't get too far from the ocean bottom," d'Artois continued, repeating an instruction that the Ghost Trader and Forefather had already hammered into them. "The Maelstrom will be looking for enemies approaching him. The one-eyed one says as long as you keep to the bottom, he won't discover you. It would be best if you actually walk, and only swim in emergencies." He shook his head as if he were sorry to be parroting rules that he didn't understand himself. "You should be careful of strong currents, of changing pressure, and so forth. These all could be signs that the Maelstrom is reaching straight at you."

Jolly nodded numbly. She'd already heard all that at least a hundred times in the last few days. But to hear it now, explained by someone like d'Artois, who didn't accept magic as a given, made the terror ahead even more palpable and threatening.

Soledad had said hardly anything during the last few

minutes, and she kept still now, too. Jolly knew the princess felt guilty at the thought of the burden being placed on the polliwogs. That she herself could do nothing and knew of no better solution made her wild with helplessness.

The rays were now flying in a southerly direction again, where the sea wasn't so rough. During the flight they'd seen kobalin hosts in the deep, seething dark swarms like ants that were moving under the surface in the direction of Aelenium. Kobalins as far as the eye could see. Once they'd flown through a zone where it was raining fish cadavers out of a clear sky, and all knew that somewhere beneath them there was a creature of the Maelstrom, a monstrosity like the Acherus, who had killed Munk's parents. Possibly they'd even passed over the lord of the kobalins himself, a creature that none of them had seen as yet but whom Jolly had already twice been close enough to touch. Once on the open sea during their trip to Tortuga, a second time with Griffin on the island of the shape changer. Both times it had rained dead fish in his vicinity.

Gradually the waves under them settled into smoothness, and finally d'Artois gave another wave to the second ray. The animals slowed their flight and began to circle. Jolly looked over her shoulder. The dark stripe on the horizon was still visible, but the arms of the Maelstrom did not reach this far. And the kobalin hordes had long since passed this spot, so there was at least a chance for them to push their way to the sea bottom unhindered.

"D'Artois!" Soledad cried suddenly. "Up ahead there!"

"I see it," growled the captain.

Jolly looked to the south and discovered what the two of them meant. A dark spot was approaching them on the water, so fast that it was flying over the surface.

"Is that a sea horse?" she asked.

"His rider must be riding it almost to death to go so fast," replied d'Artois, frowning.

"A servant of the Maelstrom?" Soledad said what they were all thinking.

D'Artois whistled in the direction of the second ray, but its riders had already caught sight of the spot in the distance. The captain pulled a small crossbow from its halter on the saddle and stretched it with one practiced hand. An old-fashioned weapon like this was easier to handle from the back of a ray than a pistol, which first had to be rammed and loaded.

Soon the new arrival had come so near that its outlines allowed no more doubt. It was a sea horse. But its rider wore thrown-together clothing in the fashion of a pirate, not the leather uniform of the guards of Aelenium.

"Who the devil is that?" asked Soledad. Judging by her tone, she would probably have liked to be holding a weapon in her hands herself.

"I know the animal," said d'Artois a moment later. "That's Matador."

A tremor ran through Jolly. Her breath stopped, her heartbeat altered. "Griffin's sea horse?"

The captain nodded.

Pirate Wars

And then the rider raised an arm and waved excitedly to them, and although his voice could not be heard over the rushing of the rays' wings and the distant roaring of the Maelstrom, and although his face was still just as small as the head of a knitting needle, Jolly knew who he was.

"That *is* Griffin!" Her voice broke, she sounded shrill with excitement. "Go down, d'Artois! Please—go lower!"

Circling, the ray lost altitude. When it was still four or five fathoms over the water, Jolly recognized Griffin's blond braids, then his smile. He was now waving so exaggeratedly that for a moment she believed it might be a hallucination, something conjured up by her longing.

"Griffin!" she cried, waving back. Softly she whispered into the wind, "Oh, Griffin, thank God. . . ."

She paid no attention to the others anymore, not to Munk, who was looking over at her stony-faced, not to the lines of concern on the Ghost Trader's forehead, not to d'Artois's warning, or to Soledad's good-natured murmuring. In a flash she opened her safety belt, stood up on the saddle, ran two steps across the broad wing of the ray—and slid into the water in a head dive.

The excited cries of her companions faded as she broke through the surface, in a confusion of dancing bubbles and foam. For moments she heard only bubbling and roaring, then she turned beneath the water and poked her head above the waves. Griffin steered Matador in her direction, reined in the seahorse two or three paces away, frantically opened the fastenings of his saddle girt, and jumped down into the water. With one powerful stroke he was beside her, and then they hugged and kissed and felt as though the Maelstrom and the kobalins and the whole world around them had vanished into air.

"I followed the ship," he got out breathlessly, while the water kept splashing into his face. "When you left Aelenium . . . with the *Carfax* . . ." He gulped for air. "And now I almost came too late again . . . you were just about to start off."

She kissed him again, more vehemently this time, and they both threatened to go under, because in their joy they forgot to swim. Jolly had almost forgotten that Griffin, in contrast to her, couldn't breathe underwater.

D'Artois's ray was now circling low over the surface. The crests of waves lapped at the animal's belly. Jolly saw that Soledad was smiling in satisfaction, and for some reason that appeared to her hugely generous and understanding in light of the situation. She became aware for the first time of how very much the princess meant to her.

Something splashed into the water not far away from her, and then Munk popped up beside them.

"Hello, Griffin," he said and spat out salt water. He smiled, perhaps a little grimly.

"Munk." Griffin nodded to him, then turned once more to Jolly and gave her a—much too short—kiss. Then he let her go. She knew why he did that: He didn't want the wedge that, against his will, he'd driven between her and Munk to get any larger. Not considering what lay before them.

Now the Ghost Trader's ray was also hovering over the

water. The animals circled around the two boys and the girl, while Matador swam in the waves several yards away. The draft of the ray's wings blew cool in Jolly's face. Perhaps that was the reason she was shivering. Or was it the certainty of leaving?

Well, it was there, the moment she'd been fearing for weeks. In a few minutes she'd be alone with Munk, down in the deep. Only the two of them, entirely on their own.

Griffin gave her an encouraging smile, but she saw through the facade: He didn't care about the Maelstrom, about Aelenium, or about the fate of the world at all—he only wanted her to return home to him safely. At that moment, in those few intense seconds, she made the irrevocable decision to fulfill that wish: Come what might, she would not give up. She would do what must be done. And then she would return—to him.

"Jolly, Munk—look out!"

Knapsacks of oiled leather fell from the rays into the water. They both grabbed them and fastened them tightly to their backs. Griffin helped them with it, Munk too, who let him only after a short hesitation. The bundles contained waterproof boxes with pickled meat, fruit, and raw vegetables, as well as coconut pieces—food that could be unpacked below the surface without immediately spoiling or becoming soaked with salt water. When they spoke or ate no water passed the lips of the polliwogs, but that also made drinking water more difficult: The knapsacks held bottles with narrow, corked openings through which they could suck up the contents, as if with a straw. They'd practiced all that, as they had so much else, so that their mission wouldn't founder on something as ordinary as eating and drinking.

"Keep in mind," the Ghost Trader called to them when they were ready to start out, "always stay close to the ground. Don't be tempted to swim over impassable terrain. The Maelstrom will send out currents in all directions, and he'll discover you if they encounter any unexpected resistance."

"How does the Ghost Trader know all that?" murmured Griffin.

Jolly grasped his hand underwater. "I think he's experienced all this before, that time when the first polliwogs conquered the Maelstrom in the Crustal Breach and shut him into his mussel shell."

"But that was thousands of years ago!"

Jolly nodded. She had no more time to inform him of all she'd learned, so she only said, "Talk with Soledad. She knows about everything."

He looked at her uncertainly, then he also nodded.

The voice of the Ghost Trader pushed between them like a separating hand. "It's time to start!" he called down from his ray.

"Yes," said Munk, with a sideways glance at the two of them.

Jolly tried to read his eyes, but he turned away quickly. She looked at Griffin, kissed him one last time, then let go of his hand.

"Farewell," she said, thinking it was terrible that nothing

better occurred to her, something that expressed everything she felt and felt for him.

"Good luck," said Griffin. "Come back soon, the two of you." He glided over to Munk in one stroke and shook his hand below the water. "Take care of yourselves."

Munk nodded to him abruptly.

A moment later, when the sun illuminated that spot where the polliwogs had just been treading water, they'd both vanished.

The feeling was not new anymore and had long lost its charm. With outstretched arms and legs Jolly and Munk rushed down, unaffected by the water pressure, which would have killed any other human after the first few minutes. Their polliwog vision allowed them to see several hundred feet ahead of them, but down here there was nothing that could have held their glance.

They fell through a nowhere of gray into gray, for polliwog vision emptied all things of most of their color, making them pale and plain and ugly—even if there'd been things there to see. But around them there was nothing, only empty water, in which a swarm of tiny particles floated now and then. No fish. No trace of light. The armies of the kobalins had driven all living things out of this part of the sea.

"Do you think there are any here?" asked Jolly. "Kobalins, I mean."

Munk shrugged, while they floated ever downward.

"Maybe. But that really doesn't make any sense. They'd be more needed in Aelenium than out here."

Jolly thought over what the Ghost Trader had said. About the currents the Maelstrom could use to seek and find them. Once they got down on the sea bottom, they might perhaps be safer from them. But what about now, while they were still sinking even farther downward? Weren't they helplessly exposed to the searching currents of the Maelstrom the whole time?

She hastily repressed the thought and concentrated on finding something in her surroundings on which she could fasten her gaze. But there was nothing except Munk, who was floating along on a level with her. She didn't even have the feeling of sinking, really, since the water offered them no trace of resistance and there was never anything to see that would allow them to estimate their speed. Were they sinking slowly? Or at a breakneck speed?

During the practices in the waters around Aelenium there had always been the undercity nearby, the formation of sharp-pointed coral structures on the underside of the giant sea star. The sight of it had made it easier to orient themselves. But out here there was nothing like that.

Jolly's dejection grew harder and harder to bear. Looking at Munk, she saw that it was the same with him. His features were closed, as if he were caught in the suction of his own gloomy thoughts. At some point she groped for his hand as they sank deeper side by side. He returned the gesture so gratefully that for the first time she felt a hope that he could forget their quarrel and again become the old Munk, the same lovable, playful Munk she'd first met on his parents' island. The same Munk she'd shown how to shoot a cannon and who'd dreamed of being a pirate.

The weeks that had passed since then had changed him, made him more withdrawn, grimmer, and more opaque. But perhaps all those traits would disappear and they could be friends again as they had before. Down here they were dependent on each other, and there would be times when they needed to give each other courage and reassure themselves. How would that work if Munk still hated her because she'd fallen in love with Griffin and not with him?

Jolly lost any feeling of time as they sank into the deep hand in hand. Once something twitched forward up ahead at the edge of her field of vision, possibly just a fish. Not big enough for a kobalin, thank God.

They might have been under way one hour or several, and most of the time they had been swimming. Both avoided speaking about their rift. Sooner or later they'd have to talk about it, Jolly knew that. There was no point in keeping silent. And as little as he could excuse her for what had happened, she understood his behavior. There had been so much selfishness in him, so much anger and injured vanity.

Sometime, after half an eternity, they made out the sea bottom below them. Rocky points reached toward them in the darkness. At first sight they looked like figures in hooded capes. Shapeless stone structures stretched toward them like bony fingers. The cliffs rose out of a dark, rocky underground, a plain that led gently downward—down to the Crustal Breach.

Thirty miles, went through Jolly icily. She felt deathly sick.

"That place up ahead looks good," said Munk.

"Good?" she asked scornfully, but at once she was sorry. Who was the one picking a quarrel now?

The place Munk was pointing to lay a bit farther north—provided that north was the direction where the land fell away. They knew only that the Crustal Breach was the deepest point far and wide, at least Forefather had claimed that.

With quick strokes they moved sideways and let themselves sink to the ground. Both were wearing sandals with firm soles, which offered hardly any resistance to the water and protected them from rough surfaces underfoot, as long as the undersea wasn't too different from land. But who could know whether everything might look very different in such a place? Did any of the laws of the surface apply here at all?

Shivering, Jolly realized that they were the first humans who'd gone this deep in the ocean. Or no, not the very first—polliwogs had set out to conquer the Maelstrom before, thousands of years ago. That was the first time he'd tried to tear down the borders to the Mare Tenebrosum. The polliwogs, so it was said, had shut him into the mussel in the Crustal Breach, until fourteen years ago he'd managed to burst his prison. Right afterwards new polliwogs were born, all of whom had perished since then except for two. Only Jolly and Munk were left. It was now their responsibility to walk the path of the polliwogs once again and to overcome the Maelstrom.

The landscape was impressive in its absolute desolation. The ground looked like a mixture of cooled lava and firmly baked ashes. There were no plants far and wide. Forefather said they couldn't survive at such depths. The stone wasn't even covered with lichens; all was bare and desolate like the tip of a volcanic island, which Jolly knew from her travels with Bannon.

They also saw no fish, although Jolly couldn't shake off the feeling that they were being observed from the splits and cracks in the porous rock surface. There must be life down here, and with a shudder she thought of all the stories of giant krakens and other monsters that were said to live on the bottom of the sea.

From the ground, the rock needles around them seemed even higher and more bizarre. Some looked as if someone had piled black cinders on top of each other and had let them set, half liquid. Others were so sharp-edged that it hurt her just to look at them. Not a few resembled grotesque, distorted bodies, which bent over them like giants and showed teeth of dark stone. Those that lay on the edge of their vision appeared to move if you weren't looking at them directly.

Jolly bit her lower lip in the hope that the pain would turn her from her fears. Unsurprisingly, it didn't help. She straightened her knapsack, checked all the fastenings and belts, then turned to Munk.

"Let's go," she said, and with that she sucked a deep breath of fresh salt water into her lungs.

"Yes," he said softly. "Let's get on the road."

The Threshold of War

On his return to Aelenium, Griffin was struck by how very much the city had changed. He'd barely noticed it earlier, in his frenzy to find Matador and chase after Jolly—even if only to say good-bye.

The coral mountain bristled with weapons and war machines. The markets that had still existed at numerous places in the labyrinth of streets one or two weeks before had vanished. The storytellers' square was now piled with sandbags and chests of weapons. Soldiers patrolled in the Poets' Quarter, which lay just below the second defense wall; here, too, there were no more public lectures, readings, or singing.

At first, it seemed as though the burghers of Aelenium had vanished into thin air. Instead you saw only people in uniform in the narrow coral streets. But when he looked more closely, Griffin saw that many civilians had changed their everyday clothing for the leather uniforms of the guard.

In the city's squares and gardens they were being instructed by weapons experts in the basics of fighting with saber and pistol. All too quickly it became obvious that the inhabitants of the sea star city were not people of war. Those not responsible for the provisioning of the city as traders, fishermen, or their employees usually worked in the library—there was no one among them who'd really mastered the handling of weapons, even though the council had begun years ago to subject the citizens to regular training.

They'd known for a long time that the Maelstrom was arming for war, but now it was painfully obvious that the preparations for defense hadn't been sufficient. Count Aristotle and the other lords of the city had relied a bit too airily on the polliwogs' being found in time to fight the Maelstrom.

Griffin provided for Matador and asked the stable boy to care for the animal especially attentively after the strenuous ride. The worst was still to come for the sea horses, too. Griffin wasn't sure when action would come—but when it did, the battle in the water against the kobalins certainly wouldn't be any picnic.

Walker and Buenaventure, who'd greeted him on his arrival, had hurried away again to help reinforce the first defense wall above the breakwater. More and more wooden beams, sandbags, and pieces of coral from the undercity were heaved onto the barricades to make penetration more difficult for the kobalins. But it was questionable which was the bigger danger: the deep tribes or the fleet of the cannibal king Tyrone.

D'Artois, the Ghost Trader, and the council seemed to be divided on that. Certainly the kobalins were horrible creatures with claws and murderous sharks' teeth. But their element was the water, and no one knew yet how well they'd fight on land.

On the other hand, the cannibals and pirates Tyrone would lead into battle were ordinary men, and in great numbers. For fighting in the streets, they were the perfect allies for the Maelstrom.

Still, Tyrone and his fleet had been involved in wasting sea battles in the waters west of the Lesser Antilles. The Antilles captains, who'd ruled that region of the Caribbean for years, felt themselves betrayed by the cannibal king and swore vengeance.

This could only be a good thing for the defenders of Aelenium. Not only would Tyrone—and with him the Maelstrom—be significantly weakened by the sea battle, but he also lost valuable time as well. What had been planned as a surprise attack on the sea star city had now turned into a predictable military expedition, which the inhabitants of Aelenium could incorporate into their plans.

Griffin picked his way through the lanes and over steep steps. Along the way he passed the two defense walls and various smaller barricades.

People in uniform were everywhere—mostly men, but there were also some women among them who intended to fight for the city. Some soldiers were formed into troops and marched in formation, while others ran around in disorder, reinforcing the walls or receiving last instructions.

The Ghost Trader had vanished immediately after their return to Aelenium. He was last seen at Forefather's side, and when Griffin asked d'Artois about it, he confirmed that the two sages had withdrawn into the library. "No affair of mine," the captain had declared gruffly before he took himself off to his troops to go over last-minute strategies.

Griffin wondered what Forefather and the Ghost Trader had to discuss up there. Soledad had told him in a whisper of the water spinners Jolly met when the *Carfax* sank and also of what the three mysterious women deep on the floor of the sea had told her. Even if Soledad wasn't quite sure what Jolly thought about it, Griffin could hardly imagine that Jolly had been having a hallucination. Perhaps Aelenium really was a place where the gods had gathered before they went into oblivion and died. And perhaps Forefather actually was the creator himself, the first deity, who had created this world.

Griffin found it all just as incredible as Soledad did. But some of it definitely did fit into the picture, beginning with the existence of such an inconceivable city as Aelenium, and then to the remarkable capabilities of the Ghost Trader. Captain d'Artois had once told him that Forefather was the soul of Aelenium. Possibly that had been far more than an empty phrase.

Griffin went up the last steps and reached the palace square. The sentries who normally guarded the door had been withdrawn. Danger wasn't threatening here—high over the water—but way down below on the shores of the sea star.

Griffin met scarcely anyone in the palace, either. Most of the women and children were hiding in protective shelters deep in the heart of the city. There were no more servants in the corridors, the guest section seemed swept empty. A depressing atmosphere pervaded the abandoned passageways and salons. More than once Griffin thought he heard footsteps following him; but then there was only the echo of his own steps.

He ran past his room, deciding against changing the pirate outfit for a new leather uniform. He'd assembled his odds and ends of pirate clothes from the wreckage in the belly of the whale: a pair of leather trousers, a black shirt, and a vest into which someone had sewn a bent Spanish gold doubloon over the heart, obviously a good luck charm.

Griffin decided it didn't really matter what clothes he wore into a fight against kobalins and cannibals. Teeth and claws could go through leather, too.

He stopped at Jolly's door. It hurt to imagine that she could still be waiting for him behind it—quite aside from the fact, he thought with a melancholy smile, that it was definitely not her way to wait for *anyone at all*.

The door was not locked; he could enter unhindered. The bedclothes were all roiled up.

"Looks as if Jolly had nightmares during her last night in Aelenium," said a voice behind him.

Griffin whirled around. "So I did hear steps."

Soledad shook her head with a smile. "Certainly not mine. No one hears me if I don't want them to." That sounded a little arrogant, but Griffin knew that the princess was speaking the truth. Even when she was just walking along beside you, her movements were fluid, catlike.

With a suppressed sigh he turned again to the empty room. "I think Jolly often had bad dreams—not only last night."

It was an odd moment in which they both merely stood there, staring at the disordered bedclothes and focusing their thoughts on Jolly.

Griffin cleared his throat. "We're talking about her as if she wasn't coming back."

"She'll come back."

"Yes," he replied softly. "She will."

"No one goes on a journey like that without playing it through in her head a hundred times beforehand," Soledad said. "In dreams, too, whether she wants to or not."

Griffin shuddered at the thought of the terrors that Jolly must have painted for herself, and shivered still more at the idea of what she might actually expect down there. His imagination exhausted itself in pictures of grisly monsters before he came to a much more obvious terror: the loneliness in the black wasteland of the deep sea.

The same thoughts seemed to be worrying Soledad. "The greatest fear she had, I think, was not the Maelstrom." She turned and stared at him until he returned her gaze. "But Munk, don't you think?"

"Yes," he said. "I do think so, for sure."

"Is he a danger to her down there?"

Griffin was amazed that Soledad had thought about that. Until now he'd believed that he was the only one who saw Munk as a threat to Jolly. "If only I knew."

"That night on the *Carfax*, they almost fought with each other. He wanted to force her to remain in Aelenium." Soledad's eyes looked more shadowed than usual. It made him uneasy to see her that way; perhaps because he'd hoped she could dispel his own worries. Instead her words only confirmed what he'd secretly been fearing himself.

"Why did you come here?" she asked. "Into her room, I mean."

He hesitated. "For the same reason you did, right? To be close to her. To say good-bye."

She walked past him to an arched window. The room was very high and narrow, almost like the inside of a tower. Many rooms in Aelenium had such odd dimensions, evidence of the fact that the city had grown and not been constructed.

Griffin followed the princess and looked over the steep cliff into the city below, over the furrowed slope of lanes and roofs that led down to the points of the sea star and the water. Not much longer and then nothing would be as it once had been anymore. Death and destruction would strike the city.

The image tore at his heart. For the first time he felt a real bond with this wondrous place, and something like a feeling of responsibility rose in him. If Jolly was ready to sacrifice herself for Aelenium, then he must ask the same of himself.

"What are you going to do?" Soledad asked, as if she'd just asked herself the same question and already found an answer.

"Fight," he said. "Like Jolly."

She nodded silently.

"And you?"

Soledad shrugged. "They won't let me ride the rays because I'm a woman, those idiots. And no one seems to know yet whether they're really going to use the sea horses against the kobalins."

He nodded.

"I'm going with the divers," she went on. "I've been taking lessons the last few days. I was down at the anchor chain. The kobalins will try to cut it to detach Aelenium from the sea bottom."

"If they really try it, no one can stop them. The divers can't go to the bottom. It's too deep."

"Nevertheless, we aren't going to just look on and do nothing."

He shook his head sadly. "It's madness to confront the kobalins in their own element."

"One has to do something." The corners of her mouth twitched slightly, but no smile followed. "And you?"

"D'Artois has assigned me to the ray riders."

Suddenly the princess walked up to him and hugged him. "Then take care of yourself, Griffin. Don't make me be the one who has to tell Jolly when she comes back that the kobalins have torn you to pieces."

He returned the embrace and blushed when she gave him a kiss on the forehead.

"I'll leave you alone up here now. And give Jolly a nice greeting from me when you think about her." With a wink she went out into the corridor and pulled the door closed behind her.

Griffin stared at the door for a long moment. Then, with a heavy heart, he turned to the window again. Over the fog the rays were moving in their majestic orbits.

It was Soledad's ninth dive, but she'd been told that the constricted feeling in the diving suit never diminished, even by the fiftieth time. True, she could breathe for fifteen to twenty minutes through hoses that ran to the bubblestone in a metal container strapped under her chin. But the air was already thin and stuffy after a few minutes.

Soledad had never seen anything like the bubblestones before her arrival in the sea star city, and she wondered where they came from. The other divers seemed not to know the answer to that either. They explained to Soledad that the stones were kept in a cave near the core and carefully protected. When a stone had given up all its air, it needed several hours to dry out completely and absorb new oxygen. Because there were only several hundred of these stones in existence, the supply would inevitably run low during the battle if the fighting under water lasted too long.

Soledad and a handful of others dove down along the furrowed underside of a sea star arm. The princess had been able to sleep for a few hours to gather strength, which she would urgently need in the days to come. Although the sun was shining on the water above, it was very dark down here below. Only where the mighty anchor chain emerged from a complicated tangle of steel and branching coral was there pale light. Shafts had been driven through the sea star point and within them, above water level and at regular intervals, were placed torches. A yellow glow fell from them but was soon lost in the depths. Enough light to recognize attackers and to oppose them—but too little to, say, read the print in a book. The murky soup would make the battle down here even more difficult.

The anchor chain was so broad that it would take twenty men to encircle one of the powerful links with outstretched arms. Next to the rusty chain links, a human was as lost as a fish. Disheveled water plants floated on invisible currents and settled around the metal in many places like dense shrubbery.

Every time Soledad looked down into the deep from the chain, she grew dizzy.

It was true that the endless ribbon sank down to the edge of the field of light, out of the torchlight into darkness, but the idea that it reached to the bottom of the sea turned her stomach. Even though she was underwater, that thought gave her something like acrophobia. So much emptiness beneath her, so much nothing.

Walker had argued with her when she told him that she was going to join the divers. She hadn't let herself be budged from her decision, however, not even by him.

Soledad knew what she was letting herself in for. She

could have chosen the easy way and fought on the barricades, and no one would have reproached her for that. But she wouldn't be her father's daughter, the future empress of all the pirates between Tortuga and New Providence, if she watched passively as the kobalins streamed onto land. She wanted to fight the creatures of the Maelstrom—and as quickly as possible.

All the divers had now reached the network of metal stays and branching coral in whose center the chain was anchored to the underside of the sea star point by a mighty ring. Nowhere was the anchor chain so vulnerable as at this spot where it connected with the city.

Destroying the metal was beyond the kobalins' capabilities—they possessed neither explosives nor heavy-duty tools—but their claws were sharp enough to dig the fastening out of the coral. Therefore, the attack on the chain was expected primarily at the upper end, not down at the anchor.

The torch shafts were arranged in a wide circle around the mooring, which gave the strange place the feeling of an ancient temple—a spectral shrine that was surrounded by a ring of pillars of light.

The patrol that Soledad and the other divers were replacing returned to the surface. Soledad watched the clumsy figures swim through the shimmering columns and dissolve into darkness on the other side of them. Despite the presence of her fellow fighters, she was overcome by an anxious feeling of forlornness, and she shuddered at the thought of Jolly, who must be experiencing this feeling but a hundred times more strongly. She wished she could have found the right words before Jolly left to express how deeply she respected the girl's bravery.

Soledad and the others scattered into the jungle of coral branches and metal stays. Most took positions on the cross braces to preserve their strength for the coming battle. Bubbles of oxygen swirled around their heads like swarms of silvery insects.

The thin air was already undermining Soledad's stamina. She tried to breathe more consciously and slowly. She loosened one of the two small crossbows she carried at her belt, stretched it with the aid of a crank, pulled a bolt out of her chest strap, and pushed it into shooting position. The force of a shot under-water was not half as great as on the surface, but it was still enough to penetrate a thin kobalin body at a distance of ten feet. Firing pistols down here was of course impossible, but like the others, Soledad was armed with a multitude of daggers. The narrow stilettos were the most practical weapons. Unfortunately they were only useful in close combat—which in view of the kobalins' claws was not a comfortable idea. Therefore they all hoped to be able to keep their enemies away from them with the help of the crossbows.

Most of the divers had spent hundreds of hours in shooting practice underwater. Soledad had been repeatedly surprised at how accurate the men were, despite the adverse conditions. She wished she could have said the same for herself.

Thus they sat there, spanned crossbows in both hands,

and waited. After about twenty minutes, even the hardiest man changed his bubblestone, to then again wait silent and motionless, keeping his eyes on the darkness on the other side of the light pillars.

It was not Soledad who saw the first kobalin, but a man who was crouching on a stump of coral thorn a little way away from her. Out of the corner of her eye she saw him start into excited motion, which in spite of all the practice looked slow and strangely clumsy. In an instant the warning was passed on by signals, and at once two dozen crossbow bolts were directed out into the darkness.

At first there was only a handful of kobalins, then more, and more.

Spindle-thin figures with limbs much too long glided through the darkness. Creatures with bared teeth and narrow eyes, in which the shine from the torch shafts was refracted. It looked as if their eyes had imprisoned fire.

Soledad overcame her horror, aimed, and fired her first bolt into the dark.

Did the kobalin scream when she hit him? If so, human ears were not able to hear the sound. A cloud of dark blood enwrapped the dying creature and made the sight even worse.

Now the bolts were flashing through the water everywhere. Most hit their targets. The first wave of attack faltered, then ebbed away entirely. Soon the only kobalins still to be found within the circle of the light columns were motionless corpses with sightless eyes, floating in the emptiness like ash flakes over a fire.

Soledad didn't stop to think. Her motions were mechanical. Her breathing grew faster, now using much more of the valuable air from her bubblestone. But she kept herself under control, reloaded both crossbows, and resisted the temptation to change the stone ahead of time—it would have been a waste and furthermore would have taken much too much time.

She clenched her teeth and stared into the darkness, past the floating bodies in their billowing clouds of blood.

She thought about Walker. Thought about Jolly.

Then they came again, and Soledad gave up thinking about anything at all. The creatures avoided the light columns as if they shunned the brightness. From all directions they glided toward the divers with grotesque, lightning-swift strokes.

Soledad killed two with bolts before a third one reached her.

Claws flashed, then steel.

The war for Aelenium had begun.

The Battle for the Anchor

Griffin was at the breakwater with Ebenezer and Jasconius when the alarm bells sounded. First only one, then more and more, until finally all Aelenium resounded with the clangor of bells. The sound sped across the roofs of the sea star city like a storm wind, floated up the cliffs and down, broke on the filigreed towers and ornamented facades and the steep roof ridges of the lower quarter.

"Take care of yourself," said Ebenezer in farewell, drawing Griffin to him in his big arms. "Remember, I need you for—"

"The first floating tavern in the belly of a whale." Griffin laughed and thumped him on the back. "Sure."

Ebenezer released him. "Jasconius and I will hold the fort down here."

"Be careful out there in the water." Griffin was worried about Jasconius and the monk. The waters around Aelenium would soon be swarming with kobalins. Men could flee onto land before them, at least for a while. But the whale was at their mercy. Griffin had a terribly guilty conscience over bringing Jasconius and Ebenezer here. If anything happened to either one of them, it would be his fault.

"I know what you're thinking." The monk waved the idea away. "Jasconius and I have coped with worse." Griffin doubted that. Hadn't Ebenezer told him just a while ago that the whale had never been attacked by kobalins before?

He took a step to one side and looked over at Jasconius. The giant whale floated like a buoyant mountain beside the jetty at the end of a sea star point. His left eye looked right over the edge and seemed to return Griffin's gaze. Again the boy was seized with sadness when he looked into the depths of that eye. The whale was not a happy creature. The sight was heartrending.

Disregarding the alarm bells that were calling him and all others to their positions, he hurried over to Jasconius. He stopped at the edge of the jetty, stretched out his right arm, and bent over until he could touch the whale's skin. He laid his hand flat on the smooth surface, only six feet away from the gigantic melancholy eye.

"Good luck," he whispered so softly that not even Ebenezer could hear. "I hope that everything you want comes to pass."

He was astonished at his words, which had risen up out of his mind without asking him for permission.

A dull rumble sounded from the whale's half-open mouth, similar to the noise that occurs when you blow across the neck of a bottle. Jasconius's voice. He too was taking leave.

Griffin had to turn away to keep the tears from coming. With a shake, he collected himself and ran off.

"See you later," he called, without turning around one last time to Ebenezer and the whale.

He ran as fast as he could along the bank of the sea star arm to his ray, which was waiting for him with outspread wings on one of the lower squares. D'Artois had moved all the animals that were going to be assigned to the first waves of attack out of the ray shelter to the vicinity of the shore, to shorten the distance.

"Griffin, about time," came the greeting from Rorrick, an experienced guardsman, whom the captain had assigned to him as sharpshooter.

Rorrick was a red-haired man in his forties, who claimed to be able to hit unerringly any point on the water from the swaying back of a ray. When the kobalins dared to show their ugly mugs over the waves—and no one doubted it any-more—it was his job to target them from the ray and, it was to be hoped, keep them from going on land.

He had a mighty mustache, just as fiery red as his barely controllable hair. Besides, he had the longest fingers Griffin had ever seen on a human being. With them he handled his gun as sensitively as a musical instrument, and what he lacked in patience for handling rays and hippocampi, he made up for with his precision shooting and an incredible sense of balance. Griffin had already undertaken some practice flights with him and learned to attune himself to Rorrick's shooting. He knew when he should keep the ray low or had to slow the wing beats to guarantee Rorrick a better aim. The man was more than twice as old as Griffin, but he never gave him the feeling of lording it over him.

Griffin returned Rorrick's greeting and swung himself into the saddle, bent over the animal's head, whispered a few encouraging words, and took up the reins. Around them other rays were rising in mighty thrusts, always only a handful at once, so that the animals never crossed courses. Griffin and Rorrick were among the last to leave the square.

Everywhere swarms of rays were streaming from lanes and openings between the roofs. Like black plumes of smoke they shot up in many places over the cliff before they drifted away from each other and dispersed in the air. Then they fell into ring-shaped formations, which circled around the city in opposite directions.

There were three such ray rings in the air. The farthest out sailed just in front of the fog wall, the next halfway between the fog and the city shores, the third over the sea star points. At the last minute d'Artois had decided against the use of the sea horses, although he went against the express wish of the council in that.

"I will not send the sea horses to their certain deaths," he announced to the council members. "They haven't a chance in the waters outside. The kobalins will attack them from underneath, without our being able to get near them with our weapons." As he spoke he was probably remembering the death of his wife, who'd been pulled down with her sea horse by the kobalins.

Some of the lords of the council had argued against it, but d'Artois had turned away, with the excuse that he must concern himself with the defense of the city, and left them standing there.

Once in the air, Griffin looked over at him. The captain had placed Griffin in his own squadron, as if he wanted to make sure that Griffin stayed near him during the battle.

Griffin was still unpracticed in handling the ray. Riding Matador came much more easily to him. Also, it was easier to form a bond with a hippocampus than with a ray. The black flying giants were too big, too majestic, almost a little remote in their silent elegance. You could admire them or fear them, but you never felt really close to them—except for their caretakers in the ray shelter, who were quite beside themselves with concern for their pets and hours before had already charged each rider not to let any of the animals come to harm. This showed once again that everyone had something different to lose in this battle. Some were concerned for their lives, others for the future of the world, and some for those that they cared most about: rays, sea horses, even the chickens that ran free in the streets of the city because they couldn't all be caught in time.

The wind created by the flapping of the ray's wings on takeoff was immense. The riders who were still on the ground had to brace themselves against the wild gusts not to be lifted out of their saddles. But then all were finally in the air, and soon each ray had taken a position in one of the three defense rings.

"Why isn't it raining any dead fish?" Rorrick shouted into the blustering headwind.

"It only does that when the master of the kobalins is in the vicinity," Griffin replied over his shoulder. "Probably he's still somewhere outside the fog. Or not close enough to the surface."

"I thought the kobalins only obeyed their chieftains?"

"Sure. But the chieftains follow the orders of a being that is subordinate to the Maelstrom."

"The people say you and the polliwog, you've seen him."

"Not seen," contradicted Griffin. "I think no one's done that yet. At least no human being. You only know he's there because the dead fish are raining from the sky." He thought for a moment, then added, "I guess we should be grateful for any minute in which he *doesn't* turn up here."

"Oh, he will," replied Rorrick resignedly. "He most certainly will, if he's as powerful as you say."

Griffin strained to see down from that height. They were in the inner ring of rays, about ten yards over the water surface.

"Kobalins!" cried Rorrick suddenly, his voice hoarse. "Down there in the water!"

Behind him Griffin heard the gun hammer snap into place as the sniper brought his weapon into firing position: Three of his rifles rested in firm hangers, which were attached to the saddle of the ray and pointed backward, similar to a triple cannon. Unlike Griffin, Rorrick wasn't secured by a belt, for he had to be in a position to turn quickly in the saddle in order to fire backward as well as forward. Every movement was deft, no reach was too far. The maneuvers of a marksman had something almost mathematical about them, for the whole time he was calculating in his head: distances, angle, and the impact of his shots. This he had in common with the cannoneer aboard a pirate ship.

"Do you see them?" Rorrick asked.

Griffin guided the flying giant in a gentle slant while at the same time remaining with his orbit of rays rotating around the city. "Yes. It's begun."

Dark spots were flitting under the water surface, recognizable only with difficulty in the shimmering light on the waves. Now Griffin understood why the kobalins' attack was taking place before sundown, not at night, which he'd been considering much more likely: They'd waited until the sun sank deep enough. Now the beams broke on the wave combs, they sparkled and glittered, and their light blinded the shooters on the rays. Obviously this offered the kobalins a greater advantage than an attack by darkness.

Rorrick cursed. But while Griffin was still worrying whether the sharpshooter would hit anything at all under these conditions, the first shot cracked. The wind of their flight carried the smell of the powder and a part of the noise to the rear, away from Griffin.

The marksmen on the other rays now opened fire too. Soon the surface of the sea appeared to boil with the mass of shots. Countless pockmarks bloomed on the waves. The first kobalin corpses floated to the surface, while here and there scrawny, shimmering arms broke through the waves, pulled back a lance or a harpoon, and flung it up in the direction of the rays. In the course of his first three circuits Griffin saw only one single ray fall out of the sky: The animal hit the surface, and immediately rider and marksman were snatched from the saddle and pulled down under the waves. The kobalins attacked the ray itself like a swarm of ants, instantly burying it under scrambling bodies, and it sank into the water.

Griffin shuddered with horror, but then he was already beyond the crash spot and must again concern himself with his task. Rorrick called instructions as to where he should steer the ray, and Griffin hastened to carry out everything to his marksman's satisfaction. Once he ducked away under a kobalin harpoon; another time a lance glanced off the ray's wing, but it left only a slight scratch.

During each circuit he stole a worried look at Jasconius, who had detached himself from the jetty and thrashed under the surface as a mighty shadow. When Griffin saw him down there the first time, he was astonished at the mobility of the giant whale and at the same time deeply concerned about the mass of dark spots that crowded around him. But by the second orbit the whale clearly had fewer opponents, and by the third the kobalins were keeping at a respectful distance from the titan who raged in the middle of them. However, Griffin didn't deceive himself: If the deep tribes focused a part of their strength and took concerted action against Jasconius, he wouldn't be able to hold out against them for long.

When the rays crossed the sea star arm beneath which the

anchor chain was fastened, Griffin noticed that a particularly dense mass of kobalin swarms were clustered there. He thought with chills of Soledad, who must be down there somewhere. As long as the kobalins didn't go onto land—and until now they'd made no attempt to do so—the area around the anchor chain was the most dangerous place in the entire battle. The princess must have lost her mind to let herself be deployed right there. At the same time he admired her courage. If anyone truly deserved to lead the pirates of the Caribbean, it was she. Maybe she thought she still had to prove it.

The next harpoons flashed into the air around his ray like steel lightning. All the horrific visions of Soledad's fight in the deep faded, as he had enough to do to keep the ray under control.

From behind him came a gurgling scream.

"Rorrick?" Griffin looked over his shoulder.

He looked into the lifeless eyes of the marksman.

The man sat swaying in the saddle, hit by a kobalin lance.

Griffin screamed with shock and fury, but when he tried to reach back with one hand to hold his companion, the ray shifted unmanageably beneath him, and Rorrick lost his balance. The body slipped back, tore one of the munitions pockets with it, and plunged down through the emptiness.

Stunned, Griffin turned away from the sight as the body struck the waves and was pulled under by a dozen clawed arms.

As Griffin lost his marksman, Soledad had long ceased to fight for the anchor chain or the future of the sea star city.

She was fighting for sheer survival.

Around her reigned a chaos of kobalins, dead divers, shredded protective suits, and dark red clouds, which made it harder still for the humans to defend themselves against the attack.

The kobalins had just broken through the light pillars of the torch shafts in a mighty attack wave. They'd drawn a ring of attack around the defenders of the anchor chain like a noose of lances and claws and snapping jaws. Within one or two minutes the number of defenders had decreased by half. About a dozen humans were now fighting desperately against the attacking deep tribes.

Soledad had a handful of bolts left, but she had no chance to reload the two crossbows. A kobalin shot toward her through a cloud of blood, his claws outstretched and fangs bared. Soledad kicked her legs to rise, and at the same time was aware that her air supply was growing thinner. It was long past time to change the bubblestone, but the attackers left her no opportunity for it. Somehow she succeeded in avoiding the first attack and in pulling the corpse of another kobalin between her and her adversary. For a moment the creature was distracted and sniffed at the dead one like a hungry wolf, without taking his eyes off Soledad. With trembling hands she loaded one of the two crossbows—and was just able to aim when the kobalin shoved his dead comrade aside and shot toward her in a flowing movement.

The bolt hit its target. However, the kobalin's stroke was strong enough to get him up to Soledad as he died. In his death throes he struck and kicked about him, his clawed fingers whirled like shears in front of her face, and he almost tore the diving helmet from her head. But then she succeeded in drawing up both legs and pushing him away from her with a powerful kick. Moments later he'd already disappeared behind a wall of dark clouds.

Soledad swam through the thick, dark fog. Her vision did not reach much farther than a doubled arm's length. This hindered her, but at the same time it protected her from the malignant eyes of the kobalins. Nevertheless she was swimming farther upward, toward the danger of leaving the mist and thus becoming visible to her enemies again.

Suddenly her head struck resistance. In the first moment she was seized with panic and struck about her, fearing that she was being attacked again. But then she realized that it was only a cross brace of the labyrinthine iron-and-coral construction in whose center the anchor chain was fastened. Close by her shimmered brightness from one of the torch shafts in the underside of the sea star point.

She froze as several silhouettes flashed in front of her, kobalins in search of opponents. But the creatures didn't notice her, perhaps because their sense of smell failed in the bloody water.

Soledad pulled herself still farther up into the web of the support structure. Once she saw a second diver. She gave him a short wave and pointed up, but she couldn't tell if he'd noticed her. He also was concealing himself between the braces, obviously just about to give up.

Pirate Wars

She took a break, forced herself to be calm, and changed the bubblestone before her lack of air could save the kobalins the work. Then she began to move away. The light now became more intense and bathed the surroundings in a red glow, through which lighter and darker streaks ran.

She was aware that she was approaching the true goal of the kobalin attack, the upper end of the anchor chain. If her luck were bad, it would already be swarming with soldiers of the deep tribes who were trying to destroy the fastening.

Her fear was confirmed when the fog thinned and opened up to a view of the chain. A dozen kobalins were climbing up the mighty iron links like monkeys, pulling themselves up by the floating curtain of plants and the mussel colonies and using the chain itself like a ladder that led up from the bottom of the sea to Aelenium. However, something was still keeping them from covering the last bit. Now Soledad realized that three or four divers had taken positions up there. They received each kobalin who approached them that way with a steel bolt.

Silently Soledad wished them luck and changed her direction. She had no chance of getting past the kobalins and advancing to her comrades. She must choose another way to safety.

Again she looked up to the torch shaft and wondered where it led. To the interior of the sea star city, that much was certain. She herself had never been in one of the shafts, but she knew that stairs within their walls wound to the top. From there the countless torches were regularly renewed in their holders. She might have tried to get to the surface through one of the shafts and run on up the stairs. But the gates to the shafts were barricaded so that no kobalin could get into the city this way. There were probably gratings under the water surface as well.

Soledad was thinking feverishly and at the same time keeping an eye out for other kobalins, when suddenly an enormous silhouette poked through the murk in front of her.

In the first moment she thought it was yet another monstrosity of the Maelstrom, a gigantic monster out of the abysses of the sea, which was going to help the kobalins in the destruction of the chain.

But it was Jasconius.

The man in the whale and his titanic friend had come to the aid of the divers at the chain!

The whale plunged into the middle of the kobalin pack and whirled the attackers around with mighty blows of his tail. Even Soledad, who was some distance away from him, felt the current, was flung against a brace, and cried out in pain beneath her diving helmet.

When she opened her eyes again, she saw that panic had broken out among the kobalins. The giant head of the whale rammed them and broke all the bones in their bodies. His fins smashed them like insects. The sea giant moved with inconceivable agility. His speed gave the lie to his clumsy appearance. The kobalins could not have reckoned on such a fierce attack.

Soledad weighed her chances. The only remaining possibility

for flight was the way past the chain in the direction of the undercity. Whether there was a chance of climbing up into the upper city from there she did not know. But she had no choice.

The name *undercity* was misleading, for it described the undersea part of Aelenium, but by no means a city. The gigantic sea star that formed the base of Aelenium possessed two mountainlike outgrowths: one on the upper side, the other below. While over the course of time the upper part had more and more been brought into the form of a human settlement, with houses and towers and palaces, the formations on the underside remained untouched. Here the caves and tunnels ran as chance had created them; arms of coral grew wildly in all directions, and the surface was covered with sharp ridges, points, and thorns, which could cost a careless diver his life.

The way to the fissured coral incline was largely free. Soledad could get there unhindered, if Jasconius distracted the kobalin swarm just a little while longer. But fear made her hesitate, for she knew what she was letting herself in for. It was quite possible that she would become hopelessly lost in the twisting coral passageways and grottoes, until her air supply was used up—and never get even close to the upper surface at all.

Her eyes fell on the pack of kobalins, which had left the anchor chain and moved to safety outside the range of Jasconius's deadly blows.

Suddenly one of the kobalins raised his arm and pointed at her. Immediately ten or eleven of them started moving.

Apparently they'd received orders to leave no human in the water alive.

She cursed her indecisiveness, which might now cost her her life, then pushed off and swam with hasty strokes in the direction of the slope. A little farther, one of countless openings gaped below her, a jagged crack, wide enough for a small ship to sail through it. She ducked along coral edges and passed sharp corners and turned into the darkness. Here there was no source of light except for the pale gleam that came in through the entrance. Desperately she wished for the polliwog vision that allowed Jolly and Munk to orient themselves underwater. She herself was dependent on the weak light from outside and on her sense of touch.

Panicked, she looked around at her pursuers. The kobalins shot up to the opening to follow her inside the coral mountain. Soledad swam faster, now using much too much of her air supply. In front of her rose the rugged cave wall. There was no exit.

Then it became dark around her.

She needed a moment to grasp what had happened. A black silhouette had slid in front of the crack and plunged the grotto into complete darkness. Jasconius!

He gave her the opportunity to flee deeper into the interior, even if she couldn't see her hand before her face. But the shock had paralyzed her and kept her motionless in the water. Spellbound, she looked back at the opening. When the whale left it clear again, Soledad's pursuers were floating higgledy-piggledy, crushed and lifeless.

Moments later she came to herself and repressed the urge to swim back into the light, into open water. With a heavy heart she left the brightness behind her.

In the dusky light she now made out a second crack in the back side of the cave, which she hadn't noticed in her fear a few moments before. If she were lucky—*very* lucky—she'd have stumbled on one of the routes the divers had marked on their inspection rounds through the undercity. Xander had explained to her that the passable coral shafts were marked by glowing stones. The stones didn't give enough light to illuminate the surroundings but gleamed bright enough to serve as trail markers. If one found them. And if one knew how to read their directions.

Soledad dove through the opening deeper into the interior of the undercity. It became pitch-dark around her.

Outside, Jasconius took on another troop of kobalins, broke the bones of some of them, and squashed the others between his jaws.

Soledad stopped only briefly to take her last bubblestone out of the bag and set it into the container under her chin. Then she went on feeling her way, searching for an outlet to the surface.

The Hand of the Maelstrom

"**I wish we** could just swim over them," said Munk, looking gloomily across the labyrinth of cracks in the rock that opened before them.

Jolly nodded silently. It might be more reasonable to disregard the Ghost Trader's warning and choose the fastest way. So far they hadn't received the tiniest indication that the Maelstrom was looking for them at all. Perhaps he was simply *overlooking* them.

Munk looked at her sideways. "What do you think?"

She shrugged, unable to take her eyes off the maze of cracks and gorges. From up here, the craggy chasms looked like frozen black lightning, which touched and crossed, thus forming a sea of rock islands.

They were standing at the edge of a narrow plateau. It protruded like a nose from the slope on which they'd been steadily moving downward for the last few hours. It was an effort for them both to walk on the soft ground beneath them; the ground itself might consist of rock, but in many places dust-fine gray sand had built up, which swallowed their feet at every step, sometimes up to the ankles. It was as if you were walking over a carpet of flour that, on top of everything else, billowed up at the slightest touch. From far off it must look as though they were pulling a cloud of smoke along behind them.

But if even this cloud hadn't betrayed them yet, would they really be more noticeable if they swam a little bit instead of embarking on the burdensome trek through the labyrinth on foot?

In the beginning they'd both avoided, if possible, admitting openly that their feet hurt and that they were gradually getting charley horses in their legs. But after the first few hours they'd come to the silent agreement that it was silly to be so tough and dogged. Now they cursed together over the strenuous path, the poor vision, and the whole miserable situation they were stuck in.

Their polliwog vision ranged to several hundred feet, but the last bit was dark and blurry. The rock labyrinth at the foot of the slope extended very much farther out, its end unrecognizable in the distance. The black fissures opened out into the darkness like a river delta into an ocean of shadows. The depressing view robbed Jolly at one stroke of all the courage she'd mustered at the beginning of their trek. In the beginning the unavoidability of their fate had driven her on, even given her new strength. She'd assumed nothing could surpass the wasteland she'd found on her arrival on the bottom of the sea—until this rock wasteland had turned up out of the darkness in front of them. In an instant, the depressing panorama destroyed all hope in Jolly of ever getting to the Crustal Breach in time. They'd be stumbling around in these ravines for so long, their meager provisions would be used up. Aelenium would fall. The Maelstrom would reach the city and—

"Jolly."

She started. "Hmm? What?"

"I asked you what you think. Should we swim?"

She took a deep breath, felt the water stream through her windpipe, and finally nodded. "Otherwise we'll never get through it."

A last hesitation, then together they walked over the edge of the rock. They didn't sink down but moved forward in the emptiness with slow swimming strokes. It was still strange to float in an element that they no longer perceived as ordinary water. It was in Aelenium that Jolly learned she could not only walk on the sea but also survive in it. For them the salt water was more like air—after all, they breathed it and it didn't keep them from hearing or speaking.

Slowly they glided farther down until they were almost touching the tips of the rock towers that rose between the crevasses. They felt themselves moderately safe over the stone plateaus on the peaks, but whenever they glided over a new chasm, another broad fissure, they shivered. They could see to the bottom of the crevasses, which meant that the chasms were rarely deeper than a few hundred feet. Since there was no source of light down here and the polliwog vision illuminated everything evenly, there were no shadows, either. But that in itself didn't make the way across the labyrinth any less eerie, for there were still hundreds of overhangs under which all sorts of things might be concealing themselves. Not to mention the numberless caves and holes in the rock walls.

Although they still hadn't discovered any signs of life, Jolly couldn't shake the feeling that they were being observed. No one knew whether the kobalins could venture into these regions—after all, if Forefather's calculations were correct, they were more than twenty thousand feet under the surface of the sea. The Crustal Breach itself lay somewhat deeper still. However, there must be some reason why people called the kobalins the deep tribes.

They'd long left behind in the darkness the slope they'd climbed down. Now there was only the sea of ravines and crevasses around them, the same in any direction they looked. Most of the time they were silent, except now and then, when one warned the other if they got too far from the plateaus on the rock towers. In spite of everything, they respected the Ghost Trader's warning and tried never to get farther than six feet from the bottom. If something were to approach, they'd notice it early enough and still be able to seek protection in the ravines.

Provided that *something* hadn't better eyes than theirs and hadn't detected them long before.

"Doesn't seem as if this stops anywhere," said Munk. Even he was growing more and more disheartened at the extent of the rock labyrinth.

"No," Jolly murmured in reply. "And what if we're swimming in a circle?"

Munk's arms and legs stopped moving for a moment, but then he got hold of himself. "Impossible."

"Oh, really?"

He muttered something she didn't understand and was silent for the next few minutes.

Finally Jolly sighed in relief. "Munk!" she cried, pointing below them. "Look!"

He followed her gaze down into the chasm beneath them, but he shook his head. "I don't see anything."

"Exactly."

"Exactly?"

"We can't see the bottom anymore. The crevasses are getting deeper! That means we're still moving downward, even if the tips of the rocks appear to be staying at the same height. But really they're *growing*, while the bottom of the sea is sinking farther!"

He thought about that for a long moment, then he agreed. A relieved smile twitched at the corners of his mouth, but it hardly brightened his face. Even his joy was swallowed up in the omnipresent gray down here.

Jolly thought they really ought to have been reassured now,

but her heart was still racing. What she'd have given for a compass! Instead they had to rely on the vague hope that down here all descending paths actually led to the Crustal Breach. They could only trust that the Breach really was the deepest place in this region of the sea floor. Otherwise, all their orientation was gone.

Again a long time passed with neither of them saying anything. Jolly observed that now and then Munk would stop swimming and stroke one hand across the pouch on his belt where he kept his mussels, as if he were gaining new strength that way. She tried secretly to do the same thing herself, but touching her mussel pouch did nothing at all for her. Possibly that was because she'd never developed such a close attachment to the mussels and their magic as he had.

"Down!" he cried suddenly, immediately letting himself sink deeper.

Jolly froze, hovering in place for an instant, and then she followed him down into the protection of a rock. She'd seen it too, at the last moment before she ducked behind the edge of the stone.

Several points of light appeared in front of them in the darkness.

"Are those . . . eyes?" she asked hoarsely.

Munk's voice sounded thick. "No idea."

They hardly dared to raise their heads over the edge, but finally they did.

The bright points were coming nearer. At first there were six or seven, but the longer they looked out at them, the more there were—almost as if they were looking into a starry sky and seeing more stars with every minute.

"If they are eyes," Jolly whispered tonelessly, "there are an awful lot of them."

"Spiders have many eyes."

"Oh, thanks, Munk! *Many* thanks!"

Once he would have smiled. Not today. He didn't even look at her. Instead he held himself rigid at the height of the rock edge and stared tensely out over it.

"It's a school of fish," he said after a while.

In fact, the glowing points turned out to be tiny fish, whose bodies gave off a constant light. None of them appeared to be any larger than Jolly's thumb.

"Let's go deeper," she said.

Munk nodded, but he didn't move. He was still peering out over the rocks in fascination. The light of the fish reflected in his eyes and lent them a wild glitter that disquieted Jolly almost more than the strange school, which was now making straight for them.

She seized Munk by the hand and pulled him with her.

"Hey!" he exclaimed, but he didn't resist. The glittering in his eyes seemed to last a moment longer before it finally went out. For a few long moments it had looked as if the glow of the fish had been caught in his head and were looking through his eyes to the outside.

They sank quickly downward. The chasm must have been much deeper than Jolly assumed, for they still couldn't see the ground.

"Jolly!"

"What?" she replied gruffly, before she saw with her own eyes what he meant.

He could have spared himself the answer. "They're following us."

The school shot out over the edge of the rock, doubled back in a flowing motion, and streamed into the deep, just behind Jolly and Munk.

The two polliwogs rushed downward, headfirst, accelerated by frantic swimming. The rock walls on both sides shot past them. They had to avoid projections and spurs now and then, but they maintained their breakneck speed.

The fish were faster.

Light flowed over them, white and glassy like the shine of a rising full moon. The school seemed to take them into its arms as if it were a single massive living creature, not a mass of hundreds of tiny animals.

Jolly uttered an oath. Munk roared something like "Keep away from me!" and began to slap about him wildly.

The touch on her cheek felt like a delicate kiss, as if the fish wanted to sniff her face or explore with other senses. Jolly stopped short as other fish touched her hands and rubbed against her clothing. She had feared bites and pain. But all that she felt was that tender touching everywhere on her body.

Before their departure, they'd been given thin, dark leather clothing, which fit close to the body and whose oiled outer surface was supposed to facilitate locomotion in the deep.

THE HAND OF THE MAELSTROM

They looked a little bit like the uniforms of the guard, but without the mussel decoration and other reinforcements. Two-piece, with a wide belt, without ornament, and so dark that they also served them as camouflage.

A fine camouflage if the very first creatures they met attacked them unerringly.

Munk kept beating around him with both arms. Without success. They must reach the bottom of the ravine any minute, a narrow strip of rubble whose surface was covered with the ever-present dust of the deep sea.

Jolly touched the ground first, wrapped in her cloud of lantern fish. She'd turned herself up again and landed feet-first. Unlike Munk, she'd given up trying to defend herself. The fish covered almost her entire body. There wasn't a bare spot on her arms and legs, and there must even have been ten or twenty on her face. She repressed her panic and kept herself under control with difficulty.

The fish were sucking at her with their tiny mouths, but they still weren't biting and didn't betray by anything else that they saw Jolly and Munk as a tasty evening meal.

"Munk, hold still!" she called to him. The fish on her face wagged and billowed as she moved her lips. The brightness they gave off was astonishing, though not glaring enough to blind her.

"Munk!" she tried again. "They aren't doing anything to us!"

He stopped in mid-motion, as if she'd snatched him from his panicked Saint Vitus's dance with a slap on the face. As much as he'd been defending himself, the fish were stuck to him all over, completely unimpressed by his slapping and kicking.

"They're harmless," said Jolly gently, involuntarily giggling when one of the animals bumped against the tip of her nose and remained stuck by its mouth.

"I don't know what's so funny," Munk burst out angrily, but gradually he seemed to calm down. He created a remarkable picture, as he stood there a few steps in front of the rock wall—a dumpy figure of pure light, as if someone had cut the shape of a person from black paper and was now holding the opening against the daylight.

"Maybe they're spies or something like that." Munk was making a noticeable effort not to open his lips too wide as he spoke, for fear one of the fish could slip inside.

"Spies for the Maelstrom?" For a moment Jolly was frightened. But then she told herself that the Maelstrom wouldn't send out spies, but murderers to kill them on the spot. He'd have sent kobalins or a monster like the Acherus, not lowly little lantern fish.

She tried to push off the ground to float over to Munk, but she couldn't move. Something was keeping her fastened to the ground like a nail to a magnet.

"They're holding us!" Now panic was rising in her again. She quickly fought the feeling down, if only with moderate success.

Munk was about to say something, but then his face froze. "Do you hear that?" he asked after a short pause.

THE HAND OF THE MAELSTROM

At first she thought the noise was produced by the fish in some way: a dull droning and rolling that seemed to come from all sides. But it sounded quite different from anything they'd heard in the fish-filled waters beneath Aelenium.

Munk looked up. The upper edge of the rock wall was too high for him to be able to make out anything; polliwog vision didn't reach that far.

"Munk!"

The movement of his head produced a tail of light as the fish whirled around with it to face Jolly.

She pointed to the ground. "Look at that."

The dust layer on the rocks was moving, dancing up and down barely noticeably. Now Jolly felt it in her legs, too. The entire underground was vibrating, very slightly, but constantly.

"An earthquake!" cried Munk, instinctively pressing himself against the rock wall. Lantern fish whisked from behind his back and firmly attached themselves to him elsewhere so as not to be squashed.

Jolly listened tensely. The rolling grew louder, came closer. Now faster and faster. The dust vibrated more strongly. Their greatest concern was that pieces of rock might come loose above them. Was that why the fish were holding them fast on the bottom of the ravine? So that they'd be buried by the quake?

The deep booming now swelled to a volume that drowned out Munk's voice. Jolly saw that his mouth was moving, but she didn't understand him. Her eyes moved up to the top of the rocks.

Something was happening up there.

It looked as if the darkness itself were starting to boil. Jolly couldn't really tell what it was. The water? Or stirred-up dust? The darkness over her seemed to seethe, just at the edge of her vision. Now the sand began to rain down. Perhaps it was only a question of time until the larger pieces would also plunge down.

The noise was deafening. Jolly was going to press her hands over her ears, before she noticed that the fish had already inserted themselves into her ears and damped the noise. So in reality, the booming and rumbling must be even louder.

Munk again began to beat around him frantically. Jolly, too, lost her self-control and tried to brush the fish off her body, now utterly uncertain whether they were helping her or preventing her escape.

Something raged across the ravine. Like a storm——or a mighty hand——it stroked over the stone and set the entire area trembling. Only very gradually did it grow weaker again. Dust still sprinkled down in fine curtains, but the noise receded. The ground also quieted. The trembling died away.

Then there was only stillness.

As if on a silent command, all the fish suddenly detached themselves from the two polliwogs and streamed apart. For a moment Jolly and Munk were imprisoned in a glowing, whirling chaos, then the school rose from the bottom of the ravine in a single pulsing movement. In a minute the last fish had vanished on the other side of the rock edge.

Jolly sank to her knees and rubbed her eyes. Because of the sudden dimness, for a moment it seemed to her that she was blind. Munk took two or three stumbling steps and then leaned against the rock wall again, breathing hard.

"What the dickens was that?" He sounded hoarse, as if he had swallowed one of the fish. But it was only the fear that had settled in his throat like a lump.

"How would I know?" Jolly got wearily to her feet, supported herself on a rock with one hand, and tried to clear her head. Her thoughts arranged themselves very gradually, but she had trouble making sense out of what had just happened.

Something had stormed over the rocks. The fish had protected them from it by holding them down on the floor of the fissure. They had been saved from whatever it was.

"Was that *him*?" Munk asked.

She was about to say *I don't know*, but then she nodded. "The Ghost Trader spoke of the currents and—"

"Currents?" He clenched his fists and banged them helplessly on the stone at his back. "That thing there was . . . I don't know, something like a tidal wave!"

"At least he isn't particularly careful. The next time maybe that will warn us early enough." She tried pushing off the bottom and floated effortlessly a few feet off the ground. "What has me racking my brains much more is the question—"

Munk finished the sentence: "Who *they* were?"

"Of course."

"Not ordinary fish, were they?"

She shook her head because, much as she wanted to, she didn't know the answer to that. She could think of only one power that might have come here to help them. The water spinners. But when Jolly had met the strange old women, it hadn't seemed that they intended to intervene in events personally.

She'd have loved to have been able to talk with Munk about that and she knew very well that it would only have been fair—but something made her shy away from it. She'd told Soledad about the spinners, but not the Trader, and the reason for her silence was still unclear to her. Perhaps because the spinners had revealed things about Aelenium and the Ghost Trader, who hadn't found it necessary to reveal them himself. That he'd once been a god, for instance; about who Forefather and the other founders of the sea star city were; and that the masters of the Mare Tenebrosum were perhaps not monsters of sheer malice but only demanded for themselves what Forefather had also sought a long time ago: nothing less than a world.

Possibly it was a mistake to conceal the explanations of the spinners from Munk. On the other hand, Munk had been a close friend of the Ghost Trader for a long time, and both occupied more or less the same square on her mental game board. What Jolly didn't tell the Trader was better kept a secret from Munk as well.

If he realized what was going on in her mind, he didn't speak to her about it. Like her, he pushed off from the bottom, and together they swam upward, at first very fast, but then more cautiously, out of concern that the might of the Maelstrom could roll over the rocks again.

When they got to the top, they found not much changed. Except that the sand dust that had covered the rock towers before was now largely washed into the crevasses. The upper surfaces seemed cleaner now, some as if scoured bare. Shuddering, Jolly wondered what would have happened if they'd been in that chaos. Would the boiling sand have torn the flesh off their bodies?

"Swim or walk?" asked Munk, as they cautiously stayed close to an edge, so as to be able to dive down quickly in an emergency.

Jolly looked down. The ground in the chasm had once more sunk into the darkness, as if a deep black stream flowed there. Then she looked in the direction whence the current of the Maelstrom had come thundering. Nothing there indicated a threat of danger either. Like a stone that you throw into the water, the Maelstrom sent out waves like rings that moved in all directions and at some point ebbed again. Had they had the misfortune to encounter one of these rings, they'd probably have been killed, but at the least it would have betrayed to the Maelstrom that they were here.

"We'll swim," she answered Munk's question. "What else can we do? We have no time to lose."

He nodded but didn't seem thoroughly convinced. He must have had the same sorts of horrific visions going through his mind as she did.

"We'll just keep an eye peeled," she said with a shrug,

attempting to appear as relaxed as possible. One look in his direction was enough to reveal that he didn't buy this coolness for a second.

He took a deep breath and began to move. Lower than before, they glided away over the rock plateau.

After a while, which felt like many hours to them, they decided to take a rest in a cave in the upper part of a rock wall. It wasn't a cave, only an indentation, which offered them temporary protection but wasn't deep enough to harbor something unforeseen. Something like a slumbering giant octopus.

They ate awkwardly from their waterproofed provisions, drank even more awkwardly from the drinking tubes of their water bottles, and finally rested for a little while. Neither one had intended to fall asleep, but when sleep finally came after all, it was of the sort that leaves one even more exhausted after waking up: deep enough for bad dreams but not so deep that it provided new strength.

As they started out again, they were both too tired to speak. Day and night did not exist on the bottom of the sea, and since there was nothing else to help them determine the time—no sun, no stars, not even the ebb and flow of tides—they had soon lost any feeling for the duration of their trek.

At some time they reached the end of the rock labyrinth. Before them opened a broad plain that led gently downward to the end of the polliwog range of vision.

Jolly and Munk glided steeply down from the last plateau, and when they looked over their shoulders a little later, the rocks rose behind them like a forest of petrified giant redwoods. It was a majestic and deeply alarming sight. If they really had gone on foot as the Trader had advised, they would have become hopelessly lost in that maze.

This was a worrisome insight, but also one that gave Jolly new self-confidence. Obviously it was not so bad to take matters into one's own hands and to make one's own decisions. Until now, anyway, that had turned out well.

The plain ended very soon and changed into a pile of bizarre chunks of rock. Jagged formations reached toward them like stone hands.

"Those are corals," exclaimed Munk.

"Looks like"—Jolly hesitated—"like fragments of a giant coral!" Following an impulse, she pushed off from the ground and floated upward.

The view from above was like a blow in the face.

Suddenly Munk was beside her.

"That's rubble," she whispered. "Rubble of a sunken coral city."

Munk nodded, spellbound. "Like Aelenium," he murmured.

The remains of individual houses were clearly recognizable, grown structures that had somehow been hollowed out and reshaped; gigantic splinters with chiseled-out stairs running along them; burst towers that had exploded like porcelain on impact with the sea bottom; roofs and even the facade of a palace, which lay flat on its back like the fragments of a collapsed card house.

Munk was as pale as a ghost.

Suddenly he raised his arm and pointed into the depths and froze. "Jolly!"

"What?"

"Something moved down there!"

Her eyes followed his outstretched forefinger down into the dark mountain of coral. There was nothing to be seen in the burst and splintered confusion. The sight looked like a gigantically enlarged pile of shards.

"What was it?" Her tongue felt swollen. "A fish—or something bigger?"

Munk cleared his throat, then his brows knitted, and he met her eyes.

"A human being," he said. "A girl."

Aina

"A girl?" Jolly stared at Munk as if he'd announced that he intended to pick flowers now. "Here?"

He nodded uncomfortably. "I saw her. Down there."

Jolly surveyed him a moment longer and then looked along his outstretched arm down into the outspread rubble of the sunken coral city. It was an eerie view that filled her eye to the limits of her polliwog vision: Sand and mussel colonies had settled on the shattered ruins, though not enough to completely distort the shapes lying beneath them.

When and why had the city sunk? Who had destroyed it? And above all, why had no one told them about it?

The place where Munk was pointing lay desolate and uninviting behind the eternal veil of gray in which their vision immersed the sea bottom. It was a sandy lane between two towering pieces of rubble, the one a shapeless block full of cavities and cracks, the other obviously part of a former palace, with hewn columns and a multitude of rooms. The crash had broken the building in two, so that you could look into the open rooms like the inside of a dollhouse. They were empty and covered with mussels, all furniture disintegrated into dust eons ago.

"There's no one there," said Jolly.

"She was there, believe me." Munk gave up trying to convince Jolly, throwing up his hands in frustration. They had mounted high over the crash site to get a better view over the landscape of the ruins; now he dove downward again, straight toward the lane.

"Munk, wait!"

"You don't believe me!"

"Yes. But we have to be careful."

He stopped, floating, and turned to her. In spite of the all-encompassing gray, it seemed to her that his face was red with excitement. "If it really was a girl, Jolly, then she must be a polliwog. Just like us."

She nodded numbly. If he hadn't been mistaken, that was the only explanation.

A third polliwog.

And where there was a third one, there might be more. Lord knew how many.

"I don't like this," she said, but she followed him as he again headed downward. They were now about fifteen feet over the bottom of the lane. They were already much too close to the depressing ruins for Jolly's taste. If it had been up to her, they would have gone around the ruins. Even a longer way around might save them time in the end if danger threatened them in the ruins.

She could literally taste the threat in the water. It was as if all her senses were screaming one desperate warning at her.

Munk would not be restrained. How thoughtlessly he was jeopardizing their mission amazed Jolly and frightened her.

"If it turns out to be a kobalin . . . ," she began.

He didn't even look around at her. "I can tell a girl from a kobalin."

Munk was the first to reach the ground. Dust puffed up when he set his feet down and looked around him.

Jolly stopped above him and let her eyes roam. Even more than the box-shaped cross-section of the palace rooms that rose up to the right of them, she disliked the shapeless coral monstrosity to their left. White plants had settled in the openings, waving in the invisible currents like the fingers of corpses and appearing to be alternately waving them in or waving them away.

"Which direction did she disappear in?" Jolly asked.

"That way." Munk pointed along the course of the lane.

Good, she thought. *At least he doesn't intend to search through the holes and cracks.*

The floating plants were doughy, like the flesh of a drowned corpse. Jolly could hear the sounds they made when they rubbed against each other: a slurping and smacking, as if hidden behind them were something that was in the process of greedily devouring its prey.

Pirate Wars

The pile of rubble around them grew increasingly taller as the two approached the part of the ruin that had apparently once formed the center of the city. Obviously the coral city had not been destroyed on the surface, not completely anyway. It had only broken into hundreds of pieces on impact with the sea floor, but it had partially retained its original plan. The city must have been structured similarly to Aelenium, arranged around a kind of mountain cone or a massive coral formation in the middle. But nowhere did Jolly discover fragments of a giant sea star. If there had ever been one, its remains were buried somewhere beneath the other rubble.

"What do you think?" said Munk suddenly, while he kept straining to look in all directions.

"About the girl?"

"About the city."

"I'd love to know why no one thought it necessary to ever say something about it." She cast a sidelong glance at him. "Or *did* Forefather tell you? When I wasn't there?"

He shook his head, his face serious. "No, he didn't." Was there a spark of mistrust of his teacher for the first time? Disappointment, perhaps? Munk had always been the more intellectually curious of the two polliwogs. He'd spent much more time with Forefather than the impatient and rebellious Jolly.

He hesitated for a moment, then went on, "Is it possible that Forefather and the others didn't know anything about it?"

"Oh, come on." She uttered a scornful sound. "Of course

he knew about it. And he certainly didn't just forget to tell us about it."

"Then maybe he wanted us to find the city ourselves."

"Oh, yes?" *You're looking for an easy way out,* she thought, shaking her head. "Maybe he did think there was nothing left of it after so long. I mean, he may know a lot, but after all, he was never down here."

At least not in the last million years. She recalled what the water spinners had said. If Forefather actually had created all this, why was he so helpless today? He was nothing but an old man who was hiding away in a floating city on the sea. Hard to imagine that he'd once had the power to create a whole world out of nothing. And it was even harder to conceive that that same power was vegetating in a fragile body and waiting for an end that would perhaps never come. If Aelenium were to go under, would Forefather die with the city? *Could* he even die? Still, the spinners had said that many of the old gods were dead. But Forefather was the first, the source of everything. Other laws might apply to him. Or none at all.

"Jolly." Munk's whisper pulled her out of her musings. "Up ahead there. Do you see that?"

Slowly she nodded, but the words were hard for her to get out: "You were right."

"I told you so."

Ahead of them on the path, on the bed of gray sand on the floor of the lane, stood a girl. Not ten yards away. In spite of the currents, her hair did not move; instead it fell smoothly over her shoulders and clung to her back down to her hips.

"I am Aina," she said. "Welcome to the threshold of the Crustal Breach."

"Who are you?" Jolly asked, after they'd advanced to about ten feet away.

Aina looked like an islander. In the sunshine her body would have had a wonderful, light brown tint; but down here it was dark gray, like burned wood. Yet not even that could detract from how beautiful she was.

Doubtless Munk had noticed that as well, for he was staring at Aina as if he'd never seen someone like her in his life. Jolly was pretty too, but she acknowledged to herself that no one she knew could match Aina in beauty. Her build was delicate, almost vulnerable. Her eyes were large and dark, almost black, as if the pupils filled the entire iris. She had a small, pointed nose, which differentiated her from other islanders. Like Jolly and Munk, she also remained unaffected by the icy cold of the deep sea, for she wore no clothing. But she didn't appear to be ashamed on that account.

"Munk!" said Jolly.

A little dazed, he tore his eyes away from the strange girl. "Uhh . . . yes?"

"Don't stare at her like that."

"I wasn't staring."

Jolly still hadn't received an answer to her question,

so she tried again. "Who are you? What are you doing down here?"

"I was hiding from you."

"Why?" asked Munk, a little more collected now.

"I wasn't sure what you were. Who you were. There are others down here, not human."

"Kobalins?"

For a moment the girl looked at them blankly. Then a smile flitted across her face. "You call them that, do you? We used to call them claw men."

"Are they here?" Jolly asked cautiously, though she wasn't overly alarmed. She had been taking in the surrounding crevices and cavities the entire time and discovered no evidence at all of an ambush.

"Many have gone away," said Aina with a gentle shake of her head. "The Maelstrom has sent them away."

To Aelenium, thought Jolly, without any real relief. Had the battle already begun? Or might it even be decided?

"How long have you been down here?" Munk asked. "And who sent you?"

Jolly thought she heard a slight undertone of jealousy in his voice. Was he worried that Forefather might have secretly sent other polliwogs as well? And did that make him feel . . . yes, what, actually? Slighted? No longer so *important* as before?

"We came down here a long time ago," said Aina. "An inconceivably long time."

"We?" Jolly probed.

"I and the others, who are just like you."

"Still more polliwogs?"

"If that is your word for us, yes."

The whole thing was getting more and more baffling. And then suddenly it dawned on Jolly. "You're one of the polliwogs from *the old* time?"

Munk gave her an amazed, then increasingly somber side glance. "That's impossible," he whispered to her grimly.

"Oh, yes?" she retorted, just as tense.

"From the old time," Aina repeated sadly, and her eyes fixed on distances that Jolly dared not imagine. "It was so long ago."

How long ago might it have been that the Maelstrom was overcome the first time and imprisoned in the Crustal Breach? There had only ever been talk of thousands of years. Not once had Forefather or Count Aristotle said anything specific about the time of the first war with the powers of the Mare Tenebrosum, so inconceivably long ago had it been.

But Aina looked as if she was no older than fifteen.

Jolly's knees grew weak, and for a moment it was all she could do to stay on her feet. If Aina could live so long, what did that mean for the other polliwogs? For Jolly herself?

She cleared her throat with an effort. "Aina," she said, "are you one of those who fought against the Maelstrom in the old time? Did you imprison him in the mussel?"

The shadow of a smile crossed the girl's regular features. "I have seen the Maelstrom," she said hesitantly. "I know the way."

Munk appeared to have decided to disregard Jolly's surmise.

"Then you can show us how we can get there the fastest."

Jolly poked her elbow into his ribs. "Munk, damn it . . . !"

He whirled around, and for a moment it looked as though their long-brewing conflict would be decided here and now, in the ruins of a forgotten coral city, many thousands of feet under the sea and before the eyes of this mysterious girl. For several seconds it looked as if Munk were going to hurl himself at Jolly, not with the help of mussel magic or any other tricks, but with bare fists.

He thinks I'm superfluous, flashed through Jolly's mind. *He thinks I'm only holding him back. That I'm of no use down here anyway because he's much more powerful than I am.*

And the worst thing is, she thought, *he's right. I am superfluous.*

She'd scarcely formulated the thought when she contradicted herself: *No, I'm not. If he so innocently trusts the first one who comes along and hands over the fate of the whole world, then it's good that I'm with him. Even if it's only to keep an eye on him. On him and what he does. On his dumb tendency toward recklessness.*

He needs me, thought Jolly. *He doesn't know it, doesn't want to admit it—but he's dependent on me. And I on him, if I ever want to get out of here alive.*

"I can lead you to the Maelstrom," said Aina, but it sounded as if it were not a confirmation of what Munk had said but an idea that had just come to her. "I can help you. But will you also help me?"

How? Jolly wanted to ask, but Munk was ahead of her. "Certainly," he said.

"I will explain it to you," said Aina. Her eyes were so large and dark. Jolly tried to read the truth in them, but there was nothing there she could discern.

The girl looked around searchingly. "But not here. It's too dangerous."

"Oh?" asked Jolly mistrustfully, thus earning a warning look from Munk. But she would not be sidetracked. "If you're one of the polliwogs from the old time, you must have escaped from the Maelstrom, right? You were just running away when you ran across our path. Quite a coincidence, wasn't it?"

Aina looked to Munk for help.

"Jolly," he said sharply. But he wasn't completely blinded yet and turned again to Aina. "Have you some sort of . . . proof for what you say?"

Thank goodness, thought Jolly, relieved.

"Proof?" Aina opened her eyes wide in alarm. "Look at me—I don't even have clothes. How can I prove anything?"

That beast! flashed through Jolly's mind.

Munk looked over at Jolly. "She's right about that."

"Oh, Munk, surely you're not serious!"

Aina frowned. Obviously she was uncomfortable being in the firing line of an argument between the two. She quickly began to speak again. "Please listen to me. And then decide for yourselves." She was silent for a moment, looking worriedly up at the slopes of rubble to the left and right of the lane.

Munk walked up beside her. "Don't worry." His voice sounded gentle and reassuring. "We'll find a hiding place.

Some kind of a place where no one can see us from above so easily. And then you can tell us everything."

"I've seen a place like that," said Aina. "A little farther down. There's an overhang, I've rested there."

Jolly looked thoughtfully from one to the other. She still couldn't shake off her mistrust of the girl. But she had to admit that it was only fair to listen to Aina. The girl didn't actually appear too dangerous. Quite the contrary: She felt Aina's vulnerability arousing pity in her, too.

After hesitating briefly, she followed Aina and Munk downward along the lane. Here and there she noticed small creatures between the rubble pushing themselves along the ocean floor with difficulty. Obviously the deep sea wasn't as dead as she'd thought in the beginning. Even the ugly albino plants that grew everywhere among the ruins and fished invisible nutrients out of the water with their stumpy out-growths spoke for that.

The lane broadened and led on over a bottomless crack between two mighty fragments. They swam over it and reached a kind of plateau, which in truth was the mirror-smooth broken edge of a gigantic coral piece. All around it lay rubble.

"Behind there is the place." Aina pointed across the bizarre plaza, where more coral mountains arose at the edge of their polliwog vision.

"The area is too open," said Jolly to Munk. "If one of the currents comes now, we're unprotected."

He agreed, if reluctantly, and so they went around the

plaza in the protection of the heaps of debris. Aina had nothing against that. She even appeared to be a little frightened to realize that she'd already risked crossing the open surface.

Finally they reached the place the mysterious girl had meant. Jolly had to admit that it was a solid hideout. Not perfect. Not secure through and through. But it was a place in which they could take cover for the moment.

It was a tower that was still standing almost upright and whose upper half had caved in with the crash onto the sea floor. Inside, a funnel-shaped slope of debris had formed. Here there were no plants and no crabs. But the best thing was that other rubble had fallen onto the opening above and closed it like a roof. There were two entrances: the old entry and a window opening farther up to which they could easily swim in an emergency.

"Looks good," said Munk when they'd made themselves fairly comfortable on the coral heap.

"One hour," said Jolly. "No more. We don't have time."

He nodded, and the two turned to Aina, who knelt not even an arm's length from them, her hands crossed on her thighs. Her long hair fell down into her lap.

"It's strange," began Aina. Her eyes were turned toward them. "It's already so long ago now. But I can remember it as if it were only a few years." She was silent for a moment before she went on. "At that time we were sent out to close the Maelstrom. There were three of us, two boys and a girl. We were good friends."

Jolly and Munk exchanged a brief look, almost a little ashamed.

"We succeeded. We closed in the Maelstrom, but also ourselves."

"Into the mussel?" exclaimed Munk with a groan.

"Yes. The Maelstrom was not dead, you know. He wasn't even asleep. He was simply locked in the whole time. And we with him."

Jolly had a number of questions burning on her tongue, but she hesitated. Gradually her pity for Aina was growing into real sympathy. She tried to imagine what it would be like to be closed in with your greatest enemy in a narrow space for thousands of years.

"What did he do to you?" Munk wanted to know.

"First we resisted. We were all three powerful mussel magicians, and in the beginning we could keep him from doing anything to us. It even looked as though we could keep him away from us forever. But the Maelstrom was superior to us in one thing —he had all the time and patience in the world. He wasn't strong enough to break the mussel magic, but he didn't mind waiting. Sometime our vigilance must diminish, and that's what happened. When the years had worn us down, he struck unexpectedly. And from then on we were at his mercy." Aina moved uncomfortably back and forth on her knees. It was a wonder that the sharp edges of the coral didn't cut her skin. "First he tortured us. Then, when the pain could no longer be any greater, he suddenly left us alone. He simply lost the pleasure in harming us. Perhaps we weren't important to him any longer, for presumably by that time he'd already begun to plan his return. We were only his past, but he wanted the future. He separated us from each other and must have hoped that we would perish of boredom. Or go mad."

Jolly couldn't utter a word. She was ashamed to have met Aina with such mistrust. Had the girl experienced what was also in store for them? An eternal imprisonment at the side of the Maelstrom? Was that why Forefather had claimed that he didn't know what actually awaited them at the end of their road into the Crustal Breach?

Munk stretched out a hand to touch Aina. Very carefully only, on the arm. Perhaps he wanted to be sure that they weren't merely dreaming the girl, that something hadn't taken shape out of their fear to warn them.

His hand went right through Aina's arm. She offered no resistance.

Munk shrank back with a gasp. Jolly leaped up. But the girl only looked sadly up at them without moving.

"I am fading," said Aina.

Munk stumbled to his feet. "She's a ghost," he whispered tonelessly.

"No." For the first time Aina sounded energetic, as if all the sorrow and all the pain were gone with one stroke. "No ghost! I am I. I am Aina. And I live."

A spark glowed in her eyes that hadn't been there before. "Perhaps that's enough proof that I'm telling you the truth." She was silent for a moment and then went on in a quieter voice. "I'd like for you to believe me. Since I succeeded in escaping the spell of the Maelstrom, I've lost . . . substantiality. I'm fading, and it's going faster and faster, the farther I go from the Crustal Breach. Perhaps because in the world outside there, in the *time* outside there, I really oughtn't to exist anymore."

That was crazy—and at the same time it sounded so plausible that this time it was Jolly who was the first to get over her suspicion.

Poor thing, she thought sympathetically. "Why didn't the others flee with you? Your friends."

"I don't even know if they're still alive. The Maelstrom separated us. I haven't seen them for an eternity. But I can feel them. That sounds crazy, doesn't it?"

Automatically both of them shook their heads. They were polliwogs, no matter how things stood among them. Aina was right: There was a connection among them, unseen and incomprehensible.

"Will you help me?" Aina's eyes glowed. "Will you help me to free them?"

Munk looked at Jolly. "What do you think?"

She nodded. "We'll try."

Munk sounded a little hesitant as he turned to Aina. "Good. Agreed. We'll help you if you help us. You know the way."

Jolly looked at his face. It was closed, as so often in recent days. She didn't understand him. Just a minute ago he was ready to quarrel with her in order to support Aina. But now it was as if *she* had to convince *him*, not the other way around. Was it because of disappointment that after Jolly, for the second time a girl had become unreachable for him?

For now she gave up trying to understand him. Everything was confusing enough without trying to figure out a boy's mind.

"So, shall we go together?" asked Aina hopefully through the strands of black hair that kept falling into her face. They looked a little like strands of dark water plants.

Jolly nodded. Munk did as well.

Silently they sat in their hiding place, each of them lost in thought. And although Jolly had a multitude of questions going through her head, she was reluctant to ask them aloud. Did she really want to know more about what the girl had lived through? Or would the answers be worse than all the unknowns?

Somehow she fell into a restless sleep, perhaps several hours long. When she awakened, Aina was still with them, sitting above them in the window of the tower ruin with her knees drawn up and looking out into the black deep sea, lost in her own thoughts.

The Second Wave

"Buenaventure! Here they come!"

The pit bull man didn't look up as Walker pointed over the wall toward the water. With his keen canine senses he'd already scented the kobalins not far from the shore before anyone else could have seen them.

The rays were still wheeling in three wide orbits around the city, but soon their mission would be at an end. Even d'Artois and the other commanders must know that. It had been clear from the beginning that the Maelstrom's hosts couldn't be halted from the air forever.

This task would fall to the men and women on the shore, the defenders of the first wall. Most of them were frozen with horror when the first kobalins crept onto the land.

Skinny, almost skeleton-like bodies with arms much too long; hard-bitten gargoyles of faces with receding foreheads, dark slits for eyes, and mouths so large that they could dive into fish schools with wide-open jaws and swallow dozens of prey at once; scaly skins that shimmered in all colors of the rainbow and in their fascinating play of color were a bizarre contrast to the ugliness of these creatures; and not least, the knife-sharp claws on bony fingers, some of which held weapons: primitive harpoon lances replete with barbs, rusty sabers from the bottom of the sea, the odd dagger that had once belonged to a sailor.

The kobalins were creeping out of the water in oil-slick-lustered waves, as if the spume itself were spitting them up. Creatures that had not been created to leave the sea, and nevertheless now dared to. Buenaventure might almost have admired them for their determination—if it weren't for the certainty that they were not acting of their own free will but were being incited by their chieftains and driven forward with threats. Chieftains who were under the influence of their lord, who himself obeyed the Maelstrom.

With many others, Buenaventure and Walker were manning a defense line on the north side of Aelenium: a twelve-foot-high wall of coral pieces, which had been broken out of the undercity and strengthened by sandbags, wooden beams, and even furniture that the inhabitants had dragged there from the nearby houses. To the right and left of the barricade rose the walls of a wide street. All the accesses to the sea were closed with similar blockades.

The first row of defenders awaited the kobalins above on the wall, with loaded rifles and flintlock pistols, which were discharged at the attackers nearly simultaneously on command.

The noise hurt Buenaventure's ears, and the powder dust stung his eyes. When the smoke cleared, he saw that the front row of kobalins was down, some dead, others wounded and still screaming. Their comrades, pressing forward behind them, climbed heedlessly over the fallen—they had no choice, for behind them still new fighters of the deep tribes rose from the surf, an incredible flow of bodies and claws and bared teeth.

Buenaventure, Walker, and many others quickly took the places of the shooters on the wall while the latter sprang down to reload their weapons. In his right hand, the pit bull man carried his saber with the broad, toothed blade that had already given him good service in the fighting pits of Antigua; in his left he held a dagger long enough to be a passable sword for an ordinary person.

Buenaventure exchanged a brief look with his friend— that had to be enough to wish each other luck. Then they plunged into the battle side by side, as they had countless times before. And yet they'd never had to face opponents like these. They'd dueled on land and ship, not seldom against a superior force of Spanish soldiers who far surpassed them in weapons and numbers; they'd fought in the alleys of Tortuga and New Providence, in the great prison uprising of Caracas, and on the burning tobacco fields of Jamaica. In the fighting pits Buenaventure had more than once found himself in hopeless situations, but in spite of everything he'd always escaped with his life.

Pirate Wars

Today it might turn out differently.

He dealt out blows like a dervish, mowed down two, even three kobalins with one blow, avoided their hooked lances and claws, broke the scrawny neck of one, and with a kick sent another flying back into the advancing masses. At the same time he kept his eye on Walker, who was no less skillful than he was with a blade, to be sure, but might well have been inferior to him in strength. Buenaventure would go to his aid if he got into difficulty, as he always had.

The plan had been to fight in an orderly formation. But after the first encounter with the enemy, all plans and wishes went up in smoke. Everyone fought as he could, always in the hope to be a little faster, a little more unpredictable than the enemy. In the hurly-burly of a battle, fighting possesses no elegance, no matter what the chroniclers claim: It is cruel and brutish.

The kobalins possessed no bodily strength. Their advantage was in their sheer mass. When one died, two others slid forward into his place. When one was wounded and fell to the ground, those behind did not trouble about him but jumped, climbed, and crept on over him. Thus they trampled many of their own fighters to death and filled the hearts of the defenders with horror at their cold-bloodedness and cruelty.

Buenaventure no longer counted how many he killed. Again and again he slashed a broad swathe in the flood of attackers. After a while his opponents grew fewer; it was as if more and more of them made a detour around him and instead turned against Walker and the other men. So

Buenaventure had time to take a breath, and in that brief moment when time was frozen, he realized the truth about the alleged strategy of the kobalins: There was none! They followed no strategy, no elaborate battle plan. And it wasn't the will to victory that drove them up to the enemy walls, but sheer panic. Whatever it was that their leader had threatened them with in case of defeat, it must be much worse than death by a saber blade.

Buenaventure caught sight of one of their chieftains under the water. He wore a head ornament of a set of open shark's jaws, which he'd put over his head like a helmet. His ugly face peered out between the open jaws. On both sides he'd fastened the arms of an octopus, which hung down from his head like braids. He was screeching and gesticulating excitedly, and with every movement of his head the octopus arms dangled and whirled crazily.

With one leap Buenaventure jumped from the crest of the defense wall into the water, in the midst of the squealing, roaring, shimmering mass of the kobalins. He heard Walker call after him and swear, but he had no time to look around. Again he let both blades whirl, the short straight one and the curved toothed one, and both cut into fishy kobalin flesh and sowed death in the ranks of the enemy. He wasn't proud of the many small victories; he felt no triumph when they avoided him and fled before him. All was only a means to the end, steps on his way to the goal.

And that goal was the chieftain.

The kobalin with the shark head ornament noticed the

doom that was approaching him when he briefly stopped screaming orders and let his arms drop. For a moment he looked a little dumbfounded, his slits of eyes widened and revealed coin-sized fish pupils. Then he called over his soldiers in his chattering, exhorting speech.

Too late.

Buenaventure reached him on a trail of lifeless kobalins. The lane that the pit bull man had slashed clear around him had closed behind him again after a few steps. And yet none dared to fall on him from behind. Instead the kobalins stormed unbroken up the wall, where they were received by the blades of the defenders, but as far as they were concerned, they chose one skirmish over the other.

Buenaventure had eyes only for the chieftain. The creature bared his teeth, and now the pit bull man realized what barbaric purpose the shark jaws had: As an additional pair of jaws around the kobalin's head, it doubled the fearsome sight of his own horrible teeth. The chieftain might have put another opponent to flight that way. But not a veteran of the fighting pits.

The pit bull man's saber whistled down, cut through the lifeless octopus arms, splintered the shark's jaw, and beheaded the chieftain in a single blow.

A high whimpering and wailing arose, and the wave of attackers stopped. The death of the chieftain didn't decide the battle, wasn't even the fraction of a victory. And yet it gained the defenders of the northern wall a moment of rest.

The kobalins withdrew. Those who'd just emerged from

the water slid under the waves. Others whirled themselves round and rushed back into the surf. And many who were not fast enough to follow the stream of their brothers to the water were killed by the men and women on the walls.

A moment's pause, no more. It wouldn't be long before another chieftain took the place of the dead one, browbeat the attackers again, and formed them into further assaults. But for a moment the fighting on this part of the foremost wall died down.

Walker leaped down from the barricade, killed a straggler, and ran to Buenaventure. With an exuberant mixture of curses and jubilant cries he hugged his friend, and the two returned to the wall together, gathered their strength, cleaned their wounds, and waited together for the next wave of attackers.

They knew it was coming when the first dead fish rained down from the sky. Sparkling silver, as if the stars themselves were plunging into the sea.

Griffin clutched the reins of the flying ray. The shock of his marksman's death had struck him so hard that he'd almost broken out of the ray riders' ring formation. But then he got himself and the animal under control again, and for a few seconds he was too busy guiding the ray back into his path to think about Rorrick.

Only when he had the flight stabilized did the knowledge of his marksman's death overwhelm him again. He could still see Rorrick sitting behind him, even feel him, although his body had long vanished under the waves. The picture was overlaid by Rorrick's last seconds, the lance, then the fall.

Griffin's muscles were cramped. His knuckles showed white, as if they'd burst the skin at any moment. Thousands of thoughts were shooting through his head. Fear of a second lance. Despair that everything they were doing was in vain. And above all, the certainty that he bore the blame for Rorrick's fate.

If he'd made the ray fly faster; if he'd flown higher or deeper; if he'd paid attention to where in the water most of the lances were coming from—well, then Rorrick would probably still be alive. But he hadn't done any such thing. And Rorrick was dead.

He was on the brink of just giving up. He was a pirate, not a soldier. He'd often fought—if not so often as he might have claimed earlier—and he'd seen men die and ships sink. But this was something different. This was a war. Not a skirmish at sea, not a raid on sluggish, ponderous trader galleons.

War, he thought once again. And suddenly the idea of killing and being killed had nothing daredevil about it anymore, and certainly nothing heroic. In these moments it didn't matter who felt himself in the right, who was forced to fight, or who followed a lofty ideal.

We'll all die, he thought. Then an unexpected objectivity came over him, which frightened him almost more than the despair that had held him in its spell first.

We all will, went through his mind. *Every one of us.*

Jolly too.

He took his hands from the reins and rubbed his eyes with his palms, so hard that it hurt and he saw fiery wheels rotating before his eyes. Then a bit more of his reason came back.

"Griffin!"

D'Artois's voice made him look to the right. The captain had brought his ray right alongside Griffin. The wings of both animals were almost touching, a chasm of emptiness yawning between them.

"Griffin, you must go back to the shore. There are more marksmen there. You mustn't give up now!" The captain's face was dead serious, his cheek muscles working determinedly. "Do it, Griffin! Now!"

Griffin nodded jerkily, then he let his ray drop six feet down and turned it around. At a narrow angle, really too sharp for such a placid animal, he broke out of the ray orbit toward the inside and flew up toward the coral cliffs of Aelenium. Beneath him, in the waters between the two sea star arms, the waves looked as if they were boiling, while everywhere skinny kobalin arms poked up through the surf and flung lances into the sky. None came close enough to Griffin to threaten him.

The place where Griffin had started out lay on the opposite side of the city. He had the choice of going around the cliff, with its gables and towers, or gaining altitude and flying over. He decided on the second choice.

The ray shot over the gaps between the houses of the city, over narrow lanes and steep gables, tower points with twiglike coral battlements, and the outermost roofs of the palace. Griffin saw the familiar buildings beneath him to his right and the Poets' Quarter, in which the Hexhermetic Shipworm continued to dream in his silken cocoon. He also could see—far away—the lower defense wall, just above the place where the sea star point ended in the massive mountain cone. Somewhere there Walker and Buenaventure were fighting, but at that distance he couldn't make them out anywhere.

On that side of the city, in the north, beyond the water and over the fog, black clouds of smoke were rising, and occasionally the booming echo of distant cannon thunder drifted over. The Antilles captains were fighting against the fleet of the cannibal king. The sea battle appeared to be still undecided.

Griffin saw something else in his flyby, up in the center of the city, where the buildings were the highest. He was too shattered by Rorrick's death to be able to process the whole complex at the first look, but then he recognized it. It was the library, where Forefather's rooms were, the holiest of the holy temple of knowledge in the sea star city.

On one of the balconies, a semicircle with bizarre coral outgrowths pointing in all directions like frozen arms, two men were observing the battle.

Forefather and the Ghost Trader.

They stood side by side, motionless, not looking at each other but staring out at the rings of ray riders rotating in opposite directions around the mountain cone. At countless points within the flock there were flashes and then reports when the marksmen fired their weapons toward the water. The kobalins answered their attacks with a black hail of lances from below.

The Trader's hands were extended from beneath his dark robe and clutching the edge of the balustrade. Forefather was supporting himself with both hands on a stick that towered over him by a head. Griffin could see that their lips were moving, but the sound of the battle and the rushing of the ray's wings drowned out their words.

The ray bore him past the balustrade, barely a stone's throw from the two mysterious figures. Griffin felt a prickling on his skin, a tickling and scratching, as there sometimes was over the deck of a ship when a mighty stroke of lightning came too close. Like an invisible explosion, the certainty flared in him that there were things happening on this balcony that would decide the fate of Aelenium, perhaps of the entire world.

Suddenly the battle was only half as important and certainly not decisive. This was all taking place just to win time. Time for Jolly and Munk, but perhaps also for something else.

He shuddered as he tried to imagine what that might be. His imagination failed at the task. He was almost glad of it.

The balcony with Forefather and the Trader was behind him. He was uncertain if they'd noticed the single rider on his ray, off course outside the ring formation and near them.

Griffin shook himself, got his head clear again, and looked for his landing place in the confusion of narrow streets. What was he fighting for? To that, at least, he had an answer.

Pirate Wars

Certainly not for Aelenium. Not even for himself.

Most of all he was fighting for Jolly.

Up on the balustrade, dozens of fathoms over the turmoil of the battle, Forefather's hands clutched his long stick. The liver spots on the backs of his hands were stretched, and the Ghost Trader could imagine he heard the old man's knuckles crack.

Above them, on a coral ledge, sat the two black parrots, Hugh and Moe. Two pairs of eyes, each a different color, stared impassively down on what was happening below.

"We cannot wait any longer," Forefather said in a hoarse voice. It was even hoarser than usual from the long, sometimes excited conversation. "You must do what has to be done."

"No, not before the second wall falls," countered the Ghost Trader. "I've said it many times, and I say it again: The danger is too great. And the price . . ." He let the words die away with a somber shake of his head. "The price could be higher than we can imagine."

"Against that are hundreds of deaths. And perhaps the final destruction."

"The one can produce that as well as the other. Let's not argue about it anymore, old friend. I've made my decision. Until now they've held the first wall. After that we have the second. And only then . . ." Again he broke off.

"You're still placing all your hopes on the polliwogs." Forefather surveyed him out of eyes that had watched the eons pass the way a mortal does the ebb and flow of the tides.

"And why not?"

Forefather shook his gray head. "What makes you so sure of them that you would risk everything?"

"There's no certainty, I know that." The Ghost Trader hesitated. "But I know the boy. He has the power that is needed."

"But does he also possess the sense of responsibility and the wisdom that such a task requires?"

"That is why Jolly is with him."

"She's still a child too."

The one-eyed one smiled sadly as he looked at Forefather. Above, both parrots titled their heads. "*Still* a child, you said, not *only* a child. And you know why. You know the difference."

"But you also know what happened the last time. We both witnessed it, very much like today. We stood by and watched and were unable to change it." He sighed. "Even then we were too weak."

"Today we are wiser."

"Are we?" Forefather giggled hoarsely. "I'm older than you, but even I am still waiting for the wisdom of age. Gradually I've given up hope of ever attaining it."

The Ghost Trader smiled again. "At least you've learned to know the obstinacy of age."

"If I were as obstinate as you think, I'd force you to do everything necessary. Instead I'm trying to convince you, and I am forced to observe how unsuccessful I am."

The Trader suddenly grew serious. "It won't work. Not yet. Only if there's no other way out."

Pirate Wars

"We've seen so many die, you and I. So many squandered lives in all the ages."

Over the water the ray riders formed into a single broad ring, which moved closer around the cliffs of the city. They'd given up trying to free the waters of the kobalins as far as the fog. Instead they were concentrating on the shores and on the waves of attackers who surged up from the surf there.

"It's raining dead fish in the north," said Forefather, pointing to the flashes in front of the fog background. The evening sun bathed the edge of the clouds in a reddish yellow firelight. From a distance a rain of sparks seemed to be falling in front of the fog.

"Then he's here," said the Ghost Trader. "He comes late."

"Not late enough."

"Hardly."

Again the old man turned to the Trader. "You can change the dying into stories, my friend. But more stories have been told about the two of us than anyone could ever collect or write down. Doesn't that mean that we are, in a sense, long dead?"

The Ghost Trader thought about it, then he nodded. "Perhaps we just haven't noticed it yet."

On the Kobalin Path

Can't be much farther to the center of the earth, Jolly thought gloomily. She felt as though she and Munk had been running through this darkness for a lifetime. Aina had led them through the ruins of the sunken coral city, on a downward slope. Two or three times they'd come to the edges of dark chasms and had to dive down along the rock walls. And they were always going farther down.

Once Aina warned them not to take the direct way along a row of remarkable rock chimneys from whose tops rose something that looked like black smoke. It actually was the boiling, ash-filled water out of the maw of the earth.

"Undersea volcanoes," Aina explained, adding that the warm waters around the craters were inhabited by all kinds of animals that were better not encountered.

Jolly soon saw that Aina had been right to warn them. In

the distance, almost at the limit of her polliwog sight, Jolly saw mighty silhouettes eddying around the chimneys. The creatures resembled white-skinned morays with gigantic mouths and repellent light feelers that arose between half-blind eyes. The polliwogs might have fallen victim to them had Aina not led them in an arc around the crater. As she did so the girl kept urging them to hurry, especially if they had to deal with detours like this.

She didn't speak about it often, but she seemed to be very worried about her friends, whom she'd left behind in the clutches of the Maelstrom. Perhaps she also felt guilty for what had happened.

More than once, Jolly imagined how Aina might have been in those days when she left to go to the Maelstrom. Had she undertaken her fate as willingly as Munk? Or had she felt as Jolly had?

They left the chimneys and their warm waters behind them. Aina went first, followed by Munk and Jolly, who kept her eye on the jagged rocky landscape on both sides of them.

"Aren't you afraid?" Jolly asked the strange girl suddenly.

"Of the Maelstrom? Certainly. I—"

"No, I didn't mean that. If we really should succeed in destroying him and freeing your friends . . . then you'll come back up to the surface with us, won't you?"

Aina hesitated. Then she nodded slowly.

"The world today is a whole lot different from your time. Everything has changed."

"Not people," said Aina, and a bitter expression played around the corners of her mouth. "People never change."

Jolly exchanged a look with Munk. "What do you mean by that?"

The girl didn't answer right away. She seemed to be thinking, as if there were suddenly a wall between her and her memories that she had to overcome first. "People weren't good to me. They were afraid because I was different from them. We could do things that—"

"That they couldn't do," Munk finished her sentence.

Jolly's feelings wavered between agreement and amazement. She knew what it meant to be different. But wasn't that ultimately only a question of the people you surrounded yourself with? The pirates aboard the *Skinny Maddy* had themselves been outcasts, the lepers of society—and they'd accepted Jolly for what she was.

Munk's bitterness, on the other hand, obviously applied to the inhabitants of Aelenium. Certainly he'd enjoyed their honoring him as a savior. However, maybe their admiration had only been the mask behind which they concealed their fear of the polliwogs? Suddenly this idea didn't seem at all farfetched to Jolly. Perhaps Munk had just seen through the people much sooner than she had, and now he shared Aina's dislike.

"They beat and kicked me," the girl said, without looking around. She now sounded very depressed again, as if the old time lay not thousands of years back but only a few days. "First it was only scorn, then fear was added to that. And finally they tortured me, again and again. My own family turned me out."

Jolly nodded, lost in thought. Bannon and his crew had been her family, and they had also betrayed her. Aina must have been just as wounded and despairing as Jolly.

The longer she listened to the girl, the more ironic it seemed to her that they three, of all people, were the ones chosen to save mankind. Of all people, they, whom the inhabitants of Port Royal or Havana met only with dislike, or arrogance at best.

"Nevertheless, you came down here to destroy the Maelstrom," Jolly said to Aina.

Aina gave her a long look. "Where else was I supposed to go if I didn't?"

And then she was silent again.

The meeting with Aina had distracted Jolly from her misery at the sight of this wasteland, but now the gray, dark environment seeped into her again.

"Didn't the Maelstrom have you followed?" she asked at last in Aina's direction, just to hear a voice again.

"Oh, yes, of course. He's looking for me."

"The current?" Munk asked, and Aina nodded.

"I'm sorry," she said. "It hit you, too, did it?"

Jolly frowned. "We thought he was looking for us."

"No," said Aina. "I don't believe he knows you're here yet."

Was the girl really more important to the Maelstrom than Jolly and Munk? Perhaps he wasn't afraid of the two of them at all, perhaps they were completely unimportant to him; he knew that they couldn't harm him. Jolly surreptitiously clenched one hand into a fist. She'd rather keep on believing that the search current had been aimed at them. At least until now she'd had the feeling that the Maelstrom took them seriously. But now their whole mission looked even more hopeless. Sometimes it was an advantage to be afraid.

On the incline ahead of them now grew something that looked at first glance like the pale plant worms that thrived among the ruins of the coral city. In fact they were a very similar type of plant, only these were much bigger. It wasn't long before the worms towered over their heads, waving at them like gigantic arms and legs that someone had stuck in the ground by the wrists and ankles. They grew side by side in broad clumps, but between them there were more and more lanes, through which the three could walk without any effort. Munk suggested swimming over the bizarre forest, but Aina declined. They were too close to the Crustal Breach, she said. And she seemed to be about to add something, but then she thought better of it.

"How much farther is it?" Jolly asked.

"Not much. We've already covered more than half the distance."

How long had they been traveling? Jolly didn't know. The missing sense of time down here worried her more and more.

"Careful!" Aina stopped.

Jolly and Munk also froze. Tensely they stared first at the girl, then into their gloomy surroundings.

"What's wrong?"

"There's something here." Aina's eyes traveled over the wall of plant arms waving soundlessly back and forth. Forth and back again, disturbed by unseen currents.

Jolly looked at Munk, but he gave a barely noticeable shrug. Neither of them had seen anything.

"Down off the path," whispered Aina, and with one swift stroke she glided from the ground between the bending stems. "Quick!"

"Path?" Munk looked bewilderedly at the ground. The lanes between the plants didn't look as if they were laid out by design. Jolly signaled to him silently that she hadn't the slightest idea what the girl was talking about. Nevertheless they quickly followed Aina between the plants. The white, spongy flesh of the plants felt revolting, much more organic than Jolly liked.

"Is that really a path that you've been leading us along?" Munk asked in a hushed voice.

Aina nodded. "A path of the claw men," she whispered, then immediately indicated with a finger on her lips that he should ask no more questions.

They waited, anxious and motionless, while the plants gently stroked their bodies as if they were trying to examine the three invaders in their midst.

In the silence Jolly heard a gentle rushing and rustling— the rubbing of the plant stems against each other. After she first noticed the sound, it came from all directions at once, until it even drowned out the hammering of her heart.

Three kobalins struggled along the path, shoulders bent.

Their bodies were low and very broad, and they had shorter, more muscular legs than the kobalins on the shape changer's island. Their nostrils were deformed to fist-sized. In return, they had no eyes—mere slight depressions above the sharp cheekbones showed where the eye sockets had been in their ancient forebears. Like all animals and plants down here, they were also of a transparent whiteness, like fresh coconut milk.

Jolly's stomach twisted. She prayed that an especially strong current might close the plant stems in front of her before one of the creatures picked up her scent.

Munk grasped her hand. She nearly cried out in fright. His fingers closed so hard on hers that it almost hurt. But she understood him only too well.

Aina didn't move. Her eyes were firmly fixed on the creatures that were passing not five yards away from them. The girl's face showed deep worry.

Jolly stopped breathing. It was a strange feeling when the water stayed in her lungs and gradually warmed. But to breathe it out now appeared too dangerous to her.

One of the kobalins stopped.

He senses us, Jolly thought. *He senses that we're here.*

The edges of the giant nostrils widened, drew together again. At the same time the many-toothed mouth opened and closed as if the creature were trying to taste something out of the water.

Us, thought Jolly icily. *He's tasting* us!

The two other kobalins halted too. It occurred to Jolly that none of the three possessed webbed feet. Therefore their feet were uncommonly broad and plump, almost as if this species of kobalin were bound to the bottom of the sea.

Of course! It was so obvious: white skin, no eyes, the bent posture—everything suggested that these creatures passed their entire lives down here and for countless generations had been exposed to the pressure of the water mass.

Now they were snuffling around the area with nostrils quivering, making smacking noises with their mouths.

They're going to find us, flashed into Jolly's mind. *They simply have to find us.*

The kobalins uttered a few whispering sounds, and then they went on, following the path in the direction from which Jolly and the others had just come.

The polliwogs remained in their hiding place for a long time, until Aina finally gave the all clear with a sigh. "We're safe now," she said. "At least for the time being."

"Whatever were those?" Munk burst out as they pushed their way between the stalks.

"They live down here." Aina looked once more in all directions, checking, and then stepped out onto the path. "They're different from the ones that you know, aren't they? There aren't many of them anymore, but they're at least as dangerous as the tribes farther up. Anyway, they can't swim, at least not very well."

"Can it be that they were looking for you?" Jolly asked. "Maybe the Maelstrom sent them."

Aina starting moving ahead and downward. "Either that—or . . ."

"Or?"

"Probably they're only hunting because they're hungry." After a moment she added, "You decide which you prefer."

Jolly swallowed and said nothing.

"But they couldn't eat you," said Munk, and Jolly was annoyed with herself that she hadn't thought of that. "You don't have a solid body."

Aina's pretty face twisted slightly in pain, then she shrugged. "That wouldn't help you, would it? Two polliwogs aren't a bad catch."

Jolly felt a nausea rising in her that was almost painful.

They went on, even more watchfully than before. Soon there were no more traces of the kobalins to be seen; the dust had covered their tracks.

The forest of deep-sea plants ended at the edge of a high plain. The abyss on the other side of the rock edge billowed in uncertain blackness.

"Listen!" said Aina.

Jolly and Munk started in alarm, but the girl made a calming gesture. "Just listen over there," she repeated in a whisper.

They did so, if hesitantly, and it took a moment before Jolly realized what Aina meant. Out of the darkness in front of them came a distant roaring and thundering, like the noise of a mighty waterfall or a tidal wave.

"Search currents?" asked Munk.

"No," returned Aina, shuddering. "That is *he*."

"The Maelstrom?" Jolly strained even harder to hear. Yes, it might sound like that if an inconceivably large mass of water rotating in the deep were sucked in and spit out again. The ominous noise in the distance seemed to grab her and shake her. Jolly trembled, as though a powerful voice were speaking to her from the indistinct raging and fuming so as to intimidate her.

To her amazement she saw that Munk had squatted at the edge of the drop-off and unpacked his mussels from his belt pouch. He was deftly laying them out in front of him in the dust. Aina watched him with interest, her head tilted slightly to one side.

"What are you doing?" Jolly asked.

"I'm laying out the mussels."

"I see that! But why now?" Had she missed something? Had he noticed a danger that she didn't yet see? At the same time her hand involuntarily slid toward her own mussels in their belt pouch.

Munk didn't look up. His fingers pushed the mussels around in their circle, sorted out some, replaced them with others, or changed the order, as he sought for the one definite combination. "Forefather said we should try out how the mussels react in the vicinity of the Maelstrom. Whether they behave differently from usual. That would be important, he said." He stopped for a moment, and then he looked up at Jolly once more. "You can't know that, you weren't there."

She weighed whether to do the same as he did and take out her mussels. But then she let it be; she didn't begrudge him this triumph.

"What do they say?" asked Aina, turning to Munk.

Say? thought Jolly.

Munk looked up at Aina with a smile, clearly overjoyed that here was someone who obviously understood mussel magic better than Jolly. "They're speaking, but not clearly. It's more a . . . something like a tugging. They want us to go on, as if something were drawing them."

Jolly stared at him. Her fingers snagged in her belt pouch.

"I brought my own mussels out of the Maelstrom with me," said Aina. "I thought perhaps I could help others with them, somehow. But I didn't use them." She paused. "I was afraid he could find me more easily."

At once Munk was alert. "Those must be very old mussels if you brought them here in the old time."

Older was synonymous with power. Jolly had learned that much about mussels. The longer a mussel had lain in the sea, the greater the magic contained in it.

Aina's eyes focused on the darkness on the other side of the chasm. Her voice sounded almost wistful. "They were imprisoned in the Crustal Breach with me the whole time. Together with my friends—and with the Maelstrom."

"I could use them," said Munk with unconcealed enthusiasm. "I could try to use them against the Maelstrom. They must be much more powerful than mine." As if he wanted to lend his words additional weight, he carelessly shoved his own mussels—so painstakingly arranged a moment ago—into a heap and put them, trickling sea sand, back into his belt pouch.

Aina shook her head sadly. "It's no good," she said. "I

don't have them anymore." She looked at the ground. "I left them behind on the way."

Munk lifted his hand as if to comfort her, but then he seemed to remember that she didn't have a solid body.

Jolly frowned. She felt herself more and more excluded by the two of them. There was something between Munk and Aina that she couldn't understand. Casual movements seemed almost like secret gestures to her. And weren't there also stolen glances between them?

Delusions of persecution, she thought, remembering moments in her earlier life, lonely night watches on the deck of the *Skinny Maddy* when her mind had played similar tricks on her: movements in the dark, sneaking shadows on deck, figures hiding behind the masts—all fantasies, but no less frightening on that account.

She was silent for a moment. Suddenly Munk got to his feet. His eyes blazed. "We're going to look for Aina's mussels," he declared firmly. "We'll find them and free her friends." His face was beaming as if the fight against the Maelstrom were already decided.

Aina knit her brows, then looked over at Jolly, as if she were asking for her assent. "Perhaps Munk is right. We could look for them and use them," she said cautiously.

Munk also seemed to remember Jolly suddenly. Looking almost annoyed, he turned around to her. "What do you think?"

Do you really care? she thought, but instead she said, "Sounds reasonable." There was no point in discussing her feelings at such a moment. She had to trust to Munk's greater experience in matters of mussel magic. She hoped he knew what he was doing.

Munk turned on his heel. "Good," he said, "then let's look for them."

"They must be here somewhere," said Aina, after they'd reached the foot of the rock wall and again found themselves on a gravel slope. "I left them lying down here somewhere." She looked worriedly in the direction of the Maelstrom. "But we must hurry."

"Did you bury them?" asked Jolly, with a dubious look at the stones under her feet.

"I put a stone on top of them, about this big." She made a circular motion with both hands.

Munk's cheek muscles worked. "I hope they aren't broken." His eyes were already roving over the stones, seeking.

Jolly shook her head, sighed slightly, and began to look for a stone of the size that Aina had indicated. There were at least a thousand of them within her range of vision.

Without discussion they separated, lifting stones and looking under them. Munk went about it with special zeal. Finally he opened his belt pouch again, laid several mussels on his hand, and let himself be guided by the suction of the magic. The mussels led him to a part of the gravel slope where Aina was already searching. The girl looked frantic and no longer as convinced as she had a few minutes before.

Jolly had just rolled another stone to one side without success when Aina called, "Here! This is it, I think."

When Jolly looked over at her, the girl was just sticking her hand into a crack behind a head-sized fragment of rock.

Aina's face brightened. "I've got them!"

Munk put his own mussels back into the pouch and went over to her. Nevertheless, Jolly got to Aina before he did.

In her hand the girl was holding one mussel, larger than any of those Jolly and Munk had, and mottled in a striking play of light and dark. In daylight it would probably have been multicolored, shimmering, and wonderful to look at.

"Only one?" Munk made no secret of his disappointment.

Aina nodded, ashamed. "The others broke under the stone. But this one will be enough. It was the most powerful of them, anyway."

Jolly noticed that Munk cast a look past Aina into the crack. Was he really so mad about the magic that one mussel wasn't enough for him? However, Jolly had to admit to herself that she too could feel the powerful tingling that emanated from the shell in the girl's hand, almost a feeling of warmth, which jumped from Aina to Jolly and probably also to Munk.

"May I hold it for a minute?" Munk asked.

Aina smiled. "It's yours, if you want it."

"Of course!" Almost devoutly he took the shell and carefully weighed it in his hand. His fingers were trembling. "It feels as if it were made for me." He started and smiled at Aina guiltily. "I'm sorry, I didn't mean it that way."

The girl waved him off. "You have greater power over the mussels than I do. I can feel that."

"Or than I do," added Jolly. She was about to stretch out her hand to Aina's present.

Munk recognized her intention, and for a moment it looked as if he were going to pull the mussel out of her reach. But then he held it out to her. "Here, take it for a minute."

Jolly took the mussel between thumb and forefinger, lifted it close to her eyes, and stared at it. The strange tingling did not become stronger, which was perhaps a sign that the mussel had already decided on a new owner.

The shell was as large as a fist. Jolly had a sudden urge to hold the shell to her ear and listen to it. But for some reason she shuddered at this thought, and the idea that the shell might possibly speak to her made her uncomfortable.

Partly with regret, partly with relief, she handed the shell back to Munk. He received it with a hasty movement, as if he were afraid that Jolly might have second thoughts.

"I hope you can do more with it than I could," said Aina, jumping up. "It may be our only chance against the Maelstrom."

Munk was still staring at the mussel in his hand, but Jolly was observing the girl from the bottom of the sea. "If your body has no solidity, then how can you lift stones? And mussels?"

Aina shrugged. "The farther I go from the Maelstrom, the less substance I have. Perhaps it's the other way around too." She could see that didn't satisfy Jolly and added, "I don't know any better answer. I didn't make the rules."

Jolly looked to Munk for help, but he appeared to be still under the mussel's spell.

"We've already stopped too long here," Aina said, and she started off on the descent over the rubble slope. "Let's go on."

Jolly looked after her, not sure what to think. But then she followed the girl.

"Munk, are you coming?"

When she looked around at him, he was listening to the opening in the mussel. Their eyes met, and he nodded. But all at once she wasn't sure if this nod was for her or for the mussel that was murmuring something into his ear.

The attack came as a surprise, without any warning.

At the end of the slope, beyond a wall of fallen rock needles and sharp blocks, they came to the edge of a plain of white sand. Aina advised them not to walk on the white surface of the sand but to place their feet only on the gray slabs that, at a closer look, were sticking up through the cover of dust in numerous places.

"Quicksand," she explained, her eyes lowered and her arms clasped tightly around her body as if she suddenly were freezing. "Back then, that almost pulled us under."

Under echoed in Jolly's mind. Under where? Even deeper into the interior of the world? Could there even *be* a deeper place than this? Instinctively she turned her eyes upward, to where the surface of the sea must be somewhere, many thousands of fathoms above them. The darkness stretched over their bodies like a dome of black velvet. With a little effort, Jolly could have convinced herself that she was standing under a night sky. Except that there were no stars here. No feeling of infinity. Instead, dread-provoking heaviness, which pressed on her heart, her thoughts, her courage like a ton of weight.

The kobalins attacked just as Munk had asked, "How far is it to the Crustal Breach?" and Aina had replied with a mysterious smile, "Can't you feel it? We're already in it!"

In front of them the blurry horizon of their vision started to move as a number of kobalins emerged from the darkness in an extended line, their bodies as white as the sand on the plain. Their eyeless faces were turned in the direction of the three polliwogs, their thick hands with the swordlike claws dangling almost to the ground. Even their joints were more pointed and angular than those of humans, and Jolly involuntarily wondered if perhaps they used their knees and elbows as weapons.

"Back!" she cried when the kobalins walked out of the gloom.

Aina stood there as if rooted. Munk's right hand fumbled with the fastening of his belt pouch, which now also held the big mussel.

"Let them come," he said softly.

"Munk!" Jolly yelled. "Damn it, get moving, now!"

But he didn't move from the spot. The mussels appeared to slide from his pouch into his hand on their own, and before Jolly could say anything, he was crouching on the rocky ground, laying out the shells in front of him. He placed Aina's gift in the center, where it rose above all the other mussels like the tower of a wondrous fairy-tale palace.

"I have to find out how powerful it is," he murmured.

The kobalins came nearer, in an irregular line, following the course of the rock ledge. Jolly didn't take the time to count them, but she guessed there were at least ten. Maybe more.

"Munk, quit that! There're too many!"

But Munk paid no attention to her. Aina stood close beside him. Both were looking toward the kobalins.

A pale glow shone out of the opening of the large mussel. The circle filled with light as the largest and brightest pearl Jolly had ever seen loosed itself from the shell and floated up over the center of the circle. It was different from usual: Before, the magic power of all the mussels had concentrated in the center and flowed into a magic ball. But this time it looked as though the others were luring from the interior of the big mussel a pearl that had been waiting there the whole time. The end result might look the same as usual—a glowing pearl that floated in the heart of the circle of mussels— and yet everything was different. Jolly could feel it, and she didn't like it.

Something happened to the water around them. It looked as if it were freezing into long, finger-thick strips, which undulated over the bottom of the sea like snakes.

The magic veins! flashed into Jolly's head. The pearl had tapped into the power of the water spinners! That must multiply its powers.

ON THE KOBALIN PATH

The now visible water veins pointed, starlike, in all directions from the location of the three polliwogs. But suddenly their ends appeared to stand up somewhere in the darkness, until they formed a wall around the companions like the calyx of a flower. Then a hard, abrupt pulsing passed through the wall of water snakes. A pressure wave seemed to Jolly to come together from all sides at once. The water strands gathered themselves over her head into something that looked like a tree-thick braid of translucent strands. It began to swing like a whip, and then in a wide arc it brushed the line of kobalins to a hundred, a hundred and fifty yards away from the polliwogs.

It was as if the creatures had encountered a giant's saber.

Before the creatures even understood what was rushing at them, the water whip cracked among them and crushed them. It went so fast that Jolly couldn't take in any details— it was only moments later that she even became aware of the kobalins' deaths, when the horizon in her polliwog view was suddenly empty and lifeless once more.

The power of the mussel magic had turned the kobalins to dust and scattered their particles in all directions like fine ash. Nothing was left. Even their footprints had vanished, and the sand was smooth again.

The water strands had dissolved again at the shock—or immediately afterwards—and nothing showed that they'd ever been there. The pearl had vanished as well. Munk had closed it back into the mussel with a wave of his hand; that was necessary so that its magic didn't go out of control.

Jolly fought against the sudden impulse to retch, swallowed hard several times, and finally managed to get herself under control again. Her legs felt weak, but she remained upright and stared silently at Munk, who still squatted motionless in front of his mussels with his back to her; just like Aina, whose hand was now resting on his shoulder, even though he probably couldn't feel it.

Jolly took a deep breath and then forced herself to walk in a tight curve around the silent pair.

"Onward," she said hoarsely, as she started on her way without looking back at them.

Nothing in the world could have gotten her to look one of them in the eye.

Rain of Fire

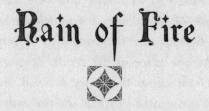

The sky over Aelenium was on fire. If the night sky had already been dyed red by the glow of the sea battle on the other side of the fog, now the defenders themselves were bathing the world in fire.

The ray riders were dousing the kobalins with flames.

They'd held the position hour after hour, but all had known that sooner or later it would come to this, and most of them were painfully aware of the consequences. Kindling a fire in the constricted confines of a city like Aelenium was a double-edged sword. And even now it was threatening to strike in both directions.

From above, Griffin saw that parts of the foremost walls were in flames, as well as some of the adjoining houses. The coral structures themselves remained largely untouched, but the wooden additions and roofs offered sufficient nourishment for the fire. It was already spreading to numerous living spaces.

The defenders had withdrawn and were lying in wait on the other side of the flames for individual kobalins who might leap through the flickering fire, driven by fear or bloodlust. At one place in the south, despite the flaming wall, a chieftain drove his hosts forward and soon the kobalins had extinguished part of the fire with their bodies. Black, greasy smoke rose between the houses, while the next ones trampled the cadavers of their incinerated comrades into the ashes and stormed over them to the wall.

"Did you see that?" cried Griffin's new marksman, a man named Ismael.

"Yes," Griffin replied, thinking, *You could almost feel sorry for them*. But he didn't say it because he was afraid Ismael might not understand sympathy. He couldn't even reconstruct it for himself very well. The kobalins were their adversaries, their deadly enemies, and dozens of men had already fallen victim to their claws down there below. And yet the fact remained that the kobalins weren't acting on their own. The true enemy was the Maelstrom. And, of course, that creature he'd sent to fight the battle for Aelenium for him, a creature for whom they had no name, whom they all called merely "the lord of the kobalins."

They were, however, quite sure that this creature was not a kobalin himself. The fish rain suggested a monstrosity like the killer of Munk's parents, the Acherus.

But so far no one had seen the kobalin lord, not even

Griffin and Jolly, who'd come closer to him than anyone else.

"Damn fish!" Ismael swore, while he whirled one of the fireballs on a long chain over his head to sling it into the deep where the wall was threatening to break. "Pull in your head, boy!"

Griffin felt the iron container filled with blazing oil circling over him, and he was almost more afraid of that than of the lances of the kobalins, which were still shooting into the air, if only sporadically. It was a wonder the rays still obeyed, despite the closeness of the flames and the heat. The chain net with the fireballs in it dangled some ten yards beneath the animal and were fastened to the saddle. D'Artois had hoped not to have to make use of these weapons, for the ray riders had had only a few practice flights with them, and Griffin himself just a single one.

Ismael, a light-haired, light-skinned giant, had upper arms like tree trunks, and he needed them too, to pull the fireballs up out of the net by their chains. He claimed that it was necessary to swing them over his head to increase the effect of the shot. Griffin wasn't so sure of that; it would have worked just as well, he thought, if they'd simply been able to hurl the balls down onto the kobalins. He had the uncomfortable feeling that Ismael was having fun with this and enjoyed the thrill. That might be all right as long as he didn't risk the lives of Griffin and the ray doing it. All the same, so far he hadn't lost one drop of the burning oil on the animal or its rider. Ismael was unusually strong and skilled and his hatred for the kobalins was deep-seated. No,

Griffin thought, probably better not to show any sympathy for the kobalins. It might be that he'd risk having Ismael throw one of the balls straight at him.

His eyes followed the fiery shot when the marksman let go of it. With chain tail clinking, it whizzed accurately down, leaving a glowing trail through the night. Before the ball crashed into the mob of kobalins, Griffin lost sight of it for a moment. But then a flaming flower hissed up among the creatures, and he knew that Ismael had once again hit his target. He felt no triumph, only deep horror.

"That was the last one," Ismael bellowed to make himself heard over the uproar. "Let's land and pick up some more balls."

Griffin shook his head. "No more balls! Look down there. Most of the places we could pick up supplies are too crowded. I don't want to circle around out of action as long as we can do in a few of the beasts another way just as well."

He felt Ismael's eyes on his back and expected a vigorous argument. But after a moment Griffin heard him loading his rifles behind him and the guns being cocked. Soon Ismael began firing below with all barrels.

They flew a second wide orbit around the embattled city, swooping fast and deep over the sea star points, where the kobalins were now swarming, and swept through the smoke clouds of the burning barricades. Griffin could not make out either Walker or Buenaventure.

In this chaos humans and kobalins alike were transformed into vague, scurrying figures, as small as toys from up here.

Griffin felt himself strangely removed from it all, although really he was caught right in the middle of it.

As they repeatedly moved out of fields of hot air into nighttime coolness and back, he thought again about Jolly. How was she making out on the bottom of the sea? Were she and Munk still under way, or had they already reached the Crustal Breach?

"Boy! Damn it all, look at that!"

For the first time Griffin was grateful to hear Ismael's hoarse voice. It tore him out of the nightmare pictures that had sprung up on their own before his inner eye.

But the reality wasn't one whit pleasanter. "That fire over there," cried Ismael, pointing to one of the sea star arms, "those are the sea horse stables, aren't they?"

Griffin's throat felt as if he'd swallowed some of Ismael's hot oil. For a moment he almost lost control of the ray. Matador and the other hippocampi! They'd all be incinerated down there!

He looked in the direction where Ismael was pointing and sighed with relief. Indeed fires were burning on the arm, but they hadn't yet jumped over to the long, extensive complex of the stables. However—and that was almost as bad—the entire arm was at the mercy of the kobalins.

But then Griffin discovered something else: The stall boys had opened the gates before their withdrawal into the interior of the city. Beneath the smoke a stream of sea horses poured out, shot between the kobalins in panic, and disappeared into the fog wall. His innards knotted until he realized that the kobalins had better things to do than to fall on the harmless sea horses. In fact, he didn't see that any hippocampus was pulled under. Obviously the servants of the Maelstrom were letting the herds pass. Griffin kept looking for Matador, but he couldn't pick him out in the flood of animals and through the clouds of smoke. He silently wished his sea horse well, holding back the tears that burned at the corners of his eyes.

Ismael emptied his rifles and pistols at the kobalins in front of the stables, and then they were beyond the sea star arm, leaving the barns and the fleeing herds behind them.

"They had damned good luck!" the marksman shouted over the noise of the weapons and the roaring headwind. His laughter sounded relieved. Like all the guardsmen of Aelenium, he too felt deep love for the elegant sea horses.

They'd half rounded the city when they again encountered a hail of fish cadavers. This time Griffin did something that until now he'd resisted: He disregarded d'Artois's order, broke out of the ring formation, and steered his mount hard to the outside.

Ismael exulted boisterously, as if this were only a singularly great prank they were indulging in. At the same time he got off a whole salvo of shots at a horde of kobalins that were just preparing to go on land. The shots struck the front row and drove the creatures back into the water. Ismael crowed with delight.

"Where are we off to, boy?" he called, while he reloaded his weapons.

"Are you interested in a *real* fight?" Griffin returned. He felt Ismael's high spirits infecting him—maybe because of his relief over the saving of the sea horses, maybe also because all this madness had finally rubbed off on him.

"Well, of course, boy." Ismael slapped him on the shoulder. "Who're we going to give it to, then?"

Griffin pointed through the clouds of dead fish down to the water. The light of the fires didn't reach this far, but the moon was illuminating a dark silhouette that showed vaguely under the waves. Down there was something large and shapeless, circling around the shores of the sea star city.

"Him," replied Griffin grimly. "We're going to kill the lord of the kobalins."

Soledad awakened feeling as though her back would break in two if she tried to move more than just her head. Her right arm burned, and when she looked she saw that the leather of her diving suit was hanging in shreds from the elbow down. However, the skin beneath it seemed to be largely undamaged.

Her head was filled with a terrible confusion of headache and a multitude of mixed-up images: the battle with the kobalins at the anchor chain, her flight into the undercity, and then complete darkness—a blackness that pressed like thumbs on Soledad's eyes. She'd tried to find a way, had put in her last bubblestone and had—as the air grew increasingly stuffy—finally stumbled on a shaft to the upper city. The last thing she remembered was the image of a mighty body that glided into the shaft and filled up the water around her, ever longer, ever more tortuous. And then—yes, then there was nothing more. Only blackness. A deep, gaping hole in her memory.

In spite of the pain in her back she tried to sit up. She was lying on something that felt like steps—and in fact, her hunch turned out to be right. It *was* a staircase.

And she slowly became aware of something else: She was no longer wearing a diving helmet. She could breathe freely without the bubblestone that had provided her with air. The reason was, of course—yet she also realized that in strangely slow motion—that she was no longer in the water.

A pale gleam lay over her surroundings, comparable to moonlight falling through a thin cloud cover: White, almost blue light flickered over the steps. Those were obviously part of a long circular staircase, which led upward and downward along the walls of a round shaft. Soledad's legs still lay up to the knees in water. Beneath the surface, plashing as it lapped against the walls of the shaft, the stairs descended farther into the deep.

The pale light came from numerous glow-stones. There was one lying on each stair in the corner between floor and wall, and this winding ribbon of light points even extended into the water below her.

This shaft must have served as access to the undercity for earlier diving expeditions of the guard. But how had she gotten here?

Slowly Soledad pulled her legs up into the dryness and

tried to right her upper body completely. It worked, if only with a lot of pulling and stabbing in her back muscles. But the pain was only because of her uncomfortable position on the steps, not from other injuries. How long had she lain there that way? Certainly several hours, for the wounds of the battle at the anchor chain had long ceased to bleed. Leather and clots were firmly stuck together.

Stand up, she told herself. *You must stand up.*

She tried it—and failed. She sank back onto the step with a groan. A renewed attempt. This time she managed it. Wobbly, but somewhat more securely, she supported herself with an arm against the wall. She didn't want to move the right one if she could help it; at least not until she was sure how badly injured it was.

She stood there for a while, out of breath, as if she'd just achieved a superhuman effort. And she'd merely gotten to her feet. Why had that cost her so much strength? Obviously she was much groggier than she'd realized at first.

She looked anxiously at the surface of the water. The shaft was almost perfectly round, which indicated that it had been artificially constructed, but in any case it had been shaped. Its diameter might be about ten yards. It wasn't possible to see how far down the spiral staircase continued, for the gleam of the glow-stones was too feeble to penetrate the water after even a short distance.

Soledad tilted her head back—amazingly free of pain this time—and looked up. There the stairs continued for seven or eight turns, although that observation wasn't reliable either;

the shine of the glow-stones was only a pale suggestion up there, and the stairs themselves might go on higher yet.

Soledad got her breathing under control again. Anyway, she was alive. And as far as she could tell, there were no kobalins here, near or far.

But there remained the question of how she'd gotten here. Someone or something had destroyed her diving suit and brought her to safety. If indeed she was in safety.

She grew dizzy, and for a moment she lost any sense of up and down. Only very gradually did her sense of balance return, and she began the ascent. Dragging herself up, painfully she managed step after step. It grew easier as her body became used to its own weight again.

Walker's face appeared in front of her in the darkness, half memory, half wishful thinking, and the thought of him gave her more strength. She must make it.

Behind her, down in the shaft, the water surface exploded.

She whirled, back against the wall, and saw a fountain of water shoot up, but she was too far away now to be able to tell what had surfaced down there. Rigid with fear, she listened to it thrashing in the water. Waves splashed against the walls, and something made the steps tremble under her feet.

She stood there for a long time, not moving, back and palms pressed against the coral wall. She tried to keep her breathing as quiet as possible, but the more she concentrated on it, the more often she needed to take a breath. She no longer had any weapons and would have to meet the creature with her bare hands, if it decided to follow her up the steps.

Panic arrived suddenly, not just fear, but real terror that stopped her breath. Now she was no longer ashamed of that. She'd been through too much in the past hours to act the proud, fearless pirate princess now. It was time to face her fear. And with this thought, she gave in to her curiosity and took one step forward, to the edge of the railingless stairs.

The water had quieted. But that did not mean that it was empty.

The creature had stopped throwing itself back and forth in the confines of the coral tube. Instead it was standing upright like a living tower in the middle of the shaft, its reptile body raised high, completely motionless, with almost hypnotic stillness. Water beaded its black scales and dropped into the deep. It was standing so still that Soledad had to take a second look to realize what it actually was: a sea serpent, black as night, as wide as the trunk of a primeval tree, with a triangular head, almost as big as Soledad herself.

Instantly the serpent rose another fathom higher. Before Soledad knew it, the eyes of the creature were on a level with her own.

And what eyes those were!

Slit serpent eyes, larger than a human head and the color of pure amber, as clear as golden glass and deep enough to become lost in within seconds.

Soledad lacked the power to move. She stood there motionless, not even moving back to the wall. The serpent's mouth would reach her in any twist of this shaft. There was no point in running away.

But still the creature made no move to devour her. Soledad's chest rose and fell, her breathing echoed against the damp walls. Silent and unmoving, they looked each other in the eyes, princess and serpent—and somehow in these moments, which extended themselves endlessly, Soledad understood. She read it in that amber gaze, in the clarity of those eyes, in the depths of that powerful intelligence.

The serpent had saved her. But it hadn't done it disinterestedly. The undercity was its kingdom, its territory, and if the kobalins were victorious and Aelenium went down, its living space would be destroyed along with her. It hadn't pulled Soledad out of the water out of charity, of course not; a term like that had no place in this ancient mind. It had done it to strengthen the city and injure the kobalins. For that reason alone.

Soledad stood there a few seconds longer. Then she slowly bent her head and bowed. "I thank you," she said, uncertain whether the serpent would understand the words. And then she quickly added something else before she could think about whether it would possibly be improper, even profane. "If you really want to help us, then protect the anchor chain."

With a calm she maintained with difficulty, she turned and continued on her ascent. Silently the body of the snake stretched up alongside her, completely soundless, remaining on a level with her for two more turnings of the staircase. Then suddenly it disappeared, so fast and quietly that Soledad only realized it two steps later. A thundering splash sounded from the bottom, then only the sloshing of the roiled-up waters against the walls.

The serpent was gone.

Soledad dragged herself on, without stopping. She felt a strange new strength inside her, as if the sight of those eyes had purified her and awakened all the reserves she had. And deep in her heart she knew that what she had just met was not an animal, not a monstrosity of the endless sea, but something entirely different.

She closed her eyes for a moment as she climbed. A tiny smile played around the corners of her mouth. Something had touched her, far more than just the teeth of that creature.

How presumptuous it had been to assume that all the gods who'd survived the ages in Aelenium were human.

The exit was in the middle of a tangle of coral streets and plazas, only a stone's throw below the second defense wall.

Soledad had stumbled up the last steps and come to a wooden door. She'd hammered on it and called for a long time until finally someone on the other side shoved a bolt and carefully opened it.

Two men in uniform stared at her with suspicion, rifles and lances pointing. Only when one of them recognized her and made clear to the other that the young woman in the diving suit couldn't be a kobalin did they let her through.

Over the shoulders of the men she saw that she'd landed in a narrow space, which was only meagerly illuminated by a single torch. A few nets were stretched on the walls to dry.

Pirate Wars

The cellar of an ordinary house, Soledad guessed, which was intended to camouflage the entrance to the undercity.

One man made a move to grab her under the arms as Soledad threatened to fall, but she pushed him away indignantly, straightened herself, and walked proudly past the sentries. She also refused the offer to bind her wounds with a silent shake of her head. Behind her the door to the undercity was closed again, the bolt squealing into its guides.

Those gigantic amber eyes—golden, bottomless pools— were still burning in Soledad's memory. And more than everything she had seen at the anchor chain, this gaze caused her fear and breathless amazement equally. Such perfection, such cold calculation. And at the same time, such superiority.

Dazedly she let them show her the exit and climbed the stairs—still more steps—until finally she was standing outside.

In the first moment she felt as if she'd just walked into the eyes of the serpent. The night sky was dyed golden, flooded with the glow of countless fires. The deadly glow of the flames was refracted by the veils of cloud and streamers of fog. She knew what this sight meant. However, she couldn't combat the fascination of the firelight. Many deaths, much destruction, and in spite of that, this light was of measureless beauty. She doubted that anyone except her saw it that way.

Soledad shook her head and rubbed her eyes as though waking from a dream. The amber eyes faded, melted into the hellish brightness of the sky and the burning city. Only now, with each further step, did she become herself again.

Before her the street opened onto a small, deserted square, which ended in a broad balustrade. From there she could look out over the deep drop-offs, over the sea of roofs, between which the shadows seethed like boiling oil. Streams of fugitives were pouring through the streets up the mountain.

The lower wall had fallen, that much she could tell right away. The fighters were pulling back, were already on the way to the second defense ring above the Poets' Quarter. Not much longer and the first ones would reach it.

Soledad raised her eyes to the sky over the water. In front of the fog wall, which almost looked like a wall of fire itself, isolated ray riders were circling, even if the majority of them now floated over the shore, keeping the flood of kobalins under fire.

On the other side of the fog wall the night was burning. Soledad couldn't tell if that was already the distant red of dawn, a reflection of the burning city, or if the inferno of the sea battle between the Antilles captains and the cannibal king Tyrone was still raging out there.

A thought came to her, and once it took hold of her, it wouldn't let her go. She detached herself from the balustrade, hurried back across the square, and turned into one of the adjoining streets.

Soon she was standing in front of the narrow house in which the Hexhermetic Shipworm slumbered. There were no longer any guards in front of the door; the entrance was closed but not locked. Soledad quickly walked inside and ran up the stairs to the attic of the house.

The cocoon had grown larger since she'd last been here. It appeared to be forming new silken layers still, and the threads that kept the bizarre tissue afloat were much more numerous. Almost two-thirds of the sharp-gabled storage space was now filled with them. Fine fibers extended from beam to beam, from floor to ceiling, and as floating curtains inside the network.

"Worm?" She made the suggestion of a bow, without really believing that he could see it. If he was still alive, his spirit was probably somewhere else, caught in a dream that was, she hoped, more agreeable than the gruesome reality of the battle.

"I'd give a lot to know what you're seeing right now," she said absently. The cocoon still seemed to be pulsing and sending vague oscillations through the net. Again and again tenuous fibers detached themselves, joined with others, and formed new layers within the net. There was a barely audible rustling and swishing in the air.

Carefully she stretched out a hand to touch the nearest layers, but she pulled back a finger's breadth before the net. She was afraid to awaken something that perhaps mightn't be ready to return yet.

"I don't really know why I came here," she said to the worm. "But I saw something down below, in the undercity . . . something that was not of this world. Jolly said that some of the people living here in Aelenium are in truth ancient gods—or what's left of them after they've lost their power. But that thing down there . . . well, I can't imagine that it was ever *more* powerful. I can feel it, you know? Something in those eyes has touched me, and there was something . . . something *truly* godlike. Sounds crazy, doesn't it?" She looked for words but found none that could express what was going through her head. "I mean, it really didn't do anything . . . anyway, not really." She cast a pain-filled look at her lower arm and went on, "It looks as though it saved my life. And I think I know why. It doesn't want Aelenium to fall into the Maelstrom's hands. It's just as stuck on this place as Forefather and the Ghost Trader. I think they all need Aelenium, perhaps because here is the only place they can still exist undisturbed."

Shaking her head, she broke off, thought for a while, and then said, "Anyway, I'm wondering what *you* really are, Worm. It wasn't a coincidence that we brought you here, was it? The wisdom of the worm you've talked about, that's nothing but a pile of sea lion crap. In reality, you're no more a worm than that snake down there is a snake." She took a resolute step up to the net, not knowing what she intended to express by it. "Right?" she asked softly.

The worm—or that which was in the cocoon—gave no answer. Not that she'd seriously expected one.

She snorted softly, then shook her head again. She was terribly tired, and the idea of now having to fight on frightened her deeply.

"Lovely that we've discussed it," she murmured mockingly, walking to the only window of the attic room. When she looked out, she could see up to the upper defense wall, now swarming with people. She took a deep breath and ran back down the stairs, leaving the net and the cocoon and whatever was in it behind.

She wondered what would happen if the kobalins entered this house. If something made them climb up to the attic.

What would *they* see in it?

And would they dare to wake it?

In the street outside it was raining dead fish. A troop of guardsmen came toward her on the way to the upper defense wall. She attached herself to them, reached the wall at a place where it crossed a former marketplace, and looked for someone she knew.

A hand touched her shoulder. As she whirled around, she was already taken into his arms.

"Walker," she whispered against his shoulder, and then she began to cry.

The Heaviness of Deep Water

The hill on the bottom of the deep sea looked like a termite hill, although a thousand times larger and strangely uniform in its proportions. Almost like an upright index finger that warned the wanderers on the sea floor against going any farther: Beyond me is nothing but death.

"What is that?" Jolly asked.

Aina lowered her voice as if she feared that someone might hear her from the hill. "That's the nest. The kobalins' nest, as they call it. They're born here."

Jolly and Munk exchanged a look. "*All* kobalins?"

The girl from the sea bottom shook her head. "Only the oldest. The fathers of the deep tribes, long before they splintered and began fighting each other." She stepped from one foot to the other. "At any rate, they did that until the Maelstrom united them again."

"We've heard that the ancestors of the kobalins came out of the Mare Tenebrosum," said Jolly, remembering what Count Aristotle had told the council. "And that the humans mixed with them. They say that the very first kobalins came into existence in the old days."

Aina shrugged her naked shoulders. "I don't know anything about that. Anyhow, that there"—she pointed to the finger-shaped rock tower—"is the place where the first of them were . . . hatched. Or born."

Jolly took a step to the edge of the narrow rock plateau. They had only just walked out of the protection of an assemblage of round stones as tall as houses onto this natural platform. From above they must look like ants creeping out between a pile of pebbles.

In front of them spread the panorama of a deep rock kettle, with jagged cracks running across it, chasms, and sharp-edged crests that must cut a sinking ship to pieces like a knife blade when it landed. The kobalin hill rose in the middle of this inhospitable landscape as sentry over the Crustal Breach, a ghostly silhouette at the edge of her perception.

Since their meeting with the albino kobalins they were no longer walking downward. It appeared that Aina had been right—they'd crossed the outer margins of the Crustal Breach and were now approaching its center.

Perhaps the kobalin hill was in fact something like a last sentry post before the heart of the breach, before that place from which the Maelstrom sprang. The roaring and raging in the darkness had become noticeably louder, but they still couldn't see anything. Polliwog vision didn't reach far enough.

"I swam over the rocks when I fled," said Aina. "We could walk, but that would take a long time and—"

"We'll swim," Munk interrupted her.

Jolly regarded him with a dark side glance. "Oh, is that so?"

He sighed, as if he were sorry to have to fight with her over each and every thing. But she only wanted him to at least ask her what she thought. "We have no time, Jolly. You know that as well as I do."

"And the search currents?" she retorted angrily. "What good will it do us to save a few hours if one of those currents catches us and either kills us or throws us a zillion miles back?"

"We can work forward bit by bit," Aina put in. "From one rock ridge to the next. And we can rest at the kobalin hill."

"Oh, good idea," Jolly answered. "We'll just ask them if they still have a warm place by the fire for us."

Aina smiled. "They told us about the hill—in the old time, before we started out. We have no danger to fear from there. The kobalins have never lived in the nest—except for one."

Aina walked to the edge of the plateau. Her right hand felt for a long strand of hair, and she rolled it thoughtfully between her fingers. "It's said she was the mother of the kobalins. Even her own children fear her. But she's been sitting there so long in her pit of slime and bones that the rocks have grown up over her and closed her in. After that she couldn't get out any-more because she was too big and fat for the cracks and tunnels."

"Too big?" Jolly repeated with terrible misgivings.

"Probably she's long dead." Aina was silent for a moment and appeared to be thinking. "We could make a detour around the hill. But that will take time."

Jolly looked up at the peak again. It was hard to estimate its height in the weak half light, but she estimated that from the place where it became visible over the rock labyrinth to its knobby top it measured around a hundred yards. But the mighty stone tower might be somewhat taller still.

"We should hurry," said Munk.

Jolly gave in and nodded. The three of them pushed off from the edge of the plateau and floated over the rocky peak with powerful swimming strokes.

The landscape beneath them resembled the one in which they'd been saved by the lantern fish at the beginning of their journey; only everything seemed to be more furrowed and sharper edged, as if in the gray prehistoric times a giant had struck the rocks with a huge hammer. Here, too, the bottom of the abyss lay too far below them, and polliwog vision did not reach to the ground. From above it looked as if wavering shadow streams flowed through the cracks. Pure black frothed around the cliffs and stone needles.

What Jolly had feared was quickly confirmed: She'd underestimated the distance to the kobalin hill and thus presumably its height as well.

Soon they'd have to rest, for swimming cost them far more energy than walking along the sea bottom. They hadn't slept for an eternity either, and their mealtimes had become irregular and without pleasure.

THE HEAVINESS OF DEEP WATER

Jolly was just chewing on a tough piece of pickled meat that tasted even saltier with seawater when Aina blurted out a warning cry. They quickly slid down behind a rock wall and cowered beside each other in a fissure. They'd barely found cover as a search current rolled over the wasteland, a tower-high swirl of stirred-up dust, whose force even made the rocks tremble. It was the fifth of these undersea tidal waves they'd experienced—the last had been not long ago, and Jolly worried that the closer they came to their goal, the more frequently they'd have to deal with them. Luckily, Aina had a good feeling for them and usually recognized the danger a little sooner than the others.

The three had just left their hiding place and were again swimming toward the top of the rocks when something unexpected happened. This time Aina was also surprised.

A second search current followed the first.

They'd scarcely risen up over the edge of the rocks when the rumbling of the invisible Maelstrom appeared to increase. But the noise didn't come from the Maelstrom itself but from a raging, whirling wall of sand and water that followed after the first with hardly a pause. It wasn't so high, but in width it extended from one edge of their sight to the other.

"Jolly!" Munk yelled. "Down!"

The warning came too late. She'd realized the danger at that very moment, but she had no time to react. She didn't even see what happened to the two others.

The search current seized her, and then it was as though

someone had stuck her into a giant container of sand and shaken the whole thing vigorously.

Dust and little stones pushed into her mouth and eyes. Up and down became meaningless. She felt herself being swept along by powers that were greater and more destructive than anything she'd thought possible. Her consciousness was wiped out by pain and panic and a darkness that obliterated polliwog vision itself.

He's separating us! was her last clear thought, hissing through her head like a flare.

Then she thought nothing more.

At least for a while.

"Jolly!"

I'm unconscious echoed through her thoughts like a strange voice.

She knew that voice. It wasn't the voice of Munk.

"Aina?" she managed haltingly. Her eyelids trembled and opened, and her vision was flooded by gray twilight, then by shapes. Sharpness returned. Recognition.

Aina's face. Over her.

"There you are again," said the girl with a smile. "About time."

Jolly stretched out a hand and reached through Aina like a dream image. And that's what she thought in those first moments, until she remembered. What Aina was. Munk. The undersea tidal wave that had carried her away. Her hand felt numb when it passed through the girl's body. That was the nearness of the Maelstrom. Aina actually gained in solidity as they advanced toward the heart of the Crustal Breach.

"I . . . I feel sick," she whispered.

Aina nodded. "The search current flung you against the rocks. You were lucky."

"Lucky?" Jolly touched her head with a groan. "My head says different." Even touching it hurt. Her scalp was sore. It felt as if thousands of hands were pulling on each single hair.

She made an effort to look around her. She was on the bottom of a ravine, at least she thought so. There was a rock wall at her back and one a few steps in front of her too. High over her arched the darkness, not a ceiling, but the limit of polliwog sight.

The current must have seized her and thrown her into a fissure. But it could have been worse. As far as she could tell right now, she hadn't broken anything. She saw merely a few scrapes, trickling blood that mixed with the seawater. The salt burned in the open places.

"Where's Munk?"

Aina pointed into the darkness behind her. "He's looking for you. He was quite desperate when you were suddenly gone. We separated."

"Then the search current didn't catch you?"

Aina shook her head. "We just made it behind the rocks."

Jolly nodded without really listening. Anyway, their mission wasn't endangered. She felt a pang that she was the one, of them all, whose mishap had delayed them.

"How much time have we lost?"

"Not much." Aina tilted her head and observed Jolly as if she were expecting a very particular reaction to this reply.

Her look made Jolly uncomfortable. "Why are you looking at me like that?"

"You don't need to worry that you're holding Munk up." Aina's voice was gentle and full of understanding. "Yet that *is* what you're thinking?"

Was she so easy to see through? Well, even if she was—what business was that of Aina's? She'd just taken a breath for a fitting reply when the girl shook her head slowly.

"You have no reason to be jealous of me," Aina said softly.

"I—"

"At least not yet."

Jolly stared at her. Then she tore her eyes from Aina's enigmatic smile and looked for Munk. He was nowhere to be seen.

"Don't worry about him. He's behind the rocks, looking for you." Aina didn't move. She was kneeling in front of Jolly on the ground, her dark eyes gleaming like spheres of polished onyx. "He's fine, and he's looking for you over there, a few crevices farther north—far enough not to be able to hear you if you call him."

Jolly pushed herself upright with her back against the wall. Finally she was standing on both feet, somewhat steady, although her sense of balance was acting crazy.

"Who are you, really?" she asked.

Aina stayed crouching and looking up at her mildly. "A polliwog like you. Only a few thousand years older."

"You're lying."

"No. Everything I told you is the truth." Her smile flickered like firelight. "I merely left out a few things."

Jolly was about to push off the floor to swim upward, but Aina shook her head and made a motion of her hand that made Jolly hesitate. "No. You won't manage to warn him. And he wouldn't listen to you anyway." Aina's hands formed a hollow, which she held to her right ear. "He has something better that gives him advice now."

"The damned mussel!"

"What I said about it was not a lie. It is more powerful than any you have ever held in your hands. Munk recognized that immediately."

"You beast!"

Jolly was all set to rush at Aina, but she knew that an attack was senseless. Her hands would go right through the girl. On the other hand, how did Aina intend to keep her from getting out of here?

A blur whizzed over her and took form a moment later. Something settled down over Jolly, and when she thrust up her hands in defense, she felt it between her fingers.

A wide, coarse-meshed net.

From niches and cracks in the rocks came white, eyeless figures.

One of them had flung the net and in one claw still held the rope by which it was fastened. Stones were knotted into the border of the net, which made it much heavier than it looked at first sight.

Jolly had no time to avoid it. The strands of plant fibers

settled down on her and Aina. But while the net lay over her head and shoulders and caught her arms in it, it sank right through Aina as if she weren't really there. The girl rose with a sigh and left the fibers of the net beneath her on the ground. Jolly, on the other hand, was so hopelessly entangled in it that the albino kobalins had enough time to shuffle over to her in their crouching gait and grab her.

"Don't resist," said Aina calmly. "They are stronger than you."

Jolly bellowed Munk's name, but she already sensed that Aina was right. He couldn't hear her, not in the middle of this maze. There was no echo down here, the water prevented that, and the stone swallowed the rest.

Two kobalins grasped her arms through the net and lifted her off the ground. The creatures might be smaller than she was and blind, but they possessed strength with which no human could compete. Under the white skin stretched wiry muscle fibers, and their long claws gripped like gigantic bird talons. Jolly cursed and swore, but she was simply carried away without the least chance of defending herself.

Aina walked lightly beside her. "No one will do you any harm."

"Right. That's how it looks," Jolly said between her teeth. Her enunciation suffered under the strands of the net, which were cutting painfully into her face. Two ran right across her mouth and kept her from being able to open her lips wider than a crack.

"No, believe me," said Aina earnestly. "You and Munk,

you're the last living polliwogs. You're much too valuable to destroy. Until there are no other possibilities, anyway."

"What about the other two polliwogs? Your friends." Jolly was not sure if her distorted words were understandable, but Aina answered matter-of-factly, as if she had no trouble understanding Jolly.

"One of them is dead. You killed him. And the other . . . I don't know if I would still call him a polliwog."

"We killed—" Jolly fell silent. Deep inside there awakened a bitter suspicion.

But before she could get around to busying herself more exhaustively with the thought, the ravine took a sharp bend. The ground rose. When Jolly looked up the incline, she realized where Aina and the kobalins had brought her.

Over her rose the kobalin hill. From down here it looked like a gigantic tower, which was only imperceptibly wider at the base than in its upper regions. If they climbed it the zigzag way that led upward on the outside, there was a chance that Munk might see them from afar. A thin hope, certainly, but for a moment it gave her new courage.

Until she discovered a second troop of kobalins that were busy with a round boulder several fathoms above her. The creatures placed poles under the stone colossus as levers and rolled it aside. Behind it, an opening in the rock wall became visible. A gateway to the nest of the kobalins, not high, not wide—just big enough to push a human through it.

"What are you going to do with me?"

"You will remain here until I have you fetched." Aina

smiled. "Then everything will be over, and you will have the opportunity to make a decision. For or against life. Until then you have time enough to think about it."

They reached the hole in the rock, which lay far below the level of the other peaks. If Munk were swimming toward her over the ravines, he wouldn't be able to see her from up there.

The kobalins transported her through the opening, net and all. Jolly stumbled, further entangling herself in the mesh. She fell down a slope of smooth stone with a curse. Over her she heard the screams of the two kobalins who'd pushed her. As she lay there, stunned for a moment, she saw Aina standing alone in the opening.

"Excuse them," the girl said angrily. "They are uncouth creatures. I have punished them for their roughness."

Jolly didn't see what Aina had done to the kobalins, but since the two of them had disappeared, she could guess. The cold-bloodedness of her opponent terrified her anew.

She pulled the net away from her face so that Aina could see the hatred in her eyes. "How long am I supposed to stay here?"

"Not long. The battle for Aelenium will soon be decided. After that we'll overrun the settlements on the coast and then . . . well, we'll see."

"How did he do it? I mean, how did the Maelstrom get you on his side?"

Aina tilted her head again, as she often did when she was surprised about something. "You still haven't grasped it, have you?"

Jolly's gut twisted. "Then explain it to me."

"Not now." Shaking her head, Aina stepped back and gave her creatures a sign. "I will come again. Then we'll talk."

A grating noise indicated that the levers were being employed again. The crack grew narrower.

"And Munk?" roared Jolly. Her legs kicked the net away, but it was too late to run up now. "What about Munk?"

Aina made a motion of her hand and the boulder stopped for several seconds. "Munk?" she asked with genuine astonishment. "But I am his friend!"

She didn't laugh, didn't even smile, as she stepped back and finally left the opening free. The seriousness in her pale features terrified Jolly more than all the other things that were happening in those seconds.

She called Aina's name, but it was too late. At the last moment something glowing shot through the crack. Then the rock sealed the last gap with a deep rumble and lay there, a weight of tons.

Silence returned. No sounds from outside penetrated the rock, and nothing moved around Jolly either. She blinked away the tears that had filled her eyes, more from rage than fear. Blurrily she gazed at the handful of lantern fish that swam around her like a glowing swarm of insects.

"You?" she asked weakly, but she couldn't even rejoice about that. Instead she looked over her shoulder, in the only direction that was still open to her.

This was a long, extended cave, whose end she couldn't make out.

Her knees trembling, she got to her feet and looked up at the blocked opening one last time. The formation of fish exploded, for a moment they whizzed around in confusion, and then they formed a densely clustered ball of light over Jolly's head.

Jolly didn't need their help. Polliwog vision worked inside the hill, too.

First hesitantly, then more and more decidedly, she began walking deeper into the lifeless stillness of the kobalin nest.

Two Giants

The lord of the kobalins was making his circuit around the city. He glided through the churning waters not far beneath the surface, discernible from above only as a shadow.

Griffin guided the ray behind the kobalin lord, about five fathoms above the waves, and followed his course. So close to him, the rain of dead fish was a repellent, often painful business—aside from the fact that they interfered with Griffin's vision. The scaly bodies glittered and dazzled in the light of the rising sun.

Behind him Ismael had been cursing ceaselessly. Each time he raised one of the rifles, a fish cadaver fell onto the barrel and pushed it down. Getting off an accurate shot was impossible in this stinking chaos.

"I really don't know if this was such a good idea," the marksman shouted over the racket.

"It's the fear of their master that's driving the kobalins forward." Griffin twisted his head to avoid the lashing arms of an octopus as it fell from the sky in front of him. With his left hand he pushed the cadaver off the ray's body. "If we succeed in killing the lord of the kobalins, then—"

"Then is the battle over?" scoffed Ismael. "Do you really believe that?"

"No," replied Griffin coldly. "But it's a first step, isn't it? This whole battle is wheeling in circles. It's time to do something that none of us expected."

He heard himself say these words and thought they didn't sound as if they came from his own mouth. But that also was a consequence of this war. They would all be changed men when this was over, if a spark of life was still left in them. And as Griffin guided the ray over the foaming mountains of waves, he seriously questioned whether he hadn't already changed long ago, in that moment when he decided to fight on Aelenium's side. Even earlier—when he made the decision to stick with Jolly.

The dead fish pelted down onto the ray's wings. The animal had trouble maintaining its altitude. Both riders were being thoroughly shaken, their flight path careening up and down. However, Griffin succeeded in keeping the animal on the track of the mighty shadow as he pursued his course through the sea.

The shape of the creature's body was almost impossible to make out. His outline appeared to change constantly; it was sometimes extended lengthwise, then oval, then again polymorphic with numerous outgrowths. He was as big as four or five rowboats and only showed up vaguely against the blue-black of the deep, which led Griffin to suspect that his body must be transparent like dark glass.

Griffin had expected an especially large kobalin or a kind of twin of the Acherus. But now, up close, the lord of the deep tribes did not resemble that creature. He was completely different, and that caused Griffin far greater fear than any giant kobalin or a golem of body parts. So numerous were the terrors he'd met in recent weeks that he feared the unexpected more than any known monstrosity.

"What the devil sort of beast is that?" asked Ismael, who'd given up trying to target it with his weapons. Instead he was now holding on with one hand and fending off the falling fish cadavers with the other.

"I haven't the faintest idea."

"They say you and the polliwog, you already met him one time."

"We were in his vicinity. But we didn't see him. Maybe we wouldn't be here if we had."

"You know how to encourage a fellow."

Griffin reined in the ray, for the lord of the kobalins had slowed under the water. Had he noticed that his trail was being followed from the air?

They received the answer in the form of half a dozen lances whizzing in their direction. Through the fish rain, Griffin hadn't been able to see the kobalins swimming in the waves near their master. Ismael cried out as one of the barb points grazed his shoulder, but it wasn't a serious hit. All the others missed their target, for the kobalins couldn't aim in the midst of this hail of dead fish either.

"All right?" Griffin called back worriedly. "Or shall I turn around?"

Ismael gave a pained laugh. "Not for anything in the world! As long as my head's still on my shoulders, we're staying in the air."

"Don't tempt fate." And with that Griffin pulled on the ray's reins and made it sink steeply down until its underside touched the waves. It was a dangerous maneuver, especially for the animal, but Griffin's calculation worked out. Two kobalins were rammed by the ray's gigantic head, torn from the water by the force of the impact, and flung away. The others instantly dove and scattered in all directions.

Griffin pulled the ray up again, but kept it at an angle behind the gigantic dark shadow under the surface.

"Can you fly the ray?" he roared into the headwind.

"Of course," retorted Ismael, and then his tone of voice changed. "Hey, wait a minute, you aren't serious!"

Griffin pulled his long guardsman's dagger out of his belt. "What else? You'll never get him from up here with bullets."

"You can't do that! That's madness!"

"Any other suggestions?"

"They'll shred you before you ever get near that thing."

"At the moment he's alone."

"It may look that way from up here. But all the same he's

something like their commander of the army. No general goes into battle without his bodyguard."

"The battle isn't out here, Ismael. The shores are lost, the first wall breached. The battle is raging up there in the streets now. This dirty beast is just watching it all from a distance. And it really doesn't seem as if it's swarming with kobalins here."

"Don't do it!"

But Griffin ignored the marksman's objections. He turned halfway around in the saddle. "When I jump, you slide forward in the saddle and take the reins. Hear?"

"You're crazy!" Ismael sounded as if he were seriously considering hammering reason into Griffin with the rifle barrel.

Before the marksman could stop him, Griffin stood up in the saddle. Straddle-legged he stood on the ray's shoulders, the reins still in his hands. The wind blew his many braids back; they rustled at his ears like palm fronds in a monsoon.

He looked down past the ray's head. Any minute they'd be exactly over the lord of the kobalins. Griffin was now convinced that the lance attack had been an accident—if the creature really had noticed them, he would certainly have dived.

Or else . . . he was waiting for Griffin. Perhaps he was hungry to get involved in the battle himself. Even if he could only demonstrate his power over a pirate boy.

"Griffin!"

He'd figured that Ismael would try once more to hold him back. He paid no attention to the shout.

The marksman grabbed him by the trouser leg. "Griffin, damn it, wait and look at that!"

For a moment Griffin's determination wavered—and then he also saw what was approaching them in the water from the left. He had to hold on tightly to the tautened reins or he would certainly have lost his balance as he stood there.

A gigantic dark phantom shot through the waves toward the lord of the kobalins, many times larger than he and incomparably more massive. Like a triumphant blast on the trumpet, a mighty column of water rose above the waves.

"Jasconius!" Griffin exclaimed.

"Your whale friend." Ismael's voice broke. "By my faith, he sooner makes a fair opponent for that bastard!"

Griffin still hesitated. Then he realized that it would have been suicide to plunge into the deep now. He would inevitably be crushed in the collision of the two giants. He quickly slid back into the saddle and guided the ray in a tight circle around the arena of the duel.

The whale and the lord of the kobalins came together. It happened too far under the surface for Griffin to be able to see the details. He saw only that the transparent figure of the monster changed again shortly before the collision and flowed to a kind of star, as if he intended to hurl his sharp extensions against Jasconius. But his points did not possess enough solidity to stop the whale. Powerfully and with murderous strength Jasconius crashed against the creature, and then both disappeared under a boiling carpet of foam and three-foot waves.

TWO GIANTS

Ismael swore again. "I can't see them anymore!"

Griffin didn't utter a sound. He was afraid for Jasconius and Ebenezer, and instantly he became aware of how crazy it was to have planned to throw himself on the lord of the kobalins with only a dagger. A voice inside him whispered that even the whale might not have a chance against an army leader of the Maelstrom. Not even he.

Griffin would have given anything to have been able to intervene in the fight. But there was nothing to see in the raging waves. The sea boiled. Cries floated on the wind, and this time they were not wafting from the city. They came from everywhere at the same time, a screeching and bellowing that made Griffin desperately want to press his hands over his ears. Stiff and pale, his fingers clutched the leather, and the euphoria he'd felt just moments before at Jasconius's appearance turned to blind panic. At the same time he was aware how narrowly he'd escaped death.

"Jasconius!" he cried, but he knew that the whale couldn't hear him.

Ismael seemed to regain his reason faster than Griffin. "Let's fly back to the city. We can do more there than here. That isn't our fight any longer."

The ocean surface broke apart. A circular fountain blossomed beneath them and reached with glittering fingers of water toward the ray and its two riders. In its center appeared Jasconius and something else that covered part of him, a runny, gelatinous mass like jelly. Or like a gigantic jellyfish that had fastened itself to the body of the whale.

"That's him." Griffin gasped.

"What?" Ismael's voice trembled. "That . . . stuff?"

"That's his body. That's why he kept changing his form all the time."

The silvery jellyfish creature was obviously trying to close itself around Jasconius's body and thus squeeze him to death. But there was something more. Griffin saw it only when he looked a second time. And although it was now directly in front of him, he hardly believed his eyes.

"Holy Mother of God!" Ismael exclaimed. "Do you see that too?"

"Yes . . . yes, of course."

"Is that a human being?"

Griffin patted the back of the ray so that it flew more calmly. The water fountains had long collapsed, but the whale and his opponent were still on the surface. Jasconius thrashed and shook himself, struck with his house-high tail fin, and expelled angry water fountains from his blowhole; that wasn't yet covered by the gelatinous mass, although the edges of the mass were pushing together with smacking sounds. Soon they were going to close around the whale's body.

What so unsettled Griffin and Ismael, however, was the human form resting within the jelly mass, with arms and legs outstretched, unclothed, the gaze turned upward. The silvery slime pressed his back against the whale's body.

"That's a child!" cried Ismael.

"Is that one of us? From Aelenium?"

"Never seen him before."

TWO GIANTS

It was a boy, perhaps a little younger than Griffin, although it couldn't be said with any certainty at that distance. He had coal black hair, and his skin was darker than that of Griffin or Ismael. One of the natives of the islands. The transparent mass flowed and pushed over him, pressed him against the whale's back, and according to all the laws of nature the boy should have been dead, suffocated by the milky substance of the giant jellyfish.

And yet he lived. His lips opened and closed, as if he were calling something. The mass filled his mouth. No sound came out. Normally Griffin would have assumed that the boy was caught in the sticky substance, perhaps was being sucked up by it—but the changing expressions on the stranger's face made him suspicious.

The boy appeared to be angry. His features expressed sheer hatred, and the words he was uttering were perhaps not cries for help at all but commands.

Was *he* the lord of the kobalins? A human, still a child, who was only using the jellyfish mass as a means of transport, as armor for his own weak body?

Was it he who commanded the deep tribes and now prodded the giant jellyfish to greater rage, to conquer the whale faster, to kill more quickly?

"Can we free him somehow?" asked Ismael, who obviously didn't share Griffin's fears. To the sharpshooter this was only a child who needed their help.

But Griffin guessed that the truth was a different matter. Together, this boy and the jellyfish body that surrounded him like an ancient insect in amber formed a single creature, no longer human but also not entirely monster. They were—together—the lord of the kobalins. The representative of the Maelstrom in this battle of men and half-forgotten gods.

Jasconius dove again and dragged the jellyfish and the boy with him. Again the waters foamed, the waves broke apart, and again both vanished beneath gray spray and the reflection of the fire tongues on the waves.

"Back to the city!" Ismael roared. For the first time there was panic in his voice, mixed with complete bewilderment.

"No," replied Griffin. "I have to see how the battle goes."

Ismael placed a hand on his shoulder. His fingers pressed painfully into Griffin's muscles. "There's no point, boy. Whatever happens, we can't do anything to change it."

"But I must *know*! I owe Jasconius that, at least."

"At the cost of both our lives?"

Griffin understood what Ismael meant when the hand of the sharpshooter let go of him and pointed to the right. There beneath the waves approached a surging throng of kobalins. Lance points plowed through the water like sharks' fins.

Once more he looked over at where Jasconius and the lord of the kobalins had sunk. The two giants could no longer be seen under the cover of the foam and seething spume.

"I can't just turn around now," he said decidedly.

"Boy!" Ismael's voice grew imploring. "That's not your battle."

"Oh yes, it is. It is all our battle. Jasconius . . . the whale, I mean, he's fighting for us. And Ebenezer . . . the man in the whale, everyone called him, called him names and said he was a murderer. And now those two are risking their lives for us." Griffin looked angrily back at Ismael. "Do you seriously intend to claim that this isn't our battle? It *is* ours. Only someone else is fighting it for us and may die doing it."

For a long moment the man's features twitched. Griffin saw that his words had hit the mark.

"The least we can do is wait for the outcome," said Griffin in a firm voice. "We two are the only ones who can tell the others about it. We at least owe Jasconius and Ebenezer a damn *remembrance*, don't you think?"

Ismael hesitated, and a trace of guilt appeared in his face. But then he looked down in alarm. "We won't be able to tell anyone else about it!" he shouted. "Turn away, boy—*turn away!*"

At the sound of Ismael's voice Griffin acted instinctively. His hands pulled on the reins, but the ray moved much too heavily. A lance rammed through its right wing and came out again through the top. The animal shook itself and let out a deep roar. Its wing beats became irregular, and for a moment it looked as though it would throw off both riders. Ismael cried out, Griffin too, but somehow they succeeded in staying in the saddle. More harpoons twitched upward, sharpened bone points full of hooks, and one grazed the animal's body, and this time Griffin lost control. Ismael bellowed and cursed, then instantly fell silent as a harpoon ate a bloody furrow into his thigh. The shock robbed his powers of speech for a few seconds. Then he cried out, a high sound of pain that went to the very marrow of Griffin's bones.

"I can't . . . hold him!" Griffin yelled. Then the reins were snatched from his hands, the ray reared, and its body completed a snakelike movement that Griffin would never have believed the colossus capable of.

"Hold on tight!" he cried to the marksman, then invisible hands tore him from the saddle, he lost his balance—and slipped off.

"Griffin!" Ismael saw the boy fall, and for a moment forgot the burning pain in his leg and tried to grab him.

He just managed to catch Griffin's right hand.

Griffin cried out as a murderous jerk went through his arm. Then he realized that the crash on the water had not come, that he was still hanging in the air. He was dangling at the side of the ray, held only by Ismael's hand.

"I'll . . . pull you . . . up," the man gasped grimly, but they both knew it was hopeless.

Down below the kobalins chattered, harpoons twitched after them. But the wavering ray had already distanced itself from the pack in the water, and the shots went awry. What nothing would change was that the animal kept shaking in pain and rearing; it was unable to coordinate the beats of its healthy and injured wings.

Griffin was being shaken back and forth. He hung there, helpless, too weak to pull himself up Ismael's arm with just one hand. The wounded marksman's strength was also ebbing, and both realized at the same time that their efforts were in vain.

"It's not going to work!" cried Griffin. Perhaps he only

thought it. He felt his fingers slide through Ismael's hand. Bit by bit, with a nightmarish slowness. And yet the end could no longer be checked.

Ismael's face was distorted into a desperate grimace. He could scarcely hold himself in the saddle. The injured ray was going completely out of control and flying in a wavering zigzag, which didn't really bring it any nearer to the city.

A wide panicked swerve, then the animal sailed wobblingly back in the direction from which they had come, again over the screaming kobalins and their sharp-toothed hooked lances.

Griffin was going to fall. He knew it.

Only seconds more.

Ismael had tears of grief and rage in his eyes when he looked down at Griffin. Their eyes met. They both knew the outcome of this hellish ride.

Griffin accepted the truth a moment sooner.

"No!" roared Ismael when he realized what the boy was going to do.

But Griffin didn't listen to him. He had the choice: He could let himself fall, a good fifty yards away from the kobalins—or he could hold out a few seconds longer and then plunge right onto their lance points.

"No!" cried the marksman again, but it was too late.

"Take the reins!" Griffin yelled, gasped for air—

—and let go.

Ismael's cries filled his ears, his head, until he hit the water hard. The waves seized him with their fingers of spume and pulled him down under. Darkness, penetrated by a red glow, surrounded Griffin as he sank down like a stone, then began to kick, first in panic, then with more confidence. He'd lost his orientation, didn't know if the kobalins were already on their way to him.

He only hoped that Ismael had succeeded in getting the wobbling ray under his control. Then it wouldn't be entirely for nothing that he drowned or was torn to pieces by the soldiers of the deep tribes. Then it would all still have some meaning, somehow.

The claws of the kobalins grabbed him. He felt he must scream, even though he didn't, even though he resisted and did his best to fight, not to give up.

Not to die. Not now.

Not without seeing Jolly one last time, holding her, hearing her voice.

Then they fell on him, a whole dozen, and they pulled him with them. In all directions at once.

The Cannibal Fleet

For a moment Griffin thought the kobalins were going to tear him to shreds. They pulled and tore at his arms and legs—until finally one of them uttered a high scream, all the others froze in fright, and the pain in Griffin's limbs slackened.

He immediately began to fight again, but there was no point. There were too many, a dozen or more—exactly how many he couldn't tell in the seething, raging waters. All around him were snapping mouths, long claws, and skinny, shimmering bodies, swirling in veils of air bubbles and whirling turbulence.

They pushed him up to the surface so that he could breathe. He gasped greedily for air and even tried to catch a glimpse of Ismael and the ray up above, but he couldn't see them.

He felt the creatures pulling on him again. At the same time a ring of ugly kobalin faces surfaced around him. Then three of them dragged him swiftly in one direction, so fast that the spume spraying into his face almost took his breath away again. Somehow he managed to get some air now and then as they rushed him toward the fog wall, which was glowing orange in the light of the early morning. Not even the smoke rising from the burning shores of Aelenium could entirely obscure the shining of the morning sun.

But when they dove into the fog, the light stayed behind. The only thing from the outside penetrating the mist was the hail of dead fish that fell around them. The lord of the kobalins must be nearby. Despair overwhelmed Griffin, not only for his own sake but because he feared that the jellyfish creature might have killed the whale and Ebenezer. He wondered what would happen to the rooms behind the magic door if Jasconius died. And to Ebenezer, if he'd managed to hide there.

But he had no more time to think seriously about the whale's defeat, for now he saw where the kobalins had brought him.

A remarkable hump rose out of the water ahead of him, half veiled in fog. At first glance it looked like a tiny island, not ten yards in diameter, which rose about three feet out of the water. As they came nearer, Griffin saw that it consisted of large mussel halves; the shape was similar to a gigantic turtle shell. He was very close to it when he discovered that each of the mussel shells was held over the head of a kobalin—

on the underside of the hump it was swarming with kobalin soldiers who bore the artificial island on their clawed hands. On top stood a figure, half concealed by veils of fog.

Two of the kobalins sprang onto the shell, seized Griffin by the arms, and pulled him out of the water. The mussels scraped and crunched under his feet but held together without a gap. It wasn't very easy to stand steadily on them, for the two kobalins were leading him to face the figure that stood waiting for him on the highest point of the mussel shells.

Griffin's breath stopped when he looked into the face of the person opposite him.

It was his own.

Almost, anyway. For another face mixed in with the image of his features like ink trails in the water, narrower, more finely cut—and feminine.

Griffin didn't utter a sound. What he saw in front of him, constantly in motion, incomplete like a half-finished clay bust, was his double, over which, in quick succession, repeatedly flitted the face of a girl.

Jolly's face.

And then he understood. It was the wyvern, the shape changer, which he and Jolly had met on the burning bridge between worlds. That time the creature had met them in the shape of the bridge builder Agostini. The wyvern had taken flight when the bridge had gone up in flames. Griffin had hardly given it a thought since then.

The wyvern smiled—a bizarre mixture of Jolly's and

Griffin's own smiles. Obviously the creature hadn't decided yet which form it wanted to take. Not only did the two faces alternate on the creature's head, they also appeared anything but complete. The nose somehow resembled neither Griffin's nor Jolly's, and the wyvern was having a hard time replicating Jolly's long black hair. But its difficulties with the numerous rings in Jolly's ears and the silver pin through the skin at the bridge of her nose were even greater.

The time before, when Agostini's double had dissolved before his very eyes, Griffin had been able to get a look at the true form of this creature. Now, in this condition of indecisive transformation, the wyvern's real makeup was also visible. For it was not a single creature but a throng of thousands upon thousands of tiny beetles. They came together like seething grains of sand in a skinlike surface, taking on various tones of color like a chameleon, and thus could give the impression of a human or any other living creature.

So now it would be Griffin. Or Jolly. One of the two. Griffin's capture had probably decided the issue.

Wordlessly the wyvern stretched a pulsating hand toward him.

Griffin pushed off the ground with all his strength. He wouldn't permit the wyvern, camouflaged as his double, to be slipped behind the defense walls of Aelenium. Because of his adventures at the side of the polliwogs, Griffin had access to all the defense installations and dignitaries of the sea star city. It was unthinkable what damage the wyvern could wreak in his form.

But evidently the finishing touch was missing. Something that required Griffin himself, the living, breathing model.

And that, whatever it was, Griffin did not intend to give the creature.

He stumbled backward, pulling the two kobalins with him, and his sudden movement caused the entire mussel island to begin rocking. Again the edges of the shell grated over each other. For an instant, a broad crack opened beside him. Furious jabbering arose from the bunch of kobalins beneath the mussel shells.

The wyvern gave a high, long-drawn-out cry, which penetrated all Griffin's bones like an icy storm wind. It started after him, but because of its unfinished body it didn't have complete control over its movements. It reeled, stopped, and swayed for a moment before it found new stability and straightened up.

Griffin rammed his left elbow behind him, felt the teeth of one of the kobalins shatter under the impact, and shook him off. Squealing, the kobalin slid backward into the water. The second kobalin, who'd pulled Griffin up, didn't let himself be outwitted so easily. Griffin also struck at him, but the creature ducked, sprang crouching beneath the blow, and tried to grab him by the hips. Griffin was just able to turn sideways and escape one of the kobalin's paws; the other struck his side with its claws. The points of the long talons dug into his skin, and he cried out in pain and rage. He seized the kobalin's outstretched arm and slung the creature over the edge of the mussel island. Gibbering, the kobalin slapped into the water.

Something had fastened onto the back of Griffin's head. A stabbing pain like the touch of stinging jellyfish spread through his skull. Then there was scrambling movement on his temples, his neck, his forehead. Griffin roared, shook himself in revulsion, and threw himself on his side. The wyvern was pulled to the ground with him, while the tiny beetle creatures swarmed over Griffin's face to study its form and transfer it to the swarm.

Somehow Griffin succeeded in drawing the knife from his belt. The blade passed through the body of the wyvern like butter, but there was no wound—it was as if he'd plunged the blade into a heap of sand. When he withdrew the weapon, the swarming insects closed the opening like trickling sand.

The heads of the kobalins appeared around the mussel hump. They'd encircled the strange island, and after a brief hesitation they pushed themselves over the edge of the platform. The first pulled themselves out of the water with bared fangs, which shimmered yellow-white through the mist of the fog.

But Griffin paid no attention to them. His battle was hopeless, he knew that. Nevertheless he refused to give up. He ran his hand over his face and wiped a broad furrow in the layer of beetles that were about to close over his features like a mask. The wyvern bellowed with pain. Griffin realized that the beetles were very probably elements of a single organism. When he separated some of them from the rest, it was if he cut off part of the wyvern's body.

Armed with this new knowledge, Griffin fought merci-lessly. The wyvern screeched and screamed as Griffin did his best to rip entire clumps of beetles out of the monster and throw them out onto the water.

He didn't have much time left. And yet in all this tumult, as he tried not to be enclosed by the beetles, the behavior of the kobalins was puzzling. They'd surrounded him, and almost all had now climbed up onto the mussel shells. And yet they didn't seize him. It was almost as if they were watch-ing him—and awaiting the outcome of his grotesque duel with the wyvern.

The shape changer struck at him with crawling, seething limbs. Gradually Griffin's strength was flagging. All the hours in the ray's saddle, the tension, the fear; then the plunge into the sea, his hopeless struggling with the soldiers of the deep tribes, and now, last of all, his fight with the wyvern, were accompanied by the never-ending rain of dead fish.

To the right of him the waves broke apart, an eruption of dark saltwater, followed by a transparent ball of gelatin, which soon towered out of the waves like a glassy finger. Twelve feet high and clear as crystal. And in its interior, standing upright, with crossed arms and a malicious smile at the corners of his mouth—the boy.

The same boy that Griffin had seen from the ray when the jellyfish creature had encircled Jasconius. Black-haired, dark, and very delicate. Younger than he was. Really a pretty child—had there not been the smile that changed his face into a malignant grimace.

Griffin and the wyvern were knitted into a grotesque embrace, half standing, half on the ground. On the water, nests of wriggling beetles were floating everywhere, trying blindly and frantically to return to their swarm. The wyvern suffered terrible pain, but it had not yet given up its plan to take Griffin's form.

But then it caught sight of the boy, who towered over the mussel island in his jellyfish sphere. It cried out harshly from a dozen body openings at the same time, orders perhaps, demands for support. But the boy only looked on and smiled.

What's going on here? thought Griffin. *Who's fighting whom? What have I gotten into?*

The shape changer bellowed again, but the boy in the jellyfish shook his head barely perceptibly. He made a short hand motion in the direction of the kobalins. The ones that had climbed onto the mussel shells were waiting with dangling claws and bared teeth to fall upon Griffin. Now their master gave them the silent order to withdraw. Swiftly the soldiers of the deep tribes slid into the water. A few seconds later Griffin and the wyvern were alone on the backs of the mussel shells.

Griffin closed his eyes. That the lord of the kobalins surfaced here, uninjured, could only mean that he'd triumphed over the whale.

Griffin gave vent to his rage and despair with a scream. And it might have been his anger or a last rebellion that gave him the strength to break the wyvern's resistance. Griffin drove his fist into the blurry face of the shape changer; he felt his fingers penetrate it and come up against something like a hard pit in the center of the teeming skull. He couldn't be certain that he'd actually found the wyvern's brain. He trusted his intuition alone and his luck.

His hand closed around the firm substance——and he pulled it out of the whirling chaos of beetles with a wild yell.

Instantly the swarm collapsed on itself, hitting the mussel shells and spraying out in a firework of colors. Then, as a cascade of beetles, it flowed into the cracks and over the edges of the island.

Seconds later Griffin was alone, crouching exhausted on his knees and closing his right hand around the brain of the wyvern with all the strength he had left. The black organ, which resembled a clump of earth, was not firm enough to withstand his grip. Silently it crumbled between his fingers.

The boy inside the jellyfish laughed.

His mouth opened like a portrait coming to life behind glass. His hands twitched with excitement. Only his eyes remained unchanged, wide open, staring at Griffin. He looked like a puppet that is manipulated by too few hands to move naturally——each movement looked incomplete, every motion lacked the details: eyes that didn't laugh with the mouth; fists on which the thumbs remained spread, as if paralyzed; and when he opened his mouth to speak, no sound came out.

He speaks with them through his thoughts, Griffin decided. Then all at once the mussel shells under his feet shifted closer together again and all the gaps closed. And the kobalins in the water formed themselves into a perfect circle around the hump.

The jellyfish towered upright over the waves behind the kobalins. The waves struck against its sides, but they didn't bounce off. They were absorbed by the gelatin, as if it drew its strength from the ocean itself.

So that was why Jasconius hadn't been able to overcome him, Griffin thought in grim sorrow. No matter how much the whale attacked the jellyfish monster, as long as it was in the water, its reserves of strength were inexhaustible.

"What do you want of me?" Griffin roared at the boy. The wounds that he'd suffered in this and the previous fights hurt. He was dizzy, and his legs were threatening to buckle. But no wound, no matter how severe, would make him fall on his knees before this monster.

Some of the kobalins were growing restless. Griffin saw them only blurrily, but he noticed that their jabbering sounded more excited. Some were paddling nervously back and forth, others ducked their heads under the water and looked into the depths.

The boy inside the jellyfish opened his mouth wide, as if in a piercing scream.

And the sea exploded.

Griffin saw the water surface under the jellyfish curve upward. The jaws of a giant whale rose up around the lord of the kobalins like a black wall, enclosed him completely—and swallowed him. But still Jasconius continued to rise from the sea like a black tower, rushing quickly but at the same time in slow motion, as if time itself had slowed so that everyone could appreciate the majesty of the whale rising from the waves.

The kobalins under the mussel platform scattered, screeching. Suddenly Griffin no longer had a floor under his feet. The mussels slid apart in all directions, and a mighty tidal wave swirled over him and the soldiers of the deep tribes.

Jasconius's gigantic body twisted itself ever higher, until more than half his body towered out of the ocean. Then the whale reached the highest point, seemed to float free for a fraction of a second—and let himself fall on his side.

In a mighty eruption of water, foam, and tossed-about kobalins, Jasconius plunged back into the sea. His mouth was now closed, the jellyfish and the boy vanished inside. While Griffin kicked desperately to stay on the surface, he saw that the entire body of the whale was covered with lifeless kobalins and countless harpoons. The jellyfish boy must have thrown the combined might of the deep tribes against his adversary. But he hadn't reckoned with the tenacity of the giant whale.

Griffin saw Jasconius sink with his prey and he guessed— hoped, prayed—that the duel was decided: In Jasconius's stomach the lord of the kobalins was only a gigantic jellyfish without the opportunity to renew itself in the water. Griffin had seen a thousand times what happened to jellyfish that were thrown onto land: They dried out and finally dissolved.

But that meant that no more water could get into Jasconius's body. And suddenly Griffin understood what the whale and Ebenezer had done.

Jasconius was dying. Hundreds of harpoons were sticking into his body. The claws and teeth of the kobalins had torn deep wounds in his skin. His attack on the lord of the kobalins was a last convulsion, a final, determined effort of will.

"*No!*" Griffin howled so loudly that even the fog scarcely muffled his voice. Shattered, he floated in the churning waters, oblivious to the fleeing kobalins and incapable of following his dying friend to the bottom. He wanted to be there when the end came, wanted to thank Jasconius one last time for everything that he'd done. And Ebenezer . . . just the thought of him burrowed into Griffin's entrails like sharp steel.

He struck his fist on the water in desperation. Then he dove under, headfirst, swam down into darkness, as deep as he could. The need for air was unbearable, and the pain of the water pressure raged in his ears. But he kept sinking deeper, although he knew that it was pointless.

He'd never see Jasconius again. The whale had taken the lord of the kobalins to death with him.

He cried out, this time into the water, and his rage and grief turned into a last burst of air bubbles, which pushed quickly upward. He couldn't help it, he had to get to the surface. Right now.

He let himself be moved by water pressure, without using his arms and legs, for at this moment he didn't care if he arrived on the surface living or dead. He'd lost Jolly, perhaps forever; Aelenium was sinking in fire and the attacks of the deep tribes; Soledad had possibly fallen in the battle at the anchor chain; and now Jasconius and Ebenezer . . . especially those two, whom he'd drawn into this business and who'd joined the fight for his sake.

They'd sacrificed themselves. For him. For all the others.

His head broke the surface in the midst of the fog. In anguish he gulped air and bellowed angrily once more. Then he relaxed, let himself drift. It didn't matter where. Deeper into the fog or out onto the battlefield again. It didn't matter at all.

But something happened that roused him. Instantly his will to survive returned, and this time it was not the thought of Jolly.

A dark silhouette was moving through the fog not far from him, was coming right up to him. For one rapturous moment he hoped it was Jasconius, to whom nothing had happened, who was still alive and—

It was the bow of a ship.

Wild shouting was coming down from the deck of the galleon. The sails hung slack on the yards, and the ship itself moved painfully slowly. It wasn't hard for Griffin to reach it with a few strokes. His heart thumping, he looked up at the high plank wall.

Heads were dangling from the bowsprit. They were the severed heads of men, and he recognized at least two of them from his years as a ship's boy.

One was Rouquette, the oldest of the council of the Antilles captains. Beside him dangled the head of his fellow captain, Galliano.

The battle between the cannibal king and the Antilles

captains was decided. Tyrone's fleet had finally set its course for Aelenium.

The ship that was moving through the fog ring in front of Griffin must be the flagship of the cannibal king. No other was entitled to ornament his prow with the heads of fallen enemies.

Griffin glided over to the hull of the ship and let it pass by him for a short distance. Then he grabbed hold of a rope that might have been left dangling into the sea after the last keelhauling and was being dragged along through the waves. The ship lay low in the water; it must be filled to bursting with fighters, cannibals, and cannon.

Griffin clenched his teeth and climbed up the rope hand over hand. He'd done the same thing a dozen times, but today the wound in his side slowed him; it hurt hellishly. An arm's length below the railing, he waited until the ship moved forward into the interior of the fog ring and all the seamen were distracted by the sight of the burning sea star city.

Then he pulled himself soundlessly aboard, scurried over to a chest full of weapons, and took cover behind it, unnoticed.

"The kobalins are running away!" shouted someone in the line of defenders, and soon other voices took up the cry: "They're quitting! They're getting out of here!"

Soledad had been fighting at Walker's side for the past few hours, in the middle of a wall of harried, tattered, exhausted figures. The stink of fire, blood, and sweat hung in the air.

Buenaventure was right beside them, grim and silent. He must have slain more kobalins than any other, and the only thing he ever said was a curse now and then that his saber was getting too dull to kill three of them with one blow.

They were standing on the second defense wall, above the Poets' Quarter. Smoke rose up to them from far below, but the fires along the shores didn't appear to have spread.

"They're right," Walker murmured. "The kobalins are making tracks. Devil take me, well, I'll be damned!"

His long locks were matted, his face smeared with kobalin blood and dirt. Like the clothing of all the others, his shirt and his trousers had turned a muddy brown; in many places the cloth was shredded by the claws of the enemy, showing deep scratches underneath.

"Soledad!"

She turned around to him. Only unwillingly and still with a trace of disbelief could she take her eyes off the kobalin masses now turning from the wall and plunging head over heels through the streets back toward the shore. A stampede of scaled bodies, fanged teeth, and scraping claws, the deep tribes surged down to the water.

Soledad repressed the urge to fall on Walker's neck in relief—she still didn't trust the sudden peace. Maybe the unexpected retreat was a trick, some kind of devilishness that was supposed to lull the defenders into a sense of security. But why was the withdrawal so disorderly then? Why did the kobalins trample each other in their flight, scratching and biting in their struggle to be the first to jump back into the sea?

"As if they were afraid of something," growled Buenaventure. He was breathing hard. During the fight, Soledad had looked over at the pit bull man a few times and observed his tongue hanging out of his mouth as he panted.

"It seems to me it's the other way around," said Walker.

Buenaventure looked at him with a frown. "Huh?"

"It looks as though suddenly they *aren't* afraid anymore—of their captains or even of the Maelstrom."

"You think"—Soledad swallowed—"they've lost their commander?" She didn't look at him but stared out over the fleeing army of the deep tribes.

"So it would seem," said Walker. "Without him they're following their instinct and rushing back into the water. They detest land and air."

"And fire," said Buenaventure, sniffing the smoke.

Soledad let herself sink down with her back against the defense wall. "But that would mean that the lord of the kobalins is beaten."

Some of the soldiers wanted to follow the kobalins and fell those in the last lines, but the officers of the guard held them back. No one trusted what he was seeing yet, especially not the actions of kobalins.

Soledad turned from the congested streets and looked up at the sky over the water. A handful of rays was circling there; the others were busy transporting the injured from the wall up to the entrances of the refuge halls. Had one of the ray riders out there killed the lord of the kobalins? And where was Griffin? Through the smoke, aglow with the beams of the morning sun, she couldn't distinguish the individual riders on the rays—they were hardly more than bright dots on the backs of the mighty animals. Soledad sent a fervent prayer to heaven that nothing had happened to the boy.

Uncertainty nagged at her, in spite of the great relief she felt at the withdrawal of the deep tribes. Were they really gone?

The defenders got busy binding up each other's wounds. Water bottles were passed from hand to hand, and all greedily quenched their thirst. Those who'd managed to stay on their feet with their last strength were helped down from the wall by their comrades.

"What now?" asked Buenaventure helplessly. He hadn't even lowered his saber yet, as if he still couldn't believe that the battle had come to an end. Even the deafening jubilation that echoed from all parts of the wall couldn't convince him.

Walker took a step forward. "I think," said the captain, "we—"

A shout interrupted him. Before he could finish the sentence, the general congratulation turned into cries of alarm. Somewhere in the streets above them the alarm bells were sounded, and very close to Soledad a young man began to weep heartrendingly.

She followed the direction of the others' gaze and saw what had so suddenly put an end to the relieved atmosphere.

Only vaguely discernible through the walls of smoke, ships were breaking out of the fog. Black flags flapped at the mast tops, and the wind carried a dull chorus of war cries over to Aelenium's cliffs.

Pirate Wars

"That's Tyrone!" exclaimed Walker, his face stony. "From the frying pan into the fire, I'll be goddamned."

The galleons emerged from the fog ring like ghost ships. Their decks swarmed with gruesomely decorated tribesmen and saber-wielding pirates.

"Are those the cannibals?" whispered the weeping boy near Soledad.

No one answered him.

A Conversation in the Deep

The cave in the kobalin hill was extensive, quite narrow, and not especially high. But Jolly's hope that the angular rock tube would be a tunnel that led somewhere turned out to be false.

After thirty or forty paces Jolly's polliwog vision saw the back wall emerge from the darkness, first only as a blur, then as a steep scree of boulders and small stones. At some time the roof must have fallen in at that spot. There must be earthquakes down here that you didn't feel on the surface, and this realization made Jolly's sense of isolation intolerable. If she were to die in this place, there wouldn't even be a wave up there on the sea. No one would learn of it.

Oddly, she thought of the sky as she looked up at the rock roof—of a bright blue open sky, which now lay thirty thousand feet above her, as unreachable as the moon and the stars. She thought of the Caribbean wind, which had blown in her face countless times and filled the slapping sails. She thought of the freedom of the endless ocean. And she remembered her old life on the *Skinny Maddy*, her foster father Bannon, how it used to be, before his betrayal, which had started all this.

And then the memory of a single face flashed through her like a sharp pain. Griffin. It was almost as if something from him stretched out to her, a hand that waved to her one last time, a farewell forever.

Jolly sank to her knees and burst into tears.

It was too much, definitely too much. She'd borne pain, the sorrow of separation, the loneliness, and Munk's enmity. She'd swallowed all that. But now the moment had come when she gave in, and everything that she'd repressed for so long overwhelmed her.

For a long time she cowered there on the floor, her eyes closed, curled up like a child who didn't know where to turn, and she wept until she could no longer tell if the tears were still coming because they were one with the sea and left no trace behind them.

Something bumped the tip of her nose.

When she opened her eyes, she was blinded by the brightness of the light from the little fish. The rest of the school were dancing in front of her face, while pairs of tiny dark eyes looked at her expressionlessly.

"Leave me alone," she whispered, weakly batting her hand at them. The fish darted apart, but they immediately reformed again. Again one of them bumped her nose; two others stroked along her cheeks. This time she felt almost as if hands were gently stroking her face.

In her memory, an image assembled itself from swirling light and darkness: Three old women, their long hair binding them together, sat at spinning wheels on the bottom of the sea and spun the water into a transparent, sparkling yarn. The fibers, some single, others bundled, extended out into the distance. Woven apparently at random, they formed a tissue of glistening strands that stretched in all directions; the spinners sat at the center of a worldwide network of veins.

Then the image detached itself from what Jolly had seen with her own eyes and took her with it on a journey. At breakneck speed her gaze whizzed along a fat bundle of the magic strands, over undersea mountains, dusty wastelands on the sea bottom, and forests of bizarre plants. Finally it went over rugged gorges and crevasses, along mighty stones that might be sunken ruins, again through gray wasteland until . . . yes, to this rock cone, the nest of the kobalins. Here the magic yarn crossed other strands, a host of them, and Jolly understood: The hill towered over a crossroads of magic, a place where the veins from many other directions met one another, saturating the environs with their power.

The lantern fish swam apart, whirled around Jolly's head, and came together in a glittering cluster that bobbed up and down on invisible currents.

The vision faded at the end of her journey into the kobalin nest, and Jolly's hand involuntarily moved to her belt pouch. She'd lost her knapsack and all her provisions, but the pouch on her hip was still there. And in it, her mussels.

She got to her feet and blinked a few times, as if this were the only way she could be sure that her surroundings were real. The fish twirled restlessly among one another, seized by a hard-to-comprehend excitement.

"You can't help me, I take it," said Jolly, "so I have to do it myself, don't I?" She sniffled one last time, gulped, and felt new strength coursing through her.

She crouched down, laid out the mussels in a circle around her, and waited for them to speak to her. It wasn't long, and then she felt her hands going through motions that were only partly guided by her. Her fingers sorted out the mussels, added others to them, and changed the pattern again and again. Finally satisfied, she let go of the shells, regarded the arrangement, and nodded slowly.

She shut her eyes for an instant, and when she opened them again, the magic pearl was there, almost without her help. She couldn't remember when it had ever been so easy to call up the magic of the mussels. It must be due to the power of this place. Jolly didn't let herself imagine how dense the network of magic yarns must be in the Crustal Breach itself, how interwoven the magic, how concentrated its power.

The pearl in the center of the mussel pattern glowed and sparkled. Then it moved from its position and floated up the steep hill of rubble, exploring cracks and crevices, and diving into hollows and holes. The lantern fish fol-lowed along behind it in a wavy row, like the sparkling tail of a meteor. Jolly was enchanted by so much beauty in the middle of this desert.

Finally the pearl disappeared into a dark corner, where the incline and the roof came together. It glided into an opening that was not discernible from down on the floor. Jolly's heart made a leap. The pearl had found a way through, an opening that led behind the debris of the caved-in rock ceiling.

A little later the pearl reappeared, shot down to Jolly, and again placed itself in the middle of the mussel pattern. There it floated back and forth and waited impatiently for her to lead it back into one of the mussels. Jolly obliged it with eyes closed and conjuring hands outstretched. When she looked down again, the pearl was gone and all the mussels were closed.

Never had she felt so powerful. For the first time she understood how Munk felt when he commanded the magic of the mussels. It was an enlivening, wonderful euphoria, but it also hid within it the danger of forgetting oneself and everyone else to feel completely unfettered and omnipotent.

It pleased her, flattered her, but it also frightened her. In the silence she swore to herself never to give in to this temptation. She hoped that in the end she would be able to make this choice for herself.

She quickly gathered up her mussels, stuffed them into her belt pouch, and climbed up the rock slope. The fish were still dancing around the newly discovered opening. With their silver light they marked the place, which otherwise Jolly would have lost sight of entirely.

The hole was bigger than she'd supposed, and it wasn't hard for her to crawl through it. More caves awaited her on the other side, the remainder of the blocked rock tunnel.

She climbed down to the floor and went on her way, down deeper into the silent caverns of the kobalin nest. The fish followed her, emitting a barely audible crackling and rustling, perhaps the sound of their rubbing scales, perhaps also a babble of voices, a joyous, relieved giggling of these tiny creatures.

Eventually she lost track of how many forks she'd taken, how many turns of the path. The floor kept sloping down the entire time, sometimes gently, sometimes steeply again, and it seemed to her that the water around her was gradually becoming warmer. What if she were stumbling straight into a settlement of kobalins? Into an undersea cave city of the deep tribes? However, she'd already discovered numerous small and larger caverns. If the kobalins had intended to settle in these rocks, they'd surely have already done it farther up.

Something else was waiting for her down there. And in light of what Aina had said, there was very little doubt about what that would be. Or who.

Nevertheless, there was only this one direction. Until now she'd found no way leading upward. There'd been forks, certainly, but all the other tunnels had led down even more steeply.

Had Munk and Aina already reached the heart of the Crustal Breach? *Don't think about it,* she drummed into herself. *Rather, give some thought to how you're going to get out of here.*

The passageway widened. Its walls ended abruptly and

released Jolly into a gigantic grotto, so big that the end of it was beyond the range of her polliwog sight.

The cave appeared to be empty. The floor fell steeply away at Jolly's feet, though only one or two yards deep, and then there was the bottom, even more furrowed and dark. This surface appeared to curve gently up, like a hill, at the middle of the cave.

For a moment Jolly thought that at one time the grotto must have been full of molten lava, which had hardened there. The ground was black and wrinkled and looked quite different from the cave walls or the floor of the tunnel from which she'd come. She hesitated briefly; then she took a step over the edge and landed with legs astride on the sunken cave floor. To her surprise it gave under her feet and was springy. It was as soft and resilient as tar that hadn't yet cooled.

A bone-chilling shrieking filled the air, rebounded from the walls, and pierced Jolly's ears like needles. Terrified, she pushed off from the floor and shot up to the ceiling of the grotto. She hovered there.

From here she had a good view over the floor of the cave, at least as far as the limits of her sight. And she realized that what she'd been standing on was not floor.

It was a body.

A doughy, gigantic body, which filled the entire grotto and . . . yes, was stuck in it like a cork.

The shrieking came from a mouth as big as a well shaft, in the middle of a corpulent, very wide face that was located at the end of the monstrous body without recognizable neck or shoulders. Black skin folds and half-rotten teeth surrounded the throat, and a little above it—or rather, next to it, for the face was lying horizontal and staring up at the ceiling—she recognized two eye slits, framed by fleshy bulges.

The gruesome creature looked like an infinitely fat kobalin that a powerful fist had mashed flat and somehow pressed into this grotto. In truth the cave must be a mighty rock cathedral, very deep, so that there was room enough down below for the rest of the giant kobalin. What Jolly was looking at was the upper end of this living, shrieking cork. Her imagination wasn't able to picture what kind of power had forced this creature into the rock shaft.

"What? What? Whatttt?" came spitting out of the mouth. Oily saliva fell straight down in blurry strings, looking like smoky air flickering in the heat. "What are you? Whatttt are you?"

"Jolly," said Jolly.

She was careful not to sink a fraction of an inch deeper. Her head was almost bumping against the cave roof. The hill of spongy kobalin flesh was a good fifty yards below her.

The mother of the kobalins—for it must be she, if Aina had spoken the truth—uttered a gurgling sound that turned without pause into something that might be a repetition of Jolly's name.

"Whatttt are you doing here?" asked the monster.

"I'm trapped," said Jolly. "Just like you."

Again there came a hideous roaring and shrieking. The ceiling trembled slightly, dust sprinkled out of cracks and recesses. But the creature didn't move from the spot. She was stuck as firmly as if someone had walled her in.

"Trapped, yes, yessss. I am that. By that hateful, dreadful brood." The black, wrinkled flesh around the eyes was so swollen that it was impossible to say if the creature was directing her gaze at Jolly. "My miserable, cowardly, corrupted brood. Cowardly and corrupted is what they are."

Jolly considered whether she should swim nearer to the contorted giant mouth, but then she decided to remain where she was. The kobalin mother might be stuck fast, and perhaps she no longer had the strength to free herself after all the millennia—but Jolly didn't trust the truce. She saw neither arms nor legs; they must be stuck with the lower part of the fat colossus. But the appearance of the gigantic mouth was unquestionably reason enough to maintain her distance.

"The kobalins are your children?" she asked.

"Yes, yes, yessss!" The gurgling, hissing voice sounded impatient. No wonder, after such a long time. "Will you free me?"

I can hardly wait, thought Jolly with a shudder, but instead she said, "Possibly."

"Then do it! Then do itttt!" murmured the beast.

"I told you my name, so it would only be polite if you tell me yours."

"Kangussssssta," roared the maw. "Kangusta the Greatttt!"

"Kangusta . . . And you can't free yourself?"

"No, no, no."

"How shall I help you?"

"Pull down the accursed mountain! The whole accurssssed mountain!"

"I'm too small for that. And if *you* can't even do it . . ."

Kangusta let out a snarl that produced a strong current in the grotto. The lantern fish, which had clustered anxiously around Jolly, were whirled apart by it.

"I'm stuck fasssst!"

"I can see that."

"He did this to me. Incited my brood to turn against their own mother. . . ."

The beast might seem ponderous, but Jolly took care not to underestimate her. A trapped colossus, certainly—but there was also cunning in her voice, an undertone of cruel wiliness.

"Is there another way out of here?" That was clumsy and probably too early, but she could no longer bear the presence of this monstrosity. "A way that we could escape together?"

A rumble came through the mouth. It sounded like lava shooting up out of a volcano.

She's laughing, Jolly realized with horror. *She's laughing at me.*

"I can see you, little animal. You're like her. Like that which she once wassss."

Jolly had already begun to search for a second opening in the grotto walls when Kangusta's words roused her. "Who do you mean?" she asked, now not quite as firmly as before.

"She! *She!* The little animals who came . . . Little animals like you. And then . . . And then . . ." She fell silent, but the mouth still remained wide open.

"What happened then?"

"Why do you ask such questions, little animal?" She said it *questionsssss*, and it sounded smacking and ghastly. "You should know that. You're like her."

"How many of them came here in the old time?"

"One and two little animals. First one. Later two."

There was hardly any doubt that she was speaking of Aina and the two other polliwogs who'd come in ancient times to subdue the Maelstrom. Perhaps not all the girl had said had been lies.

Kangusta's voice grew softer and stealthy. "You must help me, little animal. Then perhaps . . . yes, perhaps I will tell you everything." *Yessss, perhapssss*, she said.

"I'm too weak. I can't destroy the mountain."

"Then find a way to do it."

"I haven't the power to do that."

"Power?" Again that rumbling, stony-sounding laughter. "Oh, that you certainly have. I saw it, in the old time. Saw how the animals fought. Imprisoned him. Saw it."

Kangusta must already have been imprisoned here at that time. So how could she have watched something going on outside?

"I see much," said the kobalin mother, as if she intended to answer Jolly's unspoken question. "Can look through the rocks, taste it in the water. Everything that happens. Tasted how the other little animal shut you in here with me. Oh, yes." Her voice became darker, deeper. "And I taste you, little animal. Mmmmmm."

In the grayness of polliwog vision Jolly saw it nearly a moment too late—something twitched up out of the kobalin mother's throat, a warty strand of black muscle!

She just succeeded in escaping the powerful tongue. The tip smacked against the rocks beside her, felt over the stone, twitching and trembling, and then pulled back with a whip-snapping sound.

A roar of rage rose from Kangusta's body, then the tongue shot forward again, as long as a topmast, but not very much wider. Presumably this was the only body part the kobalin mother could still move freely.

The cries of the monster faded away, the tongue disappeared.

Jolly had to force herself not to flee in panic. Instead she stayed on the ceiling, just out of range of the tongue. "That's no way to close a deal," she said in a thick voice. Her entire body was trembling, and she hoped that Kangusta didn't see it.

"Little, nimble, quick animal!" thundered from the mouth. "Little, tender, tasty animal!"

"Tell me which way leads to the outside, and I'll do what I can for you." The lantern fish had vanished from her sight and were now floating anxiously behind her.

"There's only one way. Not the one you came by. The other. Leads up, leads outside. They bring me food that way. Living, kicking, fat food."

Jolly shuddered, feeling her stomach turn over. *Don't think about it. Just don't think about it anymore.*

The second tunnel Kangusta was talking about must lie

on the other side of the grotto, too distant for her polliwog eyes to see it. Now that Jolly knew how far Kangusta's tongue reached, it would be easy to get there unharmed.

But there was something else she wanted to know. About what the kobalin mother had said in the beginning. About Aina and the others. Jolly had to find out what had happened to the polliwogs. Why had Aina betrayed her?

"If you've tasted that I was shut in here by another . . . animal, then you also know that she was no friend of mine."

"Tasted it. I surely did."

"Why is she obeying the Maelstrom now? She is doing that, isn't she?"

Kangusta's laughter made the rock vault shake. "Obeying? *Obeying?* You know nothing, little animal. Nothing of the truth. The Maelstrom is powerful, that he is. United my brood, in fear of him. If he were dead, wiped out . . . then my children would again fight to gain my favor. The way it used to be. But fear welds them together and makes them lose all respect for me. Makes them even leave the water!" An indignant roar followed these words, for it appeared to Kangusta quite unthinkable that a kobalin could voluntarily go onto the land. "If he were destroyed, then yes, there would be some who were there for me again. Who would free me. And others who would be envious of my favor and would fight for it. The way it used to be. In the good times. The fat, tasty times." The kobalin mother expelled a moan filled with self-pity. "But today . . . He spoiled them. Made them forget their own mother. He did that."

The tongue flicked out, whipped through the empty grotto at a mad tempo, and finally fell limp across Kangusta's face. It lay there for a long time, and there wasn't a sound except for the sniffling of the kobalin mother.

Jolly waited until the monster had grown calm again. Only when the tongue began moving and retreated into the throat like a dying sea serpent did she speak.

"I will destroy the Maelstrom so that everything is the way it used to be again." Hesitating, she added, "In the good times."

"The tasty times."

Jolly cleared her throat. "Exactly."

"You're too weak." Kangusta sounded tired now. "You said so yourself. Besides, I don't trust you. You'll find the way to the top, leave here, and forget me."

How could I do that? Jolly thought with disgust. She felt no pity for Kangusta, but she could understand what was going on in the brain of this ancient being. Once the deep tribes had revered her, but now she was in danger of going into oblivion down here.

"I will destroy him." Jolly was amazed at her own certainty. "I will put an end to all this."

The swollen flesh hills around one of the eyes twitched. "Will you really do that?"

"Or I will die in the attempt."

"A brave little animal. Or a dumb one. Perhaps both."

Without thinking about it, Jolly cried, "Better than to be stuck fast in these rocks, lazy and fat and helpless!"

A CONVERSATION IN THE DEEP

Kangusta was so quiet that Jolly concluded she was planning another nasty trick. But then words rose from the black throat again, very slowly this time, and they were heralded by something like an echo in advance, which hurried ahead of the actual sentences.

"You're right, little animal. There were times, you should know, when I was strong and powerful. Times when all trembled before me, whether kobalin or animal or the wooden fish on which your kind ride over the waves."

Then the island dwellers must already have been traveling from island to island by boat thousands of years ago, Jolly thought. But why was hardly anything left of that culture? She thought of the answer herself: Presumably the islanders never recovered from the first war against the Maelstrom. Even though they'd *won* it. So what would be left of the present-day Caribbean after all this business?

Kangusta continued, "You think the Maelstrom comes from over there, from the *other* sea, don't you? But that's not true. The Maelstrom comes from this world. He was once a little animal like you. That he was."

"Like me?" Jolly repeated, perplexed.

"A little animal with great power. You've seen her. The same one that imprisoned you here. The first little animal that came down here."

"Aina!"

"If you call her so . . . yes."

"But she's a human. A polliwog."

"She was like you." *Ssshe,* hissed Kangusta.

"And she came to conquer the Maelstrom."

The monster laughed angrily. "There was no Maelstrom when she arrived. She has become that. She *is* the Maelstrom."

For a moment Jolly forgot to swim and threatened to sink. The lantern fish whirled excitedly around her face, startling her. With a rowing motion, Jolly got herself up to the cave ceiling again.

"How can Aina be the Maelstrom?"

"I don't taste everything from the water," said Kangusta slowly. "But in the very beginning, right after she set my children against me, she came into the hill. She wanted to torment me. Torment me, she did." She was silent for a moment. "Told me everything, the little animal. How she was cast out by the other animals because she was different, more powerful. At that time the powers of the other sea were breaking through to us. Into my realm! The little animal came and became a slave to the ideas and promises of the foreigners. She tried to open a gateway for them . . . to become *herself* a gateway for them, through which they could get into our world." The longer Kangusta spoke, the clearer her voice became. It was as if with each sentence a part of her memory of that time was returning—of the Maelstrom, the war against the Mare Tenebrosum, but above all, of herself. She remembered how it had been to speak with another living being and to exchange knowledge. It did not make her more human, but less monstrous.

"Under the prompting of the others, the little animal

became the Maelstrom. I could do nothing against it, for I possessed no magic powers at that time, and I do not possess them today. . . . But don't tell anyone else that."

"Don't worry," said Jolly somberly.

"The Maelstrom seized power over my kingdom and my children."

Jolly thought over Kangusta's words. As unbelievable as it all sounded, it made sense. Aina was expelled by the humans—she'd told them that herself. And as for the temptations that the masters of the Mare employed—Jolly had felt them on her own body. She remembered her visions that time on the deck of the *Carfax*. If Buenaventure hadn't been there . . .

She shook herself, as if to shake the images out of her head. She'd almost forgotten where she was. She gazed thoughtfully at the gigantic head of the kobalin mother. Perhaps she had to revise her opinion of Kangusta. Certainly she was malicious and hideous-looking—but she wasn't stupid. The pity Jolly had been resisting the entire time now spread through her—mixed with the fear she continued to feel facing this monster.

Kangusta went on, "The little animal you saw . . . that led you here . . . she was not real. Only a copy of her earlier self, before she turned into the Maelstrom."

"That's why we could reach through her!"

"Yes."

"What happened to the other two polliwogs? You said there were two more like me back then."

"They came a while later, when the Maelstrom stood at the height of his power. They fought him in order to stop him. And with him the powers from the other sea."

Jolly nodded. "They were shut inside the mussel with him, Aina said. Was that a lie too?"

"No. They sacrificed themselves to imprison him there. Brave little animals they were. For a long, long time they were gone, imprisoned in the great mussel. Until it opened again, much, much later, and the Maelstrom began to grow in power. Then they also crept outside, but they were no longer what they had been. He had conquered them during all the ages and made them into his creatures. He formed the one anew, of mud and algae and the remains of those who sank down into the deep to us from the wooden fish."

"The Acherus!"

"I don't know that word," said Kangusta.

"What became of the second?"

The black, barklike skin of the kobalin mother rippled in a burst of anger. "He took the power over my brood to himself. He united the tribes in the name of the Maelstrom. He also was changed, but different from the first one."

The lord of the kobalins. In retrospect it explained everything. Even the fact that the Ghost Trader had always spoken of only one Acherus, not of several. He'd told them that the Acherus was created by the Maelstrom—not, however, from what.

He knew it, she thought, and tears of rage came to her eyes. The Ghost Trader had known the whole time what the

Maelstrom and his two most powerful servants had been. And he'd told Jolly and Munk nothing of it so they couldn't see the danger that threatened them. A danger much worse than death: Possibly the same fate awaited them as the polliwogs who'd shut up Aina.

The longer Jolly thought about it, the more it became obvious to her that Munk was already well on his way there.

That was why Aina chose him. She wanted to make him into her servant to substitute for the Acherus, whom Munk himself had destroyed. And she also had plans for Jolly, which was why Aina hadn't killed her but locked her in here. She intended to make Jolly into her slave and misuse Jolly's magic for her own purposes.

Until now they'd assumed they were fighting against a creature from the Mare Tenebrosum. But that was wrong—their enemy had once been a polliwog like themselves. Cast off by her own people, gone over to the other side, and now its strongest weapon.

"I must get to her." She spoke her thoughts aloud. "I must free Munk and stop Aina."

"You cannot stop the Maelstrom," said Kangusta angrily. "No one can do that. I tried—and look at me. I have not always been as I am today—not always."

"If I defeat the Maelstrom, will you rule over the deep tribes again?"

Kangusta hesitated. "If he is truly destroyed and not just shut in, the way he was before . . . yes, then they will see me again as that which I once was."

"Then promise me something."

"Why?"

"Because I'm going to establish your old power again."
Anyway, I'm going to try, she added silently.

"What kind of a promise shall I give you, little animal?"

"That you will keep the deep tribes away from us humans.
Away from the surface. That there will be no more attacks,
not on our shi—on our wooden fish and not on the sea star
city or the coasts of the mainland. Down here you can do
and allow what you want—but there must be no more war
between you and us."

"I could promise that. I could."

"But will you also hold to your promise?"

A muffled gurgling and rumbling rose from Kangusta's
throat. "You don't trust me, do you, little animal?"

"No."

"Then you will not believe my promise, either."

"Do I have any other choice?"

The rumbling in the kobalin mother's throat repeated
itself. "So you want me to let you go. To destroy him."

"That's the plan, anyway."

"It will not succeed."

"Perhaps not. But perhaps yes."

Kangusta was silent for a moment. "You are brave, little
animal."

Jolly sighed. "Actually, I'm scared to death of you, of the
Maelstrom, and of this whole horrible place down here."

This time Kangusta's rumbling sounded almost like

human laughter. "Well, little animal, you can stop being afraid of Kangusta. If it succeeds, there will be no more war between you and the deep tribes. So shall it be."

Jolly heaved a sigh of relief. The warm water of this cave streamed through her lungs, and for a moment it made her feel almost comfortable.

"Go now," said Kangusta. "I will describe to you the way by which they bring me prey." She was quiet for a moment, as her giant mouth opened and closed with a smack. "Hurry. I taste mischief in the water."

Tyrone

"The fish rain has stopped," announced the Ghost Trader as he looked down at the shore from the library balcony. Forefather's eyes were no longer the best, and the Trader had to describe for him what was going on. "The kobalins have withdrawn into the water. But that won't help us. Tyrone's fleet is placing the city under fire."

Cannon thunder rolled up from the sea. The smoke of the guns mixed with the black smoke from the ruins on the bank. The eyes of both the men on the balcony were burning. Forefather's were red and teary. His appearance made the Ghost Trader aware once again of how human his colleague had grown over all the eons.

They withdrew together to the interior of one of the book rooms, closing the door to the outside behind them. The rumbling of the guns was dulled, but the sharp smell of the battle had long since filled even the library's high-ceilinged halls.

"Is it possible that's the only point for the Maelstrom?" asked the Trader, while his black parrots settled on piles of books to the right and left of him. "Does he intend to drive us into a corner so that we ourselves take the last step?"

"Not we, my friend. Only you have the power to do that. Mine is long gone. But in you there's still enough left of what we once were." Forefather laughed softly and sadly. "In comparison to me, you're young."

"You could have remained so yourself, if you hadn't preferred to hole up in this place. The humans in the outside world have almost forgotten you. They revere something that they call god, but they don't even give him a name anymore. If you'd stayed with them and shown them . . . then perhaps you'd still have all your powers."

"I didn't want that anymore, you know that. In those days, after the destruction of the first sea star city . . . ah, sometimes I'd be glad if the memory had deserted me along with my powers."

The Ghost Trader supported himself on a tower of leather-bound folios. "If I do what you wish, it will bring the Maelstrom even closer to his goal."

"He has only the mind of a little girl, my friend, don't forget that. It's the hate of a child that drives him. I'd call it spite if there weren't so much riding on it. You're the only one who still has the power to stop him."

"You're asking me to let the spirits of the other gods come

to life again. But they wouldn't obey me for long," said the Ghost Trader. "They're not like men, whose souls I can call out of the depths as I will. They're gods! They're like *us!*"

Forefather's bony fingers clenched his stick. "Nevertheless, they will decide the battle for us! Ah, if I could only do it myself . . ."

The Ghost Trader walked over to the old man, with a gentle smile now, and took his hand. "You've used your power for better things, my friend. You have created an entire world."

"And now shall I watch while the anger of a single girl destroys it? Tell me, is that really *godlike?*"

"Aina has not been a girl for a long time. The masters of the Mare Tenebrosum have made her into the Maelstrom, and she has been that for thousands of years."

"But she still acts like a child. At first she felt she was betrayed by humans who drove her out because of her abilities. They didn't know any better. And today she feels deceived by the masters of the Mare because they didn't stand by her when the first polliwogs defeated her." Forefather let out a despairing sigh. "She can't annihilate the Mare Tenebrosum, but she can destroy what the masters want most ardently for their own: my creation. This world! Aina will reduce it to ashes, and all because a few stiff-necked humans threw her out of her village and she got mixed up with powers that were too great for her."

The Trader nodded thoughtfully. "She will annihilate us."

"If you do not stop her." Forefather groaned and, supported by his stick, began to hobble back and forth in the pathways between the walls of books. "We've been going in circles for days now." He stopped, and his eyes met the gaze of the Trader. "We've become like her, don't you see that? We argue like two children who never tire of pulling on two ends of a rope, back and forth." Shaking his head, he lowered his voice to a whisper. "Back and forth, over and over."

The Ghost Trader pulled his silver ring out of his dark robe. Gently he stroked the cool metal. "I could waken the gods," he said. "I could throw them against Tyrone and his vassals. Even against the Maelstrom himself. But who would direct them back into the shadows after their victory? I'm not capable of that. The powers that I awaken would be too great for me. They would fall upon each other, and what was left of the world would be torn to pieces—for hate of the creatures by whom they were forgotten in earlier times, or simply because it pleased them to." The Trader let himself sink wearily against the edge of a table and propped himself on it with both hands. "Whichever way we choose, both lead to destruction."

"But they are gods!" contradicted Forefather. "They have the right to destroy. The Maelstrom does not have it. He is only . . . a sport of nature. A running sore that we have the spinners to thank for."

"The spinners?" The Trader's voice grew sharper. "They were created by this world, without your help. They don't need human belief in them, because the world itself believes in them, every stone and every blade of grass. That is why you scorn them."

Pirate Wars

"They are——"

The Trader took a step toward Forefather, his eye appearing to blaze. "When the Mare Tenebrosum stirred the first time, the spinners only did what appeared right to them in view of the danger. They created the polliwogs, in order to fend off the masters of the Mare. Do you intend to blame them for that?"

"Nevertheless, Aina was the first of these polliwogs, and she has become the Maelstrom! Perhaps the greatest failure the world has ever seen."

"But it was the failure of humans, not of the spinners. You do the three a disservice, my friend. They tried to protect the world."

Forefather lowered his eyes. "Because he who created the world could not protect it," he said guiltily.

Side by side, Soledad, Walker, and Buenaventure hastened over the coral bridges and stepped streets of the devastated city. They'd joined a troop of guardsmen who were supposed to scout out the fighting morale of the cannibal king's army. How hard had the long sea battle hit them? What sort of cooperation was there within this army of native tribal fighters thrown together with the scum of the Old World?

In the meantime, the cannibals' fleet had stopped firing on the city, likely because the ships' cannons couldn't angle wide enough to hit the targets that lay higher up Aelenium's steep cliffs. All the balls had reached only the already destroyed shores.

The reconnaissance patrol made its way downward, and the lower they went, the thicker grew the smoke of the smoldering fires. Soon they came to the first ruins. In many of the houses and villas, only the walls were left, reaching skyward like blackened rib cages.

None of them said a word, and it wasn't the fire and smoke alone that made them speechless. Soledad had taken part in many battles at sea, but only rarely did one see more than a few dead in the water; often the dead adversaries went down along with their ships. But walking through a city that had turned into a giant battlefield was like a nightmare.

She cast a side glance at Walker and was surprised to discover how much the sight of all the destruction also affected him. Wordlessly she took his hand as they walked.

"Look!"

The cry startled them. They stopped. One of the soldiers had run to a coral railing that bordered a small plaza to the south. From there a smoke-veiled view opened out over the waterfront. Soledad and the others hurried to his side.

On the embankment of the sea star arms, the first attackers were just jumping onto land from their rowboats with wild war shouts and storming in disorder into the openings to side streets.

One of the guardsmen, a man with a white, neatly cropped beard, now sprinkled with kobalin blood, made a disgusted face. "Pirates and savages aren't even soldiers. They only understand plundering, not how to fight a war."

Walker was about to contradict him energetically, but he noticed that neither Soledad nor Buenaventure were protesting.

"Is that an advantage for us?" asked Soledad.

The soldier shook his head. "With so many of the enemy? Before the first ones get to the wall, the streets will be swarming with them. They'll probably just continue there where the kobalins left off."

Buenaventure growled agreement. "They're going to overrun us."

Soledad massaged her wrist thoughtfully. "Well, scarcely. Tyrone must have had around two hundred ships. I can see no more than half of that."

"A quarter, at most," said Walker. "Provided there aren't more waiting out there in the fog."

"I don't believe that. Tyrone will throw everything he has left into battle." Soledad smiled coldly. "The Antilles captains took care of him quite nicely."

The white-bearded soldier spoke up impatiently. "That's all well and good, but the fact remains that they far outnumber us. I suggest we go back to the wall. Soon they're going to need every man there. And," he added, with the suggestion of a formal nod in Soledad's direction, "every woman."

"You go ahead with your men," said Soledad. "Walker, Buenaventure, and I will try to get at Tyrone."

Walker raised an eyebrow. "Oh, yes?"

"Soledad is right," Buenaventure agreed. "It sounds like a plan, anyway. In any case, better than waiting up there on the wall until they trample us under."

The soldier grew pale, but he continued to hold the gaze of the pit bull man. Then he nodded. Perhaps he was glad to get free of the three pirates.

Soledad turned to Walker. "Let's at least try."

He sighed softly, then shrugged. "A beautiful woman is always right, my father said."

Soledad flashed a smile. "I thought you never knew your father."

The white-bearded soldier cleared his throat in disapproval. "Very well," he said firmly, "my men and I will make our way back. Good luck, you three—and I mean that sincerely."

The steps of the soldiers quickly died out beyond the crackling of the fire and the cries from the shore. A few moments later the three set out. Soledad and Walker went ahead, Buenaventure remained directly behind them.

In some streets the fire burned so hotly that they had to turn around and look for another way. In several passages, on the other hand, the smoke was so thick that it was almost impossible to breathe.

Finally they crossed a narrow, railingless coral bridge that led over one of the wider streets. Below them a pack of pirates and cannibals in garish war paint stormed up the mountain, followed by a troop that moved in an orderly formation, suspiciously eyeing the burned-out windows on both sides of the road. Some also looked up at the bridge, and Soledad, Walker, and Buenaventure were just able to throw themselves to the ground in time not to be discovered.

Pirate Wars

In the midst of the band of pirates strode a black figure. The cannibal king's head was shaved bald up to a long, black ponytail at the back of his head. In contrast to the other pirates, he'd assumed the war paint of the savages he'd made his subjects years before. His black, flowing clothing was that of a nobleman, with knee-high, wide-cuffed boots and a wide cape, which looked as if Tyrone were pulling a dark trail of smoke behind him. From up here the three couldn't see his filed teeth, but the mere knowledge of them made Soledad feel sick.

She feared him. There was no reason not to admit that to herself. Tyrone was cruel, without any scruples, and thus an outstanding fighter. Even when he was still sailing the Caribbean as a pirate, the stories of his raids had been legend. After his disappearance into the jungles of the Orinoco and later when he returned as the leader of the cannibal tribes, the rumor mills worked overtime. There was no grisliness, no barbarity that he hadn't surpassed long since.

His officers hurried up through the smoke-filled streets in his wake, big men with scarred, hardened faces. Another swarm of pirates followed them, ragged cutthroats who protected their masters' backs.

Behind them was someone who looked like—

"Griffin?" Soledad's jaw dropped. "Look! Down there! Isn't that Griffin?"

"Impossible," growled Buenaventure.

"Yet you're right!" Walker's voice sounded excited, and he tried to damp it even as he spoke. He didn't like to show how very fond he'd become of the pirate boy in the weeks they'd been under way together.

Griffin was walking in the middle of the pirates. He wore a dirty shirt, red-and-white-striped trousers, and a black cloth on his head. He had a nicked saber over his shoulder like a hiking stick.

Soledad stretched her head a little too far over the edge of the bridge; for a moment she had to be clearly visible from below. But only one of them raised his eyes, almost as if he'd felt her presence.

Griffin concealed his surprise and tried hard not to betray his excitement. The strain of moving in the midst of his enemies was getting on his nerves. His face twitched.

"What a devil of a fellow," growled Buenaventure.

"And with the devil is just where he's going to land if he doesn't look sharp right now!" Walter sounded alarmed, and the two others saw at once what he meant. Soledad smothered a frightened exclamation.

Two pirates walking right behind Griffin had clearly noticed that he didn't belong among them. One pirate pulled his dagger, and the other stretched out his arm to grab the boy by the shoulder.

In a fraction of a second Soledad was on her feet, pushed off, and jumped. While still in the air she knocked the weapon out of the hands of one foe and struck at him with her own. Walker and Buenaventure landed to the right and left of her and immediately went on the attack. They'd landed in the middle of the mob of pirates, almost ten yards from the place where Griffin had just fallen to the ground.

Soledad had no time to keep an eye out for the boy. She had enough to do to take out as many pirates and cannibals as possible before her opponents could realize that they weren't facing an army but only three desperadoes.

Buenaventure's fighting technique resembled that of the two others, with the noteworthy difference that the striking power of his gigantic toothed sword measured severalfold more than Soledad's own blows. Leaping over yelling men as they fell to the ground wounded, he dashed to the edge of the narrow street, and with his left hand he grabbed a beam that had become unsound in the fires of the night. The roof frame of the shed, which had been built onto one of the coral houses, was still burning. "Walker! Soledad! . . . Look out!" Buenaventure called—then the shed leaned in an eruption of flames and flickering wood, before it landed on the pirate mob as a rain of fire. Suddenly most of them were busy defending themselves, not against blades any longer but flaming timbers. Several pieces of timber at once landed on Buenaventure himself. A furious howling came from his throat. Walker was hit too, a little more lightly, and Soledad was the only one to entirely escape the inferno. Her immediate opponent was also unharmed, and so they fought on in the midst of the flames, the circling men, and the billows of smoke, which soon embraced them all. With one saber blow out of a whirl of them she succeeded in striking the man down. In a sudden panic she looked for

Walker and saw him, his hair smoking, dueling with a cannibal. Buenaventure was standing on two feet again, an ugly burn on his left upper arm, but otherwise more or less unharmed.

And Griffin? Where was the boy?

Most of the pirates had left the fire-saturated street for the adjoining ruins. Some had probably also gone on their way up the mountain. It was senseless to wear themselves out down here if the main forces of the defense were waiting on the upper wall. Tyrone had also disappeared.

But when a blond man stumbled out of the wall of smoke toward Soledad, coughing wildly, she suddenly recognized him and immediately went on the attack.

"Bannon!" she cried, as their blades met, striking sparks. "It ought not to have come to this."

He gave no answer, just struck harder at her and drove her several steps backward through the acrid vapor toward the shore.

The smoke grew thicker and thicker. The stench hurt her throat and robbed her of breath.

Soledad had no choice but to save her skin, and she was almost grateful that it was Bannon, in particular, with whom she confronted that fate. She despised him for his betrayal and because he'd tried to surrender his foster daughter Jolly to Tyrone and the Maelstrom.

Bannon fought silently and grimly. Again and again their blades met. He was her superior in strength, but she was faster and more skilled with the saber than he was. The attacks that hit him between his parries were brutal. Once she believed that her blade would surely break under the weight of his blows, yet the steel held out. But the vibration of the weapon went all the way to her shoulder, so that for a moment she could no longer lift her arm.

Bannon got ready for a lethal blow. He didn't smile the way they used to say he did when facing a defeated opponent, and he avoided any mockery. Obviously he intended to bring this business to an end as quickly as possible.

Soledad groaned as she tried again to lift her lame arm and parry his blow.

There was a slashing sound. Bannon winced, stopped short, looked down at himself, and stared in surprise at the blade sticking out of his chest. His eyes slowly widened, his mouth dropped open. "A hundred thousand hellhounds!" he whispered. Then he collapsed, as silently as he'd dueled, fell on his face, and was still. An old, nicked saber was sticking out of his back.

A figure in red and white trousers leaped over the corpse, crashed against Soledad, and embraced her.

"Griffin!"

"Princess!" They hugged each other as if it had been years since their leave-taking, rather than several hours. It felt good to know he was back with them. When she let go of him, he reeled. Shortly afterwards his legs buckled.

"Griffin?" In an instant she was bending over him. "What's wrong? Are you wounded?"

He tried to smile, but it only made him look more tired

and sick. None of them had had enough sleep for an eternity, but it wasn't only exhaustion that robbed him of his strength now.

"You're bleeding!" She carefully pushed his arm to one side and stared at the dark red spot in horror. The dirty pirate shirt was completely soaked through.

"Not deep," he murmured. "Not dangerous."

Soledad didn't listen to him and raised her head. "Walker! Buenaventure!" she called out into the smoke. Her eyes burned, breathing was increasingly difficult, but at the moment she was thinking only about the boy. "I need one of you here with me!"

A shout like an answer resounded through the smoke, then Buenaventure came stomping up, followed by a disheveled Walker covered with scratches. There was a gaping burn hole in his shirt, but he appeared not to be seriously wounded.

"Most of them have gone on," he gasped in between coughs. "But this smoke is going to kill us if we—" Walker broke off as he saw the blood on Griffin's side. "Goddamn it!"

Griffin's mouth twitched again, but this time there wasn't even the shadow of a smile. "It isn't bad. Only it hurts . . . a little. . . ."

"Come here, boy." Buenaventure pushed Soledad aside and lifted Griffin from the ground like a flyweight, very gently, so as not to cause him any more pain.

"We have to get behind the wall," said Soledad. "He needs help."

"I do not."

She wouldn't allow herself to be distracted. "Do you think we can do it?"

"No." Walker spoke candidly, as always. "We're behind enemy lines now. I wouldn't be surprised if there's already fighting at the wall. And there are still more of Tyrone's people down on the shore. As soon as the smoke clears, they'll be coming through here." He shot a concerned look at Griffin, who lay like a child in Buenaventure's muscular arms. "I guess we have to find ourselves a hiding place right now and wait until it's more opportune to push through to the others. So far we've just had good luck."

He's right, Soledad thought. *The skirmish with Tyrone's people would have turned out differently if Buenaventure hadn't made the shed collapse.*

"I can walk," gasped Griffin unconvincingly.

"Of course you can." Buenaventure hurried off without setting him down on the ground. He bore Griffin uphill through the smoke, until the billows thinned a little and they could see more clearly what the situation was. Soledad and Walker stayed beside him.

The stepped street in front of them was empty, but the sounds of the battle reached their ears from above. The fighting around the defense wall had been reignited. This time, however, it was men against men.

"Looks as if we're exactly between two attack waves," Buenaventure said. "The rest of the crews from the ships will be coming along pretty soon. We've got to hurry."

They stormed up the steps, striding breathlessly over the

bodies of kobalins and fallen defenders, and very soon they reached the Poets' Quarter.

The shouting and stamping behind them was growing louder.

"They'll be here soon!" Walker whispered, adding a formidable oath.

"Let's duck into one of the houses." Buenaventure was about to run into an entry and kick in the door, but Soledad held him back.

"Wait! Just a little bit farther."

Walker threw a doubtful look over his shoulder. The smoke at the foot of the stepped street was swirling in bizarre eddies, the billows moving erratically. Behind the smoke it was dense with human silhouettes. Any minute the first ones would break through the haze and discover the fugitives.

"To the left!" Soledad ran ahead. There was nothing for the two men to do but follow her. In Buenaventure's arms, Griffin clenched his teeth. Despite his pain and the wild shaking, his eyelids threatened to close.

Soledad ran down a narrow alley, came to a crossing, and turned upward again. Even here it was going to be swarming with Tyrone's people any minute.

"Soledad! We *must* get inside somewhere, now!" She was almost persuaded by Walker's call, but she stormed on, turned off again, and suddenly stopped, gasping, at a front door. At the end of the street she saw the cannibal king's men, headed their way.

Walker came up beside her, snorting, at the front of a narrow coral house. The facade was only a few feet wide. He recognized the place right away.

Buenaventure reached them and didn't even stop. "They're right behind us!" He kicked in the door with a thundering blow before Soledad could point out that it wasn't locked.

The two followed him, but inside Walker held Soledad back by the arm. "Is there a special reason you led us here?"

She slammed the door behind them. The two half doors bounced back because the broken lock didn't catch anymore. "In a minute—help me here first!"

Together they pulled a wooden chest against the door. That wouldn't stop the pirates for long if they'd noticed the four, but now it wouldn't show from the outside that someone had just run into this house.

"So?" asked Walker.

"For one thing, it's higher than all the other buildings," Soledad said. "You can almost see to the upper wall from the roof. I know, I was here just a little while ago."

"You were here to see the worm?" Walker raised an eyebrow, but Soledad wasn't sure if that meant he disapproved or simply didn't understand.

"It's hard to explain." She avoided his eyes. "I saw something in the undercity. And I had an idea that it could be something like—"

"Quick!" came Buenaventure's rumbling voice. "Come up!"

They hadn't noticed that he'd already hurried up the stairs to the gable room.

Soledad saw that something wasn't right while they were still on the stairs, before they could see into the attic room. But she didn't realize what it was until the last few steps. It was too light.

Much too much light was coming through the door, as if up there were—

"Where's the roof?" Walker asked, as they squeezed, stumbling, through the doorway to the storeroom.

Over them yawned a gray-blue emptiness, streaked with clouds of smoke that the sunshine dipped in gold. The two gable walls were still standing, but all that was left of the slanting roof were a few jagged remains.

"And where the devil is the worm?" asked Buenaventure. He stared up at the sky for a moment longer, then remembered Griffin in his arms. He gently laid the boy down in front of him. The floor was covered with scraps of the web in which the Hexhermetic Shipworm had pupated. White and gray clumps drifted around, collected in fibrous heaps in the corners, or hung like sea foam on the remains of the roof. Buenaventure gathered a little of it with both hands and pushed it under the back of Griffin's head as a cushion.

"I'm not . . . I'm all right," the boy said softly, and Buenaventure nodded seriously.

"You only need a little sleep . . . like all of us."

"But we have no time to . . ." Griffin's voice trailed off and then he was silent.

Soledad bent over him worriedly. "What's wrong with him?"

"He's sleeping, that's all," said the pit bull man. "Let him rest. That will relieve the pain, a little anyway."

While Walker inspected the debris of the roof and looked in vain for the shipworm in the remains of the nest, Soledad carefully opened Griffin's shirt and examined the wound in his side. It didn't look that bad: a row of short cuts, not deep enough to injure him seriously. He'd bled a great deal, but not so much that it would kill him. The worst of it was probably the pain. The wounds were on his side over the ribs and might go down to the bone.

She blotted the sleeping boy's forehead with her sleeve and left him in the pit bull man's care.

"Here," said Walker, who was crouching in the farthest corner of the attic and examining something on the floor in front of him. "Look at that."

Her eyes narrowed. "Is that the cocoon?"

"What's left of it. There are more pieces over here. The wind probably blew the rest into the courtyard or who knows where."

The fibrous white webbing looked like the shredded edges of a gigantic eggshell.

Walker poked one of the remnants with his finger. Rustling, it rocked back and forth. "Doesn't look like cut edges, does it?"

"No," Soledad agreed. "It looks as if the thing burst open. He hatched by himself."

She looked at the walls towering into emptiness. It looked as if an explosion had taken place. The shock wave must have flung all the debris outward. It was probably spread over half the district or there would have been more rubble lying in the street. The force had literally pulverized the roof.

"What did you mean before?" Walker asked. "When you said you had an idea about the worm."

With a shiver she recalled the serpent in the undercity, that wondrous creature whose gaze had convinced her that she was facing not an animal but one of the old gods of Aelenium. Even now, in the midst of all this destruction, she still felt that she'd sensed something quite similar at the sight of the dreaming worm in his cocoon.

"The worm," she said, "is no worm. I think, anyway."

"But?"

"A god."

Walker looked at her without any expression. *If he laughs now*, she thought, *I'll paste him one.*

But Walker squatted there motionless, just staring at her. "A god?" he repeated somberly. "Our *shipworm*?"

"The ancient Egyptians worshipped beetles. And the Indians, toads. And the Indians in the jungle even—"

He gestured to her to be quiet.

"But he . . . I mean, he's a pain in the neck. A plague. He almost ate up my ship!"

"Other gods are said to have eaten *people*." She smiled without humor. "Would you have preferred that?"

"Then I could believe you, at least." Quickly he added, "I mean, I really do believe you . . . somehow . . . but that . . . that thing! Good grief!"

"Doubt is the privilege of the faithful," said a voice behind them. It sounded familiar in a strange way—and yet different. "Without belief there can be no doubt."

Soledad and Walker whirled around. Buenaventure was still holding Griffin's right hand in his huge one, but now he looked up from the boy to the creature floating on the other side of the shattered edge of the roof. It rose majestically from the depths of the back courtyard, where it had perhaps been waiting or sleeping or emerging from the remainder of its dream.

Light poured over the debris of the roof. The four pirates were bathed in the glowing brightness. For a moment the glow even outshone the shimmering beams of morning sunshine that strayed through the smoke.

"Have no fear," said the newborn god solemnly in the midst of his dazzling aureole. And softly, almost under his breath: "Zigzag-striped rock newt! I'm so hungry I could eat a whole ship."

The Breach

The kobalin mother's nest was behind Jolly. As the rock dissolved into the darkness, she did her best to banish it from her memory.

Her strokes hasty, she swam toward the heart of the Crustal Breach, closely followed by the lantern fish, which imitated each of her movements.

Kangusta had described the path to the outside to her, and so Jolly lost no time in escaping from the interior of the kobalin nest. She left the mountain at the top through a jagged crack near the peak, which had been just wide enough for her shoulders. Again she realized that Kangusta had been imprisoned down there first, and then they'd piled the rocks on top of her. So that was the dimension of the power Jolly was confronting.

Strangely, the thought of it no longer terrified her. Her

mind was long past all intimidation and her resolve was unshakable. She'd never thought to arrive at a point at which courage, despair, and indifference were one. She felt now as if other powers were moving her on a chessboard, to the last square finally. The place where the outcome would be decided.

She floated over the labyrinth of cliffs and chasms surrounding the kobalin mountain, with the fluttering particles of the deep sea dancing around her. The school of lantern fish followed her at some distance, until she wondered worriedly whether the tiny little creatures mightn't draw the Maelstrom's attention to them all the sooner. She saw no more of the blind albino kobalins beneath her, but most of the crevasses were too deep for her vision, so what might be romping around on their bottoms remained unknown. Neither did she discover any trace of Munk and Aina, who'd most likely reached the source of the Maelstrom long since.

The rocks in front of her appeared to become lower. Maybe the sea floor was sinking down even farther. But finally the rugged rock land ended and the view opened out over a wide, sandy plain.

Somewhere there, she sensed, lay the end of her journey. It was still beyond her view, but she thought she already felt the suction emanating from there. It couldn't be the actual suction of the vortex, for then she'd long ago have been crushed by its force. It was more a sort of pressure inside her: She wanted this to end, one way or another.

She felt that she was at the height of her powers, and for the first time she felt a gentle pulsing when she placed her hand on the pouch holding her mussels. Almost as if they were pushing to be freed and to open to the magic powers.

Jolly sank till she was just over the floor of the plain. The rocks fell away into the darkness behind her. Now gray, dead sand stretched around her in all directions, stroked smooth as if by a titanic paw, perhaps a consequence of the search currents that swept over the sea floor at irregular intervals.

Very gradually something peeled out of the darkness in front of her. At first sight it looked like a mighty tower that was rotating around itself at inconceivable speed. It arose from what she slowly realized was a gigantic white mussel, half-buried in the ground: The two halves were wide open, so that only their edges showed out of the ground. They extended from one edge of her polliwog sight to the other.

The giant mussel was surrounded by a sea of smaller shells, whose number grew the closer Jolly came to the center of the Crustal Breach. Soon she was floating over thousands of fist-sized mussels, a solid carpet under which the sand vanished completely.

The foot of the Maelstrom, that column of raging water, was no wider than the watchtowers of the cliff forts that the Spaniards, English, and French had erected on the islands of the Caribbean. But there was a difference between confronting a tower of solid stone and one of whirling, rushing water. Clouds of churned-up sand billowed at its foot, in the center of the open mussel giant. They were the only sign that the powers of the Maelstrom affected his immediate surroundings at all. Jolly still felt no physical suction. Only the tugging in her mind remained constant, as if the sight of the Maelstrom had released an almost uncontrollable desire to swim closer to him.

Even though the foot of the funnel-shaped Maelstrom might be narrow compared to his mile-wide extent on the sea surface, the sight of this whirling water column was enough to evoke in Jolly a feeling of boundless respect. Sometimes during her journey through the deep she'd imagined what it would be like to face the Maelstrom. Now she finally knew: The panorama took her breath away, made her feel tiny and powerless, and even the impatient pulsing in her belt pouch did nothing to change that.

Her mussels were urgently demanding to be set free at last. The magic in their shells was restive and rampaging, and Jolly wondered apprehensively if these powers couldn't be turned against her, faced with the giant mussel. The sea of mussels beneath her made her doubt her own capabilities. Did the Maelstrom use the magic from all these thousands upon thousands of mussels to increase his own strength?

She saw no sign of kobalins, no fortresses or other defenses. This was no fortress where Aina resided, not like an enchanted castle. How many magic pearls had arisen from these mussels, and what powers had they lent to their new possessor? For one thing, the strength to subjugate the ocean itself, to form it into an all-engulfing vortex. For another, the power to open a portal between the worlds.

And in the process—Jolly was certain—the real Aina had ceased to exist thousands of years ago. The powers that the girl had once called up had long since devoured her. Like a snake that bites its own tail. All that was left was the head, her spirit, a bundle of hopes, memories, and vengeful thoughts. From them the Maelstrom had formed that bodiless image he'd sent to beguile Munk.

A figure detached itself from the several-stories-high cloud of dust in the center of the mussel where the halves separated and the Maelstrom's funnel twisted upward, so infinitesimal in front of the breathtaking background that Jolly almost overlooked it.

Jolly hovered. She'd come here to . . . yes, to do what? Something about unpacking her mussels, laying out a small circle, and hoping that the sliver of magic she had at her command would affect something down here?

The figure floated toward her just a few feet over the carpet of mussels. Now Jolly saw that it was Munk. The suction of the Maelstrom at his back left him completely unaffected.

"Are you coming to fight with me?" she called out to him. Her voice wavered, but there was no point in trying to conceal her uncertainty. He knew her much too well for that.

"It grieves me to see you like that," he said as he came closer, almost motionless, as if he were floating on a current.

"To see me like this?"

"Alone. And so vulnerable."

"Hurt, Munk—not vulnerable."

He tilted his head slightly—almost the way Aina had done—as his fingertips danced in casual play around each other. "Perhaps because Aina imprisoned you?"

"Being betrayed is much worse than suffering a defeat," she retorted.

She'd figured that he would have fallen under the Maelstrom's influence by the time she arrived here. And yet it flustered her that he still looked the way he always had. Not pale or ailing, without glowing eyes or the other signs of possession she'd imagined. Quite the contrary— Jolly had to admit that it was far more painful to see him so vigorous and content, rather than facing a weary, dazed boy who hadn't been able to prevent Aina from taking control over him.

He was here voluntarily. What he said, what he was going to do—it was all happening of his own free will and his own conviction.

Jolly was so disturbed by this that her swimming strokes went awry, and she plunged to the ground. Mussel shells broke under her feet. Quickly she pushed off and fought for seconds to float calmly again.

"Don't be afraid," said Munk. "If she'd wanted to kill you, it would already have happened. She told me. She wants you as an ally, Jolly, not an opponent."

"What did she promise you to make you fall in with her?"

"Promise?" For a moment he seemed genuinely surprised. "Do you really think she had to promise me something? She's only explained to me the necessity of everything. The inevitability of the whole thing, no matter what you or I try to do about it."

"Then it's much worse than I feared," she said scornfully.

"You haven't simply given up—you've crossed over to her side! To *his* side—the Maelstrom's side."

"You're still seeing all this as a war, aren't you? The good on one side and the bad on the other."

"No." She'd learned from the words of the spinners, and she'd long known that it wasn't so simple. "But to kill others or to enslave them, that can't be good, Munk. You know that. Or has the Maelstrom also wiped out your memory along with your conscience? He murdered your parents. Have you really forgotten that?"

She saw by his look that her words had struck him. Good, she'd meant them to. He floated closer to her. Now there were about thirty yards between them.

"That was a mistake," he said with an obviously conscious effort. Or was she only imagining that? "An oversight," he added.

She stared at him, openmouthed, and for a second was unable to reply. An oversight? The murder of his parents? She shook her head and put her right hand to her mussels in the pouch. There was hardly enough room in the narrow leather case, and she had to be careful not to damage any of the fragile shells. A comfortable warmth rose through her arm and reached her chest.

"You're not yourself anymore," she said numbly. "How did you get the idea that it could be good to summon the masters of the Mare Tenebrosum into our world? Hang it all, what do you see being right about that?"

Munk was silent for a long moment. His face twitched.

Pirate Wars

"The Mare Tenebrosum hasn't much to do with all this anymore," he said finally. "It began with the Mare, but it won't end with it."

He halted scarcely ten yards away from her. They were now at the same height over the sea of mussels. Behind Munk the water column of the Maelstrom rotated endlessly around itself, an untiring cycle that never lost momentum. It roared and boiled, but the raging wasn't loud enough to drown out their words. Not only were the laws of nature out of kilter down here, they were completely suspended.

"Aina explained everything to me," said Munk. He looked nervously about him. "The masters of the Mare Tenebrosum made her into the Maelstrom so that she could serve them as a gate into our world. But when the Maelstrom was defeated by the other polliwogs, the masters didn't lift a finger to help her. Instead, they looked on while she was imprisoned. Time meant nothing to those beings, not a few thousand years, and so they decided to wait. They didn't have to undergo the torments the Maelstrom suffered . . . or Aina."

Devil take it, Jolly thought, *that sneak has totally warped his mind.*

He went on, "Then when the Maelstrom gained power again and broke out of his prison, the masters of the Mare demanded that he serve them. But he decided to make himself the master of this world—without being of use to those who'd created him and then betrayed him." He motioned his hand toward her. "Aina was just defending herself, Jolly. And it was almost the same with you. Remember when you were stranded on the shape changer's island with Griffin? That was no accident. The shape changer obeys the Mare. And his bridge was built for only one purpose: to take you to the masters. With you they would have had a new Maelstrom, could have formed a new gateway, this time into their world." He lowered his voice. "You were lucky. Aina sent you the kobalins to destroy the bridge in time. That's all that saved you."

Jolly stared at him. The bridge stretched before her eyes— and with it the indescribable look into the sea of darkness. What had the shape changer said to her that time on the island? *You are expected.*

Now his words made sense. She shuddered. What if the kobalins hadn't attacked? Would it then have been she who opened the gate to the masters? Would she have let catastrophe into the world? Munk was right, the kobalins had saved her from that fate.

Involuntarily she took a step backward, but Munk took a step forward.

Jolly blazed at him, "Don't you understand what's going on here, Munk? Don't you see what the Maelstrom is doing to us? The same fate awaits us as the first polliwogs! He changed one of them into the Acherus—the same monster that killed your parents!" She rammed the words against him like a blade. "He used to be like us too. The Maelstrom intends to do the same thing with us. We're supposed to help him, just not in the same form, but as slaves without will." She almost clenched her fist around the mussels in her pouch in her anger. "Do you want to become like the Acherus? Do you really want that?"

Munk was silent for a moment, as if he were listening to new promptings in his mind, for an answer that someone else was giving him.

"I . . . ," he began, but he fell silent immediately when a second figure appeared behind him. She emerged from the raging column of the Maelstrom, as if the water itself had produced her. In the first moments Aina's body was transparent, but it gained in color and consistency as she came closer.

Jolly felt as if the sea were freezing around her, she was suddenly so cold. Yet she'd expected that sooner or later someone . . . *something* in the shape of the girl would appear.

Aina's image floated out of the Maelstrom, and at that moment the whirling wall opened for a second, like a curtain. Through the crack Jolly was able to get a brief look into the interior of the water column, a lightning-quick view straight into the soul of the Maelstrom.

There was nothing inside there except darkness, a night-black chasm of emptiness.

"Munk!" Jolly called imploringly before Aina was close enough to stop her. The sea of mussels on the ground beneath them appeared to vibrate, as though the aftershock of an earthquake raged underneath them. "She's going to make both of us into slaves. You can't want that."

The Maelstrom girl was only a stone's throw away. She needed no swimming strokes to come closer; she rode on a current that the roaring water column had sent out like a gust of wind.

Jolly crossed the distance to Munk in one instant. At first it looked as though he was going to draw back to avoid her, but then he kept floating in the same spot, holding her eyes with a visible effort. There was a pleading in his eyes that she didn't want to see. She didn't understand it, didn't understand *him*.

She grabbed him by the upper arm. "Munk, please . . . she's going to make something like the Acherus out of you. Out of us both."

"She showed me that I belong here," he said dully. "We're polliwogs. The sea made us. And this is the place where the most magic veins cross."

No, Jolly thought, *that is not so*. She'd seen with her own eyes the place where the veins began, and it wasn't here. Nowhere else could so many strands of the magic come together than among the spinning stools of the three old women at the bottom of the sea. But how could she make him understand that? He hadn't been there when she had; he didn't know the water spinners. To explain to him that there was a corner of the ocean where even greater powers operated and where the true source of the polliwogs lay appeared impossible in view of the infernal scenery at his back.

Aina stopped beside them. Her lips opened, and Jolly was able to watch teeth and tongue developing behind her lips. She was taking shape only as necessary, not a moment too soon.

Why was the Maelstrom being so stingy with his power? Didn't he have enough of it? Or had he used a major part of his strength in the battle for Aelenium? Was that why he was so bent on making use of their polliwog power? Jolly sucked a deep breath of water into her lungs. She might have this fact alone to thank that she was still alive: the Maelstrom needed her.

Jolly was becoming more and more excited, but she tried not to show it.

"Why are you resisting so hard?" asked Aina, and even her voice only became really her own as she continued to speak; the syllables developed from something vague and blurry into the voice of a girl. Was that carelessness because it was no longer necessary to deceive Jolly? Or did Aina really lack the strength?

As fascinating as this idea was, it made Jolly even more anxious. If her enemy were in a hurry to draw her to his side, he would strike quickly and brutally and not wait for her counterattack.

Aina's features coagulated into a smile. "Munk has understood that his place is here at my side. Why do you resist that? The humans don't want us polliwogs. They hate us."

"You say that because they expelled you in the old time."

"And what about all the polliwogs they killed? Why are you two the last ones still alive? Don't you realize how stupid humans are? They lack any wide vision, any openness to the unknown. They fear what they don't understand. They whisper about you behind your back, they point their fingers at you and think of ways to get rid of you when you've fulfilled your purpose. You may be trying not to let yourself notice, but secretly you know the truth."

Jolly shook her head. "They accepted Munk and me and treated us like their own."

"That's not true," contradicted Aina, looking at Munk as if she expected a confirmation from him.

After a short hesitation he nodded. "They always said that we're different from them. They stared at us on the streets of Aelenium and whispered when we passed by."

Jolly's eyes grew cold. "And you *enjoyed* it, if I remember correctly. Lord God, Munk! You even tried to keep me there when I wanted to go to look for Bannon."

"Because . . ." His voice became softer. "Because I didn't want to stay there alone."

"Because he was afraid," said Aina. "Isn't that how it was, Munk?"

He nodded hesitantly. "Yes."

"Here in the Crustal Breach you need never be alone again. Here you are among your own kind."

Jolly made a movement with her legs that drove her a short distance from Aina and Munk. "Munk," she said imploringly. "She's lying! She made the two polliwogs who followed her into her creatures. Into monsters!"

He didn't reply, only chewed silently on his lower lip.

Aina altered her strategy, and now her face grew harder. Her voice took on a commanding tone, which warned Jolly that the time for discussion was running out. The Maelstrom was in a hurry, for reasons that she could still only guess.

"Aelenium has fallen," said Aina. "There's nothing more awaiting you up there."

"If that were so, you wouldn't need us," retorted Jolly, suppressing the trembling in her voice. What if Aina spoke the truth? It simply must not be. "Aelenium is still fighting, that I know."

"You saw what happened to the first sea star city. It went down and broke into thousands of pieces. Many people lost their lives, and so will it be again today. That was the first time they tried to imprison me, and they were almost clever enough—but at least I was able to destroy the city." Aina stretched out her hand as if to touch Munk. "Show her whose side you're on, Munk."

Jolly shoved her fingers to the mussels in her belt pouch, a handful of grating shells that at the moment were completely useless. She would have had to lay them out and then call up a pearl—all things that took much too much time.

"Don't do it," she said to Munk.

"He wants you to stay with him," said Aina. "Isn't that so, Munk?"

"Yes," he said.

"You can force her to do that," said Aina. "You must only want to."

"You already tried that once before," said Jolly. "To force me to stay, do you remember?" Perhaps it was wrong to remind him of his defeat on the *Carfax*. But the devil with that! It pained her to see him this way. Despite all their differences he was still Munk. The farm boy who'd fished her out of the water and saved her. Her friend.

Aina lost patience. "Do it!" she snarled in Munk's direction. "Or I will do it myself!"

Jolly looked around her. The school of lantern fish danced

behind her in front of the gray of the deep sea. She couldn't expect help from them this time. She must try to think of something herself. She looked down, over the endless carpet of mussels on the ground. Her thoughts felt into the deep, down into the crust of empty shells.

What she felt there shocked her: There was no more magic in those mussels, no sign of their own life or remains of their former power. The Maelstrom had sucked them all out, had taken all their power and misused it for his own devilish purposes. What Jolly had taken for a collection of immeasurable magic was in reality a graveyard. The magic of all these mussels was irrevocably lost. Sorrow clutched her heart. It was as if she herself had been cheated of the most valuable thing she possessed, gnawed down to the bones. And she realized that that was what lay ahead of her and Munk: The Maelstrom would swallow their magic, would consume their talent and their powers and leave nothing of them. It would not be they themselves who would take the places of the Acherus and the lord of the kobalins but their spent shells. That was why the servants of the Maelstrom were dependent on new bodies, for they could not move at all under their own power.

Even that thing floating there in front of Jolly was no longer Aina herself, only an image that the Maelstrom had spit out to deceive them and to mock them.

Jolly felt deeper, under the layer of mussels, to the real floor of the Crustal Breach. And there finally she found what she sought.

The magic strands. The ancient, powerful vein network of the water spinners. Branching thousands of times, it ran through the Crustal Breach, many times intertwined and interwoven.

At the sinking of the *Carfax*, the spinners had drawn Jolly to them through a tunnel of water that had borne her to their undersea nest as fast as a storm wind. Could they do that again? And would they do it to save her from the Maelstrom—and from Munk?

She tried to grasp one of the magic veins with her mind, but then she was suddenly seized herself and pulled away from the strands. Her link to the spinners' yarn was snapped like a too-tightly-stretched rope, snapped whip-fast up out of the deep, and paled in the twilight of the Crustal Breach. Jolly shook herself, her vision cleared.

She saw that Munk was sitting cross-legged on the ground, in the middle of the emptied mussel sea. He had his eyes closed in deepest concentration.

And she realized something else.

She'd deceived herself when she assumed that all the mussels under her had gone dead. There were still some, only a few, in which power seethed. Munk's mussels! And among them, the greatest and most beautiful of all—the mussel Aina had given him.

Munk must have laid them out in a pattern before Jolly arrived at the foot of the Maelstrom. He and Aina had lured Jolly into the center of this circle. A pearl had arisen under her feet, just above the ground, hissing and spitting with power—and glowing more than any Jolly had ever seen. Munk could only have made such a powerful thing arise with the help of Aina's ancient mussel.

Aina smiled, and any innocence was now gone from her face. Her features distorted, turned, formed a vortex that led directly into the interior of her skull. Jolly stared at her and at the same time fought to tear herself away from the sight. But Munk's powers held her fast, as if he'd wrapped her in a paralyzing crust of ice. Below her the glowing pearl grew larger and larger, now touched her feet and traveled up her body while it inflated around Jolly.

It's engulfing me! flashed through Jolly's mind. But not even her panic lent her the necessary strength to resist it.

She tried to speak, but her mouth didn't belong to her. Jaw and tongue were frozen. Her eyes were only able to look straight ahead, at the rotating maw into which Aina's features had transformed themselves.

Bright light points rose up to the right and left of Jolly's vision, were drawn past her. The lantern fish of the Spinners were caught in the suction of Aina's skull vortex, shot helplessly up to it—and were swallowed. Their light went out in the depths of the gray whirl, and Jolly felt a sharp pain, as if someone had rammed a needle between her ribs. Then the light of the pearl reached her face and enwrapped her. Jolly was now caught in the center of the flaming sphere.

A desperate scream rose in her, blazing fury and hatred for the Maelstrom and infinite anger at Munk, who was too weak or too dumb or simply too wounded by her love for Griffin to listen to her anymore.

He appeared not to have noticed the change that had taken place in Aina at all. Nothing remained of the body of the girl, only a whirling spiral, rotating swiftly around itself. At the lower end, the vortex lengthened to a whipping water worm, which slithered to the mighty Maelstrom column and melted into it. Soon the great pearl would be also caught, with Jolly trapped and huddled inside. She had to watch helplessly as she was sucked toward the vortex, straight into the interior of the Maelstrom.

When Gods Weep

The flood of light pouring over the destroyed roof of the house blinded them all. Even while the worm—or what he had become—was speaking with them, Soledad wasn't able to tell what he'd really changed into. Only very gradually, as he again cursed and complained that he was hungry and asked if there wasn't a sturdy tree trunk for a starving god anywhere, her eyes got used to the glittering and glow and she made out what was hovering in the center of the light.

The worm had turned into a winged serpent whose mighty body coiled incessantly in the air, borne by wings that were wide enough to cover the entire attic. Their fanning sent warm, humid breezes over the ruins of the attic and whirled the remains of the web around like snowflakes. The creature's scales gleamed a dark crimson, almost black. His wings were the same color and thickly feathered, like the wings of a predatory bird; they were set in the upper third of the serpent body, which might measure about twenty feet when stretched out, although all the coiling and whipping made it hard to estimate.

Walker let out a roar, and Buenaventure shoved himself protectively in front of the weaponless Griffin. But Soledad stood fast. Inside she was just as upset as her friends, but she had one advantage over them: She'd already met such a creature once. It hadn't been winged, but it was just as enormous. Even the triangular reptile head was the spitting image of that of the sea serpent of the undercity. Had she not known better, she might have supposed that the creature from the depths of Aelenium had grown wings and flown to the surface.

But for all the elegance and size it was still plainly the Hexhermetic Shipworm who was speaking to them. God more or less, his complaining and cursing was reminiscent of a badly brought-up child. "By the treacherous breath of Tetzcatlipoca, is there no one here who can bring a newly hatched serpent god a serving of wood?" He fell silent, seemed to be thinking, and then expelled a sigh of utter self-pity. "I've finished up everything that was lying down in the courtyard, but that wouldn't even have been enough to satisfy a worm, not to mention——" He broke off, for his slit snake eyes had just discovered Griffin. The pointed head shot forward, over Soledad, wove effortlessly past Buenaventure, and swinging, bent solicitously over the boy. At first the pit bull man looked as if he were going to bash the serpent god's head away with his bare fist, but then he took a deep breath and let him do as he wished.

"Boy!" the creature exclaimed with concern. His voice sounded lisping and was amazingly like the worm's, though much more powerful. "What's wrong with you?" The serpent body made an arc and, without intending it, formed a loose loop around Buenaventure. The gaze of the narrow pupils was again directed at Soledad. "He isn't dead, is he?"

"No," she said. "He's not dead. Only exhausted and wounded."

The reptile head ducked, then the amber-colored eyes blinked down at Griffin again. The glow billowing around the mighty serpent body now also embraced Buenaventure and the unconscious boy. Soledad almost expected that the light would heal Griffin, but when the creature unknotted itself and unmade the loop around the cursing pit bull man, Griffin hadn't awakened. The crusted cuts in his side still shone dark red.

"Where's the girl?" asked the serpent. "Where's Jolly?"

"Still in the Crustal Breach," said Soledad. At least she hoped so.

"The Crustal Breach . . . of course." The creature's voice sounded thoughtful, as if he were slowly remembering what had happened before his pupation.

Soledad saw Walker frowning. "By Morgan's beard, what's that supposed to be?" he asked undiplomatically, pointing at the winged serpent. The question wasn't directed at anyone in particular, but then he planted himself in front of the creature, chin raised, placed his hands on his hips, and looked at the gigantic head. "What's this you've turned into, Worm? Looks to me like something you'd find under a stone."

"Walker," Soledad warned him gently.

"Zzzssss," hissed the serpent. Its forked tongue shot out, darted through the empty air, and disappeared again between the scaly jaws. "That would have had to be a bigger stone than you could carry—don't strain yourself, my friend."

Was that a warning? *No*, Soledad thought, *probably not*. In his old form the Hexhermetic Shipworm had been gluttonous, deceitful, and self-seeking through and through, but there'd been a good heart in his . . . well, breast.

"I am the Great Serpent," said the creature, and now he sounded almost as if he were commanding reverence. "I fly on the winds between the worlds and devour the enemies of the Ancient People."

Soledad knew the myths of the Indians' serpent god that were told by the native inhabitants of the islands. She'd also seen drawings and reliefs of the winged serpent in the ruins of the jungle temple of Yucatan, where her father had once taken her many years before. Now she wondered if the mythical deity of the Indians was in fact the same as that creature opposite them. That would have been incredible in itself. But to have to accept that it and the shipworm were one and the same creature was completely mad.

"Devour enemies." Walker repeated the serpent's words. "Sounds like a good idea."

The head of the serpent swung, but it wasn't possible to tell if the movement was supposed to be a nod.

"Can you carry Griffin behind the wall?" Soledad asked.

A mighty gust of wind buffeted her, making her hair dance around her face. But this time it wasn't the serpent's wings that were stirring the air by the roof.

"We'll take care of that," d'Artois called down from his ray. The animal's angular silhouette darkened the sky over them, but it cast no shadows because the serpent's light was illuminating the attic. No one had noticed the rays descending, so fascinated were they all by the serpentine creature.

Two other flying rays, manned by riders and marksmen, hovered in the captain's party. The serpent god's glow was reflected in the mussel decorations of their black leather uniforms. The soldiers were staring in distress at the creature in the center of the light. One of the marksmen had aimed his rifle at the serpent, but d'Artois quickly raised a hand and made him lower the weapon again.

"I've seen weirder things in this city than a snake with wings," he said. Soledad shuddered at the picture of what creatures the captain might have met during his years in Aelenium. Even older, even larger than the sea serpent in the undercity?

She had a thought. "You knew what he was going to turn into!" The words were directed at d'Artois, but she was pointing at the flying serpent as she spoke.

"Not when he arrived," replied the captain. "But when the pupation started . . . well, let's just say, Aelenium has quite an astonishing effect on some. It brings out things in some of us that elsewhere might have remained latent."

And that was such a pertinent observation that they all left it at that, and even Walker refrained from any further remarks. For one thing was clear: D'Artois's statement didn't apply just to the worm but in certain ways to each one of them.

There was noise down in the chasm of streets under the ray riders. The gathering in the air over the house had attracted the enemy's attention, and now the second attack wave of Tyrone's troops arrived. Shots whistled past, and one of the rays shook itself as a bullet struck its underside. With an animal of this size, a single shot wasn't necessarily fatal, but several would bring the giant down.

D'Artois shouted commands, and at once the three rays fanned away from each other. As always their movements were phlegmatic, their reactions unhurried. The marksmen opened fire onto the ground—but they weren't the first to avert the danger.

Like a lightning bolt the winged serpent shot forward, turned in flight between the rays still drifting apart, and whizzed away over the edge of the attic and steeply down toward the street.

Horrifying cries rose from the street, screams from many throats. But when Soledad overcame her paralysis, ran with the others to the edge of the roof, and looked down, the battle was almost over—if you could call what had happened down there a battle at all. The serpent had mowed down the military host of cannibals and pirates in seconds. Soledad got gooseflesh when she saw the remains of a body at both sides of the serpent's mouth fall to the ground.

A second attack from below never came. If other men from Tyrone's fleet had been watching what happened, they stayed at a distance. However, Soledad doubted that there were very many witnesses. The serpent's attack had been swift and thorough, and at greater distances the smoke still veiled the city.

A remarkably pale d'Artois gave a brief command to his men. He guided his ray down, and Buenaventure helped to secure the mumbling but still not completely awake Griffin in the saddle between the soldiers. The animal lifted off again, carrying Griffin away, up the mountain, in the direction of the tumult of battle at the wall.

Soledad, Walker, and Buenaventure divided up on the two remaining rays, and soon they all were sailing away over the coral gables of Aelenium, toward the upper defense wall.

The winged serpent followed a short distance behind them. He had not spoken again since his attack on Tyrone's people. The light that flickered around him gradually paled, as if that had also been part of his magical rebirth.

It appeared that the transformation of the worm was not yet completed.

The Ghost Trader didn't notice the departure of the companions for the wall. He'd walked out onto the library balcony alone and was observing the course of the battle between the plumes of smoke. Like termites, the masses of attackers were surging through the streets of the sea star city, and it was this sight that finally decided the issue.

"It's wrong," said the Ghost Trader, "and perhaps even stupid and irresponsible. But I will do what must be done." He said the words aloud, for his next step was too important and momentous for him to want to confide his thoughts to the grave of silence.

He stood there outside, isolated, with flakes of ash whirling around him on the wind and the noise of the battle far, far below him.

The Ghost Trader was in despair, and he could no longer conceal his discouragement.

Forefather had stayed with the books, the thousands and thousands of books that for a long time had been much closer to his heart than the humans he'd once created. His spirit had suffered in all the years. It had begun after the destruction of the first sea star city. Or even earlier? It was not a public decline, nothing that showed in the words or actions of the old man, whose passivity had scarcely changed in the last millennia. Much more it was a vague feeling, a whiff of decline and death, that floated through the halls of books. And since there was nothing else that could die here, there could be no doubt as to where this presentiment originated.

Everything was tending toward the end, one way or the other.

The Maelstrom was about to swallow up the world. And if he didn't do it, the resurrected gods would.

The Ghost Trader had decided to awaken their spirits again—the spirits of those deities who'd once withdrawn to Aelenium and had died there in the forgetfulness of the humans. He knew no other remedy than to battle the one catastrophe with the other. Jolly and Munk must long since have reached the Crustal Breach, and there was still no sign that they'd defeated the Maelstrom. The defenders of Aelenium had paid a high toll to buy time for the polliwogs.

But the grace period had run out. Aelenium would fall under the assault of the cannibal king, and with him the Maelstrom would reach his goal. For a long time it had no longer been about the masters of the Mare Tenebrosum, as the Trader once assumed it to be: The Maelstrom had served them in order to build up his power, but he had no intention of opening a gate for them. This world was now his, and he would shape it as he wished.

And that included making it a world without humans. The revenge of the girl Aina on her race would be realized.

The Ghost Trader hadn't decided on his step because he shared Forefather's weariness and indifference. The fate of humankind was no game. The Ghost Trader had walked among them too long to believe anything different.

And if nevertheless he was now going do what he alone could, then it was only because he was despairing and helpless—perhaps for the first time in his immeasurable existence.

He inhaled the stench of war once more, like an admonition not to weaken now. Then he turned back into the library. His black parrots fluttered somewhere in the heights of the coral dome. Yet not even they could provide him with solace.

"Have you made your decision?" asked Forefather, looking up from a book whose writing had long ago faded. Forefather knew the words once visible there by heart.

"I will do it," said the Ghost Trader.

Forefather closed the book and stood up. The sound echoed through the hall like a cannon shot. "I'm not going with you," he said wearily.

He was silent for a moment before he began to speak again. "My road ends here."

The Ghost Trader nodded. "I know. You can't help me."

Forefather shook his head. "That's not what I mean," he said.

The Ghost Trader was startled, but with a wave, Forefather motioned him to be silent. "I'm like the writing on this paper." He pointed to the book with the empty pages that he'd just closed. "Without even noticing it myself, I've been faded for a long time. It only looks as if the writing were still there because we know the words by heart, you and I and a few of the people in this city. But in truth"——he took a deep breath——"in truth, no one can read me anymore."

The Ghost Trader tried to contradict him, but again Forefather gestured for him to be quiet. "Don't try to claim that I'm still needed here!" As vehement as these words sounded, the old man punctuated them with a gentle smile. "I created this world, that is so, but I have never been able to protect it—not from dangers from the outside and not from itself. My place is no longer here. Let me depart, old friend, before I must experience the end with my own eyes."

"I'm to—"

"I beg you to."

The Ghost Trader took a step back, clutching at a table edge with one hand. His elbow struck against a pile of books and made it fall. Neither of the two men even looked as the heavy volumes fell to the floor in a cloud of dust and lay there like dead doves with outspread wings.

"You alone are able to do me this last favor," said Forefather urgently. "If I ever knew how to do it myself, it was long ago—I cannot remember how. But you, my friend, you know it."

Forefather might sound to others as if he were speaking in riddles, but the Ghost Trader understood his every word. Their meaning lay before him as clearly as if someone had cut them into glass with a diamond. And their sound was just as painful to his ears.

"You ask much."

"No," said Forefather. "Only resolution."

"It's more than that. You are—"

"Old."

"That we all are."

"Old and faded. And as good as forgotten. They might revere something of what they believe I am. The nameless creator, the father of all, the word at the beginning of time. But I am not really that. They've forgotten the truth, and soon it will fare with me as with all the other forgotten gods, whom I myself once created. I will disappear."

"You want me to change you into a story? The way I did with Munk's mother?" asked the Ghost Trader in a trembling voice. "But that's as if I were to kill you!"

"No. You would give me a future, if there can still be such a thing in this world. Do it, my friend."

"But it's wrong."

Forefather shook his head with an amused smile. "How can stories be wrong? You know better than that. I beg you. And afterwards . . ."

"You will live on as stories," said the Ghost Trader somberly. Perhaps Forefather was right. What were they, the gods, in the eyes of men other than stories?

Forefather read his thoughts. "I knew you would understand." Without waiting for an answer, he sank back onto the chair. He placed his right hand on the binding of the book, as if he felt more connected to its empty pages than ever. "Step behind me," he said, closing his eyes.

Still the Ghost Trader hesitated. Then he made a conscious effort, took a step behind Forefather, and placed both hands on his shoulders. Tears gathered in his one eye, and it wasn't long before they were running down his cheek. It was the second time within minutes that he'd wept. Before that, centuries had passed without even one tear appearing, but now they dropped freely on Forefather's shoulders and were soaked up by his robe.

"I make you into a story," he said gently. "You will be a

story in which light emerges from darkness. In which people are born and die. In which sorrow and injustice happen, but also good fortune and great joy. A story of being born and passing away, of ascent and decline, and the constant hope of a new beginning. Of fathers and sons and spirits and the life in eternity. And of the humans you have created and who will tell themselves these stories, for they are part of them and forevermore one with you."

The fragile body did not collapse, did not even twitch. But when the Ghost Trader carefully lifted his hands from Forefather's shoulders, he saw that the life had slipped out of the old man's body like a young bird leaving its nest. And with it flew the stories of Forefather, out into the world to be told and heard and told again.

"Farewell, my friend," the Trader whispered, and he bent over and kissed the old man on the forehead. "Your road was hard, but today it is the easier, for it goes on elsewhere without burden and guilt and grief."

The Ghost Trader buried his face in his hands and wept until his tears finally stopped.

Then he went on his way to the highest point of the city, where Aelenium almost touched the sky. As he walked he drew the silver ring from beneath his robe. His fingers stroked the metal, feeling the invisible current of power.

He did not look back at Forefather as he left the library. He felt as though he were hearing a thousand voices in the distance, and they were all telling one story. And thus it would become true.

The Old Ray

The sound of the battle penetrated Griffin's consciousness as a distant rumble. First it was a muffled booming and roaring like the wind at night beating against the hull and making the sails flap spookily. Then voices emerged, screams, the clattering of blades, and the thundering of pistol and rifle fire.

Griffin started awake. He was lying on the hard floor of a house, among groaning wounded, who'd been laid out in rows side by side in a field hospital, most of them only on blankets, some—like him—on the hard, bare floor.

Someone had placed a few old pieces of clothing under his head. The air was humid and heavy, the emanations of blood, sweat, and fear of death mixed to a rancid stench.

Griffin got up with difficulty and staggered dazedly once on his feet. He moved drunkenly toward the exit. He had to be careful not to trip over the other men—and a few women—on the floor. A doctor who was bending over a wounded man in soaking bandages cast an exhausted glance toward Griffin, then turned again to the one who was more in need of his help.

The wounds in Griffin's side hurt, primarily because he'd stood up too quickly. He told himself it wasn't bad, and he felt ashamed that they'd brought him here because of these scratches.

Had he been so weakened? He could hardly remember. Before his eyes he saw Soledad as she'd leaped from the coral bridge into the middle of Tyrone's men. And there'd also been Buenaventure and Walker. But then? A desperate battle. Acrid smoke. And some sort of bright light, with something moving inside it that looked like a gigantic snake.

Yes, he remembered the serpent. And its feathered wings.

Very vaguely also the men who'd held him firm on the back of a ray while the turmoil of a battle passed beneath him. Then nothing more. That hadn't been sleep but unconsciousness.

As he stumbled through the door into the open air, still more images crowded up in his mind. The kobalins in the water. The shape changer dissolving before his eyes into thousands of tiny beetles. And then Jasconius shooting out of the deep with mouth wide open and swallowing the jellyfish boy.

Jasconius, who had sacrificed himself for Griffin and defeated the lord of the kobalins.

Griffin ran out into the street. He was instantly surrounded by the tumult that prevails behind the lines of any battle: Figures swarmed in confusion like ants; wounded who'd been borne from the battlefield, some silent, others screaming; occasional men who'd lost their nerve and now ran frantically back and forth, murmuring wild snatches of conversation or bursting into tears.

In vain he kept his eyes peeled for his friends. Before him lay one of the largest squares of the city. In former times, dealers had offered their wares from tents and stands, wares they'd shopped for in their ships in Haiti or the Antilles Islands. There'd been cheerful crowds, fragrant spices, and exotic foods, even in those last tense days before the invasion.

Today the square was covered with wounded or exhausted fighters who were seeking rest here for a moment. The real battlefield was about fifty yards away, where three broad streets opened into the square.

Griffin turned and looked up at the top of the mountain. There was no smoke rising anywhere. That meant that at least so far the upper third of the city remained undamaged.

Suddenly the dust was whipped up around him, and a mighty shadow sank down onto the square next to him.

"Griffin!" called d'Artois from the saddle of his ray. "You're on your feet again, then."

"Yes, Captain. How bad is it?"

D'Artois looked as weary as all the fighters in this battle, but in his exhaustion he registered something that Griffin recognized with dismay as a shade of resignation. "Not good," said the captain. Behind him his marksman was using the pause to reload his rifles and pistols.

When he'd awakened, in those strange, blurry moments in which thoughts gain a life of their own, one question kept running through Griffin's head over and over. Now he spoke it aloud. "Why doesn't the Ghost Trader help us?"

"What's he supposed to do, boy?"

"He could awaken the spirits of all the fallen and let them fight on our side!"

D'Artois let out something that sounded like a mixture of laughing and yelping and might rather have fitted Buenaventure. "If it were only so simple. . . . How are the spirits supposed to decide who's their friend and who's their enemy? Believe me, this has been talked about more than once, but it's pointless. The Trader has to explain to each individual ghost who he's supposed to fight with. If we had an army of conjurors who could keep the ghosts under control . . . But he alone? Impossible."

"Is there a ray around here anywhere for me?" Griffin looked up at the sky, where fewer than a handful of the powerful creatures floated. Their sharpshooters were firing bullets down onto the attackers from the air.

"Most of us are fighting on the other side of the city," said d'Artois. "They've broken through the wall over there. Count Aristotle has fallen and many good men with him. But as well as we can, we're keeping Tyrone's people from the road to the upper quarter from the air. So far we're still managing." He looked over his shoulder and saw that his marksman was finished reloading. "Climb on, Griffin! I can set you down on the landing area."

Griffin didn't wait to be asked twice. He hurried over the outspread wings of the ray and climbed into the saddle between d'Artois and the marksman. "Thanks," he said. "I think I'm more useful as a ray rider than on the wall."

"We may be desperate," replied d'Artois, as he made the ray ascend, "but we're only defeated when we give up. You're a brave fellow, Griffin. I—and many others as well—have heard what you did for us out there. It's a wonder that you survived—but perhaps there's more behind it. If you infect us all with your luck and your courage, boy, maybe we still have a chance."

Griffin had turned red as the captain spoke, and he was glad that neither d'Artois nor his marksman could see his face now.

The ray bore them a little way up the mountain, away from the embattled wall and the broad square. Then it began to circle the coral mountain. Griffin saw that the battle was raging around the entire city like a boiling whitecap. On the other side, the throng of dueling and shooting men had moved up the mountain, but a whole crowd of ray riders were holding the attackers in check. The wall was broken, but Tyrone's men had no chance against the concentrated attacks from the air. As long as the defensive positions didn't give in other places so the ray riders had to divide up, the damage below remained limited.

"Captain?" Griffin asked.

THE OLD RAY

"We're just there. There'll be a ray for you down in that square."

"While I was gone, did you hear anything about Jolly?"

The soldier shook his head. "I'm sorry."

"No sign at all? No weakening of the Maelstrom? Or . . . I don't know . . ."

D'Artois shrugged and let the ray descend. "We have no scouts outside anymore. I have no idea what would happen if the Maelstrom were to suddenly close. If the polliwogs' mission had succeeded and had some sort of direct consequences for us, we'd probably notice it in one way or another, don't you think?"

Griffin nodded thoughtfully, but in truth his thoughts were already elsewhere: outside over the sea, over a roaring chasm of rotating, foaming masses of water. And with a girl who was opposing that all alone.

The captain let him climb down to the ground and then guided his ray up into the air again.

Griffin waved to him, then turned to the handful of rays lying with wings outspread on the north edge of the small square. Their riders were dead or wounded, and not a few of the animals had been wounded by kobalin lances or pistol shots.

He chose a ray that was only slightly injured, scratched it on its shallow head, and climbed into the saddle.

"Here, catch!" cried one of the stall boys taking care of the animals. He threw Griffin a saber. "We have no more sharp-shooters left on the ground. You'll have to manage alone."

Pirate Wars

Griffin shoved the saber into a sheath on the saddle. With a whistle and a whispered command he made the ray rise in a narrow semicircle. Dust puffed up beneath him as the broad wings whipped up the air over the ground.

Moments later he was on his way to the other side of the city. From above he cast a last look at the defenders fighting on the wall. Finally he turned the ray around, flew out over the water, and rode over the fuzzy roof of the fog ring as over a meadow of white grass, until he saw the open sea lying beneath him.

In the far distance mist veiled the horizon like a gray mountain, whose tip constantly shifted, rose, and then collapsed, flowing apart and again taking shape. The creeping fingers of the Maelstrom would soon reach Aelenium.

"Fly as fast as you can," he cried to the ray, but really it was more a command to himself. "Take me to the Maelstrom."

Soledad ran a pirate through with her saber as he climbed the wall waving his blade in the certainty of victory.

What a blockhead, she thought bitterly. *It's really an army of blockheads that's going to defeat us.* That made the defeat even more painful, even though the outcome was still the same.

Walker and Buenaventure were fighting on the crest of the wall, as if they'd just hurried fresh into the battle. Yet they were as exhausted as Soledad, and the strength they were using and throwing at their adversaries was nothing but a last spasm.

Many defenders had fallen, first in the battle with the

kobalins and now in the battle against the pirates and the cannibals. Parts of the wall, it was said, were already over-run, over on the other side of the city. Count Aristotle, who was leading the defense there, had been killed, and with him several human members of the council. It was only a question of time as to when the first enemies would get up to the top and would storm into the refuge halls in the center. With the women and children, Aelenium's last hopes would die. What sense would it make to duel for victory on the wall if those for whom they were fighting were killed by the barbarian hordes?

Soledad was accustomed to pirate raids, but she had never seen a battle of this scale. Nothing of all this had to do with honor, with pride, or with heroism.

Soledad didn't feel like a heroine when she killed an antagonist, only like someone who'd won another minute or two; she doubted that it was any different with her enemies. The cannibals who'd been stripped of all humanity by rumors and legends finally showed themselves to be ordinary men who fought and fell for their cause.

Certainly they were horrible to look at, with their painted bodies and grisly trophies dangling at their shoulders and hips. But in certain ways they resembled the kobalins, for they also were being driven into battle by others.

Tyrone had drawn the leaders of the tribes to his side, had taken part in their rituals, honored their customs, and finally made himself their king.

And now his subjects were dying for him in droves,

blinded by his promises, led astray and made use of. Victory might await them at the end, but at what price? The Maelstrom would make no distinction between them and the other humans. He would brush them from the face of the earth before they could recognize the extent of his deceit.

All the while the winged serpent god raged among them like a demon, spreading the same horror among friend and foe. The inhabitants of the city had him to thank that the wall was still standing on this side of Aelenium. Many arrows were sticking out of his scaly body, but his pointed tail and, even more, his fearsome jaws sowed multiple deaths among the attackers.

Soledad had expected that the cannibals would panic at the appearance of the serpent, but that had quickly proven to be rash hope. When the first arrows pierced the serpent skin, the tribal warriors lost their reverence and threw themselves against the creature in desperate waves. Some inflicted wounds on him, others bagged a crimson feather from his wings. But there was no time for any of them to savor the triumph.

Soledad's arm gradually grew numb, her wounds became harder to ignore. Her entire body hurt, and her sight dimmed even in the midst of a duel. Her reserves were dwindling.

Something had to happen. Otherwise far more than just her life would end on this day.

The ray shelter at the top of the coral mountain cone was empty when the Ghost Trader walked through the great door. Even the young animals were taking part in the battle.

THE OLD RAY

All the stable boys were down in the city with their charges to provide for the wounded rays in squares and in broad streets. All that was left behind up here was a damp, slightly fishy smell.

Outside it was long after noon and the sun was deep, so that its beams only reached the edge of the circular, fifty-foot-wide opening in the ceiling. Up there the edge glowed like a golden ring and reflected in the pools of water on the floor.

The Ghost Trader strode across the empty hall and approached the stairs that led in a broad sweep up the curving walls to the opening. He'd just climbed the first few steps when his eye fell on one of the pits that gaped all along the base of the walls.

He'd been mistaken when he assumed that all the ray berths were empty. A single animal was still there, in a pit at a slant under the stairs, and even from the steps the Trader could tell by the leathery skin and the wheezing breathing that this was a particularly old ray. Obviously it was too weak to fly outside with the others.

The Ghost Trader hesitated for a moment, then he climbed down the stairs again, went to the edge of the pit, and squatted down. His knees ached with the motion, his entire body seemed to groan and to creak.

The animal was lying comfortably in the water, with outspread wings, through which went a gentle waving motion with each panting breath.

"Well, old fellow," said the Trader, and he had the irritating feeling that he was talking to himself. "I guess you'd have liked to be outside with the others, wouldn't you? That's the hard thing once you learn where and to whom you belong—you can never get free of it, whether you want to or not." He smiled sadly. "It's no different with me."

He looked up and along the course of the stairs to the roof opening. A plateau extended all around it, the highest point of the sea star city. In order to really call up all the spirits of the dead gods, he had to see the entire city spread out below him, with every corner in which one of them had died.

The animal wheezed even louder when it noticed the visitor. The Ghost Trader didn't know if the ray sensed his meaning. Probably not really, he thought, for he was a god of men, not of animals. This differentiated him and all other gods of Aelenium from the three spinner women, who had arisen from this world itself, from every plant, every stone, and every animal.

They were born of the dreams, wishes, and necessities of every fiber of this world—out of things over which Forefather had never had real influence. He'd created the world, but he hadn't understood it.

The Ghost Trader knew that Forefather had envied the spinners. They had been this world's first step into independence from its creator. The child had detached itself from its father and chosen its own way.

He stood up with a sigh, when he saw that the ray was moving on the bottom of the pit. Wearily it tried several beats of its wings, which after several failed attempts finally lifted it from the ground. Water dripped from its body down into the puddles as it rose out of the pit until its head was at a level with the Trader's face.

"Are you trying to tell me something, my friend?" The Trader felt the gaze of the dark eyes, which still seemed young in comparison to him, yet must be ancient for a ray. A strange excitement seized him as he watched this animal rise above itself and its infirmity.

The ray's wings beat very slowly, just enough to hold the heavy body over the pit. Now the animal sank a little and turned itself with its left wing toward the Ghost Trader.

"I should mount?" He considered it briefly, then nodded. "Why not? If you carry me up to the plateau."

He took a seat on the unsaddled back of the old ray and thought once more as he did so how similar he and this animal were. He also was leaning against fate and nature, just like this ray under him. Warmth went through him at the idea and something almost like a feeling of friendship toward the brave animal.

They rose through the opening in the ceiling into the outdoor air. The beams of the late afternoon sun caught them and cast them in bronze as the ray flew forward and set the handler on the edge of the wide plateau. With rattling breath, the animal lay down on the ground again.

A few heartbeats later it was dead. It was not the strain that had ended its life but its own wish: It had been of use one last time, then fell asleep contented and peaceful.

The Ghost Trader crouched down again, stroked the

motionless body, and silently took leave of it. If this meeting was a sign, it couldn't have been any clearer.

It was time to say farewell to everything here.

He stood up and turned his gaze to the north, toward the broad band of whirling mists that announced the monstrous breadth of the Maelstrom. In front of it a dark dot was moving through the air, a ray that was quickly distancing itself from the sea star city and riding toward the Maelstrom. On the ray sat a figure.

The Ghost Trader surmised who it was. Griffin might have felt that things in Aelenium were approaching their end. Probably he couldn't stand waiting and doing nothing while Jolly wrestled against the powers of the Maelstrom.

If she was still alive.

The Ghost Trader was gradually coming to doubt that.

With the silver ring in his hand, he approached the outer edge of the ledge and began to circle the plateau once. As he went, his eye skimmed over all the quarters of Aelenium, over the roofs and the crooked streets, through the plumes of smoke and swarms of gulls and ray riders.

Murmuring, he began the invocation.

Where All Magic Ends

Rolled up like a baby in its mother's womb, eyes closed, lips pressed firmly together, Jolly floated inside the glowing pearl just large enough to carry a human being. Warmth surrounded her, a comfortable feeling of safety. She'd reached the place she'd been trying to get to all along, a place where she felt welcome, that filled her with happiness and peace and security.

The magic pearl had broken through the thundering wall of the water column and was now in the heart of the Maelstrom, in a black abyss, which no longer filled Jolly with fear, for the darkness only strengthened the light of the pearl and the beauty inherent in it.

Jolly dreamed once more all the dreams of her former life, rolled up together in a rush of millions of pictures, pressed into one single moment, a powerful explosion of colors, smells, and sounds. Voices in her head, many faces, circling her like mosquitoes around a blazing fire. And yes, she felt herself blazing, burning hot with power, boiling over in the storm of feelings that she had once felt and that now welled up in her again, happiness and sorrow and suffering and—

So much suffering.

Her friends were dying.

Blinking, Jolly opened her eyes, and the light, which until then had only come through her eyelids filtered, blinded her like a glowing blade. Instead of brightness there was suddenly darkness. And in this moment of blindness, of seeing absolutely nothing, she knew the truth.

She was caught. The Maelstrom had swallowed her.

The dreams turned to nightmares, no more pictures, only the bundled power of all anxieties and cares that descended upon her. Memories tormented her, not the emotions of long-forgotten dream images but the thoughts of things just past: Aina's likeness, which dissolved to a rotating vortex and sucked her into itself together with the pearl. And Munk, who'd called up the pearl, blinded on his part, not by magical light but by the Maelstrom's enticements. It wasn't power that he was seeking but—and in that he resembled all others, Jolly too—only his place in the world and a little security.

Jolly opened her mouth and screamed. It was a long, shrill scream, and it broke through the close curvature of the pearl and echoed out into the dense darkness.

She kicked and hit around her, but nothing helped. She saw no up and no down, only emptiness around her. She

guessed what this was, recognized that a piece of the Mare
Tenebrosum dwelled in the interior of the Maelstrom,
whether the whirlpool had repudiated the masters of that
world or not. Where did the water go that he sucked into
himself? Quite certainly not to the bottom of the sea, for
then they couldn't have approached him for many miles. So
there was still a connection to the Mare whether the
Maelstrom wanted it or not, and of course, because he himself was the connection. He might live, think, plan the
destruction of an entire world—but he'd still been created at
one time as a passage, as a tool for crossing, as the portal for
the masters of the Mare Tenebrosum. Something of them
was also in him, and the darkness was part of their world.

Though she couldn't be certain, Jolly imagined that she
was floating between the worlds, in the middle of a whirling
tunnel connecting the one plane of existence with the other.

Suddenly she saw a point of light glow in the darkness,
become larger, unfold itself. Trapped in the pearl, she had to
watch as he rushed toward her.

It was Munk. The glowing brightness surrounding him
came from the mussel he was holding in his right hand. It
was the same mussel that Aina had given him, the wonderful, dangerous thing that whispered to him when he held
it to his ear.

"Jolly, don't be afraid," said a voice, which she only recognized as his after a moment. He came to a stop a mere arm's
length away from the pearl, floating in the middle of the
darkness. His lips were moving without another word being

audible. It was as if she heard what he said *before* he said it, and it took her a while to understand that the pearl was the reason for it. The glowing sphere that imprisoned her refracted and distorted time; what she heard might be being said at precisely the same time, but what she *saw* had really happened a little bit earlier. That seemed a meaningless detail, given the situation she was in, but it intensified Jolly's feeling that she'd been transplanted into a dream.

"I'd never do anything to you." Munk's voice sounded in her ears, and only then did his mouth move outside the pearl.

"Where are we?" she asked, after she'd swallowed down the flood of vituperation that had been the first thing to come to her mind.

"Inside the Maelstrom."

"I know that." Did she really know that? Anyway, it had been her first supposition. "But what is this, this darkness?"

His voice sounded as if he were smiling as he spoke, but the corners of his mouth only turned up after she'd heard his words. "You've gotten too used to polliwog vision, that's all. We're not in the water anymore . . . anyway, not in the seawater of our world. Polliwog vision is useless here. It's dark because . . . well, because it's just dark. It was just as dark outside in the Crustal Breach—only not for us."

That sounded clear, but at the moment not important enough to be worth more than a thought. Maybe he was right or maybe he wasn't. It didn't matter to her.

"I want to get out of here, Munk. You have to help me."

"Try it yourself," he said, to her amazement.

"What?"

"You can destroy it." Again it took a moment until she saw him smile. Then he added, "Trust me."

Which she found somewhat strange. But she didn't wait to be asked twice. She hit her fist against the inside of the pearl and was astounded to discover that she struck through the light. She tried to move her fingers, and it disturbed her that she could feel them move but it was only a little later that she could see them; even though her hand was now outside the pearl and thus in a different time plane.

She wondered if it was the same with Munk. Did he also see her movements within the pearl several seconds after they'd actually taken place? Then unquestionably she offered a bizarre sight from the outside, for to his eyes her hand and her body must be moving separately.

She shoved the second hand after it.

"Tear it," she heard Munk say.

With a jerk she tore the walls of the pearl apart, so quickly that the darkness struck against her like a gust of wind. Then she pushed herself out through the gap to Munk. The shine of the mussel in his hand distorted his features to a grimace of shadow and light.

Jolly pulled her other leg through the gap. Like Munk, she was now floating in nothingness. This wasn't water. It felt oilier, more viscous, which made moving a little more difficult. But perhaps this remarkable slowness was only a consequence of the falsified time conditions that prevailed here.

"Don't be afraid," said Munk yet again. Now she saw how

exhausted he looked. Completely worn out and pale. "Aina can't come here."

Jolly didn't understand what he intended with his new behavior. But at least one thing she did understand: Aina couldn't turn up here because they were *in* Aina—in the middle of the Maelstrom.

"But why——," she began.

Munk pointed to the pearl, which floated, glowing, at Jolly's back. The crack had closed again. "In spite of everything, Aina's magic is still the magic of a polliwog. A thousand times enlarged and warped, of course. But there are certain rules that apply to her, too."

Jolly shook her head, not understanding. She was so terribly angry at Munk, but at the same time confused, too. What sort of a game was he playing? Whose side was he really on?

"Polliwog magic can work only in the sea or near it," he said. "On the waves, on the beach, sometimes a little way inland. But this isn't the sea anymore. Not here, inside the Maelstrom."

Very slowly it began to dawn on her. This *was* a place between the worlds. She again imagined it as a tunnel, as the tail of the Maelstrom, reaching over into the Mare Tenebrosum. If that were so, the polliwog magic was slowly losing its effect here. That was the only reason Jolly had been able to free herself.

"But you shut me into the pearl," she said, although all indignation had left her voice.

He nodded. "Because Aina's magic couldn't do anything to you here."

"Then that was a trick?" she asked without real conviction.

Munk tried a grin, but he no longer had the necessary strength even for that. "For one thing, so that she'd trust me. For another, to protect you from her." He looked past Jolly, straight into the brightness behind her. "But above all, to smuggle *that* inside here."

Jolly whirled around. The pearl glowed like a moon in the darkness. She stretched out her hand and poked the thing with her finger. The light shell indented like a bag made of animal skin floating in the water. Now Jolly became aware that the light of the pearl was fading. Of course—for it, too, was created with polliwog magic.

She frowned as she turned to Munk again. "You shut me into the pearl so that Aina would suck it and me inside her?"

He nodded, but his eyes were held by the wavering light image. "I knew that she was lying to us. That is, I thought so. I first knew it when she told us that all her mussels except the one were crushed under the stone. You remember I stayed behind a moment when you and Aina walked on? I looked under the stone. And there was nothing at all there. Not a single fragment."

"You knew it the whole time? And didn't say anything to me about it?"

"She had to not notice anything. She had to believe I was on her side," Munk said. But the words didn't sound arrogant anymore, the way they used to. This was the old Munk speaking again, though infinitely drained and weary. "Otherwise she wouldn't have let us come any closer. Her kobalins could have torn us to pieces at any time." He stopped for a minute and appeared to listen into the darkness. "It almost went wrong when she shut you into the kobalin hill." He was silent and looked at Aina's mussel, as if he was regarding a tremendously precious object. "She gave me her most dangerous weapon to convince me of her goodwill and because it whispers things into your ear—if you listen to it. But to use it against her I needed a pretext—something so she wouldn't notice what I was doing. And for that I needed you. If you hadn't freed yourself . . ." He shrugged and left the rest unsaid.

She still didn't understand where he was heading, what his plan actually looked like; she was too confused. He'd shut her into the pearl because he knew or at least hoped that the Maelstrom would swallow her. But how did he intend to harm Aina with it?

She waited for him to go on or to do something, but then his face darkened suddenly. He turned around at once and his eyes darted through the blackness. A deep crease appeared in his forehead, which made him look older. "Do you feel that too?"

She was much too excited to be able to think of anything except all her open questions. So she shrugged.

"There, outside," he said softly.

The lump in her throat thickened her voice. "What do you mean?"

"There's something there."

Jolly took a deep breath. "Aina?"

He shook his head slowly without looking at her. "No, not her."

"Who, then?"

"I don't know." He moved backward, closer to Jolly, but the current that suddenly brushed her didn't come from him.

"Something is circling us," he whispered.

Jolly was going to reply, but she couldn't get a sound out. The glow of the pearl at her back grew weaker.

"What is it?" Jolly breathed out as her eyes searched in vain for a clue in the blackness.

"Then you feel it too?" In the fading light of the giant pearl, Munk looked like a shallow sandstone relief; his body had lost all depth. The glow bathed them both in a brownish yellow.

"I can feel it, but I don't see it," Jolly replied. "And you really don't know what it is?"

"No."

She had to get used to trusting him again, and it wasn't easy for her. "What do we do now?"

He didn't answer. Suddenly his eyes widened and stared as if spellbound into the darkness outside the dwindling glow of the pearl.

She turned around and followed his eyes, but now there was nothing more to see. "Did you see something?" she asked excitedly.

He nodded stiffly. "Yes."

"What?" Still she kept straining to try to make something out herself.

Pirate Wars

"It was big."

"How big?"

He was about to answer when again something slid by at the edge of the area of brightness for the fraction of a moment. This time Jolly saw it too. It was gone again at once in a flowing, shadowy movement suggesting that she had seen only a portion of an incomparably gigantic body.

"By Morgan's beard!" Munk swore. She hadn't heard him say that for a very long time. In spite of everything that had happened in the Crustal Breach, it brought back a pleasant memory of the past.

"Is it one of the masters of the Mare?" Her voice was now only a whisper. She wasn't certain if Munk could understand, but then he nodded.

"Perhaps. Originally the Maelstrom was their gate, after all."

Jolly closed her eyes for two or three moments. Almost these same thoughts had gone through her head just before. If this place was something like a between-kingdom, a kind of tunnel between her world and the Mare Tenebrosum, and if one or several of the masters of the Mare Tenebrosum were already in the tunnel, then the Maelstrom wasn't as powerful as Aina had pretended. Kangusta had said that the Maelstrom didn't intend to serve as a portal for the masters. But if some of them had succeeded in slipping through, that must mean that the Maelstrom had lost some power. But what had weakened him? He hadn't taken part in the attack on Aelenium himself, so it must be something else.

Think, she flogged herself.

WHERE ALL MAGIC ENDS

Perhaps Munk had struck a much bigger wound than they'd all guessed when he killed the Acherus. In the final analysis the Maelstrom made use of the magic power of his polliwog servants. After the Acherus was dead, there still remained the second polliwog from the last time, the lord of the kobalins. What if he'd been wiped out during the battle for Aelenium? Wouldn't that mean that the Maelstrom had lost two-thirds of his power?

"Jolly!"

She started, figuring that something huge was rushing at her. But it was only Munk.

"The light of the pearl is getting weaker all the time!" he said excitedly. "It's going out. You understand?"

"Certainly. And when it goes out entirely, that thing will grab us and—"

"I don't mean that!"

She looked at him without understanding. "What, then?"

"This pearl was the greatest concentration of magic I've ever called up," he said. "I mean, it was . . . *powerful*. Since that light is still there, it also means that its magic can't disappear entirely."

"We've already established that inside here polliwog magic doesn't—"

"Yes. Maybe, anyway. But the pearl is glowing and that means its magic is still alive."

"And so?" She surmised that all this was part of his original plan when he smuggled her and the pearl in here. But what *was* his plan?

He looked past her into the darkness, but the shadowy being remained at a distance. It was circling them way outside the light of the pearl, almost as if it feared the weak light.

"Do you still remember what I told you that time on the island about my parents?" he asked her, and his words sounded strained. "About the first time, when I didn't get a magic pearl closed back into a mussel at the end of the magic?"

"The palms on your island had red leaves afterwards. And once the roof of your farm burned. But what has that—"

He nodded excitedly. "And when you kept me from closing up the pearl again on the *Carfax*, the magic went crazy and hurt my back."

Then she began to understand.

"What do you think might happen," Munk asked, "if the largest and most powerful pearl I've ever created weren't put back into its mussel?" He swallowed, and in the dying light she saw his Adam's apple move.

"The other mussels are lying outside in the Crustal Breach somewhere," Munk went on. "This one is the only one the magic can go back into." He pointed to Aina's mussel in his hand.

"If such a powerful pearl isn't shut into its mussel," said Jolly, with growing excitement, "then there might be . . . something very *bad*, mightn't there? A catastrophe."

He nodded and looked enormously sad as he did so.

"And," Jolly went on, her voice trembling, "it would look for the next best mussel to disappear into—and it would have to be quite a *large* mussel to contain so much wild magic."

"The Maelstrom's mussel," said Munk. "Its root."

Jolly cast a glance at the sagging pearl, which now looked like a shapeless pig's bladder. The light was only a sort of pitiful afterglow. It was going to go out completely any minute.

Munk flinched. "There it was again!" He pointed to the blackness, which inched closer.

There was no doubt that the being would rush at them as soon as the magic light went out.

Jolly had eyes only for the dying pearl. "It will explode like a thousand barrels of black powder. Or . . . do something else crazy!"

Munk lowered his eyes dejectedly. "If it's only half as strong as I think, then it will tear everything in a radius of many miles to pieces."

"Us too?" She knew the answer. But suddenly the idea of her own death hardly hurt at all. It seemed to her that it had been established from the beginning that she would never return from here alive. As she sought after the truth in her heart, she knew that she'd known it the whole time. Suspected it, at least.

A strange calm descended on her. Almost a feeling of . . . yes, contentment.

She nodded to him and he raised his hand with Aina's mussel, cast a last look at it—and hit it so hard with his other fist that the shell burst into a cloud of tiny splinters. A sound rang out, like a scream carried from afar by a gale wind.

Jolly reached out and took Munk's hand.

At the same moment it was as if his face were sucked backward into the darkness. But he didn't move away at all—instead, the darkness suddenly came nearer and closed around them like a flood of black ink.

The pearl paled.

"Jolly?" she heard him call. Then she was seized by a powerful current. Their hands were torn apart.

Something large rushed at her.

And the magic of the pearl, hardly visible at all, exploded.

Within seconds the absolute blackness turned into its opposite. The freed magic flamed up like a spark reaching the end of a fuse.

Silence.

And then—

The ray bore Griffin over the outrunners of the Maelstrom as if over a mountain of water. From the great height the churning masses of water did in fact look like a landscape that was constantly changing. The floods moved in broad lanes, broke over and into each other, mixed in numerous smaller whirlpools that were still big enough to swallow a whole fleet. Foaming hillcrests arched up and flowed away again. Gigantic hands of salt water and spray curled up out of the sea and seemed to be trying to snatch the ray and its rider from the sky.

Griffin was sailing a good two hundred fathoms over the ocean. He'd never climbed so high on a ray before. Since he'd left Aelenium he'd not only moved forward but also upward at the same time, so that he reached the height necessary to be able to look over at least a portion of this whirling, raging beast.

But he'd erred in thinking that he could grasp the absolute size of the Maelstrom even from up here. The rapidly advancing water masses already filled his entire field of vision, and still he couldn't see the real center of the whirlpool, the eye of the monster.

After a while he noticed that in the distance the world appeared to curve down, as if the globe of the earth had suddenly become much smaller and its curvature visible. So there was where it went down into the abyss, straight into the heart of this inconceivable, monumental monstrosity.

He'd long ago ceased to perceive the noise as actually noise. His ears gave up the task of filtering out details or even variations from this chaos. Everything had become one, a constant rushing and thundering that filled his head and almost brought it to bursting.

The ray was afraid of that thing stretching away under it. Occasionally it bucked and jerked so hard that Griffin feared he might slide out of the saddle despite the safety belts. On Tortuga he'd once heard a one-legged priest preaching about the apocalypse, of the end of the world and the hellish beast that would rise from the sea on the Day of Judgment. How wrong that picture of the end of all things had been. For now it was clear that it was the sea itself that rose and that it could be more dreadful and cruel than any creature of flesh and blood.

Pirate Wars

The wave crests of the Maelstrom stretched in all directions, and now the slopes of the boiling surface became steeper. Soon beneath him it was going down vertically, and again he was conscious of what power must be at work to curve the ocean itself like the back of a giant creature.

With the reins he signaled the ray to climb even higher. The animal obeyed willingly. It would probably have flown to the moon if Griffin asked it to, just as long as it got out of reach of that chasm opening beneath them mile after mile.

After the slopes had become a steep wall and a cloud cover of seething steam and spray stretched out beneath him, Griffin caught sight of the opposite side of the abyss in the distance. He was now exactly over the Maelstrom's center. Treacherous eddy winds tugged at the ray's wings, and dangerous air currents threatened to suck him into the pit. It was hard to gauge the diameter of this titanic funnel, but from one curving edge to the other must measure many miles. It surpassed Griffin's imagination that this maw in the framework of the world stretched some thirty thousand feet into the deep, becoming narrower and narrower as it went down so that at its deepest point on the bottom of the sea it could vanish into a mussel.

Somewhere down there was Jolly.

If she ever got that far, whispered a voice in the back of his mind. He did his best to repress this thought, but he didn't succeed entirely. Jolly had ventured into regions that lay beyond human experience. And her only companion was someone who had at one time become almost her worst enemy.

There was no point in fooling himself. Her chances were not good. And yet he was glad that he was here now, at this place that was closer to Jolly than any other place in the world. He could only hope, perhaps even pray, that she was still alive.

For a moment he weighed actually plunging into the deep with the ray and just seeing how far they got. How deep could he thrust into the Maelstrom without being caught by the rotating walls of water? But he rejected the idea, for what good would it have done to take his own life in the bargain? He would help neither Jolly nor his friends in Aelenium that way.

In a curious way he was almost relieved, in spite of everything. He was finally seeing with his own eyes what they had only talked about for so long. He looked at the Maelstrom lying below him, heard its roaring, felt its terrible suction. He felt the nearness of the enemy, and that spurred his hatred again. Determination rose in him, and if he succeeded in returning safely to Aelenium, he would fight for the freedom of mankind until there were only two possible ways left—survival or going straight to the end.

Before he turned around and started back, however, he couldn't resist the temptation to go a little lower. It was as if the suction of the Maelstrom also had an effect on his thoughts, as if there were a pull there that drew him down like a magnet.

Come closer, hissed up out of the throat of the Maelstrom. *You cannot escape me.*

While he was still wrestling with himself, trying to resist the temptation, he saw something that startled him alert in an instant.

Pirate Wars

Deep below him, beyond the cover of water vapor and the arcs of splashing water that now and again formed over the abyss like bridges, a glittering brightness flared up.

At first he took it for another cloud of water droplets, snowy white and denser than the others. But then he realized that the entire cloud cover was glowing, as if lightning had struck and ignited the whole world for the fraction of a second.

A fountain of light shot up out of the depths and stood only a few stone's throws removed from Griffin in the center of the Maelstrom like a pillar of glittering, blazing fire.

The ray reared as if it had flown against an invisible wall. Griffin hollered in fright, slumped in his safety belt, and for seconds fought to keep from falling out of the saddle. The wounds in his side burned. When the animal was horizontal again and Griffin had managed to pull himself together in his pain and regain his balance, the pillar of light dissolved before his eyes into a cascade of glittering points of fire.

From deep, deep below an enormous rumbling thundered up, entirely drowning out the roaring of the water masses and seeming to rotate in common with the walls of the Maelstrom, at one moment on this side, the next moment on the other side. The ray fell into a panic, but it no longer shook, rather it shot forward with powerful wing beats, faster than Griffin had ever experienced with one of these animals. It was looking for the shortest way to the edge of the Maelstrom, away from his center and the swarm of light points that were still dancing and sparking there.

The rumbling grew louder, and suddenly it appeared to

Griffin as though the edge of the funnel kept moving away from them, as though it intended to keep the ray and rider from ever reaching it. And while a bizarre competition broke out between the ray and the curvature of the Maelstrom, Griffin looked down over the animal's wings into the deep.

The waves of vapor flew apart and with them the water masses around the chasm in the sea. The funnel grew wider and broader, while the bestial rumbling filled the world with a sound quite different from the noise of the raging water.

The wings of the ray flapped up and down, faster and faster now, as if the animal were still not yet at the end of its strength. Gradually the edge of the abyss came closer, that whirling steepness that somewhere merged into the level of the ocean.

But before they arrived there, Griffin saw something else.

Beneath him there was no more water vapor. The clouds had pulled away and the walls of the funnel were glowing on their own, as if the water had turned to glowing lava.

Down below them gaped a shaft in the water that reached all the way to the bottom of the sea.

He grew dizzy and then sick, but when he retched, nothing but gall came up. No wonder—he hadn't eaten anything for an eternity.

Under him lay the Crustal Breach.

Six miles deep and at least two miles wide yawned the abyss. On its bottom was a white surface, sand perhaps, like a piece of desert in the midst of the sea. Something shimmered in its center, a dot, which might be anything. Much too big for a human being. Perhaps a shipwreck.

Or a closed mussel.

The ray let out a strange sound, a muttering cry of alarm, and a moment later Griffin realized the reason.

The abyss was closing again! From all sides at once the rotating walls of the Maelstrom stormed closed. The bottom of the sea was already invisible now. The waves circled ever faster, drew together, filled the emptiness with the floods of ocean.

"Faster!" Griffin screamed in panic. "Faster!"

The ray now had a speed almost approaching that of a sea horse. Its wings beat in an unprecedented rhythm, and its heart was pumping so hard that Griffin was bouncing up and down in the saddle.

They made it.

Somehow they made it.

When the Maelstrom closed behind them and a colossal column of water rose into the sky, they were just far enough away not to be caught by the flood.

Griffin closed his eyes and shouted, and the water thrown up plunged from the sky in crystal curtains around him.

Beneath him the sea surface curved up in a tidal wave several hundred feet high. For a moment it almost appeared to freeze. Then it rolled apart in an eruption of gigantic force in rings in all directions, to bury the shores of the world beneath it.

The voices of innumerable gods were swirling through the Ghost Trader's consciousness when he caught sight of the light on the horizon. Like a finger of glittering brightness it shot up over the horizon and bored into the gray-blue of the heavens like a glowing dagger.

The Trader was distracted for a moment, and the connection to the forgotten ones was snapped. An angry bellowing arose, forcing its way out of fields where they were impatiently awaiting their rebirth—and was suddenly cut off.

An invisible fist struck the Ghost Trader and flung him to the ground. The silver ring slid from his hand and rolled to the edge of the ledge. The Trader was lucky that he'd stumbled only a few steps backward; the impact had almost thrown him over the edge of the plateau, down into the depths of the ray shelter. But he remained lying there, groaning, then lifted his head again and stared out at the horizon.

The light in the midst of the wavering walls of mist paled again. The world seemed to be holding its breath. Silence sealed his ears like liquid wax. The only thing the Trader heard was the blood pounding in his temples. Even the noise of the battle seemed to have halted, perhaps because the fighters also felt that something had happened that no one expected.

The door through which the ghosts of the dead gods of this world had intended to enter was closed. It would cost much strength and conviction to reopen it and begin the invocation all over again.

But perhaps it wouldn't be necessary anymore.

Out of the heart of the Maelstrom, so many miles away, a gray tower of water twisted up, which was clearly recognizable even at this distance. Its point touched the sky, blossomed out like the cup of a flower, and finally broke apart in an explosion of water cascades.

The Ghost Trader saw all this and realized at the same moment that the tidal wave would come. Knew it before he finally saw a wall of seawater under which the ocean curved up, bucked like a stubborn animal, and made the air itself tremble.

Over the Ghost Trader the two parrots shot up into the heavens, ascending until they were only two dark dots.

He struggled to his feet, looked for a hold, and found the body of the old ray. Without taking his eyes off the tidal wave thundering toward Aelenium, he ran over to the dead animal, leaned his back against it, and closed his eyes in anxious expectation.

Silent and motionless he waited for the end.

Destruction

A few minutes before the mysterious light burst the Maelstrom, before the Ghost Trader broke off his invocation, and before Griffin's ray reached a safe height over the tidal wave with its last strength, the defense wall for the upper third of Aelenium broke for the second time.

As in the case of the south side, the attackers succeeded in making a gash in the desperate defense of the guard on the west side. Pouring over the wall now were ragged figures who'd stayed all day long in the darkness of the storerooms of Tyrone's fleet, awaiting the outcome of the sea battle against the Antilles captains. Several cannon that had been brought on land and rolled up the streets had torn a breach in the defenses. Many of the inhabitants of Aelenium would have been killed, had the responsible commander not seen the situation in time and got his people to safety in the adjoining streets.

Pirate Wars

Now pirates and cannibals were streaming through the dense smoke from the guns, stumbling over broken splinters of coral and wooden debris, yelling and waving sabers, and trampling across a square where children used to play and people would sit in the evenings with wine and songs.

The first wave of the attackers came to a halt when the guardsmen opened fire behind a corner of the street and a few makeshift barricades. But those who fell back used the moments in which rifles and pistols were being reloaded to engage the defenders in fierce hand-to-hand fighting.

From the air, the ray riders saw what was happening, and d'Artois immediately felt compelled to divide his ray force and send a troop out of the hotly contested south to the new breach in the west. The result was that the attackers there were stopped, certainly, but those in the south now encountered less opposition and gradually won the upper hand.

"It's hopeless," said the captain to his sharpshooter. As commander, he couldn't show his despair openly, but he and his marksman had known each other for years and had no secrets from each other. "They'll take the city," he said dejectedly, "before the sun goes down."

The marksman fired a salvo down to the ground from several rifles. As the smoke of his weapons cleared, his eyes fell on the fog in the north.

"Look at that!" he cried, thumping d'Artois on the shoulder. The captain followed his outstretched hand and saw what he meant. On the other side of the fog ring, high over the ragged strands of mist, the sky colored brilliant white for

DESTRUCTION

a moment, as if a second sun had risen somewhere over the Atlantic. An instant of gloomy dusk followed the light a moment later, before an unearthly rumbling sounded like the eruption of a volcano.

Then something high and gray rent the captain's vision, as if an ax had split the horizon. It was as if someone had stood the world on its head: The water of the ocean shot into the sky with a roar.

Soledad had long stopped counting how many arrows were protruding from the flying serpent's body. The creature that had once been the Hexhermetic Shipworm was still fighting with the recklessness of a predator, but even his strength was gradually being weakened by the many wounds. Certainly the serpent was big, his bites and the blows with the end of his body were lethal, but he offered an easy target for the arrows of the cannibals and the bullets of the pirates.

From her place behind the wall, where Soledad had withdrawn to rest for a moment, she could clearly see that the flying reptile was bleeding from many wounds even where no arrows were sticking out between his scales. And as great as the panic that he spread among the attackers was, the triumphant cries when another arrow hit its mark were loud as well, and the courage and determination of the invaders was kindled anew.

Soledad was just about to jump up and plunge into the battle again when suddenly Buenaventure was standing next to her, panting, his tongue hanging out of his dog muzzle. The toothed saber now had more nicks than teeth.

"Walker's wounded!" he shouted to her.

Her heart almost stopped beating.

"I carried him away from the wall," the pit bull man went on, "into an empty house at the edge of the square. The one with the little windows over there."

"How bad is it?"

"Not too bad. A wound in the side. And a deep knife cut in the left upper arm. Nothing that will kill someone like him. But he's lost a lot of blood and can't fight anymore."

"Take over my place. I'll be right back." She pointed to one of the houses. "That one there?"

Buenaventure growled agreement; then he plunged into the battle with a wild war cry.

Soledad ran as fast up the steep square as she could. Several times she had to avoid wounded who were being carried from the wall to the field hospital. In the beginning there were still plenty of reinforcements moving up across the square, but that was long past. Anyone who could hold a weapon was now fighting at the very front.

She reached the entrance of the house, stormed into a hallway, and looked into the open doors right and left.

"Walker?"

"Soledad?" came a voice from the second floor. "Up here. That hairy, stinking monster of a friend has laid me aside here like an old man. Help me get back——"

He broke off as she came flying through the door of a room on the second floor, her face pale with alarm.

"Damn it," he said with a pain-filled grin, "you were

worried about me!" He lay on the floor, a single pillow under his head. The rest of the room was empty—all the furniture had been taken out to strengthen the wall.

"Not in the least," she retorted. Then she leaped over beside him and embraced him hard. "When he said you were wounded, I thought . . ."

He tried to raise himself from his supine position. "Nothing happened to me. It just makes me sick to lie here uselessly, while—"

The rest of his words were lost in a terrible din that came in through both windows and even overwhelmed the noise of the battlefield.

Soledad jumped up. "What the devil . . ." She couldn't hear her own voice, it had grown so loud outside suddenly. The floor trembled, and then she was thrown off her feet as if by a gale wind and tumbled through the room in a somersault.

Chance willed it that she crashed against the wall beside one of the windows. Groaning, she tried to get to her feet, but for some reason her sense of balance wasn't cooperating. Then she understood: The floor was no longer level. The whole house was lying on a slant like a ship in a storm!

The wooden shutters had been smashed by a ricochet, probably hours ago, and so her eyes fell on the square unhindered.

At first she didn't take in what she was seeing.

Something like a hurricane had hit the city. Everywhere there was water, spray, gray foam, and people in panic. But that was only a foretaste of what was approaching from the other side.

A gray wall.

The Maelstrom, shot through her mind, almost matter-of-factly. *He's here. He's come to get us all.*

But it was not the Maelstrom. It was the ocean itself that rose against them.

And then, in those endless, unreal fragments of seconds, before the tidal wave hit Aelenium, she saw something else.

The defense wall had vanished, torn away by the first surging water masses. And with it all the people who had been on it. The place where Soledad herself had just been fighting was now only emptiness.

Buenaventure and all the others were gone.

The tidal wave looked like water, acted like water, and for the drowning it even tasted like water during their last, terrible moments. Yet in that second when it hit Aelenium, it seemed hewn out of solid stone and ground up beneath it people, coral, and ships on the shore equally.

The great miracle in the midst of all this misfortune and death and the absolute feeling of being at the end was the fact that the anchor chain held.

There was a list of other miracles, though certainly lesser in comparison, that were for some people just as marvelous and merciful.

There was the little girl who had stolen out of the refuge hall with her brother to watch the battle from above; at the

DESTRUCTION

last moment she was caught by a ray's wing as a water fountain poured down on her from a rooftop.

There was the cannibal who got himself to safety on a statue and was able to grab a guardsman as he was torn away by the flood; the tribesman pulled the man up beside him on the shoulders of the statue and there they sat silently side by side, deadly enemies just before who now faced a common, incomprehensible opponent.

There was the cook of a pirate ship who only survived because at the last moment he fell headfirst into a half-empty apple barrel. And while the hull of the ship broke into pieces beneath him, he remained unharmed for some mysterious reason and was found unconscious but alive, floating in his barrel, still with his head down; he never went to sea or touched an apple again in his life.

Then there was the small troop of guardsmen who were able to save themselves on the roof of the only house that remained undestroyed in the Poets' Quarter. And the old woman who in spite of her great age was hobbling to the wall and approached the first waves with stick raised like a soldier swinging a saber against a superior enemy force; even she survived, half-drowned, of course, but sturdy enough to save herself. And the doctor who in his despair kept his back against the door of the hospital to protect the many wounded from the water with his own body; actually, the waves flowed around the house, which might have been because some god or other had saved it or because the building was sited unnoticeably higher than the land around it.

Pirate Wars

There were many such episodes, but also far more of those with the unhappy ending of death and the disappearance of many people without a trace.

It affected the attackers most of all. The tidal wave was high enough to lay waste to the lower two-thirds of Aelenium, and by that time the area was exclusively occupied by the cannibals and pirates who were hurrying up to the upper wall. They were all swept away. Of the dozens of ships at the shoreline not one was left, and the few men who'd remained aboard during the battle were miserably drowned, except for a handful.

Also, the defense wall was destroyed. Fighters of both sides died on it.

Only the people above the wall were almost completely unscathed: countless wounded guardsmen and citizens of the sea star city, but also those who had fled up the mountain just in time as the water approached.

No one ever found out how many people lost their lives on that day. Later, tallies were taken in the sea star city, but it remained uncertain how many pirates and cannibals had died.

Tyrone's fleet was wiped out at one stroke.

As the tidal wave rushed toward the Lesser Antilles and finally the mainland, slowly lost its force, and ebbed away, Soledad and Walker were sitting pressed close together in the bedroom of the house where Buenaventure had brought the captain.

They huddled in a corner, not speaking, keeping their eyes

closed, listening to the breathing of the other and the gradually diminishing noise outside.

At some point they separated from each other, and Soledad helped Walker to the window.

"I'm going out to look for him," the princess breathed tonelessly. "I'll find him. He must be somewhere."

"I'm coming along," said Walker.

"No!"

"He's my friend."

"I'll find him for you," she said gently. "You're too badly wounded to be running around."

"My right arm is working. I can duel and shoot and——"

She placed a finger on his lips. "With that wound in your side? Let me look around first to see how it really looks outside. Then I'll come and get you."

She jumped up and quickly took two steps backward so that he couldn't hold her. It hurt to see how he struggled to his feet, tried to follow her, and then had to give up, his face twisted in pain.

"Please," she said, "stay here. I couldn't bear to lose you."

Their eyes met again. He gave up and leaned against the wall, exhausted. "He's bound to be out there somewhere."

She gave him a reassuring smile and ran down the stairs and out of the house. Torrents were still rushing through the streets, and the whole city was rocking like a loaded galleon on a heavy sea. Soledad wasn't sure what had caused the tidal wave, but she was increasingly doubtful that it could be a weapon of the Maelstrom. Tyrone's men had been on the brink of victory. Why would the Maelstrom have included their deaths in the bargain?

Because human life meant nothing to him, she thought icily. And because the attack wasn't going fast enough.

But what had the Maelstrom gained? Aelenium had not gone down to defeat, which in all probability was thanks to the anchor chain. And to that which protected it. Soledad recalled her meeting in the undercity, the sparkling eyes of the sea serpent, yet now she was only overcome with gratitude at this memory.

In the square she found most of the wounded still where they'd been lying before the wave. Some had been thrown about higgledy-piggledy, and a few were probably washed away as well—Soledad wasn't sure. The first relief workers were gradually venturing down from the upper streets, many with stricken faces and groping, uncertain steps. Almost everyone kept looking to the north, where the sky now showed itself blue and beaming. If a second wave were going to come, there was no sign of it.

Soledad hurried past the confused and injured men in the square. Soon she reached the three street openings where the wall had been situated. There was some debris lying there, but the wall itself had disappeared almost entirely.

She looked through the center opening and down the street, which after a few dozen paces was no longer there. The tidal wave had destroyed a majority of the buildings in the central part of Aelenium, had torn down walls, ripped off roofs, and left only ruins standing. Water ran from all openings and flowed into branching gutters and down to the sea.

But it was even worse farther down.

The districts in the lower third of the Aelenium, down to the water, were washed away. Where hundreds of houses had stood before, there was now only emptiness. All that was left were smooth, white cliffs, looking as if they were covered with broken ice floes—the remains of the crooked and tightly crowded buildings that had once risen there. From where she stood Soledad could also see a sea star arm, and it, too, was completely empty. As though polished clean.

Tyrone's army had vanished without a trace. Soledad had gooseflesh, and tears scalded her eyes. She wept for the beauty of Aelenium and the deaths of so many people.

"Princess?" A question, then a jubilant exclamation. "Soledad, it's you!"

She whirled around, saw no one in front of her, but at the same time caught sight of the silhouette yawning over her like a dark crack in the sky. There floated the winged serpent with disheveled wing feathers; broken arrow shafts sticking out of his scaled body like quills.

"Have you seen Buenaventure?" Soledad burst out. "God, you look horrible. Somehow we have to get those arrows out of you—"

"Never mind," the serpent interrupted her. "They're scratches. And no, I haven't seen him." He lowered his voice. "He was up on the wall when . . . when it happened, wasn't he?"

"I have to find him!" Soledad tried to shake off her horror over the destroyed city districts, but she couldn't forget all the dead. Once again she turned to the ruins of the destroyed houses. "The worst thing is that they're simply all gone. As if they were still alive somewhere else."

The serpent blinked at her out of his dark eyes, then he rose a bit higher with a mighty beat of his wings. "I'll help you look," he said and rose straight up over the roofs and walls to the east, while Soledad ran west.

Soon she came upon the first wounded who'd been flung by the leading edges of the flood wave through windows and doors, into back courtyards, and against walls. Some had saved themselves in the corners of streets, whirled along like flotsam. Quite possible, she thought, that it had been thus with Buenaventure.

But as doggedly as she looked, she didn't find him. Sometimes she asked after him, but she got replies only rarely, for many were too shocked to grasp the meaning of her words. Soledad helped some of the wounded and stayed impatiently at their sides until other rescuers appeared. Only then did she run on.

All in vain.

She found no trace of Buenaventure. Exhausted and unhappy, she turned back to the large square where she'd seen him the last time. There she met the serpent again, returning from his search in the east.

"Nothing," the creature called to her between two flaps of his wings. "What about you?"

DESTRUCTION

Soledad shook her head silently, considering how she was going to give the bad news to Walker. What words should she use to make clear to him that his best friend had been washed away in the sea and drowned? That he'd never see Buenaventure again?

She murmured hoarse thanks to the serpent, then went heavily across the square in the direction of the house where she'd left Walker.

The square was full of people now. Most had laid aside their weapons and were doing their best to help others. There were also a few cannibals being led away by disheveled guardsmen. No one appeared to be in the condition to fight anymore, as if what this battle really had been fought for had suddenly become something unclear, blurred in their minds. It was no different with Soledad. All that seemed long, long ago, although scarcely one or two hours had passed since the last duels.

The scenery had become unreal. This city, the wind, the people—all were different from before the catastrophe. Soledad couldn't bring herself to look up at the blue sky; she felt as if it were mocking her with its clear, pure beauty.

She reached the door of the house and wondered whether she had in fact left it open. No, she was sure she'd pulled it closed when she went out. Did Walker follow her after all? She went faster as she leaped up the stairs: Was Buenaventure alive, and had he made his way to his wounded friend first of all?

But she had still another thought. More a feeling, a vague

sense of danger. Her hand gripped the hilt of her sword as she approached the door of the bedroom.

Her heart was racing as she turned into the room. "Walker?"

A man stood at the end of the room, broad-shouldered, in black clothing. He held an unsheathed sword in his right hand, a cocked pistol in the left. His coat was encrusted with dirt and blood, but he himself appeared to be unwounded. The long, black ponytail on his bald head was disheveled and looked as if he'd gotten too close to a fire. But the most fearsome was the war paint, which the water had made run on his face; as if his features had melted and been fixed in bizarre new shapes.

Walker lay lifeless before him on the floor. Tyrone had placed his right foot on the captain's chest, like a general posing for a victory statue.

"I've been waiting for you, Princess," said the cannibal king, baring the points of his filed teeth in a grin.

Where's Jolly?

Griffin sensed that the ray beneath him was growing tired.

The animal's wing beats were slower and slower, and it was having trouble maintaining their high altitude as they floated over the ocean.

The cascades of water from the eruption had nearly swept Griffin out of the saddle. The ray had been almost far enough from the center of the Maelstrom, but even the outermost margins of the titanic water explosion had poured down around them in fountains that felt as if they weighed tons.

But now, since the great column of water had collapsed and the tidal waves rolled out in all directions, the sea beneath them gradually smoothed. From up here—six or seven hundred feet above the waves—it almost looked as if nothing had happened. Certainly the waves were stormy, and that appeared even stranger because there were no clouds in the sky and it wasn't particularly windy.

Most amazing, though, more astounding than waves without wind, was the fact that the Maelstrom had vanished.

At first Griffin had thought that the flood was a weapon that their enemies had used to devastate Aelenium and the Caribbean islands. But he was gradually coming to the realization that the Maelstrom no longer existed. He was destroyed. Their greatest adversary had simply ceased to be.

Something appeared to have exploded deep in the interior of the whirlpool, causing the brilliant light that had shot up from the heart of the vortex; and then the very power of the Maelstrom had blown up like an empty husk and finally collapsed into itself. The raging walls of the water tunnel had fallen in on each other from a height of thirty thousand feet like the walls of a building of inconceivable size. The force of that had caused the wave.

Where had Jolly been in all this chaos? And what had become of Aelenium and his friends?

The wave had rushed toward the sea star city like a moving mountain. Griffin had been at sea long enough to know how hard water can be. What hit the city must have felt like a wall of diamond, from which you couldn't escape and against which there was no defense, a thing that, so close to the center of the detonation, released colossal power and must have pulverized everything in its path.

When he looked to the south, the horizon there was blurry and gray. At least the fog ring around Aelenium was still there. But what lay behind it? He didn't dare imagine the extent of the destruction.

He felt very alone up here on his ray. What if he were the only survivor of the sea star city? If all the others were crushed or drowned?

His hands clenched the reins, his fingernails cut into his fists. The wounds the kobalin had inflicted on him were now hurting hellishly again. His left side was burning in alternating hot and cold fire.

And then he saw a single dark dot down on the water.

A piece of debris—or a human being?

"Lower!" he cried to the ray.

The animal sank in a wide arc toward the blue-green surface of the water. White crests of foam covered the sea with a fine mist, looking from above like a fisherman's net.

In the middle of this net, floating on the waves, was a figure.

No, it was *walking* on the waves and having the utmost difficulty keeping on its feet. The surface was rocking so vigorously that every step presented a challenge. During his circling descent, Griffin saw the figure stumble several times and get onto its feet again only after repeated attempts, merely to lose its balance once more after just a few steps on the hills and valleys of the sea.

He called out Jolly's name, but the headwind tore the cry from his lips. The polliwog down there hadn't noticed him yet; it was having too much to do to move forward on the boiling ocean.

"Jolly!" he roared again.

But then he fell silent. That figure down there was not Jolly, even if it was wearing the oiled leather clothing in which the two polliwogs had set out from the sea star city.

It was Munk who raised his head and blinked up at the sky. He must have noticed the gigantic dark outline of the ray and stopped. A wave rose under his feet, but it didn't throw him down. His lips formed Griffin's name.

"Munk!" cried Griffin excitedly. A hideous suspicion rose in him. With trembling hands he guided the ray into a circle around the boy in the water. "Where's Jolly?"

Munk looked at him as if he needed a moment to grasp the meaning of the words. "Jolly?" he asked dazedly.

"Where is she?" Griffin asked again. He was scarcely able to control himself. Instantly he saw all his worst fears confirmed. He'd warned Jolly about Munk, but she wouldn't listen to him. "What have you done with her?"

"I . . . nothing. She's . . . she's not here."

"Then is she still down there?"

"I . . . don't know." Munk had to turn around on the water in order to follow the ray's flight path. He wavered and almost fell again.

"You don't *know*?" Griffin could no longer hold back the fury that rose in him. Something inside him boiled over. The desperation of the past hours, all the sorrow and loss, the pain, and now this—it was simply too much. "What have you done, Munk? . . . Damn it, I knew you'd betray her!"

Munk stared at him, his eyes wide. He looked pale and ill. Perhaps he was just too exhausted to contradict Griffin.

WHERE'S JOLLY?

Anger and grief blinded Griffin. His wounds burned even more, and the blood thundered in his ears like a torrent. A single thought ruled him: Munk had returned—and left Jolly down there. She was dead. And Munk was to blame for it.

Griffin pulled on the reins and made the ray shoot over the surface toward his adversary.

Munk threw himself to one side at the last moment, before the animal could ram into him. He fell flat on a wave and groaned in pain.

Griffin uttered an oath, brought the ray to a halt too abruptly, and was almost flung out of the saddle. His wounds broke open again, but he ignored them.

He turned and aimed at Munk again, now lower over the water. He'd get him this time.

Soledad stared at the lifeless form in front of her. Tyrone didn't move from the spot. From where she stood, she couldn't tell if Walker was dead. But why would Tyrone have left him alive?

Bellowing with fury, she raised her saber high and plunged forward. For a moment Tyrone appeared surprised by the vehemence of her reaction, then he waved the pistol in her direction. But Soledad didn't let herself be deflected by that. She wasted no thought on the danger as she swiftly covered the last few steps. Her blade thrust in Tyrone's direction, but the cannibal king leaped back and parried with his own weapon.

Sparks sprayed when the sabers met. Soledad was now

directly in front of him. Walker's body lay motionless between her feet and Tyrone's. Was there fresh blood anywhere? Was he still breathing? The cannibal king gave her no time to find the answers to her questions. Instead he attacked, aiming to knock the saber out of her hand.

Soledad avoided the blow with a leap backward and noticed with relief that Tyrone followed her. With his left hand he shoved the pistol into his belt. Didn't he intend to kill her? Anyway, Walker remained behind, unheeded, and that had been the foremost goal of her retreat: to lure her opponent away from Walker. Either Tyrone had lost interest in the captain——or Walker was already dead.

With another yell she parried Tyrone's next saber attack. She was now quite close to the door and moved backward out into the hall.

"I saw the dog man carry your friend Walker into this house," Tyrone said between blows. "After the water was gone, I came here because I thought that I'd find you here sooner or later, Princess."

The sabers met with tremendous force, nicking both blades.

"Imagine how disappointed I was to find only this scum. And so wounded that he wasn't even a suitable opponent."

Soledad's next thrust surprised him, but he quickly caught himself and returned the attack. They'd left the room now. Tyrone was driving Soledad toward the stairs, perhaps because he hoped he'd have an easy game with her if she had to move backward on the stairs.

WHERE'S JOLLY?

"Is he dead?" she said grimly.

His grin was so cold that even the filed points of his teeth couldn't make it any more frightening.

She stabbed and wounded him on the shoulder. With a surprised gasp he leaped one step back. She'd had a glimpse of his two black-stained tongue points just then, the result of a ritual of the Orinoco tribes. Soledad sent a fervent prayer to heaven that she'd have a chance to cut them off.

He smiled again. The wound in his shoulder was bleeding, but it appeared not to hinder him. "I'm not going to kill you, Princess. I only need a hostage to get me out of this city. Don't you think they'll hand over a ray for me if I threaten to cut up your pretty face?"

She snorted scornfully. "I'd rather die here on the spot."

He shrugged. "If you leave me no choice." His hand moved in the direction of his belt—only a threat for the time being. But Soledad's eyes fell on the pistol again. The hammer was still cocked.

How careless, she thought, and she took a lunging step, ducked under his sideways blow, and targeted the pistol with the tip of her saber.

The blade scraped against the weapon and touched the trigger.

Tyrone howled when the pistol went off. The black powder exploded in a green flame. At the same time a stream of smoke shot down his left leg. The cannibal king's knee half buckled, and then there was blood on the floor. The bullet had buried itself deep in his thigh.

"You . . . witch," he exclaimed, his voice filled with pain, but with remarkable willpower he stayed on his feet. He leaned his back against the hall wall and successfully parried her next blow.

"Give up, Tyrone," she demanded between gasping breaths. "You aren't going anywhere with that wound."

His smeared face twisted into a demonic mask, only his eyes remaining human in the midst of the devilish face. "I have the power of the shamans," he said sharply. "I met the Maelstrom in a dream. In *his* dream. No one has ever penetrated there. He chose me. And he is also . . . even now . . . my master." He pressed his left hand to his wound. The smoke had dissipated, and now Soledad saw what the bullet had done on its way down his leg. "He will . . . stand by me," he gasped, and his back slid down the wall.

Soledad was about to go to him to disarm him, but he struck so hard with his saber in her direction that he almost hit her lower body. She drew back, but she quickly realized that he was helpless. However, he was blocking the hall between her and the room where Walker lay.

"What did you do to him?" she asked coldly.

Tyrone didn't answer, only laughed, even louder now.

"What's the matter with Walker?" she asked again, but as she dared a step in his direction, he struck again with his saber and drove her back.

She lost the remainder of her patience, feigned a new lunge, but leaped over his thrusting blade and landed with her right foot on his injured leg. Tyrone's scream was so loud that it must have been audible outside in the square.

Good, she thought, *perhaps someone will come and take the dirty work from me.*

With her left foot she finally kicked the sword out of his hand and poked her sword point at his chest. "One false move," she warned him.

And Tyrone laughed again.

Laughed and laughed, until it turned to hoarse coughing.

Soledad hauled off—and at the last moment had a different idea. Instead of killing him, she struck the pommel of her weapon on his skull with all her might. The coughing stopped short, his features melted, and his chin fell onto his chest. He collapsed, unconscious.

Soledad stepped over him and weakly dragged herself to the door of the room. Tyrone's laughter seemed to follow her like a ghostly echo as she entered the room and bent over the lifeless Walker.

Munk yelled something as he threw himself to one side, avoiding the deadly mass of the ray by a hairsbreadth. Griffin didn't catch his words, just cursed because he'd missed his adversary again.

Munk had Jolly on his conscience, of that Griffin had no doubt. All the helplessness he'd felt in the last days and hours, even the emptiness after his battle with the wyvern, came over him anew. Munk wasn't to blame for everything—somehow that still did get through to him—but now even that had ceased to matter. What Griffin had endured during the long battle he'd endured for Jolly, in order to see her smile again someday. By his betrayal Munk had not just destroyed any possibility of seeing her again. It seemed to Griffin as though everything else had become meaningless too.

Whether the wyvern was dead or alive; whether the lord of the kobalins was still there or not; yes, even whether Aelenium still existed or lay on the bottom of the sea—suddenly it had all become unimportant. Griffin was simply unable to think clearly about any of it.

He wanted to pay Munk back for what he'd done. At the moment that seemed to him more important than anything else, and he was surprised that he had such a thirst for vengeance, so much despair.

You're going crazy, something whispered inside him. *You've lost your mind.*

What of it?

He turned the ray for the third time. Munk vanished behind a mountain of a wave, but that wouldn't save him.

Walker's eyelids began to flutter when Soledad shook him. She could only hold on to him, staring at him, as if what she was seeing were not possible.

She'd been convinced that Tyrone had killed him.

But he was alive.

Walker was alive!

"My head hurts," he croaked dazedly.

Her jaw dropped. "Your . . . your . . . head hurts?" Then

she pulled him to her so that he groaned with pain, but she didn't bother about that. She pressed him to her, weeping as she had last done at her father's death, and somewhere deep inside her she was surprised that you wept the same tears whether a person has just died or has returned to you.

At some point he took her head between both hands, very gently, and kissed her. She thought how strange it was that she felt so much for, of all people, this uncouth, stubble-bearded pirate, but then she gave up trying to figure it out.

"I thought you were dead," she whispered a moment later, still very close to his ear.

He hesitated until he gradually began to remember what happened. "Tyrone . . . he was here. Where is he?"

"He's lying out there in the hall."

He stroked her hair with his uninjured hand. "You fought with him?"

She nodded. "He's wounded. And unconscious."

Walker smiled. "I noticed outside there on the wall . . . you left a whole crowd of those cutthroats alive. Discovered you love them, hmm?"

For a moment she avoided his eyes, almost as if she were a little ashamed, but then she looked him in the eye and, smiling, kissed him once more.

As she pulled back, she noticed that his eyes had changed. His face had turned ashen, but even before he said anything, his arm shot forward and pushed her away from him. Completely confused, she flew to one side and crashed against the wall, was going to protest—and saw the figure who stood bent behind her, the saber raised to split her skull with a single blow.

Tyrone's eyes were dull, his mouth hung slightly open.

He turned toward her. His superior smile was gone, and now there was only hatred in his face. The runny war paint looked as if someone had clawed deep furrows with his fingers in a face of clay.

"No!" Walker roared when he realized that Tyrone was going to fling his saber at Soledad like a lance.

"Go to hell!" whispered the cannibal king.

She tried to roll to one side, when something distracted her and made her hesitate for a second.

Something thundered in through the door like an angry steer. Steel flashed.

Tyrone threw the saber.

She turned at the last moment, but not far enough. The blade bored into her right shoulder and flung her upper body back against the floor.

The powerful figure who ran forward behind Tyrone struck at him as he ran. A toothed saber blade cut through Tyrone's black ponytail. There were two clatters when the dead cannibal king fell to the floor.

The pain in her shoulder robbed Soledad of her wits. She groaned softly, raised her head once more, and looked at the steel stuck in her shoulder.

"Oh, damn," she whispered tonelessly.

Walker slid across to her on his belly and just caught the

back of her head as she lost consciousness. Before everything went black, she saw him bending over her, his face frightened and filled with concern.

Beside him was a second face.

To her surprise, it was that of a dog.

"Griffin!" Munk stumbled onto his feet again. "Stop this nonsense!"

"Nonsense" was really much too friendly a word for what Griffin had in mind. However, as he was making the ray just brush over Munk for the third time, serious doubts came to him. Was he mentally still in the middle of a battle where you blindly struck out in all directions, without any thought about guilt or innocence? What had become of principles like fairness or justice?

In short, had he completely lost his mind?

Shocked at himself, he reined in the ray and made it come around again, but much more slowly this time. He flew until he was a few yards away from Munk, who was crouching on the waves, out of breath and on all fours and looking up at him.

Griffin cleared his throat. He felt a little of his tension and aggression fall away, but not the panicked fear about Jolly.

"Where is she?" he called down to the boy beneath him.

"I don't know, damn it." Munk looked as if he were close to bursting into tears. But he kept himself under control. "When suddenly everything . . . got bright, then she . . . then we were separated. It went so fast. Water came from everywhere, and at the same moment . . . I don't know, it was as if something grabbed at me—like a tunnel through the sea—and pulled me away . . . somewhere. And all at once I was on the surface and . . . and I have no idea where she is, Griffin. I simply do not know."

"You were together down there?" asked Griffin. "In the Maelstrom?"

"Right in the middle of it." Munk's face now mirrored his despair and rage. "And damn it all, I didn't manage to get up here alive, only to be knocked down by a ray! I didn't do anything to Jolly. The pearl . . . the magic . . . I don't know, exploded and there was light everywhere, and then . . . and then . . ." He gulped and was silent.

Bad conscience welled up in Griffin full force, and he suddenly felt rotten. Had he really intended to kill Munk? Good Lord, what had this filthy war done to them that now even friends were going at each other?

"If I can get down close enough to the water, can you climb on?" Griffin asked.

"I think so."

Griffin made the ray heave to by several degrees and descend so low that the crests of the waves almost splashed against the animal's belly. Munk was able to grab the edge of a wing and pull himself up on it. Breathless and weak, he climbed into the saddle behind Griffin.

"I'm sorry," said Griffin, and he honestly meant it. "I . . . I don't know what got into me."

WHERE'S JOLLY?

"You did it because of Jolly," Munk got out feebly. It didn't sound like an accusation, only a statement.

"Yes," said Griffin uncomfortably.

Munk placed a hand on his shoulder. "Then let's go," he said. "We'll find her!"

Magic Yarn

Somewhere in the depths of the ocean Jolly was rushing through a tube of water, not a vortex like the Maelstrom, but something that went through the sea horizontally. Light and dark brushed past her, sometimes individual blobs of color, perhaps swarms of fish or banks of coral or even creatures that no one had ever seen before. In the beginning she'd fallen into a panic, tried to move more slowly, to resist, but without success. Then she remembered that she'd already traveled in this same manner once before, and she understood that though she was rushing through the sea, she might also be rushing through something that just looked like it.

She still wasn't sure if the home of the water spinners lay on the bottom of an ordinary ocean; just as the Olympus of the Greek gods had been no ordinary mountain and the Asgard of the Norsemen was not at the end of a real rainbow.

At last she just let herself be carried along, closed her eyes, and concentrated on not letting this speed make her feel sick. She didn't want to meet the spinners with a green face and bloodshot eyes.

The past few minutes—or hours?—were unreeling in a strange whirl around her, as if she were standing outside events. The last thing she could remember clearly was the fading pearl in the darkness of the Maelstrom. Or no, there was more: The light was extinguished, the pearl sank into darkness. Then an enormous movement, which she only felt, did not see. Something had moved up to her with hellish speed, something so big that the water was pushed back around her and tore her with it, somewhere else, away from the pearl, and probably also from Munk.

Munk! What had become of him? The thought of him hurt, as if . . . yes, as if she might never see him again.

And then there'd been the light, far away, for the water pressure had flung her away. And in front of the light she'd seen for a moment, really only for a fraction of a second, a gigantic silhouette—the outline of the being that had circled them and had moved toward them when the light was extinguished. But it had all happened much too fast for her to have seen any kind of detail. She was left with an impression of gigantic size and alienness—an intimation of the being's astonishment over the power that was set free there.

Afterwards the light had turned to darkness, probably not really, but in her recollection. She guessed that she'd lost consciousness for a moment. Perhaps, however, what had happened before her eyes was too strange, too mighty, for her mind to deal with. It was as if her intellect had simply made fast the hatches and refused to take in any more, the way a certain measure of cargo just fit into a galleon's hold. Her ability to comprehend was overflowing, like a rain barrel. More simply would not fit inside.

And now the water spinners, too.

It was strange how matter-of-factly she awaited the meeting with the three. She'd reached the end of her journey. She didn't know if the magic set free by the pearl had destroyed the Maelstrom or not. But one way or the other, this was the end.

Perhaps she was dead.

"Not dead," said a female voice in her thoughts, and when she opened her eyes, she sank the last few handsbreadths onto the sand of an undersea plain.

In front of her stood three mussel-encrusted spinning wheels, arranged as points of a triangle. At them, their backs to each other and their ancient faces turned outward, sat the three water spinners. Like the first time they'd called Jolly to them, they were grown together by their long hair. The white strands stretched across the five feet of distance among them like bundles of fine spiderwebs.

"You are not dead," repeated the voice. The last time it had irritated Jolly that she never could tell which of the three was speaking. Not one of them lifted her head, nor did any of them stop her work. Their fingers tirelessly worked the spinning wheels and from pure water spun the yarn with which they wove the magic net. The finger-thick strands, as transparently clear as crystal, stretched in all directions of the plain and far out beyond it, through all the depths and shallows of the ocean.

"You are back," declared one of the old women.

"That is good," said another.

"Very good," said the third.

"That means the Maelstrom is destroyed."

"The passage to the Mare Tenebrosum is closed."

"The danger from the masters is banished."

"For the time being."

"Yes, for the time being."

"Not forever."

"Well, hardly."

Jolly's head swam at the speed with which the spinners were firing the sentences in her direction. Her knees gave, she sank down on her haunches. Sand billowed up and settled again. She was dizzy, and now she was feeling sick, too.

"That will soon pass," said one of the old ones.

"Have no fear."

Jolly lifted her head and stubbornly scrambled up again. "I don't. Not of you."

The three were silent. Their fingers danced over the spindles, they sorted fibers of water, and they kept their gaze down.

"May I ask you something?"

"Whatever you will," replied one of the women.

Jolly thought for a bit. "Aina became the Maelstrom

because she got mixed up with the masters of the Mare Tenebrosum, is that right?"

"They gave her the power to become the Maelstrom."

That was a difference, but one that was no longer important. Jolly went on, "And then she . . . the Maelstrom refused to cooperate with the masters of the Mare. He wanted to carry out his revenge on the humans alone. Aina's revenge. Is that right?"

"That is one explanation, yes."

"But then where did the shape changer come in?" Jolly asked.

"He was a creature of the masters. They called him over the borders of the worlds and outside the magic of the Maelstrom."

A second spinner took up the thread. "When the Maelstrom noticed that, it was almost too late. The wyvern had built the bridge over which you were supposed to go into the Mare."

"That is why the Maelstrom sent the kobalins," said the third woman.

"However, he was not capable of attacking the wyvern directly. To some extent, he even helped it. The wyvern was formed out of a part of himself. The Maelstrom would have had to turn his magic against himself to destroy it."

"And yet the wyvern has been destroyed."

"Your friend has killed it."

"My friend?" Jolly exclaimed excitedly. "You mean . . . *Griffin?* . . . How is he?"

"He lives."

She was so relieved that her knees almost gave out a second time.

"He has destroyed the wyvern," said a spinner, unmoved, "and with that done what the Maelstrom himself could not accomplish."

Jolly protested. "He certainly didn't do it to help the Maelstrom."

"Of course not."

"But nonetheless the wyvern's death suited the Maelstrom. For with that, the masters of the Mare Tenebrosum had no more influence on the battle for Aelenium."

"What's happened to Aelenium? Are they all well?" That was a shallow hope, and she knew it. It couldn't be that simple.

"Aelenium will be built up again."

"And my friends?" asked Jolly hesitantly. She was afraid of the answer, terribly afraid.

"Many have survived the battle."

"But . . . that means that some are dead, doesn't it?" she asked tentatively, although the relief that Griffin was all right still outweighed all other feelings.

"Yes."

She swallowed down a lump in her throat. "And Munk?"

"The second polliwog is alive."

She sighed deeply.

"Others are dead," said one spinner.

"The One is gone."

The One? thought Jolly. Then she understood. "Forefather is dead?"

"The Creator has gone away."

"And he has left the world behind."

"In our care."

The thoughts in Jolly's head were swirling like a swarm of mosquitos. She suspected that she was forgetting things—things she should ask now, for this might be her last opportunity to do it. But she could think of only one more question. It sounded like an accusation. "Why didn't you help me in the Crustal Breach?"

"But we did."

"As well as we could."

"We sent the lantern fish."

Jolly nodded slowly. "The Maelstrom swallowed them."

"Yes, that is sad."

"But when everything looked so bad, why didn't you get me out of there?" Jolly asked. "Just like before."

"We were not able to do that."

"Not so close to the Maelstrom."

"Not as long as he was alive."

"He would have sucked up our strength and become even stronger."

"And even if we had been able to, why should we have gotten you out of there?"

All Jolly's limbs hurt, and the dizziness simply would not go away. Slowly she walked up to one of the spinners. "Why?" she repeated. "Because I almost died. That's why."

"But then who would have destroyed the Maelstrom?" asked one of the old ones disarmingly.

Jolly lowered her voice. "I didn't destroy him. That was Munk. It was his idea and also his magic."

"He would not have done it if you had not been with him. You brought him to reason."

"It was all part of your fate."

"You were the trigger."

"Who is more important?" asked one spinner. "The gun or the cannoneer who lights the fuse?"

"The saber or the soldier who wields it?"

"The soldier or the general who leads him into battle?"

Everything was revolving around Jolly, even the words of the old women: They seemed to assume vague shapes, a whirl of syllables and letters that lulled her and made her sleepy.

"We thank you, Jolly."

"You are exhausted and must rest now."

She nodded numbly. "I would like to do that with my friends."

"Farewell, Jolly. You have done more than you believe."

"So much more."

She was about to contradict, when she felt herself again seized by an invisible suction. Something snatched her from the ground, away from the spinners, until the three women were only pale dots in the distance, the blurry, mysterious source of the yarn. It occurred to Jolly that *yarn* was another word for *story*. And had not this story also had its source in the works of the spinners? They had created the polliwogs, also Aina, and thus in a way the Maelstrom itself. It seemed to Jolly that she'd stumbled on the trace of an even greater truth. But as so often happens when you notice that you're very close to something important, it escapes you before you can grasp it. And so Jolly too forgot her observation and didn't give it a second thought.

Once more the water became a narrow tunnel around her, through which she rushed away, and for the first time she understood that it was the magic veins themselves through which she moved. Straight through the yarn to one of its ends.

Griffin and Munk spoke not a word as the exhausted ray carried them back to Aelenium.

They'd spent hours circling over the sea, first where the Maelstrom had been, then in ever-larger circles. At some point Munk had observed that they were moving in the form of a spiral, or a vortex, as if the Maelstrom still held them in his power. These words made Griffin so uncomfortable that he had the ray fly in arbitrary zigzags for the remainder of their search and was slightly relieved not to feel any uncanny suction drawing them back into their old spiral course.

It was all for nothing. They hadn't found Jolly. It had grown dark quickly, but they'd continued to search anyway, while the moon transformed the sea into a landscape of gray peaks and deep black shadow valleys.

They would probably have flown on until the next day and even afterwards, but soon it had become clear to them that the exhausted ray wouldn't carry them much longer. It had spent many hours in the tumult of the battle and had scarcely any time to rest before Griffin had flown to the

Maelstrom. But now it had finally reached the end of its strength.

"It will crash if we don't turn around," Griffin said, and Munk wordlessly agreed with him. They would not find Jolly.

Now, quite a while later, they were approaching the fog ring. At first sight it looked as if nothing had changed—if there hadn't been the innumerable floating bits of wreckage. Sometimes they caught sight of corpses in the water and girded themselves for a picture of horrors that might await them on the other side of the fog.

When the mist thinned, it was worse than their worst expectations. The sight of the devastated coral cliffs was dreadful, a white-gray landscape of ruin, which reminded Griffin of the fissured lava flows on the flanks of the volcanoes rising on some Caribbean islands. But the most terrible thing was that nowhere in this wasteland did he see any people. He'd expected that they would be strolling through the ruins singly or in groups, searching for survivors or things that were still useful. But the cliffs were empty, completely desolate.

Only when they came closer did he see in the moonlight that the upper third of the city had remained unharmed. There stood undamaged houses, towers, and palaces; streets and squares were spanned by filigreed bridges, as they'd been before; and the glowing points flickering at many places revealed themselves to be campfires around which numerous people crowded.

Munk said nothing the whole time, and when Griffin

spoke to him, only a few disconnected words came from him in answer. Munk had probably hoped the destruction of the Maelstrom might have kept the worst from Aelenium, but now he was painfully undeceived.

Yet they had—for all the horror, all the pain—reason enough to be grateful that the city still lay in its anchor place and that there were people who could build again what the war and the waves had destroyed.

The ray drifted, reeling slightly, over the roofs of the undamaged quarter and, in a last effort, soared up to the shelter.

Two people stood on the ledge that ran around the opening. One was the Ghost Trader. His wide, bulging mantle covered the other figure. Both appeared to be facing the new arrivals, but the ray was too exhausted to slow so close to its goal or even to hover in place. Completely worn out, it sank down into the opening and landed on the ground of the ray hall with a bump.

Stall boys hurried forward from several sides to take care of the animal. Griffin and Munk helped each other out of their belts before the men reached them. Both were just as exhausted as the ray, and Griffin's wounds were throbbing painfully, as if they'd become infected. He hadn't lost much blood, but his shirt was sticking crustily to the wounds, and they were sore and stung as he made the difficult effort to stay on his feet.

Munk saw him stumble and tried to hold him, but then the two of them fell and remained sitting wearily on the ground. Griffin buried his face in his hands.

"Griffin, my boy." The voice of the Ghost Trader penetrated the fog of self-reproach and grief that had settled around Griffin. "I'm glad you're here with us again."

Griffin took his hands down and looked at the one-eyed man. The two parrots sat on his shoulders with heads tilted. Numbly he wondered why the Trader was smiling.

A hand was placed on Griffin's shoulder. It belonged to Munk.

Slowly, as in a dream, Griffin turned his head. And now Munk was also smiling. What the devil—

"Griffin," said the Trader as he stepped aside. "Look who's here."

Behind him the figure who'd been standing on the ledge with him came into view.

Griffin burst into tears.

Jolly dropped down next to him and kissed him.

The New World

Two days later the sea horses returned.

Jolly was standing on a balcony with Griffin and looking out over the devastated cliffs down to the water. The Caribbean sun burned down out of the clear sky and turned the crests of the waves below to flames. In the middle of the glittering and glistening the hippocampi were recognizable as dots, which first individually and then in a mighty herd broke through the fog wall and approached the arm of the sea star where their stalls had once been. The first ones had reached the shore and were already assembled in front of the opening in the arm that had formerly marked the gates.

"So d'Artois was right," said Griffin. "He was sure they'd find their way back."

Jolly had difficulty taking her eyes off the majestic sight of the hippocampus herds. She smiled sideways at Griffin.

"Why aren't you already on your way?" she asked, laughing. "You can hardly wait any longer."

"I only want to see if Matador is there."

"He's sure to be."

"Yes . . . I hope." With that he turned around, gave her a quick grin over his shoulder, and disappeared into the interior of the palace. Considering that his torso was bandaged beneath his clothing, he moved quite agilely.

Jolly looked after him. His few dozen blond braids whirled behind him like a comet's tail. She'd told him how glad she was to be with him again more than once since her return. But somehow that couldn't even begin to express how much she really felt for him.

Sighing softly, she turned to the water again. Some of the foremost sea horses had been caught at the shore. A few saddles that had been found in workshops in the upper quarter were hastily fastened onto their backs. Now the first riders were sallying out to bring some order to the chaotic herd of hippocampi. More and more kept pushing through the fog. The animals hadn't separated from one another during the last few days. Presumably they'd dived way down, so they'd escaped harm from the tidal wave.

"Jolly?" Soledad's voice came from the interior of the building. She sounded concerned. "What's going on? Griffin just ran past here as though a thousand kobalins were after him."

Jolly went inside. Soledad was lying in her bed in her room, her left arm and right shoulder bandaged, and looking as if she wanted to shred the covers in her impatience. A deep frown of worry creased her forehead.

"God!" she groaned. "I've had enough of lying around here while—"

Jolly silenced her with a soothing gesture and sat down on the edge of the bed. In the last few days she and Griffin had spent a lot of time with the princess. The three had recounted their experiences, shared their excitement and astonishment, and noted how good it was for them to talk over everything, almost as if that turned the events into a mad adventure story that somebody or other made up. Munk looked in occasionally too, but he would soon withdraw into the library again, where the Ghost Trader was doing his best to initiate Munk into the secrets of Forefather's book room. Munk had asked to be allowed to remain in Aelenium to dedicate his time to the books. Soledad commented that maybe he was just trying to dodge helping to clear up the destroyed parts of the city, but Jolly knew better: Munk had been fascinated by books and old knowledge before, and even Forefather's death and the end of the Maelstrom hadn't changed that. The possibilities for study in Aelenium's library were unlimited.

The polliwogs avoided speaking about their journey to the bottom of the sea. The time would come when they'd be able to tell about it. Now, however, the memories of what they'd experienced were still too fresh.

"So," said Soledad seriously, after Jolly had settled down beside her, "what happened? I hope you aren't so dumb as to fight with Griffin when the two of you are just back—"

Jolly took Soledad's hand and smilingly shook her head. "Don't worry. Not everybody shows how very much they like someone else by quarreling from morning till night."

"If you're referring to that little business between Walker and me this morning, let it be said that people can like each other even if they . . . well, have a difference of opinion once in a while."

"Buenaventure said that you two were growling at each other like two street curs scuffling over a bone."

"He should know, after all." Soledad smiled. "Anyway, that wasn't a quarrel. But lying around in bed doing nothing drives me crazy—and poor Walker probably catches that now and then. Nevertheless, as for you and Griffin—"

"Everything is just wonderful, don't you worry." Jolly told her of the return of the sea horses, and the princess's face brightened.

"Thank God. The people here have lost enough. It's good that they at least have the hippocampi left."

Jolly was about to reply when her gaze fell on the balcony through the open door. The sky was darkened by an echelon of flying rays diving steeply in front of the balustrade. At the same time a distant cry came up from below.

"What's going on now?" Jolly jumped up and ran outside.

"Well?" Soledad called impatiently before Jolly got outside. "Can you see anything?"

"Just a minute, I—oh, no!"

A moment later Jolly stormed past the bed to the door, the same way Griffin had before. And almost as fast.

Soledad raised herself with an effort. "Could someone just tell me what's going—"

Jolly stopped, one hand trembling on the door handle. Her face had turned ashy. "It's the whale. His body just popped up out of the ocean."

She didn't catch up with Griffin on the way down, and when she got to the water she saw him standing in the front row and pushed her way through to him. His face was gray and tense.

She followed his gaze out to the body of the giant whale. Half a stone's throw from shore, the body of the whale curved over the waves like an island that had just raised itself from the flood. Several rays and their riders were circling in the sky, and a sea horse rider had left the hippocampus herd and was hurrying over to Jasconius.

The whale was floating on his side. From here they could see one of his eyes, which looked dully at the sky. For a moment Jolly believed there was life in it, movement, but then she realized that it was only the reflection of the rays in the gigantic black pupil.

She put her arms around Griffin and felt how tense his body was. At first he didn't react at all, but after a few moments he returned her embrace.

"I am so sorry," Jolly whispered.

"I knew he was dead," he said, his voice thick. Then he

gently detached himself from her and called over to one of the sea horse riders. The first time his voice threatened to break with grief, but at the second try the rider heard him and came over. After some hesitation, the man climbed out of the saddle onto the embankment and handed the animal over to Griffin.

Jolly looked after him as he rode over to the dead whale. Paying no attention to his bandaged wounds, he slid out of the saddle into the water. A little clumsily, hindered by the tight bandage, he clambered out of the waves onto the whale's body.

The crowd gathered on shore didn't utter a sound. All were staring in fascination at the boy who, first on all fours, then slightly bent, moved over the massive cadaver.

Jolly jumped from the shore onto the waves. She strode over the water, reached the whale, and climbed up the smooth skin until she'd overtaken Griffin.

He was crouching beside Jasconius's eye. His face was all wet, and she couldn't tell if he was crying. Wordlessly she knelt beside him, took his hand, and held it during the time he needed to take leave of Jasconius. No one disturbed him, neither the men on the bank nor the ray riders, who at last turned and flew up to the refuge again.

"He was my friend, you know?" said Griffin softly after a while, not taking his gaze from the great dark eye.

"I know," she said, swallowing. "And he certainly knew it too."

Griffin nodded slowly. "He saved my life. And all the

others' in the city. Without him the kobalins wouldn't . . ." He broke off and dropped his head.

Jolly weighed putting her arm around his shoulder and pulling him to her, but then she let it be. He'd come to her if he needed her. But this was his moment. His and Jasconius's.

A sea horse was reined in not far from the whale. Captain d'Artois had his arm in a sling. He looked over at Griffin sympathetically. "No one here will forget him," he said, so softly that it was barely audible over the murmuring surf around the dead whale, almost as if he was afraid of startling the boy in his grief.

Griffin lifted his head. The water on his face had dried, but his eyes were still red. "Jasconius was very old. And very lonely until Ebenezer came to him." He was silent for a moment, then he said, "He knew what he was sacrificing himself for. Ebenezer showed him that there were humans who were different."

Suddenly there came the sound of splashing and paddling from the half-open mouth of the whale, then a string of frantic gasps. Griffin started and then slid excitedly down the curve of the whale's skull to the corner of his mouth.

Jolly followed him when she saw how his face brightened.

"Ebenezer!" he cried, and then he slid halfway over the opening and grabbed into the recess. "Ebenezer! Thank God . . . !"

Jolly slid next to him and seized the other arm of the older man, who was lifted, coughing and panting, out of the whale's throat. Together they pulled him up between the gigantic teeth. D'Artois had difficulty keeping his sea horse quiet; it appeared to be just as excited as its rider.

Ebenezer stared at them dumbfounded, then Griffin fell on his neck with a joyous cry. The monk laughed. "Gently, gently, boy!" He returned the hug warmly and heartily, though feebly.

Griffin let go of him reluctantly. "We thought you were dead. . . ."

"I was behind the door," Ebenezer gasped out. "And then I was . . . swamped, when I noticed that we were moving upward. . . . I saw the dead boy and the . . . the remains of the jellyfish . . . and then I swam up into the light. . . ."

Griffin embraced him again, so hard that the monk wheezed. But then his eyes fell on the lifeless eye of the whale and his face darkened again.

Helpless, Jolly looked to d'Artois. With a gentle motion he indicated that it was best to do nothing, simply to sit there and wait.

Leave the two of them alone for a moment, his eyes seemed to say. *Let them grieve for a friend together.*

And so they crouched together while the waves broke against the whale and wind brushed over the desolate sea star points. The faint sound of hammer blows wafted down from the cliffs; someone called something. The fog formed ghostly whirlpools, and the rays in the sky shimmered in the sunlight.

It was Munk who had the idea of the book.

Jasconius was bade farewell with all the honors of Aelenium

and sent to the bottom of the sea for the last time with heavy weights. The day after, Ebenezer asked to be allowed to tour the library of Aelenium, and Munk readily offered to show him around. In the course of the afternoon Ebenezer told him of his exploratory work along the coast some thirty years before, of his writings about the insect world of Orinoco, of his drawings. And of course, how much he regretted that all that work had been lost after his apparent drowning.

Munk remembered what Jolly had told him about her search for the poison spiders of the *Skinny Maddy*. In the library she'd stumbled on a book written by a missionary three decades ago, which had, however, only been taken to Europe and printed there after the author's reported death in a shipwreck.

After the tour with Ebenezer, Munk located the book in a corner of the library and took it to Jolly. She and Griffin were beside themselves with joy when they discovered the author's name on the title page. Griffin, especially, was so happy about the find that he immediately ran to Soledad, who was just taking a first timid walk with Walker along the balustrade outside the palace. Griffin told her everything, and she rejoiced with him. Even Walker murmured a few approving words.

That evening, when they were all eating together and the winged serpent was cozily curled up under the window, his feathers illuminated by moonlight, Griffin suddenly stood up, asked for silence, and proposed a toast to the dead Jasconius and to Ebenezer. Then he ceremoniously handed the monk the book from the library.

THE NEW WORLD

Ebenezer, who'd spent thirty years in the belly of a whale, opened the leather cover and saw his name. Overcome, he sank into his chair and burrowed feverishly in the pages, while Jolly and Griffin held hands under the table. Buenaventure walked up behind Munk, thumped him on the shoulder, and whispered in his growling dog voice that there were great heroes' deeds, like conquering a maelstrom, and small ones, like making a grieving man extremely happy, and one was hardly inferior to the other.

On that evening they sat together for a long time, enjoying each other's company, telling stories, making plans, and dreaming of the future here in Aelenium and elsewhere. The whole time, Ebenezer held the book firmly pressed to his breast like a long-lost son, and when he thought no one was looking at him, he ran his hand over it and wiped a tear from the corner of his eye.

Several weeks after the battle around the sea star city and the end of the Maelstrom, Soledad put on one of the diving suits again, furnished it with a bubblestone, and dove down into the deep with Jolly. Her shoulder still hurt a little, making her right arm move more stiffly than her left, but on the whole she was amazed at how well it went.

For a while they sat on one of the steel links of the anchor chain, with legs dangling over the dark blue abyss. Jolly could hear what Soledad was saying behind her mask, and although she already knew the story of the meeting in the undercity, she gladly listened a second time, for now Soledad described every detail and also what she'd asked of the giant serpent. Jolly remembered the feeling that had overtaken her and Munk when they'd explored the undercity together during her first days in Aelenium, the panic and the knowledge that something was behind them, very close to the edge of polliwog vision. Suddenly there was a meaning to all that, and she realized that the thing that followed them hadn't necessarily meant them harm.

She looked over at the steep coral walls of the undercity, which vanished jaggedly somewhere deep below. The holes and splits, but also the beauty of these tortuous shapes, moved her, though differently from the first time.

At last she nodded to Soledad, and together they went on their way. The princess led Jolly to a cavern and through it they entered the undercity. Now it was Jolly who swam ahead, her polliwog vision making it easy for her to orient herself in the dark caves and tunnels. Soledad had some of the lantern stones with her and used them to mark their return.

It didn't take long for them to reach a deep vertical shaft. Jolly was quite certain that it was the same one through which she'd dived with Munk.

Soledad exchanged the bubblestone under her diving helmet, and then she looked down into the darkness. Jolly tried to imagine how frightening this bottomless blackness must be without polliwog vision—even she felt uneasy, though she could see a hundred times farther than Soledad.

She was all the more astonished when the princess suddenly said, "It's coming."

Jolly was about to ask what made her so certain, but at that moment she knew it herself.

Beneath them, where the shaft merged with the darkness at the edge of Jolly's vision, something was moving. The darkness billowed, and then something emerged from it, a mighty reptilian head, triangular, with slit pupils, followed by a monstrously long serpent body. The creature shot up to them, outstretched like an arrow, displacing such a quantity of water that the pressure on the two intruders pushed them two or three fathoms upward.

Soledad remained very calm, while Jolly had to fight with herself not to flee before the swiftly approaching sea serpent. The crack in the wall through which they'd glided out into the shaft appeared to be unreachable now.

Then the serpent slowed its ascent, the currents ebbed. The head rose up in front of them and stopped on a level with their faces.

"We've come to thank you," said Soledad under her helmet.

The serpent regarded her for a long time without any recognizable reaction. Then its gaze swung over to Jolly. The mouth opened a crack and a fine forked tongue groped forward, straight to Jolly.

"Don't be afraid, it won't do anything to you." Soledad's voice sounded so muffled under the helmet that it wasn't at all clear how convinced she was of her own words.

But then something strange happened. One moment Jolly was about to recoil from the tongue—yet immediately afterwards all fear fell away from her. It happened at the same moment that both tongue points touched her cheek, stroked down it, velvety soft, wandered under her chin, along her neck, and over her leather clothing down to her heart. There it stopped for two or three breaths, then with lightning speed withdrew into the snake mouth.

Jolly didn't even sigh. All her fear was wiped away. She now understood what Soledad had felt when she faced this creature the first time. It was a feeling in such overwhelming contrast to the fearsome appearance of this giant reptile that it made her quite dizzy.

"Soledad said you protected the anchor chain from the kobalins," said Jolly to the serpent. Was she deceiving herself or did understanding flare in the cold serpent eyes? "Without you the city would have been annihilated by the tidal wave." She thought for a second, but then she couldn't think of anything else except to bow in the water. "Thank you," she said.

The serpent's head whipped up and down several times, which might be a gesture or only the result of an occasional current. Finally its tongue was thrust out a second time, touched Jolly, then Soledad, and vanished into its mouth again. The serpent body made a tight loop in front of them, rushed past them endlessly, and shot back into the deep.

Jolly and Soledad floated in the shaft a little longer, gazing silently into the darkness below their feet. Finally the princess said, "I wanted you to see it yourself. So I know that I didn't just dream it."

"It's very beautiful," said Jolly. "And very old, I think." She remembered Jasconius, who now rested somewhere on the sea bottom, and she wondered how many such creatures there might still be down there in the darkness. Creatures whose looks instilled fear in any human and yet in truth were completely different from what everyone saw in them. A shiver ran down her back, but this time it was a comfortable feeling, born of the certainty that even her meetings with gods and water spinners were only a glimmer of all the wonders that awaited her in the world.

They turned around, crossed the undercity on their marked route, and soon were swimming through a curtain of sunbeams that reached down into the water, refracted a million times and sparkling.

"Do you think the worm can dive in his new body?" asked Soledad, just before they broke through the surface. "If so, there's someone down there he should arrange to meet."

Laughing, Jolly grabbed the rung of the iron ladder and climbed up onto the arm of the sea star.

Griffin was waiting for her on the embankment. Walker and Buenaventure were with him, and all three were eagerly awaiting what Soledad and Jolly had to tell them. Later they had to repeat it for Munk and the Hexhermetic Shipworm and a third time for the Ghost Trader, who nodded abstractedly at their words and then silently walked back into the library, supported by Forefather's staff, as if recent events had robbed him of years of strength.

His parrots sat on each of his shoulders, one with red eyes, the other with yellow, and they didn't even move when he walked out onto Forefather's balcony alone, looked over the night sea, and thoughtfully breathed deeply. He looked down at the coral cliffs, from which new buildings were already being carved, then up to the plateau at the peak where several rays wheeled like shadows that swallowed the stars.

At last he looked down at the shore, at the water between the edges of the sea star and the fog ring, and his gaze penetrated the depths of the ocean, where he saw many creatures, the mighty and the very tiny. He saw Jasconius dreaming in darkness, and he also saw the magic veins, newly woven where they had been torn apart.

Hugh and Moe whispered softly in his ear. The Ghost Trader turned and went inside. His staff clacked at every step; the sound followed him like an unseen companion.

He closed the door to the balustrade softly behind him and made his way into the labyrinth of books. Munk and Ebenezer were waiting for him with thousands of questions to which there were ten thousand answers.

Presently the three of them were sitting in the midst of all these stories, a boy, a monk, and a god. When the Ghost Trader became aware of this, he laughed aloud, and when they asked why, he murmured something about fate and age and knowledge, and he acted secretive and mysterious, so that they wouldn't realize what moved him. But the truth was that he enjoyed their company and, for the first time in a long time, his own as well.

Far removed, behind coral walls, corridors, and halls, Jolly and Griffin were kissing. They watched Soledad and Walker at their gibing, listened to the serpent under the high arching window grooming his feathers with whispering tongue, and finally looked over Buenaventure's shoulder as, by candlelight, on a huge sheet of paper, he refined his plans for a new ship, a three-master like the *Carfax*, but slimmer and faster, he hoped.

Later they walked out into the moonlight, wandered along an arcade of columns outside the palace, smelled the salty sea, and watched the campfires of the workers down on the cliffs.

And that night, finally, Griffin completed the coral picture on Jolly's back.

About the Author

Kai Meyer is the author of many highly acclaimed and popular books for adults and young adults in his native Germany. The first book in his Dark Reflections Trilogy, *The Water Mirror*, was a *School Library Journal* Best Book, a Book Sense Pick, and a *Locus* magazine Recommended Read. It also received starred reviews in *School Library Journal* and *Publishers Weekly*. His novels have been translated into twenty-seven languages. Kai Meyer lives in Germany.

About the Translator

Elizabeth D. Crawford is the distinguished translator of the Batchelder Award–winning novels *The Robber and Me* by Josef Holub and *Crutches* by Peter Hartling. She lives in Orange, Connecticut.